MASTER OF THE MOUNTAIN

Dragon Core Chronicles Book Two

LARS MACHMÜLLER

MOUNTAINDALE
PRESS

ACKNOWLEDGMENTS

There are so many people who have supported me along the way, it is absolutely ridiculous. Listing them all would be impossible. So here are just a few honorable mentions:

Maria, for encouraging me to start writing in the first place.

Tina, for having my back every single day!

My kids, for being so terribly understanding of me being on "their" computer when they want to play Minecraft.

Lunatic's Asylum (you know who you are) for keeping me company during the daily wordings.

Everybody in the Office Discord for entertainment, good company and loads and loads of wisdom.

Dakota, Danielle and everybody at Mountaindale for taking a chance on me.

Nick, Evan and everybody else who try to help me improve my writings.

Michael for keeping me sane and distracted from bad moods.

I love you all! May you never change!

CHAPTER ONE

Prior preparation prevents poor performance. - James Baker

Home, sweet home. It wasn't a thought I'd ever figured I would come to associate with a creepy underground dungeon complete with a huge throne, deadly traps, and a glimmering, shiny hoard. But there it was. The pang that hit me as I walked through the throne room was undeniably the same as I'd had back on Earth whenever I took in the splendor of my house. Pride, satisfaction, and that feeling of "Mine. It's all mine." The domain of Carl... or should I say Onyx, my new name in this realm?

Heh. Nothing ever changes. A man's home is his castle. Back on Earth, I'd only had to protect the house from my debtors, and once, my ex-wife. Here... I was looking over my troops through the mini-map as I was preparing to defend my home from a very real threat.

Through the mini map, I admired the recent addition to my home. At first glance, it was nothing special. It used to be that, entering my domain, before you'd even make it to the Farm, you'd have to go through a route of winding tunnels with lots of dead ends and doubling back before you'd reach the steep descent down to the entrance hallway. These tunnels had now been blown completely open, and the network of criss-crossing tunnels had been incorporated into our new Gallery of Illusions.

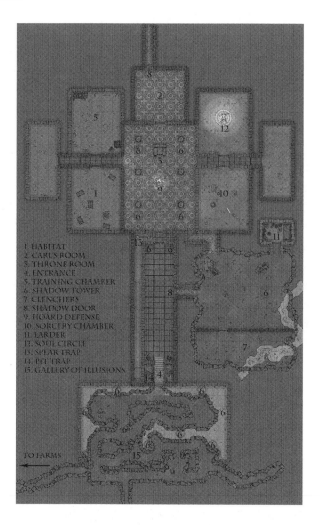

I took a look at the description.

[Gallery of Illusions

This construction applies an illusionary field to a large area of

300 x 300 feet. Within this field, shadow magic will pool and swirl, forming mental illusions to affect any intruders. Effects are set by the owner of the domain and come with several different possibilities. Can be turned off at will.]

Compared to the description, the actual look of the room was underwhelming. The hard work of the Talpi had changed what used to be a single tunnel with multiple exits. Now, the main tunnel had been enlarged into one large room, huge rock constellations breaking up the room to make the approach to the lair less straightforward. There were only three actual exits: the old trapped tunnels and the single entrance to the domain.

For any inhabitants, it was a matter of half a minute to navigate the tunnels and reach the entrance. For interlopers... heh. My experimentation with the settings of the Gallery had been limited, but intriguing. The current settings enabled the Gallery to be set to either "Confuse," "Hide," or "Off." Also, I had the choice between having it affect "everybody" and "non-minions only."

So far, the chances to test it out in practice had been non-existent. Our frequent forays into the lower layer of the mountain had done away with a lot of the more dangerous monsters, and the Talpi were becoming hardened enough to handle a good deal of the remaining solitary beasts by themselves. Today, we had our chance.

I took a good look at my forces. Arthor and Creziel were waiting side by side. The two Talpus Shamans were as different as day and night. Arthor was tall, self-confident, and stood out with his patterned brown and white fur. Absent-mindedly, he manipulated a single rock with either hand, pushing them floating away from him and beckoning them back in. Meanwhile, the tiny Creziel slouched, looking like he just wanted to be elsewhere. Right now, however, both stood silent and serious, waiting for the signal.

I closed the mini map and glanced behind me. Aelis stood at the center of a group, having a last-minute discussion with the fighters. Her sleek, jet-black fur and upright demeanor made her look strict and elegant. Even her missing paw failed to detract from the image of control, as she waved away an objection with a cool smile. Roth, our main trainer, stood next to her, but I highly doubted that he was paying attention. The wide, muscled Talpus was bouncing on his feet, fingering the pommel of his massive two-handed sword, glancing with longing at the entrance.

Next to the well-groomed forms of the Talpi stood my... less charismatic minions - my Crawls and Clenchers. The Crawls were medium-sized, brutish humanoids with rolls of hardened skin for armor and shit for brains. Currently, their leader, Erk was also listening to Aelis' explanation, but the vapid expressions on his coarse, ugly features made me doubt that any of the information was getting through. Sometimes, I debated my wisdom in taking them in as minions.

The huge, hairless forms of the bearlike Clenchers stood heads taller than the Crawls. While they'd started out as nothing more than mindless, slavering monsters to be dominated and eaten, these days, they were closer to pets. Dangerous, hungry pets. They looked like they were enjoying the outing.

Jumping back to the mini map, I spotted the threat immediately. A wandering Orugal had made its way into the Gallery. Our scouts had noticed the dangerous monster in good time, and I was waiting on the far side in case my assistance was needed. I shouldn't have worried, though. I initially set the choice to "hide" and watched from inside the mini map in satisfaction as the large monster sniffled around the Gallery.

He looked to me like what would happen if a giant alligator decided to breed with a mutant bulldog--his long body was all teeth and wiry muscles, and he sported a matching bad temper. His well-developed sense of smell was clearly confused by the strong scents that had led him here, but not once did he amble his way toward the domain entrance. Every single time he turned the right way, inexplicably, he'd start veering off course within a couple of tunnels. I decided it was time to experiment a bit and changed the setting to "Confuse."

The effect was immediate and hilarious. The large monster went berserk right away, attacking a nearby fleck of dust. Watching the stupid beast go through different grades of frenzy, confusion, and bewilderment was excellent entertainment. With that knowledge came an overwhelming sense of relief that my minions would be able to stay safe, even if I was away with the fighters. A grin spread across my face. It was time to implement the second phase of our plan and see how it would work in combat.

My mental shout went out through the dungeon: "Slide the windows open!" I grinned as rectangular sections opened on the outer walls of the Gallery at eight different positions. Beyond the openings rested the activated tops of eight Shadow Towers as well as my battle-ready shamans and ranged fighters. Split seconds later, the towers started taking potshots at the Orugal every time it got closer to one of the outside walls.

The effect was brutal. The moment the first Shadow Tower hit, the weakening effect kicked in. But the confused senses of the beast did not allow it to locate the attacker. Instead, it raged about the place, visibly weakening each time one of the towers managed to tag it. Once, it managed to focus on one of the towers through the confusing effects of the Gallery and charged in that direction, but the Talpus in charge acted sensibly and slid his window closed again. Right away, the huge Orugal was distracted by something else, forgetting all about the attacker.

The efficacy of the Gallery was undeniable. Even with our shamans and ranged fighters ready to attack at a moment's notice, we had prepared for the possibility of having to hold the huge beast further back in the domain. Totally unnecessary--it hadn't even managed to find the entrance.

Still, the Gallery was not foolproof. I wasn't too sure how it would hold up in the case of groups of attackers. The main thing was that it worked. It would keep the workers safe from most everything while the remainder of us were out touring the mountain and give us a huge advantage in larger battles. And in case somebody managed to proceed, well... I smiled. If somebody managed to force their way further on inside the domain, the walls and ceilings held other, more deadly surprises.

I led my people out to inflict tiny wounds on the Orugal from a distance. This way we would share the experience of the animal when we slaughtered it. Or not so tiny wounds, in some cases. I grinned to see the large monster finally succumb to our newest experimental weaponry.

That one had been tough. Roth and I had almost broken our brains trying to come up with a functional ranged weapon that would allow the strength-challenged Talpi to deal some damage at range. We ruled out crossbows and most throwing weapons right away. Crossbows, because stone weaponry, even combined with carved bone for the bow itself, wouldn't be able to provide the tension needed for proper damage and still hold up well to repeated usage.

Regular throwing weapons because, well, they were weak. We debated bows for a good while. In the end, we decided against them, though. It wasn't like I really knew much about bows, but from the books I'd read, you needed to find the right wood for it. Bone would probably be a bad replacement. Also, the winding, low-ceilinged tunnels that were the usual haunt of the Talpi wouldn't allow them to make proper use of the range a longbow would grant.

No, they needed something with a shorter range with more impact. As a result, right now, part of the Training Chamber had been turned into a shooting gallery, holding freshly carved, slim, stone-tipped bone throwing spears along with a couple of *atlatls* - handheld devices that allowed the Talpi to throw the spears a lot harder than they would be able otherwise.

As I passed the descent from the Gallery into the entrance hallway and the bowels of my domain, I thought of the well-hidden death ready to be unleashed on any attackers to brave the rough, boring hallway. Four Shadow Towers, a wall with hidden crawl spaces, the spiked, reusable pit trap and now, also easily disguised murder holes from where to unleash damage from a distance.

As I walked back toward my throne room, I couldn't help but give out a growl of wellbeing. Our situation was improving every day. We had just finished the last known major threat nearby yesterday--the Earth Furies. It was an exhilarating fight, and a mentally exhausting one, as the Furies had limited shapeshifting abilities.

We kept having to adapt to changing methods of attack. Even so, they had been unable to force their way through the combined bulk of the Clenchers and myself, and we'd whittled them down little by little, with tons of experience to our forces as a result. In short, we might not have any long-term plans right now, but things were fun and as safe as they came inside the mountain. I loved it.

The ample experience gave me enough to hit level 17 myself. This had been the first fight in almost four weeks since the final showdown against the green dragon who had slain Jazinth. We had not been sitting on our asses since then, but had, for the most part, stayed inside my domain.

Defeating the Earth Furies, on top of the fight with the vile green dragon, had given me a lot of goodies. Treasures, to begin with. Five new mana crystals that were now snugly installed in my own hoard at home, bringing my mana regen to 724 a day, more than a full mana pool for me. A lot of nice weapons and armor. Most of them were way too large, given that they were made for the heavy Urten. Some jewelry lay scattered around, baubles the green had decided to keep for himself.

There was also one massive stretch of cured animal leather I was unable to see the point of, at first, until the small spikes embedded in the leather gave it away. It was a collar, large enough for a dragon. Clever goddamn green. Or, I was just the slow one for not coming up with it earlier. Of course dragons needed magical boosts as well from wearing neck bands. Right now, the collar was resting comfortably back in the hoard, waiting to gain some magical attribute that would allow me to boost myself. Meanwhile, one of the leatherworkers was toiling away on another custom order for me: a full-body harness. The green had been right, but he'd just been thinking too small.

The loot, abundant as it was, had not been the real gift from the battle. No, the real kicker had been in the rewards from leveling up. Obviously, the attribute increases had been lovely, but I had gained a new feat, an upgraded skill, *and* a new skill to boot.

The feat was a defensive one, and a tough choice. I loved every single choice on the list and wanted them all.

[Improved Defense.
The layer of skin beneath your scales hardens, granting you an extra layer of defense against physical attacks. For every subsequent level, you gain a 5 percent resistance to physical attacks. Maximum cap: 50 percent.]

[Improved Magical Resistance.
Your scales evolve to protect you against any magical and elemental damage. For every subsequent level, you gain a 5 percent resistance to magical or elemental attacks. Maximum cap: 50 percent.]

[Improved Mental Resistance.
You train your mind to protect you against any mental assaults. For every subsequent level, you gain a 5 percent resistance to mental attacks. Maximum cap: 50 percent.]

I ruled out the mental one pretty quickly. Sure, the idea of being mind controlled or whatever they could do to my brains was not a nice one. Even so, my Mental Power was already high enough that I should be pretty well protected from those kinds of attacks. If they could beat that, they could probably also brush aside what extra resistance I could come up with.

The other two were tougher to choose between. I already

had the Hardened Scales feat, and I could easily picture just how effective my physical defense would be if I added another layer of defense on top of that... except, I wasn't aiming to be a close-combat specialist. In fact, thinking back, my Agility usually allowed me to keep my distance. The real threats had come from enemies who were able to beat me down at a distance with magical or elemental attacks, like the poison from the green dragon or the red dragon's fire breath. I selected Magical Resistance, grumbling a bit at how they wouldn't let me pick both.

My improved illusion skill was just lovely on all counts.

[Skill improved:
Create Illusion.
This skill allows you to create and maintain an illusion. As long as the viewer doesn't see through the illusion, it fools all senses except touch. The chance of targets seeing through illusions is affected by the size and intricacy of the illusion as well as their mental power.

The effects, limitations and effectiveness of the skill improve as you level.

Cost: 1 mana/10 seconds.
- *Cost reduced to 1 mana/30 seconds*
- *From now on, you only need line of sight to create the illusion. You can maintain it at a distance.*]

Not that I had any issues with my mana regeneration. These days, I rarely made a dent in my mana reserves, but the utility grew by a *lot* when I didn't have to stay nearby to maintain an illusion.

The skill I gained was something else--something new, and I loved it.

[**Shadow Whorl**.

You summon a living whorl of blended shadow and illusion magic and affix it to a specific location or creature. The billow-ing, undulating mass will swirl around the center in a 10-foot radius, causing partial blindness, flickering illusions, and chaotic visions on any enemies caught within the radius. The effect will not apply to allies. Efficiency of the spell is dependent on the Mental Power of the enemy. Duration: 2 minutes.]

I couldn't wait to check it out. I would be able to toss it inside a crowded battlefield and wouldn't even have to worry about my own minions. Or, I could use it to distract any enemies I was facing myself.

The attributes I divided between Toughness and Mental Power. My fight with the green had taught me that I needed more survival power and that my breath weapon needed more oomph. Besides, Timothy, the human who was caught inside the protective Soul Circle back in my domain, was still trapped, and I needed a full 500 mana to make that circle mine. With the attributes I'd gained, I managed that, with a few attribute points to spare. With a feeling of satisfaction, I put in the points and brought up my info screen to see the result.

Personal Info:
Name: Onyx
Race: Fledgling Shadow Dragon. Level 17 – experience toward next level: 5500/17000
Size: Very large

Stats and Attributes:
Health: 480/480
Mana: 500/500
Strength: 24
Toughness: 48
Agility: 61
Mental Power: 50
Mental Control: 69

Health regeneration rate: 48/hour
Mana regeneration rate: 724/day

Woo. I was looking good. Sure, my pure strength was still negligible compared to the two dragons I'd faced, but that was by choice. My toughness was improving, and my agility and mental attributes were through the roof.

On a whim, I decided to take a look at my skills and abilities as well.

[Abilities:
Deafening Roar: You release a huge roar, affecting everyone within hearing range. The effect depends on distance, the target's level, and Mental Control. Possible effects include weakness, hearing loss, stun, and paralysis. Cooldown: three minutes

Flight: You are capable of flight. How long you can remain airborne depends on your Toughness.

Minor Telepathy: You are able to communicate your thoughts mentally to the recipient. The possible range for the telepathic bond depends on your Mental Power and that of the recipient. The clarity of the messages and ability to protect thoughts from outsiders depends on your Mental Control.

Weakening Fog: You release a cloud of mist that saps the strength of any living creature it comes in contact with. Agility, Strength, and Toughness are affected. Effects are cumulative and upon multiple applications, targets may faint or lose control of their body.

Shadow control: Within the limits of your own domain, you will be able to manipulate the shadows to a certain extent. You can remove them, deepen them, and have them move like living creatures with a single thought. The ability is limited by the size of your hoard, your Mental Power, and your Mental Control.]

Ah. My bread and butter. My basic survival kit. The abilities that had kept me alive for months now, which was more or less the average lifespan in the Scoured Mountain, according to my minions. I *really* needed to improve my flight skills, though. Still, with my new-found Shadow Whorl on top of this, I was feeling good about the tools at my disposal. As for the skills...

[Inspect: Inspect allows you to see the details of friendly items and creatures within your domain.

The power of the skill increases along with the size of your Hoard.

Apply Profession: You are able to apply professions to your minions, increasing their effectiveness. Professions are permanent, but will be regained if your minion dies or otherwise leaves your service.

The power, selections, and effectiveness of the skill increases along with the size and content of your Hoard.

Domain Map: Within your map, you can now see the entirety of your domain in realtime, along with the placement and status of your minions.

The versatility of the skill increases along with the size of your Hoard.

Construction: This skill allows you to create and upgrade buildings and other constructions inside your domain. A new Construction panel has been added to your character sheet.

The selections within the Construction panel are increased along with the size of your hoard.]

By themselves, the skills might not seem too impressive - but in conjunction, they allowed me to quickly take stock of what was happening in my domain, check out details on any attackers and react accordingly. And the professions helped me single out the core members among my minions and boost their survival capabilities. Of course, other dragons would also have these skills, but they gave us a serious edge against all monsters.

Returning to my throne room, I sighed in satisfaction. My hoard was starting to look really impressive. Weapons, jewels, and armor were carefully arrayed for the best display within the glowing blue bubble of the Hoard Defense. The room itself had been completely repaired of the damage from the early days, and the knowledge that it was all prepared for any attacker improved everything even more. One of these days, I might have Creziel look into some purely cosmetic improvements: friezes on the walls and maybe something to replace the fine lines of the blood grooves in the floor. I wasn't too sure that was the kind of message I wanted to send visitors. Heh. If I ever got any.

Off to the sides, more improvements had been made. The larder had been finally completed and dried out and, according to Aelis, they had figured out a means of creating huge jars for conservation that were practically air and water tight. That would prove well for our reserves, should we ever manage to amass some. For now, the Farm was holding up well, when it came to supplies for the plant eaters. The rest of us... my stomach growled at the thought. Good thing we'd finished off the Earth Furies, or we might be looking at the need to go out and find some animals again soon.

We had also managed to excavate the final chambers in the domain. No hidden treasuries or loot stashes to be found here, unfortunately. Either side had held one single chamber at the end of their respective corridor, high-ceilinged, dull, and empty. The westmost chamber still held a couple of clues as to its original purpose in the form of glass shards and the ruined remains of what looked like a handful of potion bottles. The eastmost one stayed unknown. What it did mean was that we, for once, had spare room for expanding, should we need it.

The westmost corridor rang with noise. It was the one that led to the Talpus Habitat, and these days it was awash with mewling and high-pitched noises. Two of the pregnant Talpi had given birth to litters, and right now, we had fifteen pups in the newly established nests. They still didn't count toward my minion count. Apparently, that only happened when they got to the age where they could contribute. But things were looking up in that department.

As a matter of fact, I might soon end up discovering what the maximum minion count would mean in practice. Right this moment, I had 66 out of a maximum of 125. 36 Talpi, 10 Crawls, and 5 Clenchers costing 4 each. But with 15 additional Talpus pups and three more Talpus mothers pregnant, we might soon reach the limit. As if that wasn't enough of a future boost, two crawls and three of the four female Clenchers were pregnant. We were looking at a serious expansion soon. I was just glad I didn't have to change any diapers. One round of that was enough for me.

I took my place inside my own room and let my mental voice ring out over my domain. "Well done, everybody. Take a break. Those who wanted to talk earlier, I'm ready now." Soon, a handful of Talpi were forming in front of me with questions and issues. Within a couple of minutes, I'd reduced the queue down to two.

The first of these to approach was Laive. I wasn't really looking forward to her visit, but at least she usually had some legitimate questions and issues. The thickset Talpus was not especially strong, clever, or pleasant company, and her affinity with the earth was rather limited, from what Aelis told me. However, there was one thing she mastered above all.

"Onyx. The plants are doing well. I need answers."

It was always like this. Abrupt and straight to the point. I liked that about her. I only had two issues with her. One was that I was rarely able to answer her detailed questions. Laive had taken over responsibility for the Farm, and she was rocking it. We'd just moved past my, very limited, knowledge on the subject. "By all means. Ask away."

Her brusque nod launched a series of farming and plant life-related questions, and I did my best to keep my attention from waning and provide her with the best answers I could. It was tough, though. I really didn't care too much about plants to begin with. My own garden had mostly been a perfectly trimmed lawn with a self-driving lawn mower and a handful of fancy plants and flowers that Cait nursed.

I kept up as best I could with topics like humidity, differences between plant types and their care, and the nutrition of different plants. I tentatively allowed her to start looking for another suitable Farm room and putting together cuttings, shoots, and seeds for the establishment. We would need it. Regardless of my intentions, it would appear that my attention did drift, because in the end, my brain kicked me, implying that I'd missed something important. I frowned. "Please repeat that last bit again?"

The squat Talpus shrugged. "I'll try different guesses so I-"

I cut her off. "No. Before that."

"Oh. I said that I am taking the room past the Nest for myself."

That was my other issue with Laive. She tended to forget that I was in charge, when it came to plants. "You will have to come up with a damn fine reason to do that. We've got plenty of other people who would love a room of their own."

She blinked at me, slowly, like an owl. "It's up to you, Onyx." She shrugged. "I thought that playing with different types of earth, poison, and food might be a bad idea inside the Farm, but... you decide, I guess."

"You want to... what?"

"You heard me. I'm supposed to make sure we always have food for all of us, right? To do that right, I need to tinker around with different types of soil, mud, and plants. I can't very well do that inside the Farm. It'll be all mixed up inside the earth."

"Sure. Let's move on, though. Poison?"

"Yeah. Aelis said you'd mentioned it to Jazinth at some point. Not the best choice."

I froze. "You had better watch what you're saying right now." Okay, so I'd thought I was over the death of the defiant shaman apprentice. Clearly, I wasn't.

The Talpus paused, then looked straight up at me in defiance. Tones of fear oozed from her, but they were packed down tight beneath the smell of confidence. "So far, you haven't been afraid of the truth. You shouldn't start now. Jazinth didn't have the temper for creating poison. She was impatient, overconfident, and prone to sudden impulses. I am not."

I could feel my lips peeled back as my teeth threatened to snap at her. I fought down my temper and forced myself to look at it from the outside. Even inside my own mind, my words sounded strained when I admitted, "You may be right there. That still doesn't mean you should talk about her like that."

She just frowned. "Why do you believe that? I am not lying. In the meantime, you should give me that room."

For a moment, I considered turning her down out of spite, but reconsidered. I'd worked with a lot of different personality types over the years. Some of them were right bastards. I'd come to the conclusion early on in my career that I would need to be able to handle all sorts of workers to make it even--no, especially if I didn't like it. I was going to make this apply here too, even if I found her cold-hearted demeanor repulsive.

Hell, I might agree with some of her words too, if only she was able to act normal. I shook my head violently. If I'd already decided that I wouldn't make something out of it, I needed to act like it. "Laive. Enlighten me. If I were to give you that room, how would you go about creating poisons?"

She scratched her arm. A thin sheen of dust floated away from her as she started talking, oblivious. "I'll need help. First, Creziel is going to help me with a number of pots and containers. I'll need a lot of them, and I'll need to mark them to make sure I know what's what. Then, I need to kick Arthor until he tells me everything the tribe has remembered about different poisons ever. Hmm. You, too, obviously. Creziel told me that the people of your world can't kill each other in the open? That must mean that you resort to ambushes and poison often?"

"That's... not how it works. Heh. Not often, at least." I tried to think back to any conversations on the topic with Creziel and failed. Wait... I did try telling him about world peace at some point. Clearly, tiny details had gotten lost in translation somewhere. "Now, I'm not by any means well-versed in poisonous plants. Anyway, your nature differs so much from ours, even if I was, it wouldn't matter."

She shrugged. "All right. Then I'll make do with Arthor."

"Not what I meant. I have read a few books on the subject." Fantasy books about assassins and the like, but still. It would have to count. "My help would probably be a little different, more about the *way* you should experiment. Strengthen your poisons. Label and store them. That's beside the point, however. You *are* getting the room, and I *am* going to help you. If you are able to end up being able to mass-produce just a single high-strength poison for our weapons, it could mean a world of difference for us. We'll just have to choose the right precautions."

"That's fair. I'll get the room and containers ready."

I took the chance to Inspect Laive, looking over her attributes:

[Personal Info:
Name: Laive
Race: Talpus. Level 9 – experience toward next level: 6800/9000
Size: Very small

Stats and Attributes:
Health: 150/150

Mana: 40/40
Strength: 12
Toughness: 23
Agility: 8
Mental Power: 6
Mental Control: 7]

Those numbers--that couldn't be right. "Laive... how on earth did you manage to get your Toughness that high? I thought Talpi started with an average of 5 in all skills?" My own Toughness at level 1 had been 20, and I was a frigging *dragon*!

She shrugged. "Got lucky and got a feat. Gives me Toughness each level. Then the dragon meat gave me some. Training gave me the rest. I'm not a slacker. Roth tells me to train agility, too, but I'm not a scout. I told him to go kiss a Drainer Fly."

I shook my head in amazement. "You're absolutely right. And I've told Roth before that people are allowed to choose for themselves. In fact, I'll have a word with him, anyway. Training with your work in mind is a lot wiser than spreading out the attributes. Also, if you're going to be experimenting with poison, we'll want you as tough and resistant as possible. Hm. one question: The very best for us would be if we found somebody who knew how to heal people. From my hoard upgrades, it looks like those classes or races should be available, but where?"

"I was a builder before. Now, I'm a farmer. Can't help you. You'll need Arthor. Anything else?"

I shook my head at her behavior, which she seemed to interpret as a dismissal. I was left looking at her back as she trudged away with not a care in the world. The last Talpus waiting for me looked at me and gave a nervous grin. "She's always been like that."

I grinned back at him. "Well, at least she knows what she wants."

The lithe beast rolled his eyes. I looked him over. Even without Inspect, I was getting a lot better at telling the Talpi apart. This one was one of the two builders who helped take care of the Clenchers. Of course, the rank scent of Clencher manure was a bit of a giveaway, but I was confident I could have remembered anyway. His name was... Eamer. Even? "Eamus. How are the big brutes? Everything progressing well?"

He bounced a bit on his feet, and I could smell the eagerness coming from him. "Better than well. In fact, I wanted to ask if you could spare a moment to come along with us and see something?"

Curious, I assented and got up. "Sure. What's the deal?"

"I'd like to show you. instead."

CHAPTER TWO

On our way to the Clencher enclosure, Eamus didn't give away the surprise, even though I prodded him a few times. He did fill me in on the training with gusto. In short, everything was progressing better than expected. I'd finally trained the Clenchers enough that they registered as minions, removing the worst fear that they should go berserk and eat my Talpi. I kept up with the daily training, and just a week ago, I'd had the next breakthrough. I finally managed to get the big beasts to listen to orders from another trainer.

Since then, I'd taken any chance I could to let Eamus and the other Talpus take the reins, all under my surveillance. The last couple of days before our excursion against the Earth Furies, I had stayed outside the room as the trainers handled the massive beasts. I wouldn't want to let them handle the large beasts in combat alone just yet, but the fact that my tiny helpers were able to prod around the massive beasts was astonishing.

The way they had changed from raving beasts into something that, on a good day, could be mistaken for pets... it was way beyond my initial hopes. I had been so goddamn lucky with my minions... except for the Crawls, who annoyed the crap out of me. If we continued in this manner, I'd be able to enjoy myself alongside the Talpi without fearing for my life all the time.

Safe. It would be something to feel safe again.

The other trainer was already inside the Clencher enclosure when I arrived. The place had been changed quite a lot since we first erected it. Creziel and Arthor had forced the nearby underground stream into a new course a while back, letting it trickle through the corner of the enclosure and create a small pool for the beasts before rushing back to its past course. The trainers had a couple of oversized scratching boards erected, allowing the big beasts to remove dried mud and any annoying bugs. Laive had helped too, planting a row of plants that were apparently good for our massive monsters.

I sat down on my haunches in anticipation. Eamus hefted a massive rod that was placed next to the door, walked right over to one of the Clenchers, and patted its big leg. Not Ursam. That big bully had somehow gotten himself attached to me and rarely accepted commands from anybody else. The four females were easier to work with. Eamus approached the big beast, talking at a low pitch all the while, and it proceeded to sit down with a big oomph. Then it lay down and turned its head to look at the trainer placidly.

The tiny Talpus gave me a cheery wave and kept talking to the Clencher. In three fluid movements, he climbed its knee, launched himself onto the wide back of the animal head-first, and brought one leg around to the other side. Then, with a triumphant grin, he sat up straight and looked down on me.

I plodded over, taking care not to spook the animal. Not that scaring them was an easy task. The Clenchers were actually rather calm and lazy, once they got over that initial 'wanting to kill and eat you'-stage. "She lets you climb her?"

This time, his grin moved past triumphant to show-off territory. "That's not all, Onyx. Watch this." He sat back down, slid a little forward with his short legs widely spread and, once his feet almost reached either side of the Clencher's massive neck, started to whisper into the animal's ear.

I looked attentively as the Clencher's body started to move. The monster itself stood completely still, but beneath the skin, bones were rearranging themselves, soundlessly moving about. I almost shouted out as the bones visibly settled around Eamus' feet and clenched - but the Talpus looked unaffected. In fact, he looked extremely satisfied with the animal and kept up his whispered words even as his feet were trapped, one by one. My mental voice was more akin to a whisper as I asked Eamus, "Whaaat the hell are you doing?"

His response was instant and filled with pride. "Learning to ride, Onyx."

"Learning to... you're really doing that? I know I told Creziel, but... You *are* aware that you're irreparably trapped right now? If the Clencher decides to smash you against a wall, you won't be able to do anything about it."

He waggled a paw in front of me. "That's where you're mistaken. See, Heiven and I figured it out the other day. A good smack right *here*," he rested his rod at the point right where the spine connected with the wide neck of the Clencher, "and she'll release everything. But for now, just look at this."

I watched in amazement as Eamus had the large animal get up and walk around the enclosure with him on top. A simple prod with the rod had him controlling which way to move and when to stop and go. For all the world, it looked like somebody teaching an elephant how to act. Except this elephant was a full-blooded predator.

Once he had finished with the ride and dropped down to the floor again, I praised him. "I'll hand it to you, Eamus. I really didn't think it was possible. And the possibilities..." I shook my head, practically drooling at the thought of Clencher cavalry. "You just made history in the Scoured Mountain." The tiny mole-wolf hybrid beamed, sharp teeth grinning his pleasure at my words. I cautioned him, "Now, please do continue with the training, but don't go too fast. If we do this right, we can end up with a massive force, but it's still easy to screw it up."

He nodded. "Don't worry, Onyx. We are being careful, and I'm not going riding on this beauty outside the enclosure until after it's had its pups." His manic grin stretched the skin back from his teeth. "Still, I can't wait to see everybody's reactions when I lead her into battle."

I shook my head. It took a certain kind of maniac to look forward to something like that, but I supposed that the thought of suddenly not being the underdog in every combat situation was a powerful drug. I spent a while longer with the two trainers, discussing the future progression and our plans. Nobody was entirely certain how long it would be until the pups arrived, but they believed it was still months away. All they knew was that Clenchers had litters of several pups. The thought of multiplying our Clencher population along with having them grow up accustomed to my other minions--yeah, the future looked bright. Speaking of bright... it was time for me to visit our glowing blue resident. My mana was full. I sure hope this would work.

Timothy was still where I'd left him. He was currently face down on the floor, hands over his head, moaning silently. I shook my head. "I can't believe how long you've suffered. I hope this works." Focusing my magic, I let it rove over the floor again as a shapeless pseudopod, assuring me that I hadn't missed anything. I still hadn't figured out any other effects, apart from being able to see through illusions, but I had a feeling there was more to be discovered here. For now, I let it lie and looked at the hidden inscription on the floor, selecting my Inspect skill.

[Protective Soul Circle - unclaimed.
This construction protects the creature sealed within. It provides the creature with all nutrients needed to sustain his existence. The protective circle is dual-layered, protecting from both physical and magical dangers.]

There it was. As opposed to my last attempts, this time, the button was not greyed out.

[Claim protective circle. Cost: 500 mana]

I tentatively pressed the button and stepped back, waiting. I felt a sinking sensation in my stomach as my entire mana pool was drained. It was like when I had my wisdom teeth pulled, with some heavy painkillers involved. There was no pain, but it still felt wrong. The sensation felt like somebody reached into my abdomen and *pulled*.

The effect as the deluge of mana rushed out of me and toward the Soul Circle was impressive. The entire room lit up as the blue strands of energy surrounding the long-suffering human slithered around on all sides of the protective circle, reaching out toward me to drink in the mana. Ignoring the blinding light, I looked closely and within seconds I could see how the strands, now sated, started their lazy circling again.

This time they did not reach into Timothy's body like they had before. Instead, they circled down into the ground, lazily reaching for the mana they so clearly needed, shining brighter when they returned to circle the surface of the circle. Inspecting the circle again, the "unclaimed" part was gone, as was the part about not being connected to a mana reserve.

Timothy was still. Catatonic, even. His moaning had stopped, too. I decided to sit back and wait patiently. An hour passed. I talked to him now and again, to no result. Two hours. Then, tiny twitches ran through his body as he slowly turned onto his side and, ever so slowly, looked at me.

I nodded at him. "Hello, Timothy."

His look turned into a stare. His eyes bulged, like his head was threatening to implode. Then it slowly settled and his mental voice emerged in a whisper. "Is this real?"

"It is. Has the pain gone?"

He didn't answer. His reaction alone was answer enough. Tears welled up in his eyes and he sat up and started bawling.

Sobs, closer to shouts, emerged from his mouth. This time, they didn't sound pained, but more... cathartic. In time, his cries abated and he relaxed. Then, suddenly, he started patting himself all over. "I'm not hurting. What is this? What happened?" His gaze fixed on mine again. "Who *are* you?"

"Carl. I'm from Earth... like you, Timothy. I... I think you're safe now."

"Carl... I would very much like to believe that. Now, please, what the *fuck* just happened?"

We sat in the large room, lit by the flickering lights of the protective circle, while I told him about what had happened. My arrival and almost death at the hands of the Talpi. The annihilation of the undead and establishment of my hoard. My increases and skills. Our slow expansion and battles. Clenchers, Salamanders and more. And, finally, the arrival of more dragons.

Haltingly, I also told him about the death of Jazinth and our crusade for revenge. I added my joy at the discovery that I was not the only person from Earth here and the following hunt for a solution for freeing the glowing man from his prison.

I finished with a shrug. "That's about it. I finally leveled up enough to reach the mana I needed to claim your Protective Circle and, well, it looks like it's reconnected and back to pulling the mana directly from the earth or this Deyra goddess, whatever it is. So, how do you feel?"

His eyes welled up again and he didn't speak for a while. "Sorry. I'm not like this normally. It's just... you know, one of my favorite writers had a quote that went something like 'If there is a God, it's a painkiller.' Total sacrilege and all, but he was right. I feel... okay. I really do." His laughter reverberated inside my head, sounding almost sane. He got up in a weird, flowing motion, but stayed encircled within the protective circle, on the clean, spotless surface of the floor.

I smiled, making sure not to show my teeth. "I'm pretty sure looking at a dragon isn't the best thing for you after an experience like yours, but I promise you, I'm not going to eat you.

Things are only going to improve from here on. How about I turn off that thing, and you come see my domain?"

The enigmatic look he gave me was hard to understand. Why was it so filled with pain? He took a step forward, still within the circle, and held up a hand. "Sorry, man. No can do. I'll show you why. Give me a high five."

I frowned at that, suddenly suspicious. What was this?

Timothy laughed with a sound that did not hold any joy. "Come on, man. Don't leave me hanging. I swear in the name of the almighty Thomas Edward Patrick Brady Jr., nothing's gonna happen."

Wait... "You're a Patriots fan? That's supposed to make me trust you?" I laughed and I could feel a tear coming to my eye, too. This tiny piece of normalcy in this crazy world... I couldn't bring myself to believe that he meant me harm and brought up my front paw, slowly bringing it closer to his outstretched hand. Entering the protective circle did nothing. There was just a tiny tingle as I broke the surface. My paw moved closer to his hand, we touched... and his hand continued right through my paw, erupting through the other side in a burst of blue color.

I backed up a few steps. "What the hell?" Then, in sudden inspiration, I cast Inspect on him. I'd tried before, but before I claimed the protective circle, I had been unable to select him. Now, however, his info popped up instantly.

Personal Info:
Name: Timothy
Race: Human Soul, Level 1 – experience toward next level: 0/1000
Size: Small

Stats and Attributes:
Health: N.A.
Mana: 100/100
Strength: N.A.
Toughness: N.A.

Agility: N.A.
Mental Power: 10
Mental Control: 10

I gasped. "No way. There's just no way. You're-"

"A ghost. Yeah." The lopsided grin on his face told me it was no surprise to him. "Talk about a shitty surprise. Thrown into this world where everybody can gain levels and become totally OP, and-"

"OP?"

"Overpowered, old-timer. Of course, I'm the only one who doesn't get a body so I can get going with the killstreaks. Still, if I was surprised, you should've seen the look on that necromancer's face when he figured out I was harder to grab a hold of than M.C. Hammer." He grinned. "Hey, I made an old people joke, so you could feel included. Like it?"

I massaged my brow and pointed a claw at him. Growling under my breath, I laced my message with all the sarcasm it could bear. "I'm so damn glad you're here. I can already tell that you're going to give me daily migraines. Now, would you mind backing the hell up to the point where you told me that you've seen the *necromancer*?"

His eyebrows shot up. "Hoo boy. Oh yeah. Have I got the tale for you! Uh. It's not really that stirring, though."

I grunted. "Try me, Timmy-boy. Now, before we get started. Are you all right? I mean, really?"

His grin dropped for a moment. "No. No, I'm probably not. I'm dead, forced into an incorporeal thing that can't affect anything whatsoever, and have had an overall shitty time of it. Still, it's the best I've been for a while, yeah? Right this moment, it beats the alternative." His grin slowly crept onto his face, covering the hurts that, moments earlier, had been clear to see. "Now, hearken the tale of this one, heroic New Yorker who braved Death to educate this simple-minded dragon in a realm of dark and dangerous forces."

"Heh. Tone it down, will ya kid?"

"Never!"

Timothy started telling me everything. Some of it, I'd already gathered. He had been pretty young. 25 years old, and lost control of his car on the way to work doing some internet thing I'd never heard about. Then, as soon as he came to his senses, he found himself trapped inside this protective circle in front of the notorious Soul Carver. "I'll tell you this much: he was *pissed*. So, apparently, he'd wasted quite a bit of time and resources in order to summon silly old me into this world, and he hadn't ever considered the fact that a soul wouldn't come with its own shell attached. Stupid old idiot. Anyway-"

"No! The necromancer's the one who summoned you? Are you kidding me?"

"You as well. Now, listen here, boomer, if you'd let me finish talking, I'd tell you what I know."

I let a growl slip from my lips, but inside, I enjoyed the back and forth. I'd had my share of cocksure workers toiling below me, and this one was no different. He wasn't half bad at it, either. "All right, young whippersnapper. I'll indulge you."

The blue, glowing form performed a sarcastic bow. "Thank thee ever so kindly. Now, this Soul Carver's a scary dude. He's also usually pretty damn composed. The very first time he summoned me, though, he was beyond furious. Spitting and screaming about all the work he'd wasted, summoning a no-good spirit like me. He was also threatening--or, more considering, really--to just let this protective circle slip and kill me himself."

I held up a paw. "Hold on there, Timmy. So the protective circle isn't just to keep you trapped?"

He frowned. "It's either Tim or Timothy, man. Timmy fell down a fucking well. And yeah, the circle both protected and trapped me. I mean, that bastard was the only real threat to me, really, but from what he said, any magic damage would also be able to harm me. So the circle kept me here, but it also provided me with what I needed to survive. It's not like I need food anymore, even though my mind's *dying* for a goddamn burger."

We shared a moment in silence, as we both drooled over that impossible vision. Then he shook himself and continued. "So, since I couldn't get any sustenance, whatever it is I need, myself, and I can't bloody *touch* things, he just kept me there."

"Okay, so why did he end up keeping you around? And what was he like?"

"Oh, textbook scary, man. Tall, brooding, and falling apart at the seams. I mean that literally, too. He must've used some of his own mojo on himself, because sometimes pieces looked ripe, know what I'm saying? Anyway, he ended up quizzing me for a full day or something. Asking questions about where I came from, what I did, what I knew about magic, all sorts of stuff. As for keeping me around, well... he ended up finding me useful and full of insight."

I'd known enough young hotheads to see when somebody was dancing around the topic. "What does that mean, though? Full of insight?"

"Well, obviously, he wanted to know about our world. I told him all he wanted because, well, he was crazy scary and threatened to kill me."

I nodded. "Of course. What about afterward? Once he figured out he'd gotten all he wanted from you? Did he chat with you or leave you alone in the dark or what?"

"He... well, most of the time, I was here alone. You wouldn't know it from looking at it, but this used to be a kinda cozy room, nice chair, huge library and all. He'd come here to relax in the evenings and, once in a while, some of his minions would shuffle in to clean or deliver something they'd found. There were always some of them around--zombies, skeletons, some weird, stitched ones.

"Mostly, they were just zoned out, standing still, if they didn't get an order. Anyway, he didn't talk much. A few times he wanted some company to discuss some theories. He kinda got annoyed at me after a while, though, because I didn't know anything about this world. Still don't know much, really. Then, one day, out of the blue, he started teaching me how to read this crazy hieroglyphic script of his.

"Then he'd throw all sorts of books or tomes at me that he couldn't be bothered to read himself. 'Find all mentions of the Scoured Mountain here.' 'Go through this, see if there is anything on runes and runic magic.' Stuff like that. He had this ratty old skeleton attached to my movements who'd hold the books, turn the pages. Sometimes he'd make me read out loud to him. Then, later on-" Timothy's voice trailed off as I tried and failed to hide an involuntary grin as a cough. He looked at me, waiting, for a while, until he came with it. "All right. Spit it out."

"Oh, it's nothing. Just..." I raised my claws in front of me. "The whole image of it. He made you read to him? The scary Soul Carver used you as a goddamn Alexa? That's hilarious."

"Can we continue?"

The blue visage stared intangible daggers at me, and I got it together, waving for him to move on.

"Okay, so those were the good days. He'd have some skeleton hold the book, I'd read some stuff, learn a little about this weird damn world, and mostly be left alone. The bad days... we're saving those for another time. Needless to say, I'm still pretty much in the dark about this world, what's happening and, well, what my part in it is."

I pondered that for a while. Really thought about it. Something was off about the whole thing. Not about Timmy's explanation. He seemed like a good guy, especially for a Patriots fan, who'd just gotten the short end of the karma stick. If I thought back to when I rolled out of the egg for the very first time... Slowly, tasting the idea, I asked, "Tim. Have you ever received a system message?"

"System message? What're you-"

"Shut up. Concentrate on the words 'Personal info.' Just think it out loud inside your mind."

"What? Why would... ooooh, shitballs." The blue appearance went unnaturally still for a while.

It was the first time I noticed that he didn't breathe. In fact, when he was still, there was *no* movement, whatsoever. It was only his constant screaming and flailing inside the protective circle that had kept me from noticing.

"Oh my God, that's frustrating. Also incredible. That's been there all along?"

"Yeah. Sorry. It sounds like, if you're native to this place, you get some sort of Introduction at birth that sticks with you, eases you into the system. You and me, we probably skipped it on account of not being part of this place. I figured it out when somebody tried to murder and eat me right out of the egg, and I sort of leveled up after I killed them and got a pop-up."

He looked rattled. "So I can level even if I'm a ghost? Wait." He spent half a minute more completely still and then chuckled. "I'm not defenseless? Whooo! I have some sort of mental attack. Hah, and it drains mana from the enemy, too! So, you're saying I can actually go out there and... do what I want? Get out of this damn cage?"

I nodded. "You can. Sort of. I mean, I'm not stopping you, and you're free to go wherever you want. There's a lot of dangerous creatures out there who'd probably be able to hurt you, though. But... you know what, that's not even important right now. Let's get you out of there." I fiddled about with my Inspect skill for a while, until I was able to switch the protective circle over to where Tim was able to select for himself whether he wanted to be inside the circle or not. "All right. Give it a shot. We'll take a tour of the premises, talk with the locals."

Now that he actually had the possibility, Tim didn't seem so eager. He stood on the edge of the circle, glancing nervously at the room. "But... what if I actually need to stay inside to survive?"

"If going outside hurts or incapacitates you in some way, I'll dump you back in the circle faster than you can say 'Belichick is a goddamn cheater.'"

"How exactly are you going to do that, if you can't touch me? Also, that kind of smacktalk sounds like something only a loser would say. A Jets fan maybe. Or worse... Fins? You with the fish? Come now, show me on the doll where the bad Belichick kicked your butt."

I took a step back and growled at him. "So it's like that? Come out here and repeat that!"

He glared at me for a moment... then his anger slowly dissipated and dissolved into laughter. After a while, the laughter subsided and he wiped at non-existent tears. "Thank you. Bastard. Sorry, I'm not old enough to really fall for the old 'chicken' trick. You really think that I'm safe, though?"

"Yeah. It sounds like the motto for this place is something like 'Go. Fight. Thrive.' or thereabouts. I doubt whatever divinity cooked that up would let you die just like that. If you want to stay in the cage, I'm not forcing you."

He visibly steeled himself and took a single step forward--to no effect whatsoever. He shrugged with a relieved look on his face. "Well that was anticlimactic."

I smiled. "I'm glad. I don't think you need too much excitement right now."

His crooked, shaky grin was response enough. "On that note, thank you. Thank you very, very much. You didn't need to help me, but you did."

"Aw, screw that. We're two Earthlings alone in this crazy place. You think I'd leave you alone?"

He shook his head with a tiny smile. "Most people would. Still, I've got a feeling you're not most people, Carl." We stood in silence for a moment until he cleared his throat. "So, you mind if we stay here for a while? I... I don't think my head's up to a lot of excitement right now."

I grinned. "No problem. Now, if you're up for it, I'll introduce you to the head honcho around here, beside myself. Arthor's a good guy. You'll get to like him... eventually."

"Ugh. Could we maybe wait a little with that? Today's been pretty eventful already. I'm not sure I can deal with a lot more. Maybe tell me a bit more about what you know about the mountain?"

We spent a while more, while I went over what I knew about the place. The dangers and monsters that lurked. The weird, game-like structures that ruled the world. Finally, I quietened, leaving the translucent figure quiet, looking at the floor, silent.

Eventually he spoke, with great finality. "I. Need. Spreadsheets."

That left me speechless. I just stood there, mouth open until my wits rejoined me. "That's your take from all of this? You're in a new world, dangers lurk on all sides, everything and everyone is out to get you, and you want spreadsheets?"

He shook his head. "I have a lot of conclusions already. You've done pretty well when it comes to sheer survival. You're not doing so hot when it comes to actually deciding what you want to do with this place and which direction you want to go. I mean, now that I have the chance, I want to live a decent life here, not just coast by. That's not the main point, though. Point is, I don't want spreadsheets. I *need* them. So, we're in a world that operates on game principles, right?"

I nodded. "Yeah. No quests or stuff like that, but the levels, skills, and feats are very game-like."

"Exactly. And you've already located a couple of cheats. That one where everybody gains full experience if they do a tiny bit of damage on a target is lovely, by the way. Still, you've only managed to scratch the surface, man. Why do people gain the feats they do? Which attributes do you need to gain which kinds of feats? Are there any limits, or is it only tied to the player's, I mean, person's experience and battles?"

His eyes had gained an intense look as he paced. "At which levels do people gain feats and skills? Can we fix in on how to trigger the exact choices? How do we build the optimal dungeon? Can we shape one of these Talpi to be the perfect mage from birth? *Can we figure out the principles to give me a goddamn body?*"

"Whoa, whoa! You need to relax a bit, son. Besides, that shaping part sounds a bit much for my liking. We're not forcing anybody to do anything."

Tim held up his hands. "Sorry. Got a bit excited there, old man. But my point still stands. With spreadsheets, I could have these answers for you within the day. That's basically what I do. I take numbers and facts and make them my bitch through spreadsheets and other programs. I'm still going to be able to do it... it's just going to be much more of a pain."

I just looked at him for a while, shaking my head. "Arthor's going to love hating you."

"Hate me? I'm adorable. And blue. Who doesn't love blue? I'm, like, a giant Smurf."

"You say that like it's somehow a good thing."

"Of course... wait. Damnit! I felt that." Without further explanation, Tim retreated into the system, leaving me to stare at him quizzically. Seconds later, he returned. "Okay, got it."

I raised an eyebrow. "Got what?"

"It. That thing I need for sustenance? It's mana. We've spent, like, an hour or two chatting, right? Well, my mana just dropped down by one. Guess what happens if it hits zero."

"Yeaaah, that's probably not a good idea."

He jumped back into the circle and, a moment later, waltzed back out. "Well, at least that works. I'll just need to go back into the circle to regenerate my mana again."

"That's good to know. You should be safe for several days, then. We'll look into it later, figure out something that works in the long run."

We spent an hour extra, just chatting about life back on earth, football, games, and life in general. To no one's surprise, Tim was a huge nerd, but he did get out into the real world now and again. It was nice to just kick back and enjoy talking to another human being. The fact that I was a dragon and he was a ghost was beside the point. In the end, we agreed that he'd take a while getting his head in order, then we'd introduce him to the rest of the gang. Meanwhile, I'd let him stay inside my chamber, and he could occupy his mind with the writings that the Soul Carver had left behind.

CHAPTER THREE

Plans are only good intentions unless they immediately degenerate into hard work. - Peter Drucker

The next day, I called in the usual people for a planning session. Today, we were arranged inside the throne room, the others lounging about on the floor in a half circle while I sat in front of my hoard. The mood was a lot better than usual, and why wouldn't it be? We'd encountered little resistance lately. Our people thrived and grew in strength at impressive rates, and it looked like we were finding new tactics and strengths on a daily basis.

On top of that, our matchup with the Orugal had granted us a nice dose of experience and taught us that the Gallery would be able to keep us safe from everything but the largest monsters and huge attacks. Our defenses were looking top notch. The same could be said for our top dogs. I looked over the assembled Talpi and Inspected every one of them, smiling at the results.

Their levels had skyrocketed lately. Aelis, Roth, and Arthor were about the same level as I was or slightly lower. Of course, Aelis had already been level 7 or thereabout when I met her, and the others even higher. If I hadn't been put through the grinder the way I had, my level would be way lower than theirs, and where I had been through every single battle, they hadn't all partaken in all of them. Their attributes were nothing to sneeze at either, especially for Talpi.

Creziel was the one with the lowest level, and he had just hit level 14. Walking the halls, I could see the progress all around me. The Talpi looked healthier, tougher, fur coats shiny with health and tiny bodies putting on lean muscle. The Crawls, in contrast, looked uglier than ever, rolls of toughened skin growing and multiplying to add to their natural protection even as they bulked out with sheer muscle.

In addition, my minions took their specialization seriously. Arthor and Creziel went down the same path, training their Toughness while they worked hard to increase their Mental Power and Control. Aelis was taking her role as a scout seriously, and her Agility was through the roof for a Talpus. With her running Feat, she would even be able to keep pace with me for a while. Hell, she might even outpace me at some point.

Roth... Roth was *buff*. He'd always been more squat than the others, but his arms were seriously starting to bulk out. If he kept at it, I believed he would be a match for a Clencher soon. A small one. Maybe one with a cold. They were chatting among themselves, and I took my time. I wasn't feeling so much stress these days. Yes, we needed to ensure that we'd be able to handle ourselves against the other dragons from the clutch and yes, we would need to get back out there, but our progress was undeniable. I almost didn't want to start this meeting. Almost.

With a sigh, I clapped my paws together, getting their attention. "All right. Let's get to it. Today, we're going to have to make some big decisions, and I need your minds sharp for it." Their collective gazes focused on me, and I couldn't help but smile. Again, I praised my luck that I hadn't eaten Aelis that very first day.

"First off, I want, no, I *need* to praise you all. You've all done an amazing job. Roth. I can see your efforts every time I walk around this place. There are no more starving, scrawny Talpi with stick-thin arms. You are keeping them active, and the results are self-evident. Keep it up! Aelis..." I shook my head in amazement. "Not a single surprise attack, and no scouts lost to wandering monsters for a full month! Well done."

My neck turned to focus on the smallest of the Talpi. "Creziel. We are safer than ever. Your efforts on the construction have been crucial in improving our defenses, and I almost *want* a large-scale attack, just so we can check out your latest inventions." I wasn't lying either. The fake windows that could be opened to let the Shadow Towers shoot into the rooms had been his idea, and he kept coming up with additional ways to perfect our setup.

I let my gaze slide over to the final furred participant, taking in his defensive posture, paws folded in front of his chest and frowning expression. "Finally you, Arthor. I doubt that anybody would be able to have handled the tribe as well as you have lately. You have set aside your own desires and helped to build a stronger, more coherent force, as well as making everybody work together better with the Crawls and Clenchers." It was true, too. While he was still cold toward me, his attitude and work to build up the tribe had been inspired.

Roth stood up and began pacing. He rarely had the patience to sit quietly for a long time. "That's good to hear, Lizard. So, those big decisions?"

I sighed. "Onyx. The name is Onyx. And you need to work on your patience, Roth. But okay." I scratched my neck with a claw, wondering exactly how to present this. "Now, I used to be a foreman, overseeing construction. You all know this. What you may not know is that I also took courses on how to actually *be* a good leader. A lot of the courses were horrible. Pointless wastes of time. A few of them had some excellent points and made you think about how you wanted to act and direct the work in order to succeed. One I took to heart was this one: 'It's possible to work all day and still not do your job.'"

Roth rolled his eyes. "Make sense, dragon. Just say what you need to."

I laughed, which my vocal chords translated into a low rumble. "I just did. But okay. The point of that saying is that you need to adjust your sights constantly in order to make sure that you're aiming at the right goal." I indicated the domain around us. "We've done an impressive job so far. Built a lot, grown even faster than what should be possible. I believe, with all my heart, that any single dragon from my clutch out there wouldn't be able to match us at this point. But from now on, unless we expand, we're going to fall behind."

Arthor nodded. He got it. Creziel, too, but he kept to himself. Roth... was Roth. "That's Clencher shit, Onyx. We're still training hard and growing strong! And those throwing spears are going to be efficient once we learn to use them well. Besides, once the next few litters come, our pups are going to grow and level like never before. We can beat *anybody* in the lower layers."

Arthor spoke up, sarcasm fully unleashed. "Pfah. What are the pups going to level up *from*, Roth? In case you haven't noticed, we've dominated our part of the lower layer to the point where there are fewer targets around."

I nodded. "That's exactly it. There are also two more aspects to it. If we stay here and do not expand, we are also going to let the other dragons and their minions gain in levels while we don't. We have made much progress, but even our Training Chamber and other improvements combined won't be able to let us keep up with enemies who keep challenging their surroundings. As for the final one--well, Aelis approached me about it the other day." I indicated for her to continue.

She stepped forward, arms behind her back. "Meat. Our Farm is delivering better than expected, and I have every expec-tation that we will be able to keep up the expansion of farms indefinitely. But with our increasing numbers, we are slowly but surely running out of meat for our carnivores."

"Well said, Aelis. We need to ensure that we become self-sufficient when it comes to meat, also. And before anybody says anything, the Clenchers are off-limits. Training has improved to the point where they can take the lead in most confrontations." I looked at each of them in turn, but there was no challenge this time. Not even from Arthor, who'd been adamant that I was making a mistake in trying to train the big animals as meat shields.

I continued. "So, I've got a couple ideas on how to expand from here, but I'd like to hear from you first. What do you think we should do? Oh, and I don't expect the perfect plan today. When we're done talking, I want us to meet again tomorrow and finish the plans. For now, I just want all of your ideas out there, however crazy."

Roth looked like lightning had hit him. Then, an excited squee escaped from him, even as his mental shout rang out. "A Training Chamber! We need a Training Chamber for the Clenchers."

Arthor's mental voice and mine clashed, as we both stated our opinion. "You're an idiot!" "Of course!" For a moment, we just stood there, looking at the other, blinking.

Then I held up a paw. "No, hear me out. Roth is onto something here. It has little to do with what I was asking, but really, it's something we should've thought of already. Clenchers are capable of using a Training Chamber, same as yourselves, and we already have two trainers who are able to make them do almost exactly what they want. We want our Clenchers to grow tougher, faster, and meaner, same as us."

Arthor's frown grew smaller while I talked, and in the end, he nodded. "I didn't realize that we would be able to have them train properly. You should have mentioned that earlier. Now, if we can focus on our future, like we discussed, I have a point. We need to expand our search for materials."

"Is it necessary?" I asked. "We already have a difficult task before us. Looking for and mining better materials will have us spread even thinner."

Creziel hesitated, but came forward. "Not only necessary. It is crucial. You said it yourself, Onyx. Our enemies won't stand still. They will gain in levels and attributes, and some of them are capable of working with tools. Our levels will not mean as much if their armors and weapons outmatch ours. Also, unless we find another solution regarding meat, we will need to range out regardless."

"Great point, Creziel. Still. Can we handle it without spreading ourselves too wide?"

"Pfah," Arthor spat. "It will not be an issue. We all know earth. Informing everybody what we are looking for and ensuring that we find the right kinds of materials on our outings will be simple. Then, when we have located a handful of good spots, Creziel or I can take an outing with a scout and some Crawls to gather what we find."

Aelis did not look as happy. "I disagree, Sire. It will slow us down. Notably. However, at later dates, when we have marked out our initial findings, it will not be as much of a hassle. I will not claim to be able to estimate the actual necessity of more materials."

"I will." Roth was quick to come forward with his opinion. " We have good spears for close combat, but our throwing spears are, on the whole, not impressive. Also, since better-quality materials result in better improvements from the hoard, we need better stone. Do that, and we'll all be bedecked head to toe with magic rings and necklaces."

I looked around at everybody and nodded. "Thanks, Roth. Now. Let's consider the issues and sleep on it. We should try to find a way to handle our situation that's as safe as possible. What else?"

Aelis stepped forward. "I do not claim to have a solution, Milord. More observations. The number of scouts we have is limited. Therefore, the major issues I see in enlarging our area are security and manpower. If we need to handle larger patrols, we will need to decrease the number of rounds we are able to take closer to home. That will leave our domain more exposed to random encounters and roving packs. In addition to this, we would not be able to handle our patrols of new areas very well, since there are too few of us."

"Good points, Aelis. Any suggestions?"

Roth shrugged. "I know a couple of lazy runts that could do with a run."

The four Talpi burst out in their high-pitched laughter, but I leaned back. "That's... an excellent idea, really." They all looked at me with questioning looks, Roth especially. "No, seriously. You're used to having to keep very good eyes on your surroundings because most enemies would be able to handle you. That's obviously not true anymore. With the Earth Furies taken care of, there are no larger groups within... How far of us, Aelis?"

"Eight hours, Sire, depending on the opponent."

"Thank you. Within eight hours' distance. So, what we need to think about is this: If we were to let our own fighters and builders take over the patrols closer to home, how should we do it? And if we, on top of that, decide to start searching for the other dragons and their minions, animals we can breed for meat..."

"...nd materials." Creziel added.

"...And new, improved materials, thank you. If we're supposed to start searching for all of this how should we best approach it in order to ensure our own safety and our success? I know, it's not an easy question. Still, I'll probably have a nice surprise tomorrow to make things easier for us here at home."

They grumbled at the short notice of the task and the scope of it but, miraculously, nobody spoke out against the importance of it. Sure, Timothy might disagree--it seemed like he was a huge fan of talking about all the philosophical stuff--but improved materials and better food, that was the kind of planning I could understand.

The rest of it would have to come in time. From what I could sense, the Talpi were in full agreement, and even better.

They had spent a lot of time at the lower end of the food chain in the mountain and now, with a chance for improvement before them, they were growing by leaps and bounds. I felt damned proud of the Talpi and their work ethic. If they kept it up like this, the goal in sight *would* be a safe haven and easy growth for the lot of us.

CHAPTER FOUR

"No, I *like* the neck band. There's nothing wrong with it, either. I just don't need a neck band, I need something even larger. And, well, where this one is fastened around my neck alone. I want the next one to be locked at several spots along my back, like this, with leather bands reaching under my stomach and vertical bands to keep them tightened and in their place."

I was right next to my hoard, talking to one of the resident leatherworkers. I was trying my very best to have a civil conversation with him about which type of harness I wanted him to construct for me in the near future. The only problem was, he wasn't having it.

"Listen here, Onyx. You said it yourself. This collar works perfectly fine. You aren't even using it, either, and it's the best Orugal leather there is. That green dragon must have had some talented minions. Now you want something that covers most of your body? Have you got any idea how hard it would be to find enough Orugal leather to create that? At this quality? You'd be better off just using this collar."

I wasn't getting through to him. By now, I had tried and failed for two minutes to tell the stubborn little critter that it wasn't a question of my disliking the first neckband or simple vanity that made me ask, but a question of functionality. I was about to tell him just that, but we were interrupted by a panicked mental shout that rang from behind me, from within my own quarters.

"Carl! Carl, damnit. No, wait, Onyx, wasn't it? I need you here, man!"

I sprinted back to my room, ready for an emergency, only to see the blue blob right next to a wall, staring at the golden scripture on the walls. Slowing down, I looked everywhere, including at the exit tunnel that led from the wall right next to Tim and up to a remote tunnel far from any main tunnels. I relaxed a bit, seeing that there was no immediate panic and said, "What's the deal, Tim? I thought we were under attack."

He turned toward me and shook his head. The cocky smile that had played on his lips constantly as we spoke yesterday was nowhere to be seen and his eyes were wide open. "No. But we are going to be. I mean, I think we are..."

I sat down on my haunches and lowered my head, attention fixed on his earnest, panicked gaze. "Okay, you've got my full attention."

He indicated the wall behind him. "So, soul or ghost or whatever I am, I don't really need to sleep much. And these writings the Soul Carver left behind--I'm freaking out! I'm not telling this right." He closed his eyes and waited. And waited. Then, maybe ten seconds later, he reopened them.

"Okay. All better now. I can't be sure, but I doubt we'll be attacked right this minute, and you need the backstory to get everything. So, before I talk about the danger, you need to know more about the Soul Carver himself." Tim stood ramrod straight, looking right at me. "I have already told you we didn't talk much. That's an understatement. In fact, once he got tired hearing about Earth, he barely talked to me at *all*, except for when he gave me an order. I'm guessing he considered me a slave, just like his other dead servants. So I didn't learn anything directly from him, with two exceptions. The first was the experiments."

"Experiments? Sorry. Please continue."

"Yeah. From time to time, the creepy bastard experimented on some of his servants. It could be anything. Like, restoring a limb that was falling apart, performing some sort of bone surgery on a joint, or just testing the sturdiness of their bodies."

I frowned. "So, damaging to see how much they could take before falling apart?"

"You got it. And then he'd repair 'em afterward, like it was the most natural thing in the world. Textbook neutral evil!"

"Neutral?"

"Don't tell me you're older than D&D." It looked like whatever had shocked Timothy out of his senses, he was slowly moving on, regaining a bit of his humor. The moment I had that thought, he shuddered and continued in a lower voice. "He'd also experiment on me now and then. My pain tolerance, how fast I'd be able to recuperate, stuff like that. And--this was the worst--he could actually control me. I'd feel his dirty, oily mind in the back of the head, then suddenly it was like I was riding coach." He grimaced. "The only thing I can say with a certainty is that he needed to be able to see me to mind-rape me. Otherwise, it felt like he was pretty damn powerful. I couldn't fight back or anything."

"Damn, Tim. So sorry you were subjected to that, man."

He waved me off with a grimace. "Don't. I'm not looking for compassion here. This is important, though. Now, the second thing I learned was when he visited Selys."

I perked up. "Oh?"

"Yeah, I didn't know who that was at the time. All I knew was that he came back from a meeting with her, and he wasn't angry. He was goddamn *livid*. He ordered one of the older skeletons inside the rooms, and he took it apart. Like, blast radius explosion. Some of the bones bounced off my circle. Anyway, once he'd gotten rid of the worst of his temper, he apparently needed to vent, and I was the only semi-living intelligent creature nearby."

"Oh. Did he hurt you?"

"No. Not that time. No, the scary-ass, crazy, high-level necro-dude used me as a shoulder to cry on. Well, rather, somebody to nod and say 'mm-hmm' at appropriate times while he ranted. And of course I did it. He'd probably have torn my transparent ass a new one otherwise."

"I believe you. So, what did he say?"

"Well, the reason he went to see her was apparently for some twisted sort of job interview. Apparently, dominating the mountain was just step one of Selys' grand plan. She was looking to use it as a stepping stone to expand elsewhere afterward. Except, that required her to have somebody to take care of the mountain while she was away. This suited the Soul Carver just fine. He basically just wanted to focus on his studies and crafts, grow his undead armies, and gather his rare materials, and the position as the leader of the mountain sounded like a grand place to do just that. Except, he didn't like the spellbound oath she wanted him to swear before she accepted him, so they came to blows."

"Ouch."

"Yeah. Don't know what the dragon managed to do to him, but he wasn't looking too good. He swore his vengeance, promised fire and brimstone and all that. And, for a while, that was that. He didn't ask me to read much to him anymore, and the books he made me go through were often about ore, crystals, and this place. I actually learned a bit about the place in the process. Eventually, I figured we'd moved past the threat. Then, months later, it happened."

"What?"

"I'd been hearing weird noises in the distance for some time. Explosions, cries, stuff like that. Then, out of the blue, he was there in the doorway. He looked at me. Must've been a handful of seconds at most, but it felt like forever. Then he shook his head and left. Seconds later, the corridor collapsed and half filled my room."

"What? Just like that? No explanation, nothing?"

Tim shrugged. "No. I had plenty of time to think about what it meant, though. Once the dust settled, the noise slowly moved away and soon, I was left here with nothing *but* time. After a while, I started feeling this occasional pulling sensation - that must've been when the protective Circle ran out of mana and started sucking me dry instead. Then, suddenly, there was only pain."

I shook my head. "That's horrible. I can't believe you were just left to die here."

"Me either. Truth be told, I can't remember much. Thank the human brain for blotting out uncomfortable memories, I guess. If I'm even human anymore..."

It looked like Timothy was heading for a dark place. I needed to derail him somehow. Maybe... "Yeah, I feel the same sometimes. Except... you know Whataburger, right?"

"...I think that non-sequitur just gave me whiplash. Yes, I know Whataburger."

"You know that feeling when you get your food and look at it? How it's basically greasy heartburn just waiting to kick you in the stomach and fill your arteries with fat, right? And you *know* those big, fat patties are going to make you spend forever on the john. Yet still... you really, really want a Whataburger right now, right?"

"Oh yeah."

I put my head really close to him, closed my eyes to slits, then nodded. "Yup. You're human. No doubt about it."

"But-"

"No buts about it. Only humans are stupid enough to know exactly how dumb we are for eating fast food and still craving it constantly."

He snorted a laugh. "Hah. I guess you're right. Sorry for being a downer."

"No need to apologize. You've been through hell and back,

47

Tim. You're allowed to not feel amazing every single second. But things are going to get a lot better now."

He blinked owlishly. "Yeaaaah. So, the thing where I was yelling and screaming? That was my way of saying that they aren't. Sorry for going about this in such a roundabout way. I tend to ramble. Thing is, I realized pretty quickly what these things were." He pointed at the shining scripts on the wall behind him. "They're crafting recipes."

"Oh. Damn. I know this sounds silly, but I kinda wanted them to be a diary. You know, the big baddy giving up all his secrets in big shiny letters, because that's a normal thing to do."

He gave a shaky grin. "Well, you're not completely out of luck, then. He does give up a few secrets." He waved at the far side. "Most if it looks pretty damn useless. How to create magic rings, detailed instructions for how to improve musculature on a Mongher, whatever that is. There's a disturbing amount of poison recipes--"

"Wait! We'll need to have you copy those down, later on."

"...Sure. Anyway, the real kicker is this one. Listen." He started reading, haltingly, from the text. "*The construction of a Soulstone is a long journey indeed. Some shortcuts can be taken. The key to the effect lies in the rune construction. Sub-par ore can be acceptable, but holding, manipulation, and integrity runes need to be immaculate.*"

He skipped to the next section. "Skipping most of it. The next part was a comparison of materials and the minimum grade needed, boring stuff. Here. Ahem. *Once a Soulstone is filled, it will grant you awareness of the subject regardless of distance and direct control within eyesight. Mental Control and Mental Power both apply, for the subject and master both. Once held, the mental powers of the subject will fade in time. Physical decay is avoidable, but mental is not. Constant reinforcement and presence reduces the need for direct control. In time, control is even possible over longer distances and without a soulstone. Current limit: three miles.*" He indicated that spot. "Used to say two miles. Apparently, he learned something while he was here. Which, at best I can tell, was several years, by the way."

I frowned. "I'm not sure what these things are supposed to

be. Actual stones for souls? Things that allow him to handle his undead folks? Huh. Aelis called the undead Flawed Souls. That's more to the point than I'd expected."

My blue friend nodded. He didn't look entertained, though, just started reading again, from a different wall. "*With rigorous experimentation, it has been confirmed. Souls can be summoned from outside this world. The curse itself is simple. Bestowed upon the target, it locates and summons a soul, when the right conditions are met. The remainder of the details are less than simple. Additional runes are needed to define the exact qualities of the soul. Theories indicate that a soul from outside this world would not be subject to mental decay. First subject confirmed. Qualities: Analytical. Intelligent. Reasonable success. Materials are rare, but a positive result will be worth it.*"

Tim shrugged. "That's me, by the way, first subject. So, apparently, it's pretty damn expensive to find somebody like me. Who knew?" His laughter sounded forced. "The rest of that one is a description of the materials needed for the different runes and then this: *Later tests have proven that summoning a soul into an already deceased or a soulless body is impossible. The same regards a body with a present soul, regardless of quality and mental power/control.*

"Then follow a number of other failures, some of them... graphic. Then he tried something new. *A breakthrough! A work-around has been located. With the right conditions imposed on the Soul stones, the curse remains dormant until the target of the curse is with offspring. Then, the soul takes over the vessel inside the womb. Second subject confirmed. Qualities: Magic Capabilities. Soul remained intact for several months, but the body deteriorated constantly. Flesh shaping could not keep up with the damage. Second subject destroyed. Conclusion: A suitable vessel is needed to handle the transition.*"

Tim looked straight at me. "This must be where things started heating up with the conflict inside the mountain, because it sounds like our friend decided to go ahead and amp up his tests. *Failures. Failures one and all. Materials are deplenishing, and Selys' armies are spreading throughout the mountain.* Then, there's a handful of other negative developments until. *The curse took. Let this be my parting gift. Qualities: Survivor mentality. Mental fortitude. If this works, it will prove her downfall.* That last phrase was under-lined several times, by the way."

I could feel a headache coming on. "Sooo that last one is me? I mean, it doesn't sound too far off, but that last line sounds kinda ominous. What am I missing here?"

He looked at me like I had just said vaccines contained 5G microchips. "Really? Dude. *The curse remains dormant until the target of the curse becomes pregnant.* Ring any bells? The necromancer somehow cast the spell on Selys years ago, and it's been lingering until now, when she finally bore offspring. That's how you got here with that nice, gargantuan body of yours."

"Crap. Are you sure? Of course you are, or we wouldn't be here." I closed my eyes, massaging the ridges on my snout. "Okay. If we imagine that's all true--I mean, it would make a lot of sense. But still, that last part, where I'll prove Selys' downfall? I really don't have any intentions of challenging the biggest, baddest dragon around. If anything, I'd like to just get rid of all the other dragons who want to kill me and try to make a nice home for us ex-humans. Maybe a spa somewhere."

He nodded. "Sure. Nice intentions; I'm a fan. Except, let me just read something aloud to you again. *Once a Soulstone is filled, it will grant you awareness of the subject regardless of distance and direct control within a short distance.*" Tim put his hands behind his back, waiting for the shoe to drop.

"Oh. Oh!" I hid my face in my paws. "So not only has the Soul Carver been able to feel me since I got here... once he's close, he can take over the wheel?"

Tim shrugged again, this time with an apologetic look. "It's the only way I can read this. Oh, and of course, he'll be able to dominate me again and put me back in the cage. It'll be just like the good old times."

"Damn." Silence grew between us, while I considered the possibilities. "If Selys actually might have accepted him as her second in command, he's probably not a pushover either, right?"

"Yeah. Unless you have an army ready, we're probably not taking him down."

"Heh. I do at that, but I doubt that we'd be tough enough. You did say that he had an army of his own?"

"Yep. It's not like I've seen it, but there was always somebody shuffling about in the hallways, and some of the minions he experimented on were downright scary. Like, horror-game-level scary."

"Damn. Damn and thrice damned. Okay, we need help." I punched the wall. The sensation was weird with my claws and all, but it felt like the thing to do.

"Help?"

"Yeah. I hope you're ready to meet the gang, because we're going to have to speed the process up right about now."

CHAPTER FIVE

Don't Panic. - Douglas Adams

"Thank you for coming so fast. I know I gave you until tomorrow to think about things but... we're in trouble."

The four Talpi assembled before me were very different personalities. Still, as I introduced Timothy and then told them what we had just learned, their faces went through roughly the same emotions, starting with shock and ending with raw, undiluted fear. Even Roth, who was usually unflappable, was visibly ill at ease at the thought of the Soul Carver returning for me and Selys.

They took the story behind Tim's spectral presence a lot easier than I had, and only shot the occasional curious glance at the blue figure next to me. Apparently, it was not too hard to accept that the Soul Carver had the powers to summon ghosts from other dimensions. Not the most comforting thought.

"So there you have it. The Soul Carver's bound to come running for me and Tim at some point with his armies. When he does, he will probably be able to control us." If only I'd

chosen that mental defense feat, things might be different, but…
no use dwelling on it.

Nobody talked. It looked like none of the Talpi wanted to
be the one to start. In the end, it was Roth, blessed Roth, who
brandished his two-handed sword. "You can't face him? Then
we'll beat him for you while you handle his armies. No
problem."

I gave him a fond smile, even as Arthor shook his head. The
three rocks floating in an elaborate pattern around his waist
bobbed as he spoke. "Pfah. Roth, you need to train less. Your
head is suffering from it. This is not anybody. This is the Soul
Carver we're talking about. One of the Powers." The capitaliza-
tion of the word was easily heard.

Roth didn't back down. "So what? We're a Power, too. We
were going to go out and hunt *dragons*, for Deyra's sake. Or are
you saying we should just run away like we used to?"

Arthor walked closer to me and looked straight up at me.
"That depends entirely on which plan our resident dragon has
concocted. You do have a plan?"

"Yes. You may not like it, however." I grimaced and blun-
dered on. "The short version is this: I plan to do exactly what
we were planning anyway. We're just pulling out all stops and
doing it a lot faster and a lot less safe. Of all the forces inside the
mountain, only Selys is likely to be able to face off against the
Soul Carver, especially since he's spent the last decade or more
licking his wounds and probably building his armies. We *need*
that big red on our side, or we're in trouble."

Arthor considered my words. "So you would be running
around the lower layers, looking for the other dragons and
hopefully kill them off.."

I interrupted, "Or ally with them."

He sneered. "Or ally with them one by one, until you can
talk Selys into handling your problems. Pfah. That's weak. What
about our domain?"

"I would leave that to the pregnant and those unsuited for
combat, with a handful of protectors. Now, remember. We

haven't got a clue how far away the Soul Carver is and how long it will take him to come after us, if he even choses to do so. He *was* chased away in the first place, remember? Now, if all goes well, we'll get Selys on our side and return to continue where we left off. Should he arrive at the domain at some point while I'm away, you can always flee through the escape tunnel and collapse it behind you."

Creziel nodded. "We finished the trap in the escape tunnel three days ago, Onyx. It is ready to collapse, should it be needed."

Arthor growled at me. "I was hoping you had something better for us."

"I would, but circumstances aren't looking too good, and we are pressed for time. This is by no means a final plan, and I'm taking any suggestions on how to improve it."

Aelis nodded. "I have a number of comments on the composition of the team that should go along with us."

I gave her a warm smile. At this point, she could see beyond the razor-sharp fangs and perceive when I was truly glad. The fact that she chose to side with me against deadly odds without even a hesitation... "I will gladly listen to any comment, Aelis, but something else needs to be decided first. Arthor. This is for you to decide. Will you join our forces or stay back here at the lair?" Our agreement was clear. The Talpi were my minions; I called the shots, and any internal decisions were for themselves to deal with.

The expression on the surly Talpus closed up. Since he started training hard in the Sorcery Chamber, his emotions had become harder for me to decipher, and right now was no different. The only thing I could sense for sure was turmoil. "I will remain here."

Ever since I first met Aelis, shaking and bloodied, she had always been reserved and coolheaded. Right now, she exploded into a, for her, unseemly display of emotion. She rounded up on Arthor, shaking her finger. "How can you say that? With what our Sire has done for us, how can you leave him to fend for himself at the first sign of danger? I will not stand for this. We-"

Arthor's mental voice betrayed that he was anything but unaffected. "Stop, Aelis. Just... stop. My first responsibility is to the tribe. Always! You know this. This is not a decision I take lightly, either. I will not diminish the importance of Onyx for our tribe. Yet, we cannot risk everybody on this outing. If something happens to you, our people need somebody to pick up the pieces and continue."

I nodded at him, meeting his eyes. He was a good leader. Not ruled by his emotions, but by logic. I nodded and started talking, but he held up a paw.

"I am in the right here. Yet, that does not mean that I believe all non-fighters should stay." His eyes smiled as he looked at me. "The prospect of a series of fights against neighboring dragons sounds suicidal. I won't deny that. Still, it's not that far from what we've been doing already, except that the targets are larger, and we don't have the luxury of just changing our minds halfway. Even so, if Onyx would be as generous with the dragon meat as he has been so far, it would be the single best chance for self-improvement our tribe has ever seen. We should send some of the builders, too."

I smiled. "Good point. We're bound to be able to use their help on the trip, too. We can keep the majority of the non-combatants and all the pregnant females back here. Then, if somebody is injured, we may be able to send them back to the safety of the domain." I took a deep breath. "Should the worst come to pass, and the Soul Carver tracks us down while we're out there, you will still be able to start over from a safe place." I grimaced. "Well, relatively safe. Obviously, the Soul Carver knows his old lair and might come back."

Aelis was still seething. "We are not unused to having to flee at a moment's notice, Sire." She turned toward Arthor. "Why did you not say that this was what you meant? This is so much more reasonable than what you implied at first. Obviously, this will further complicate the logistics for our journey. I will have to assess the qualities..."

"I know. There are many details to be handled, Aelis, and I'm honored that you chose to join me. Before we go into all that, there is one other detail I want to bring up. The question of what to do with Timothy." I gestured for the glowing figure to step forward.

He did so, shaking his head at me with a lopsided grin. "So I'm a tiny detail, eh? Next to your wide ass, maybe." He turned his grin at the assembled Talpi and shook his head again. "For the record, this is so goddamn *weird*. I used to think that humans were the only existing intelligent species, now look at me."

"The main difference between Timothy and myself is that the Soul Carver decided to leave him here for himself when he fled from Selys. What I'm considering is whether he should stay here with you in the domain. I would like your input."

Creziel spoke up for the first time. "But didn't you say that the Soul Carver can feel his presence, too? Then, him being here--wouldn't it be a beacon for him to come here first?"

I sighed. Tim and I had finished the exact same discussion right before the Talpi arrived. "It would. However, I have reasons to believe that he would choose not to. First off, Timothy has stayed in the same place since the Soul Carver left him. I'll be the one moving about the place. There is no reason for the Soul Carver to believe that Timothy is even free. Second, he needs me. Timothy, at best, would be an afterthought for him."

"Thanks, bruh. That's not at all hurtful. Hah. Just kidding. Not being noticed by that creepy bastard is a *good* thing!"

Arthor ignored his outburst. "Be that as it may, why should we take the risk? You are already hunted. Taking your friend here along with you would not add to *your* danger."

"True. It would be a risk, but a calculated one, at that. You will still have your scouts out to warn you, and it will give you some added punch. Allow me to show you. Roth? Mind taking a swing at my friend here?"

Roth just shot a look at Timothy and brandished his two-handed sword, waving it menacingly, and then he plopped down on his behind again. "I would, if I believed it would do anything. Your friend there doesn't stir up dust when he moves."

I smiled. "Nice catch. That's exactly the point. Timothy's incorporeal, but that doesn't mean he's powerless. You mind taking a shot at me then, Tim? I'm 16 levels higher than you. There's no risk here... I hope."

The blue form didn't hesitate. Within a second, a wave raced forth toward me, displacing the air and slamming into my body with full strength. I had braced myself for the pain, but what rattled through my body wasn't just painful. It also brought along a whole slew of unwanted emotions. Panic, abject confusion, a craving for sugar - a range of jarring emotions raced through me, leaving me mentally stumped for a second.

A shudder ran up my spinal ridge. "Well, that was unpleasant. It also cost me..." I checked my info, "18 health. This is at level 1, with my mental stats being through the roof. So, how effective do you believe the Shadow Gallery would be with an untouchable defender to take down any intruders?"

They looked mighty impressed. Creziel was nodding and smiling, right up until Arthor spoke up. "No. It's a bad idea." He forestalled my objection and spoke on. "This is nothing against your friend. His help could provide a fearsome addition, once he levels some. Still, I believe that we are able to fend for ourselves. The Shadow Gallery in itself will be enough to take care of most intruders. Any forces that are large enough to fight their way through will likely not be here for simple sustenance. They will be here to attack, in which case, we will likely be running away regardless. So, with that in mind, the question is simply whether the added risk changes enough for us to take that risk. To which I say again, no."

I might have become annoyed at his continued shooting down of my suggestions, if he wasn't being so stubbornly logical about it. Everything coming from the other Talpi echoed agreement. "All right. Timothy, I can't deny that Arthor makes a good point. We don't want to risk the Soul Carver aiming straight for the lair first. It sounds like you're stuck with me."

"I'll see if I can get used to the thought."

I repressed a laugh. Turning back toward Arthor, I spoke again. "There is one thing that we will need to handle once we return. We will start in on it while we walk, but you may as well prepare for it. Timothy will be creating a list of all inhabitants, their attributes, feats, and much more. With this, we can start toward creating a complete list of possible builds."

Aelis lifted her head. "Builds, Sire?"

"Yes. As far as I understand Arthor, to date nobody has had the possibility and forethought to actually map out all the different combinations of feats, spells, requirements, and the like."

"Requirements?" Arthor stepped in. "Deyra provides the feats and spells that every person blessed enough to walk her earth has earned. If a person is unworthy, he will remain cut off from what his betters might earn."

Damn. I should have seen this coming. For all his logic, Arthor had the making of a religious fanatic when it came to Deyra. Not that I blamed him. Physical, tangible evidence would be a pretty sure-fire way of increasing your faith in the gods.

"I agree. But if Deyra has seen fit to create very specific attribute requirements you need to obtain in order to unlock a certain feat or spell, would keeping that knowledge to yourself be Deyra's will... or your choice?" I shook my head. "Even though I sometimes make fun of you, Arthor, you know I respect you. You never hesitate to take the difficult choices and you take care of your own and put the tribe first every time. I respect that. But think this through. These are the possibilities of future Talpi we're talking about here. Would you really want to limit their choices? Now, I will be the first to share my details, but everybody *will* share."

For a moment, I believed that Arthor would refuse to back down.

Then Roth snorted. "Of course, we'll share. Sure, we've never shared our secrets before, except with other Talpi, but no Talpus ever killed a dragon before either. This is *all* new. Go. Fight. Thrive. Those are Deyra's words. The rest is up to us to decide." He coughed, then grinned. "Besides, if we do this, at least we won't have to worry about meat. If we make it, we'll have more food than we need. If we don't... not our problem."

I couldn't quite wrap my head around the fatalism of the brawny Talpus, but it was hard to argue with. Meanwhile, the discussion turned practical in nature. Aelis had a lot of comments regarding provisions, defenses, and the like, while I tried to get an overview of the journey we were facing.

From Aelis' description, with Arthor chiming in with lore tidbits from the past, it would take maybe two to three weeks to complete a rough circuit of the lower layers of the mountain. Meanwhile, the Talpi would start taking note of any feats, skills, and developments, so they would have something ready for when we returned.

Certain things were sure to set us back in time, and there might even be a few roaming monsters out there that we would prefer not to tangle with. Even so, looking at the rough sketch drawn in the dirt on the floor, the task looked possible. We agreed that we'd loot the hoard for each and every useful item and bring every single Clencher, except for the one who, according to Eamus, was closest to giving birth.

Once we had the overall discussions handled, we split into our separate tasks. Roth was going to talk to his trainers. Aelis had volunteered to be the one to ask every single Talpus to join us on the journey. I was truly grateful for her unwavering faith. If anybody could ensure that we get the right help for our task, it would be her. Arthor... did not explain himself as he left.

We agreed to leave early the next morning. That left me the rest of the day to figure out if I needed to create any last-minute

constructions, think of whether I'd forgotten something important and... handle the most annoying part of the entire thing.

Erk was looking up at me. I was used to that. The numerous
folds of thick skin around his naked upper body looked larger
and more disgusting than they used to. Maybe that was actually
a good sign for Crawls. It wasn't a discussion I was willing to
enter into, in any case. The unusual part of his looks were his
eyes. If I didn't know better, I would suspect that he was...
thinking. Trying to, at least.

His mental voice and emotions didn't give anything away. "I
do not know.."

I carefully did not snap out at him. "What do you not know,
Erk?"

"Your question."

"My question was, 'We are going on a three-week trip,
where we will have to fight often. What do you need?'"

"I do not know."

"*Please* try to help me here. Come up with something."

"Enemies."

Don't kill him. Do not bite his stupid face off. It's not his fault. Even
after all this time, they were just so…. stupid. No, that's not
entirely fair. So damn frustrating.

"Yes, Erk. We're sure to find enemies along the way, Erk. We
will also bring food and all magic items we can spare. Is there
anything *else* you need?"

"Oh. Yes. Armor."

I was surprised by the lucidity of his answer. That meant
that they actually did think about progress and ways to improve.
Maybe they weren't actually stupid just... really, *really* slow.
"That was a good answer. We don't have any armor now, but I
promise we will try to find some."

Without parting words, Erk turned around and plodded
back to the Training Chamber.

Regardless of how talking to him made me feel more frus-
trated than a flat-earther on a round-the-world trip, I was happy

they'd be by my side. The Crawls were undeniably tough and strong, and they did *not* hold back in battle.

The rest of the day flew by. I did a tiny bit of construction, creating a Habitat inside the Clencher enclosure. No clue why I hadn't come up with that earlier; the health regeneration and the Toughness buff the Habitat provided were brilliant complements to front line fighters. Then, I learned, to my annoyance, that there was a hard limit of one Shadow Tower per level. Ah, well.

The domain was pretty well-riddled with the weakening towers as it was. Then, I figured out a handy detail--that you could actually move already established constructions. In consequence, I moved the Protective Circle right in front of the vault and ended up establishing an Outpost right inside the Throne Room. That would ensure that any fights that made it through the Gallery had a safe spot for any fleeing Talpi to use and boosts to any fights that would take place in there, while the Shadow Towers and murder holes did their jobs.

Laive joined me for a spot, and I taught her everything I had learned from books and games, which was embarrassingly little. Mostly it was a matter of general hints and tips about how to ensure her own safety. Like: remember to be entirely certain of how you mix things. Keep containers clearly marked and airtight. If possible, get some guinea pigs you can use to test out your new poisons and keep them trapped somewhere. Maybe some of those Roaches I'd encountered.

Apparently, they were called Vourens here. I mean, if you could kill or weaken a giant Roach with poison, it'd have to be effective! My parting advice was blatantly stolen from a book. "Label clearly. Measure twice. Eat elsewhere." Apart from that, I promised that we would, on our triumphant return, do our best to work with her to create some sort of written system, or maybe just teach her how to write. That should solve the whole labeling issue.

CHAPTER SIX

We left later than we planned. In all honesty, I hadn't expected anything else. With larger projects, there were always unforeseen last-minute tasks, sequences where you wouldn't be able to get to work on task B before A had been completed and difficult people who postponed the timeline. We ended up taking almost half of our minions along. Of the current 36 adult Talpi, we took 14. We also changed our minds, asking a couple Talpi to stay, to not deprive the domain of all their talented fighters and scouts. As for the Crawls, we left the three pregnant ones, bringing all seven remaining ones along, along with four of the five Clenchers.

Goodbyes took a while as well. Everybody inside the mountain was used to the dangers, and every excursion could very well be the last. Still, half of the tribe taking off to engage in fights with not one, but several dragons and their minions? That was a first. Regardless of our results, odds were bad for every single one of us making it safely back. Hence, the farewells were both hopeful, heartfelt, and sad.

At Aelis' prodding, Arthor even got in front of everybody, climbing up on the throne to be seen by everybody and deliver a few words. His patterned brown and white fur looked horrible, like he'd been sweating profusely, and his eyelids drooped. The fire in his eyes when he spoke was unmistakable. "These last months have been horrible, and I hate almost everything that has happened."

Aelis almost choked on a bite of whatever she was busy eating. "That was not the kind of encouragement I asked for."

"Pfah. It's what I've got, Aelis. You all know me. I accept the need for change and embrace it, but I do not love it. During the past months, we've been balancing on the verge of destruction several times over. I dislike departing from our usual haunts and rhythms. Even so, I cannot in good conscience deny that we are emerging on the other side, stronger than ever. This is also why, even with my dislike, I entirely understand why so many of you are willing to risk your lives.

"Deyra is many things. Bountiful. Mysterious. Fair. She is not, however, benevolent. She helps those who help themselves. And like you, I am looking at the fog covering our future and catching glimpses of a mountain where we are not fighting for survival at the very bottom of the pile, but where we can grow to reach another level. Exactly what, that remains to be seen. But I do respect you for being ready to risk everything to reach it. Pfah!

"You're making me blabber on with witless, empty words. Must be another effect from that lizard of ours. I prefer the words of Deyra. Go. Fight. Thrive... and come back to us afterward." One side of his mouth quirked up in a lopsided smile that almost looked heartfelt. "I'm not letting you go defenseless. I like Roth's addition to our weaponry: the throwing spears and those *atlatl* will make a powerful ambush tool. Yet, the horrible quality of what we've been working with so far will not do. That's why I've gone without sleep tonight--to provide you with some much-needed spearheads that will actually be able to pierce something." He handed over a small bag to Aelis, to the merry chattering of everybody who was going. Everybody knew that Arthor created the best weapons.

At last, our procession gathered everything and started moving down the tunnel. I considered my situation and almost went off without anything more complex than a simple good-bye. In the end, something decided me against it. Not my internal sense of drama. I did not enjoy public speeches. Usually, I could get people to do what they needed to with a few words and a kick to the backside. No, again, it was all due to my old much-loathed teacher, Chad. He showed me, in his very own unpleasant way, that first impressions really did matter. And, for the record, I still hated him.

Another diatribe of his, though equally infuriating, had him ranting about how important it was for you to sell yourself and your vision. Apart from the part where he spent the entire session comparing us to hookers, he had one damn fine point. When you're unable to directly supervise your people 100% of the time, you need to be sure that they're buying into your vision and working in the exact same direction that you are.

I asked my group to stop and turned around, facing my remaining minions standing alone inside the throne room. "I have something I would like to share with you all before we leave. I have given this some thought, and I might as well say it like it is: My odds of survival, were it not for you Talpi, had been abysmal. If I had simply been thrown into the battle along with the other dragons without you to ease me into the dangers of this new world? I would have been lost. Completely and utterly. With that in mind, hearing that even somebody as gnarly as Arthor..." A few titters broke out in the crowd here. "...admits that my arrival has also helped you, is of great comfort to me. It is also something that I would like to spend a word or two on. Don't worry, it won't be long. I'll be gone in a moment to make the Soul Carver chase our tails instead of yours."

That one didn't get any laughs. Apparently it was too early to joke about the very real possibility of our impending doom. "I just wanted to leave you thinking about the world of tomorrow. Now, we'll be gone for a while. Aelis says two weeks at best, but there are bound to be complications on the way. Still, when we come back, victorious, with Selys on our side, we will be able to create something new here--something amazing. We will have a place where Talpi and Crawls are not only safe, but are on top of things. Picture that. Together, we will be able to rule the mountain, side by side, and create a utopia, for dragon, Talpi, and Crawls alike."

The silence in the throne room was deafening. Then cheers broke out everywhere. The tiny Talpi were louder than I had ever experienced them before, cries and squeaks everywhere. I hadn't convinced everybody--there was plenty of doubt and reservations mixed in with the elation and hopefulness--but they liked the idea.

Arthor nodded at me. "We appreciate those words, Lizard. The fact that you think of us, even as you go off into danger, is telling. Now, I've said this before: As a dragon, you're broken. You are neither vicious, cruel, or particularly self-serving. As an ally, however, you have been a positive surprise. May Deyra stay on your side and guide your ascent."

The first day went by without any unforeseen happenings. We kept a reasonable speed, seeing as how we were in well-known territory and didn't have to fear much. I took the time to get an overview of exactly which people I had with me and how we were going to approach this. Aelis, as always, was the perfect companion for this.

"We have four scouts, including me. Then it's five builders and Roth, three more fighters, and Creziel. On top of that, we have seven Crawls and the four Clenchers, obviously."

I nodded. "Very obvious." I lowered my wing on Ursam while we walked, enfolding him in a half-embrace. The huge, hairless beast responded with a low, pleased rumble. "So, that leaves us with a good bunch of frontline fighters and builders or diggers, but pretty short on magic and scouts. Would you agree?"

Aelis nodded. "Yes. We will be limited when it comes to

using magic for digging. Also, with the area we need to cover, all of us have to take turns working as scouts."

"Sounds about right. So, in order of importance, on this trip, you four scouts range highest, obviously, then Creziel, then... Erk, perhaps?"

"Why do you need this?" She shook her head, confusion wafting off of her. "Regardless, I would put Creziel at top and the Clenchers before Erk. The Crawls have proven themselves to be... steadfast in combat, but I still do not trust them."

I kept my mental voice subdued. "You don't *like* them, and that's an entirely different animal. Regardless..."

"Which animal?"

"A different thing. It just means that you dislike them. If I put them in front of you in a combat situation, you would not fear them turning on you, would you? Anyway, I needed to be sure. I warned Arthor yesterday, now it's time to put the changes into effect. I'm changing the professions. We need the bonuses from the professions with the people who are with us right now. Those safe back in the domain will have to make do without."

With that, I selected "Apply profession," ensuring that all Scouts had the Scout profession, Creziel remained with the Mage profession, and Erk and Ursam with the fighter profession. I took a moment to look over the details of the available professions again.

[- Fighter: Increase the damage, health, and physical attributes by +35%
- Mage: Increase magical damage and mental attributes by +35%
- Builder: Increased carrying load +65%. Increased construction capabilities by +35%
- Scout: Increase running speed and toughness by +25% Bonus to hide abilities.
- Cleric: Increase healing capabilities by +25%. Increase mental attributes by +25%.]

Nice. That would go a long way to ensuring that my scouts would survive and that Creziel and my fighters could dish out damage in a fight. I still *really* wanted to find a cleric of some sort. Being able to heal injuries could change our approach quite a lot. Still, for now, scouting and fighting proficiencies were top priority. And walking. Hiking. Plodding along.

I had never been a huge fan of trekking back on Earth, and I realized that I wasn't going to love it here, either. Especially because everybody walked so damn *slow*. After the first hour, I was already trying, and failing, to convince Aelis that I should take my turn as a scout as well. After the third, I was deep into making mental lists of all the things I could possibly work on to keep myself busy.

Fortunately, there was quite a lot to do. Learning, especially. With the rush of the initial period, where we were constantly involved in one fight or another, and the grind of the following time where we were constantly working to improve our defenses, I was way behind on actually knowing my surroundings. Or the local monsters. Or my minions.

Hell, I probably shouldn't even call them minions at this point. It wasn't like they were faceless, disposable resources. Except for the Crawls, when they annoyed me. The point was that I still needed to learn more about this world in order to make intelligent choices.

That's why I approached Roth a bit later. He was bouncing around in front of the group, practicing the use of his two-handed sword while performing dodges, weaves, and blocks. Also, he was wearing... "Roth, what *are* you wearing?"

"Sand bags," he said, like it was the most natural thing in the world. He shifted the sword around in front of himself, reacting to an invisible adversary.

"Oh, wait. I've heard about this before. It's supposed to build extra muscle or something. You came up with that yourself, from the weight training? Uh, and you aren't getting any increases while you're not in the Training Chamber, are you? "

"Of course I won't. It's not only for gains, though. When I

dump the bags, I'm faster than ever. I could run circles around a Clencher by now." True to his word, he performed a sliding motion forward, followed by a dodge roll, somehow avoiding skewering himself on the large weapon.

I looked at the tiny creature. Even though he was bulking out at an alarming rate, he was still half the height and a tenth of the mass of the huge, bear-like monsters. "Yeaaah maybe don't try that yet. Anyway, I was meaning to ask you about something."

He slashed diagonally forward, body fully committed to the swing with both hands on the haft, and I took an involuntary step back. Goddamn. That would even have penetrated *my* scales. "Okay. Ask." He didn't even sound perturbed by the heavy workout.

"Okay. So, this is probably several questions all rolled into one, heh, but I would like to know. What kind of creatures are we likely to stumble upon here, and how come we haven't had to fight anything so far? I mean, it feels like everything is hostile around here, but we're not actually meeting anything."

With a final whooshing sound, Roth completed another slash and then reined it in, putting the sword into an ugly, jury-rigged scabbard on his back. "That's a question for Aelis. Not me."

I shrugged. "Sure. But she's out scouting and... heh, don't tell me you don't know."

"Course I do. I'm not dumb. I just don't care to wrap up my words nice like Aelis does. I prefer action. So, you want to know about life in the Scoured Mountain?" He punched the air.

I nodded. "Arthor's told me something in general terms, and Aelis has told me about some monsters. I just feel we should be fighting more often... it doesn't really add up."

He grinned. "That's cause, even if Arthor is grumpy, he loves drama. Kill or be killed. Us against them. Only the strong survive. Stuff like that. Right?"

"That's... very on point."

"It's also true and very wrong at the same time." He walked

in silence for a full ten seconds. "Take us Talpi, for instance. You think we'd fight anything we met?"

I thought about it. "Well, obviously not. You'd run from anything too strong, probably avoid anything around your own strength that would risk unnecessary casualties, and probably attack only weaker creatures and others when you get a good chance."

He nodded. "Almost right. Except we don't always attack weaker creatures. Some are horrible eating. Some, like Dwellers, we'll only attack in the right timing, and some are simply not worth the time. Why spend hours digging up a Borer Bug when there's more food on Talon Rot, and Talon Rot doesn't bite."

I frowned. "So, you're saying that the number of possible targets for any creature inside the mountain isn't really that large?"

Roth kicked a rock. "Close. The number of *good* targets is small. If a monster is hungry, it will attack most anything."

I grinned. "Like some weak furballs trying to make off with a dragon egg."

"Yeah, that sounds dumb." He sniggered, the high-pitched sound traveling down the corridor to where the Crawls traveled along behind us. "Also, most animals here have a good sense of smell, hearing, or sight. We, as in us Talpi, don't get surprised much. So, stumbling into other creatures in the tunnels doesn't happen *that* often. There's always a detour, side tunnel, or hiding place to avoid unlucky fights. Of course, it helps that we've cleared out most of the creatures that did dominate the tunnels around here."

I thought about that. "Then that would mean that the actual fights take place... when?"

He didn't hesitate. "When you're tracked down, cornered, or ambushed. Or when some monster gets hungry and starts sniffing after a meal. There are some real ugly ambushers in here."

I nodded. "But if everybody does that, then... nowhere's

ever safe? Except for those few monsters or dragons who are large enough to establish and defend their own domain."

"Pretty much. You need to stay on the move, know where the enemies are, keep eyes out constantly." He shrugged. "It's a tough life, but... it's life."

"All right. So, how about weaker enemies? How do Talpi tend to level up?"

"Plant eaters, mostly. There's insects and a few fast, elusive animals that eat the same plants we do. We're pretty good at surprising them. Of course, we ambush others, but that's... not something we can count on. We have to be lucky there. Mostly, we make it by being really good at hiding and taking the right chances."

I nodded, understanding. "Thanks, Roth. Let's make sure we do keep things as boring as possible. We have plenty of food to get by, for now. Hmm, there's one thing, though. I'd like you to spread this around..."

The eyes of the squat Talpus widened as he listened to my idea, but soon he started nodding. After a bit, he sauntered off toward the others, spreading the message. I grinned at his eagerness and looked forward to seeing the result. This could, potentially, be a game-changer.

CHAPTER SEVEN

They say Rome wasn't built in a day, but I wasn't on that particular job. -
Brian Cloughe

Later that day, we got the message and the progression halted.
I'd been walking next to Tim, telling him about the mountain
and our outings. He was grilling me about the shamans' powers
and it was getting to the point where I was about to admit that
he had exhausted my knowledge and fetch Creziel. To my relief,
Roth's exuberant yell saved that discussion for another time, and
moments later, we spotted him sprinting down the low river bed
we were currently wading across. "Hah. Onyx, we got lucky
with your plan. Wreil spotted a stack of Pinheads. They're
waiting for you right now."

I smiled at him. "Great job. Was anybody hurt?"

He rolled his eyes. "Please. Pinheads are weak. They're only
trouble if they manage to get the jump on you. You'll see why.
Besides, Eamus had the Clenchers run in and grab them all.
Useful, that."

We followed him into a nearby tiny side tunnel. I had to
tuck my wings in close to my body to fit. Moments later, we

spotted Eamus standing watch near a cave opening to the side with a smug look on his face.

Timothy tagged along. Watching him move was something special. He walked normally. No ghastly sliding across the floors here. Even so, if you looked close, you could see that he didn't always get it right. Sometimes, he would be walking on a couple of inches of thin air or sink slightly down into the floor, into boulders he'd missed. Right now, however, he was getting weirded out by the detour. "Hey, so what am I missing here? Why's everybody so riled up?"

I smiled. "It's all for your sake, buddy."

"Uh huh. Sure. What's really going on?"

"No, really. I asked them to do me a favor, and they delivered. Well, the first of many, I hope. We're helping you become dangerous."

He shook his head, but got the point immediately when we reached the cavern opening. Inside the tiny cavern, all four Clenchers were present, and they were practically bedecked with small beasts that were trapped alongside their flanks and backs. Some flailed, still trying to get free, while others had given in and just lay there, trapped and shivering.

"What the... no! You're power-leveling me? I can't decide if this is the shittiest or most amazing experience of my life. Afterlife. Whatever. I say, get me my experience!" He tried to push past me and walked right through my foreleg.

I coughed a laugh. "Be my guest, Tim. I'll be honest here. It's all for the greater good. The Talpi got the point immediately. The first few levels are always the easiest, and if we can put somebody in front who's impervious to regular damage and can dish out damage to anybody who's charging out at us..."

He grinned at me and finished my sentence. "They'll be near dead by the time they reach you guys. Hell, if there's a thin wall, I could even walk through it and strike out at everybody with impunity."

"You can? What skills have you got, exactly?"

"Dude. Can we maybe... save that a bit? We're kind of in

the middle of something." He was eyeing the opening with anticipation, and I snorted.

"My mistake, Tim. My brain went off on a tangent there." Addressing Eamus, I asked, "So, what have we got? Pinheads, they said?"

He smiled. "See for yourself, Onyx. The Clenchers behaved wonderfully. Except for Ursam, who decided that he was due a little snack, even though I told him no. We'll have to work on that."

I motioned for Tim to enter the small cave. I was too large for this one, and I lay down and craned my neck to look inside. "Whaaat the hell is that? They look like broken umbrellas."

He wasn't entirely wrong. I sent a message for Ursam to come closer, and we got a closer look at the weird creatures that were contracting in pain and fear along his side. They were stick-thin and tiny, maybe half the size of a Talpus, with a bulbous, circular head sporting four sets of eyes, a thin mouth with serrated teeth and eight, no, ten jointless legs that looked like they would break if I stared too hard at them. The weirdest part was that they didn't have any bodies. The legs were attached straight to the underside of the head. One of the three creatures lay still, legs gathered in the deathlike embrace of Ursam's bone structure. With the legs gathered, looking almost like one cohesive mass, I got it.

"Pinhead. Nice. Hm. They look pretty harmless, if you don't mind me saying, Eamus? I mean, can they even walk properly?" The legs looked like they were, at most, an inch thick.

Eamus snorted. "You'd be surprised. It's confusing to look at with all the flailing limbs, and they can't keep up the speed for more than a couple of minutes, but Pinheads can actually build up a decent speed. That's not what they're really good at, though. They find a tiny crack in the ceiling--you'd be surprised at how small spaces they can fit into. Then they pile in, a whole bunch of 'em, 10. 20. More. Finally, when somebody runs under, they drop down, claw first, on the victim."

I looked at the tiny creature from closer up. It didn't look like it would weigh more than ten pounds. Still. Those legs were tipped with needle-thin claws. "Ouch. So, are they poisonous or something?"

He shook his head. "No. But when they gather their legs below them, they focus their entire body weight into those nasty claws of theirs, They might even be able to breach your scales. Then picture if there's twenty of them..."

The image of how easily a bunch of Talpi could be turned into a pincushion from that was disturbing. I suppressed a shudder. "I see your point. Good thing Wreil spotted them first. Now, I'll just take over these two. Eamus. You up to grabbing that last one that looks like it's sleeping? Good. I'm telling Ursam to let go on three. One. Two. Three."

It took a while extra. Like a dog with a toy, Ursam didn't seem to want to release the Pinheads. Eventually, he caved and I found myself with a tiny, flailing creature in each front claw.

I motioned for Tim to get closer, and he ambled up to me. His usual cocksure attitude looked rattled. "Huh. So, how do we do this?"

"You're the one with the ability. Is it all right if I just hold them down on the ground like this?"

"We'll see. Errr. Could you maybe try to, like, splay the claws a little more. Yeah. That's it."

A wave of displaced air shot out from the blue form and slammed into the Pinhead. The attacked creature shuddered in my grip, trying its best to escape. The edges of the wave splashed over my claws, and I gritted my teeth. The pain wasn't anything, but those emotions... "Hooo. That was annoying. Could we maybe avoid hitting me next time?"

"Oh. Sorry. I'm afraid I haven't really been practicing. Too many people to talk to. From the description, I should be able to...hm." His brows furrowed and another wave appeared. This time, it was tighter and slammed straight into the Pinhead, which convulsed and then relaxed entirely.

"Is it dead? Check your info?"

"Oh. Yeah. Yes it is. 90 experience points on that one. That's not bad. Is it?"

I shook my head. "Not at all. That's very solid, actually. The Talpi who tried to off me my first day were like 100 apiece."

We got to work. Tim's aim improved with every shot, and before long, he was even able to kill a few of the Pinheads with a single shot. Two minutes later, he finished off the last monster and left me standing, looking at his frozen form as he was zoned out, going through his character info.

"Woooot!" He raised both arms in victory. "You are now looking at a level 2 Human Ghost with an additional 3 Mental Power."

"Congratulations! So, your spells should hit harder now?"

"Yep. 30% harder, unless there are some effects in place I don't know about. From 10 to 13 Mental Power. That's not the only thing, though. What did you get at level 2?"

I grumbled, trying to think back. It felt like it had been ages. "Oh. My first feat. I was allowed to choose a path. Heh. Pretty nice one, too. Choose one of my attributes to get an extra +1 per level. So - what did you get?"

He grinned. "You're going to love this. But first--you wanted to hear what my skills were, right?"

We spent a while going over his attributes, skills, and his new feat. It was a bit weird for me, at first, realizing that Mental Control didn't mean mana regeneration for him. His attribute descriptions were slightly different from mine.

[Mental Control: Affects the ability to control your magic capabilities. Increased resistance to mental spells. Increased damage resistance to elemental damage. Increased control of incorporeal form]

[Mental Power: Affects the power of your magic capabilities. Affects mana pool. Increased effect of spell-like abilities. Increased speed of incorporeal form.]

He only had the two to choose from, but then again, that limited the difficulty of where to place his choices. I couldn't fault him for choosing Mental Power over Mental Control since, in essence, that gave him both additional health and power now. It was weird how he only got 3 points per level, but I attributed that to him being classed as a human ghost. Maybe all humans got 3?

His two skills were something else, too.

[Incorporeal. Souls that are linked to Deyra will return to be reborn into a new body, renewing the cycle. A few, rare souls, most often due to unfortunate circumstances or terrible rituals, break their link with Deyra. As one of these unlucky souls, you are forced into an incorporeal existence, where you will be reborn anew each time without a body until you manage to reconnect to Deyra.

As a result of being incorporeal, physical attacks cannot affect you, as you are also unable to touch anything physical. You subside only on mana, and need to siphon mana from sources around you to maintain your existence. Magical and elemental attacks will still be able to affect you. You also have a limited ability to pass through walls and physical material, depending on your Mental Control.]

[Mental attack. You send a wave of mental damage toward your adversaries, doing mental damage. On top of the damage, the psyche of the target is affected, overwhelming them with distracting emotions. The wave can be spread out wide or focused into a thin beam. The Mental Power of your target decides the damage done as well as the efficiency of the emotional onslaught.]

I adored those skills. As it stood, Tim wasn't in any danger at all. We would be able to pit him against any regular physical enemy without any danger to him at all and hopefully gain him experience at an impressive speed. Even if we didn't chance upon any enemies, he wouldn't be in any danger of suffering from mana loss. The effect of his attack was annoying, but he could always recharge his mana from me. As for the feat he got, it looked pretty familiar. Maybe the pathways toward higher levels were similar, regardless of race and attributes? Yet another thing for Tim to look into.

[Path of the Resistant. Your resistance to mental and magical attacks is increased. For every level, subtract 2 percent damage from any mental or magical attack. Cap: 90 percent]

I couldn't find any faults in his reasoning. "The others sounded great, too. I could've gotten stronger attacks, faster movement speed, or better reflexes, but I was thinking that with your help, I'm bound to level pretty fast. And if I'm able to resist most of the damage from the few attacks that are actually able to damage me in the first place? That should leave me pretty damn tough."

We continued on our path. Now that we knew that Tim was able to execute enemies swiftly, we took every chance we could to gain additional levels for Tim and did pretty well. With our numbers, most monsters were quick to avoid our path. But our scouts were efficient, tracking down hiding places with a vengeance. Fortunately, this barely caused any delays. Our scouts were well enough off in Agility and Toughness that the detours were limited to the time it took for Tim to kill the enemies.

At one point, Creziel managed to close the entrance to a tiny cave swarming with Roaches, or like the locals called them, Vourens, allowing for my blue friend to slip right through the wall and wreak havoc, reaching levels 3 *and* 4. He applied 2 points in Mental Control and the remaining 4 in Mental Power, and had almost doubled his damage already.

CHAPTER EIGHT

"I'm not saying that I'm ungrateful or anything. Just, maybe next time they turn me into a ghost, please don't make my butt itch? That sounds like some sort of karmic payback, and I'm not sure I've earned that."

Tim walked next to me, gesturing with his hands as he bemoaned his situation. He didn't look sad, though. He rarely did. All told, he took his capture, torture, and see-through situation way better than I'd ever be able to. Over the past couple of days, I'd come to realize that talking was just his standard setting. If he wasn't chatting my ear off, he'd be traipsing along next to one of the Talpi, questioning them about – anything, really. Eating habits, history, their dreams, whatever. Wreil had even complained at all the questions, but I told him to humor Tim. Even if he had a tendency to let his mouth run constantly, the young number cruncher had an undeniable intellect on him that I, for one, was unable to match.

"Same here. If we ever find whoever's in charge of this joint, I have a thing or two to discuss with them. I used to build stuff to reduce stress. Not an easy task with these rippers. Heh. I guess I also used to overeat, but I don't intend to go into history as the first ever fat dragon."

Tim gave me an understanding grin. "Yeah. I get that. It's crazy how much your mind still yearns for the flavors of the past. Like, I used to be into spicy food. There was this hot sauce, could only be bought in…"

I tuned him out, as he started reminiscing about food. Flavors of the past. He had a way with language, Timothy. There was one particular flavor I had been avoiding thinking about--that of loss. Back when I was still shell-shocked, reeling from the transition into this world, I'd made a checklist of sorts. Sloppy work. I had definitely not been in the best of mindsets when I made it.

However, there was one issue on the checklist that I could now cross off. "Get some answers." I got my answers, and I bloody well didn't like them. There was no karmic reincarnation scheme here, no coma hallucinations. My poor, defenseless soul had simply been pulled into this world to act like the instrument of vengeance of a necromancer with a grudge. Sure, it did simplify things a bit. I wouldn't have to speculate on how to get back, how to wake up or similar, but I would also have to come to terms with the fact that my former life was no more.

When it came to my ex-wife Cait, that was not that much of an issue. Any deep emotions except affection were long since gone. Mostly. To my surprise, the revelation that I was never going to see my estranged daughter, Dina, again hurt like hell. It would seem that despite my years of doing nothing to mend the gap between us, my treacherous mind still harbored a desire to reacquaint myself with her. That was never going to happen now, and it bloody *hurt*. I parted myself from my self-pitying thoughts and, with a mental effort, turned my focus outward. "Hey Tim. I'll need your help."

"Of course you will. You actually *like* meatloaf. That's a mental defect if I ever saw it."

"First of all, there's something wrong with you. Second, this is serious."

"Okay. Listening." His see-through form straightened, and he looked straight at me.

"Thanks. So, here's the deal. I'm a planner. It's always come naturally to me, and in addition, it's something I've worked on my entire life. If something needs doing, I try not to waste my time with what-ifs and pointless speculations. I make a plan, and I get to work. If I need something, I try to find somebody who can provide that."

"With you so far."

"Good. I've been doing this for a while here. Wherever I've seen an issue or a lack that might be an issue for our survival, I've tried to counteract it or plan how to do it. We are doing pretty good too, apart from the whole Soul Carver issue."

"Minor detail." Tim's crooked smile was almost convincing.

"Heh. Right. What I'm trying to say, though, is that we're progressing on all the practical issues. Considering that we actually make it on our outing here, we're looking at the possibility of being able to lead safer and longer lives than what seems to be common in this place."

"...but?"

"But that won't hack it. I'm not interested in just ensuring that I survive as the most dangerous beast out there. I want a *good* life, not just a long one. If we're going to spend our days fighting for our lives, it should be *for* something. That requires us to make some pretty large changes here, among others in the way things are run."

Timothy's head bobbed up and down in agreement. "I see your point. I mean, if we make the rules, we're in a position to change things up... but it does open up to a large number of questions."

"You *are* quick. Not just your mouth, either. That's exactly my problem. Exactly which kind of society should we aim for? I mean, we're going to try to include everybody, but that stuff is complex and not exactly my forte. How do we introduce it? How do we let things best develop? I don't know enough about the possibilities to make a good decision."

The see-through blue figure drifted down to sit cross-legged on the floor. "That's... yeah. I agree. Sort of. I mean, this isn't a cart-before-the-horse issue. This is us with a handful of acorns and a vague idea what equines look like. Sure, we might have to deal with this, but shouldn't we try to, y'know, make sure we survive long enough that it's an issue first?"

I nodded. "Definitely. And I'll make sure of that. But we need to be ready and take the discussions beforehand. Because if we mess this up, the whole thing can come tumbling down on our heads *even* if we survive to take over after Selys."

Timmy Smurf was frowning so deeply, his eyebrows pointed straight down at his nose. "Honestly, I can't say you're wrong. It's just... look at where we're at. Right now, we're about to spend weeks wading through monster-filled tunnels in the search for goddamn dragons--and probably kill them! So yeah, I'm all for planning for the future, but I'm not sure we're ready to start writing the Scoured Mountain Constitution, know what I mean?"

"Heh. That *would* be too early. Just... help me wrap my head around what the options are, and let's prepare how to present it to the others in a good way. They are obviously going to be involved too, but let's approach it in a timely manner."

He nodded. "Gotcha. I'll think on it. Hell, you already planted the idea in my mind, now the damn thing's going to focus on it for the next while regardless of what happens."

A rumble of laughter escaped my stomach. "So, that's how I'm supposed to actually make use of you? Just sow the seed and your head takes over. I like it. Does that work for other things?"

His frown was back. "What do you mean?"

"Like... what if I say, 'I'm a Barbie Girl'?"

"I... wouldn't be surprised? I mean, you don't look it, but-"

"Or 'I'm Blue'."

"You should probably... Oh no you don't! I-"

I landed the kicker. "Baby Shark!"

"Do doo do do do do." He shook his head, glaring balefully at me. "You bastard."

CHAPTER NINE

Going on the road for long stretches can seem daunting, and I certainly miss being home sometimes, but the chance to see so many different cities, let alone perform in them, is something I am really grateful for. - John Mulaney

On the third day, the terrain changed. We were traveling close to the south-western edge of the mountain. It took me a while before I noticed it. At some point, as I was discussing the different types of inhabitants inside the mountain with Aelis, when the changes stood out to me. "Hey, is it becoming warmer in here, or is it just me?"

She nodded. "I commend you on your astuteness, Milord. Other changes abound as well. Plant life is reduced, and we are seeing fewer signs of weaker lifeforms around, as well. In fact, we were looking for a safe place to establish a base for ourselves."

"A base? Do you mean--"

"Yes. This is typical of what we would see in an area containing either a domain or a dangerous group of enemies. We shall need a fall-back position in case we are discovered, but there is bound to be something nearby that has caused the lack of wildlife. I must impress upon you that it may be something as simple as a natural phenomenon. Lifeforms rarely affect the nature inside the mountain. It is usually the other way around, with animals encroaching the areas that are abundant with nature and water."

Within the hour, we had located a suitable base. After half a day's work from our builders and Creziel combined, we turned a huge, empty cavern into a spacious haven for us. It looked like a regular dead-end cave to the untrained eye, but the vast majority of the place lay hidden between two overlapping half-walls and a winding pathway.

Aelis assured me that we would keep working on the place for as long as we were there, adding an escape tunnel, traps, misleading tracks, and so forth. For the time being, our scouts were out in force, slowly circling the nearby area before expanding their search perimeter. Before she also left, Aelis told me that this was what they had done for her entire life: choosing the optimal camp and improving it as much as possible, while knowing that it would be a temporary refuge and they would move on soon. The sensation of loathing as she said it told me just how much she did not miss having to live her life on the run anymore. I mean, apart from just now.

As for me, I was delegated to playing the waiting game. Fortunately, I had plenty of company to keep me occupied. Training the Clenchers was still an ongoing process. Ursam had a lot of personality that could do with some tempering, and I still didn't entirely trust him in combat situations. Eamus was increasingly taking responsibility for the other Clenchers along with his assistant. Still, we took turns training each one, to make sure we'd never be stuck in a situation where a Clencher refused to listen to an order because it wasn't his usual trainer bossing him around.

I talked Roth into something new. I figured that just because I couldn't increase my attributes in the Training Chamber, I could still do with improving my skills. I hadn't taken the time needed to improve my combat reflexes outside of the actual combat, and it showed. Hell, I hadn't even managed to gain a decent control over my tail attacks yet. It was a bit embarrassing, to be honest. That's why I started spending some of my free hours with the agile Talpus running rings around me.

The next day our scouts widened their search as enemies stubbornly refused to appear. We continued our training, as did everybody else. After a brief talk with Roth, we restarted the tradition of holding training games that we had begun a while back in the domain. According to Roth, they were becoming pretty proficient at moving like a unit, adjusting their approach from orders and ensuring that the Crawls and Clenchers remained in front of the vulnerable Talpi to take the brunt of the damage from any attacks.

Some things just could not be taught, according to Roth. "Fighting that green dragon and his Urten was the best kind of test we could come up with. The battle was chaotic, like those things are. No fake games could replace that. It also tells us a lot about what we *can* improve with practice." The brawny Talpus took his large sword and lowered it one-handed, with but a tiny tremble, aiming the point at me. "We need to get better at facing large, scary enemies."

This was why I insisted on becoming part of the training games. That first day, we set up different scenarios and acted them out with blunt weapons, trying to teach our fighters to adjust to fighting with or against a dragon. It was anything but easy going, and we had a lot of false starts. It didn't take us long to realize that adding Clenchers to the mix was not an option. Teaching them the difference between a mock battle and a real one would take training that I definitely was incapable of providing. For now.

So, it was left to the Crawls, Talpi, and myself. After the first handful of attempts, we included Creziel, to add the confusion of magic into the mix. By my order, the first handful of attempts were from the perspective of improving survival, acting out ambushes by superior forces, what to do when the enemy involves magic, stuff like that. Then, later, I had plans to introduce other, more difficult themes. Attacking an enemy position, or maybe trying to figure out something about a shield wall. That last one was dependent on finding some better crafters first. We had one decent leatherworker with us, and most of the Talpi knew how to carve bone, but it was still nowhere near enough to create shields that could handle any sort of punishment.

My plans were pushed into the background when we found the enemy the day after. Aelis herself had located a band of minions patrolling and followed them back to their lair. She returned immediately afterward, breathing hard as she relaxed from her hard run. "I have both heartening and disheartening news, Sire."

"Good news first, please." And some day, I'd have to figure out exactly who taught her that you had to talk with the formality of an old-fashioned butler, stick up the bum included.

"Very well. Their forces appear smaller than ours and I believe the dragon is weaker than you. At the very least, it is smaller."

I glanced at her in surprise. That was the first time I'd faced off against a smaller dragon. "That *is* good news. So, hit me with the bad news."

"I figured out the reason that we have been unable to find any nearby tracks. The dragon has a flight of Imps under his wings. Even when they walk, they are small enough to leave few tracks. Also, his domain is firmly entrenched and surrounded by a lake of lava. We may be able to circumvent it with Creziel's help before we run out of food, but I doubt it. Finally, he has a Bulkbeast." Aelis sounded almost apologetic.

"Heh. Aelis. Given that I don't know Imps *or* Bulkbeasts, you'll either have to show me or be a lot less sparse with the details."

Two hours later, our entire force was staying safely back, while Aelis and I were lurking 500 feet from the red dragon's domain. We were both hidden under the veil of my Camou-flage spell, and furthermore, I half-crouched behind a range of boulders. As the size of the place became evident, I realized what Aelis had been trying to tell me on our way here. This place was *massive*. You'd be able to fill the entire Metlife Stadium into the cave and the ceiling was several hundred feet up. No way in hell were we going to be able to collapse the ceiling on them. Or even get close.

Somehow... *somehow* they'd managed to create an island in the middle of a lake of floating lava, with a single narrow dirt path leading from the only tunnel entrance and out to the island. Everything else was surrounded by lava. This time, life hadn't been kind enough to help with a conveniently placed underground river that we could dump onto the lava either. I rested my neck on a boulder and sighed. "So, what you're saying is that that hillock out there on the island is actually the Bulk-beast you're talking about?"

"Exactly. From what Arthor says, they were once domesti-cated animals from outside the mountain. Huge muscles and carrying load with a tiny brain. Inside the mountain, they evolved, became more vicious and abandoned their docile nature. They are prone to violence and not at all easy to tame."

"Unless you're a dragon." I sighed again.

"Unless you are a dragon." She commiserated.

I rapped a claw on a boulder, considering our approach. "So, you're telling me that we're not taking down that Bulkbeast in close combat?"

"Exactly."

"Even with the Clenchers?"

"Even with the Clenchers." Her answer was immediate. "Your weakening attack might be able to reduce it to a level where we can handle it eventually. Also, it has plenty of other weaknesses. It is slow, cumbersome, and too large to fit in most places. Out there, that all becomes irrelevant."

"Uh-huh. I got you. Is it impervious to the lava here, too?"

"Probably not. Bulkbeasts are still animals, regardless of their size."

"Understood. And flying is a bad idea because of the Imps?"

She nodded. "They may not amount to much by themselves, and inside the tunnels we could surely handle them, especially if we managed to ambush them. Out there in the open cavern, they demand respect. The small creatures are nimble in the air and have a ranged elemental attack that is powerful for their size."

I mulled it over. "Okay, so flying is a bad idea. I agree, by the way. I have been practicing my flight on and off, but we rarely find tunnels that are large enough. Even if I can probably outfly them, it's a different story with the dragon. No problem. Anything else?"

Aelis retained her composure, but the bafflement arising from her would amount to the mouth dropping open in shock from anybody else. "No, Sire. That should cover all the major points."

I frowned, but then I could feel a grin build on my face. "Good. I mean, with all the direct roads of advance taken care of, we'll have to resort to trickery and illusions. Remind me again... what was the Shadow Dragons' specialty supposed to be?"

We established another camp within a short distance of the red's domain. Finding the right spot took little time. This close to the dragon's domain, there were plenty of unoccupied caves, and we located one looking right down on the edge of the lava, that wasn't right in the path of anybody leaving the place. We sent our remaining troops back there to prepare the assault while the two of us prepared the plan to limit the usefulness of the Bulkbeast.

At first, we were only discussing an ambush, but this time, Tim decided to get involved in the planning session. He clearly felt ill at ease facing down the rest of us, but he did it nonetheless. "We need alliances. It may be more dangerous and take longer, but we need to at least attempt an alliance."

Roth was livid. "Tell me you're not listening to him. We're risking a lot as it is. We don't need to make things tougher."

I shrugged. "I don't know, Tim. I tried forming an alliance once, and it went belly up. I mean, I get the point, I really do - but it just makes everything all the more complicated."

The blue shape shook his head. "This is essential. If you had paid attention to our history, you would know it already. If we don't get some alliances started, we are certain to fall at some point. Once we do, the whole damn thing comes crashing down with us. The history of our world teemed with warlords and fighters trying to become conquerors, and once they inevitably died, fire and bloodshed was the result, before the struggle just started over with new participants. Is that what you want? If you mean to build something lasting, where the Talpi and Crawls can continue even if you kick the bucket, we'll have to start creating alliances."

I ground my teeth. "Yeah. You're right. Sorry, Roth, but he's right. It might be a shitty situation, but we're in this for the long haul. I'm not letting you get back to running for your lives when I die. We need allies that'll be able to support you, even if this Deyra figure decides I've spent enough time here. Now, help me plan our approach so we risk as little as possible."

Once we agreed on an approach, we went on a scouting trip to verify that it could actually be done, then we went straight to work.

Creziel and I went alone. He walked in front, and then I followed right behind him. I ignored everything else but the scenery surrounding us, my focus entirely fixed on hiding both of us behind an illusion while Creziel worked. On our scouting tour of the walkway, Creziel discovered that the material below the dirt walkway was mostly gravel and some smaller rocks. The material wasn't optimal, but Creziel's detailed breakdown amounted to the following: he could work with it, but it would take some time and effort.

We debated how close to the domain we wanted to approach and eventually decided that we needed to get at least halfway across the pathway, or we could risk the Bulkbeast just bearing the pain and crossing the magma in order to attack us regardless. Before we started, I insisted on a solo approach, sneaking close and maintaining an illusion in front of myself to hide my bulk, while I waved tendrils of Shadow magic at the walkway, searching for hidden traps or magic. Nothing. Regardless of how fortified this place was, it had not been prepared for me.

This is how the afternoon on the fourth day found Creziel and myself within 250 feet of the red dragon's domain. Now that we were closer, I could take in the place. At first glance, I had dismissed it as being like the first red dragon's domain: colorful, but with no substance. Now, I could see that this was far from the truth. All over the island, scattered constructions built with low dirt walls separated different sections of what clearly were different constructions inside the domain. One group of Imps relaxed inside a raised plateau filled with nest material and what looked like trash, while another bunch of Imps flew around an obstacle course, occasionally taking a slash at some of the jury-rigged target dolls.

Those were definitely a Habitat and a Training Chamber, respectively. Other spots held constructions I did not recognize, while every major intersection held a pillar I recognized as a twin to the Fire Tower I'd buried inside the last red dragon's lair. None of the buildings held ceilings, probably to make it easier to get airborne at short notice. Behind all the other constructions, the terrain rose into a half-hill, terminating with the most brazen display of a hoard I'd seen to date, placed right there for the world to see. "Nice trap," I thought. I judged that assaulting this place head-on would be folly. Luckily, we were planning no such thing.

We were fortunate in that neither the Imps nor the red dragon were much for flying around the place. Inside the domain, the Imps flittered about all the time, but they rarely rose high. The Bulkbeast also looked fairly placid from the distance, except for when some of the Imps made it toil, dragging burdens around the place.

As for the red dragon, he must be hidden somewhere and did not show himself. Even so, it was tense work. I had to remain constantly vigilant in case a patrol of Imps or, god forbid, the dragon himself decided to go for an outing. All of this, I had to look out for while maintaining the focus of my Illusion. While the mental toll was pretty harsh, I was feeling some definite improvement - like I was flexing my mental muscles and finding them stronger than I had figured. The tiny Talpus, for his part, ignored everything, myself included, crawling backward over the pathway while he nudged the lower layers of the pathways out into the magma itself, where they joined the roiling, burning masses surrounding us.

The heat was unpleasant, to say the least, and Creziel's fur was swiftly matted with sweat, even as I started feeling light-headed. Regardless, our progress was impressive. Within half an hour, we'd already cleared a third of the pathway, leaving behind only a thin crust of hardened dirt untouched, making it seem like we had never been there. Every so often, we let a couple of scouts rush ahead of us, clearing away our footprints. Well, all right. My footprints. With his weight, Creziel barely displaced the dust.

Once, we were forced to retreat, falling back to hide inside our new cave, while a group of five Imps went out on patrol. I watched them, transfixed, ready to attack in case any of them spotted our footprints on the dirt path. To our luck, they appeared confident and unfocused, chittering in harsh, high-pitched voices as they walked and glided along carelessly to disappear into the tunnels beyond. As soon as the scouts gave us the go ahead, we got straight back to work. 45 minutes later, Creziel sighed and stretched his back. "My mana is depleted, Sire."

I looked behind us. Only sixty feet of pathway remained. I motioned for a scout to come and take care of our tracks and started walking slowly backward. "Great job, Creziel. I'm running on empty - uh, I mean, I have almost no mana left either. Let's go back to the others and plan the attack for tomorrow. We'll remove the last bit of pathway then."

We gathered inside the impromptu camp and discussed our options. I looked down on Creziel and couldn't help but feel proud of his efforts. "You've done well today. Fifteen-twenty minutes more and we'll have the trap ready for the Bulkbeast."

Roth grimaced. "That's all nice. So we've trapped the big brute on the island, where it's protected by all the flying monsters. What are we going to do about it? I'm not dumb enough to take it on myself."

I created an illusion of an island exploding into motion, Imps and the dragon flying every which way. The illusion unraveled, and I grinned at him. "That's the fun part. We get to go piss them off. Now, you remember how, back at the lair, we talked about the dangers of entrenching ourselves and letting others attack us? This is exactly what the red out there has done. He's set the entire island up to be virtually unassailable by land *and* air. Of course, in that process, he's forgotten that he needs experience to continue growing himself - or reckons that he can catch up, once he's safe out there. Heh.

"Even with all the traps, the Imps, and the Bulkbeast, it would just be a matter of time before he's taken out by somebody who's more offensive and vicious. Now, before we get started, I have a general idea, then I want your help to make the plan foolproof. What I want to do is make sure that we don't need to face off against their entire force..."

Our council took several hours. I laid out my ideas, and we extrapolated from there, starting and discarding a number of different variations before locking in on a single scheme. It was assuredly dangerous, and being exposed at the wrong time would increase the danger manyfold, but it played to our strengths and would ensure as little danger as possible. If we played our cards right, that was. We performed a few tests to ensure the theories were sound, then we really got to work.

The day after, we were ready and my mana had recharged.

The Talpi had toiled through the night along with the builders, digging into the mountain, creating pile upon pile of loose soil, all ready for the Crawls to drag out into the tunnel to aid with our constructions. Tim stood at my side, along with Roth and Aelis, staring at the island on the far side of the lake. According to Aelis, the earlier patrol had returned, but no new patrols had ranged out from the domain. Everything was calm.

Tim was the first to speak up. "I can't believe we're doing this. I doubly can't believe I won't even be able to help you with the attack."

I looked at him with a smile. "Appreciate the sentiment, Tim. With all the magical damage from the Imps and the bloody dragon, we'd be fools to expose you to it right away. Your part comes afterward, if all goes well." Turning toward Creziel, I assessed him with a glance. The success of our plan hinged, to a great degree, upon his speed and efficiency. "You've been working hard. Do you need a break?"

He looked at the tableau in front of us. The sensations coming from him were stronger than ever - testament to my Mental Power doubling over a short period of time. Stark naked fear, a sense of being overwhelmed and, to my amazement, a hint of eagerness. His mental voice wavered a little, but his focus was strong. He talked straight to me, but glanced at his fellow Talpi and steeled himself. "No. I'm ready. I will not let you down."

Moments later, we were off. Creziel and I started out by finishing the job we'd begun the day before. Shortly, a crucial piece of the plan fell in place, as the last bit of walkway was reduced to a thin crust of soil above the lava. Then we pulled back into the tunnel entrance, scouts once again hiding our tracks to remove any trace of our presence. Now, I got to stay in the background while my people toiled.

Crawls dragged heavy loads of soil from our cave to the entrance tunnel, where our builders and Creziel created a defensive position a way inside the large tunnel leading toward the lava cave. Aelis lingered near the lava cave, ready to have me create an illusion in case another patrol arrived, but we were lucky. A couple of hours later, Creziel came up, looking like a toddler who'd played with mud. We were ready. Now, it was just a matter of waiting until the next patrol ranged out.

Our builders kept up a constant flurry of activity, as did Creziel, tightening and fortifying the tunnel to the point where even a fire-breathing red dragon would be seriously inconvenienced to pass by. The rest of our people were waiting a bit further along, holed up inside the cave where we'd passed the night. I chatted with Aelis and Tim while we waited to pass the time.

The tiny Talpus was rubbing her stump while she kept up her vigil from right inside the tunnel entrance. "You realize, Milord, that Arthor would be livid, were he here? He so dislikes these fanciful notions of alliances."

Timothy smirked. "Yeah, he does seem a stickler for tradition, that one."

I grinned. That was putting it mildly. "Yeah. Good thing he isn't here, right?"

Aelis kept her composure well, but a sensation that felt a bit like a giggle escaped from her. "True. Still, do you realize that the combined memories of our entire *tribe* has no hint of anything like an alliance between dragons?"

I frowned, releasing a deep rumble of agreement. "Sure. But... I don't know. I've been risking my life pretty often here. We could keep on doing just that--but why? Just so we can reign over a larger slice of the mountain until somebody bigger kills us? Seems stupid to not try and build something lasting. You with me, Aelis?"

The sensations coming from her warmed my old, grumpy heart. "Never doubt that, Sire."

CHAPTER TEN

The Imps looked really piteous up close. If anything, they were smaller than the Talpi, and as they lay on the ground, their dirt-colored skin and bat-like wings more than anything made them look unimpressive. Of course, the fact that we had caught the patrol by surprise, and I had downed the entire group of six Imps with a single Weakening Fog didn't help on the impression. From what Aelis told me, being charged by an airborne group of fire-wielding Imps was a different, much scarier, experience.

I grinned at Aelis. "We're committed now. We're doing this! Everybody, follow me." I could feel the adrenaline rushing to make my blood boil as I stepped out into the cavern. My wings pumped up and down, and I heard a few squeals from behind me, as Talpi were pushed back by the force--and then I was airborne.

What little practice I'd managed to get in here or there didn't hurt. The double handful of Agility and Toughness points I had gained since I last flew in a tense situation definitely helped as well. To my surprise, it felt like the warmth of the lava helped somehow, warm winds pushing me upward, limiting the need for me to pump my wings to keep me airborne. I would love nothing more than just try to fly for leisure and explore the experience, but I had a job to do.

Once I gained a decent height, I glided slowly toward the red's domain, maintaining an illusion that nothing was here. It was tough to handle, and dodgy work at best, since there was no way I could anticipate what was right behind me. My best attempt right now was creating an illusion of a blurry, dirt-colored background, hoping that I would blend in with the cavern walls far behind me.

I didn't want anybody to attack me right away and ruin the chance of a peaceful chat. When I touched down right outside the domain and let the illusion drop, my heart felt like it was about to beat its way out of my chest. I grinned a manic grin at the world and roared, letting the deep, primal tones announce my presence. "Dragon. Your brother has arrived. Let us talk!"

That sure woke them up. Within seconds, the air filled with flying Imps, and the Bulkbeast started lumbering my way. For a moment, I believed I'd be attacked without even a chance for a proper parlay, but then the encroaching monsters froze, like they were listening to another voice, and backed off a bit. Then, a smooth voice sounded in my head. "We will talk."

From the far end of the island, the dragon arose. She--because the voice inside my head had been clearly feminine--must have had some hideout built into the far end of the island to surprise any attackers, because I didn't see her until she rose up from beneath the rise holding the hoard. As she got closer, I got a good look at her. The only real comparison I had was the other red, and I must admit, she fell short.

While her body had clearly defined muscles, and she rode the air gracefully down to land at a safe distance to me, she was nowhere near as majestic or overwhelming as the other one had been. She was definitely shorter, too. Regardless of her size, her voice held the same arrogance the other one had. "Brother, he says. A shadow dragon." The sneer in her mental voice was unmistakable. "I do not lower myself to the standards of your kin, and you are definitely no clutch brother of mine. I know them all. Unless..."

I finished her sentence. "Unless I was inside the egg from the clutch that went missing. So you know of that. I am not here to reminisce about what I missed by not awakening in the clutch. I am here to propose an alliance. What is your name? I am Onyx."

She crooked her head, watching me like I was a bug who'd had the audacity to stand up in the middle of her dinner plate. Hissing, she said, "I am Ruiva. Ally? With you?" Her eyes closed to slits and she growled. "Have you killed my scouts?"

I smiled at her. "No. They are merely inconvenienced. As long as we come to an agreeable solution, I will release them."

She sat back up, looking at me intently. "They are merely Imps, but… I am listening."

"Good. So, right now, we're all competing for the title to become Selys' successor when she intends to leave the Scoured Mountain. That means we should all kill off each other until only one is left standing, right?"

"That is the ultimatum Selys gave us."

"Heh." I shook my head. "What a waste of time and resources. Now, I have no intention of roaming around the mountain constantly myself. Selys has her human sorcerers, but I would rather work with kin."

The red flared her neck. "So you would be the one to reign?"

I nodded and looked her straight in the eye. "I would. I am tougher than you, faster than you, and unless I am very wrong, higher-level than you. I also do not mind the danger involved with being the one standing in front of everybody, while you have already resigned yourself to a defensive position, hoping that your fellow dragons will break their necks on your defenses. But know this: I will not be a bad leader. If you side with me, I will swear to protect you from any challengers, and I will share any information I have regarding the rest of the mountain."

Her look was all the answer I needed. That single glance of

hers held such unspeakable arrogance that I despaired at the thought of her seeing reason. Still, her response was measured. "What will the cost be?"

"You will relinquish your claim on the throne of the Scoured Mountain. I will also keep your hoard at a level where it does not rival mine. Currently, mine is at the small medium size. Finally, you will swear an oath that you will not attack me or help anybody plot against me."

She stood up tall. "Your terms are not as unfair as I would have predicted. I smell no outright lies from you, either."

I could already feel the way it was going. "But?"

Her grin showed off her monstrous teeth, and suddenly she didn't look smaller than me. "But, you did not talk about armies, either. Please tell me, with the same conviction, that your forces outnumber mine. Go ahead."

I grinned to match hers. "I don't need to. Please feel my sincerity here: My minions *can* and *will* defeat yours, regardless of that big Bulkbeast you've got lurking back there. Besides, you have already lost. My minions hold the entrance, and we have all the time in the world to wait you out." That was my first outright lie. I felt certain that she was unable to read my mind. At times, I sensed the emotions beneath her speech, affirming my belief that my Mental Control had hers beat.

She sneered. "Do you really believe I haven't planned for a siege?"

I shook my head. "No. But I believe, with all my heart, that you haven't planned for me." With those parting words, I took to the air before she could get off a parting shot and flew with full speed at the tunnel entrance.

Ruiva's forces, along with the dragon herself, circled after me, keeping at a safe distance. I turned my neck several times to look back and ensure that I wasn't being attacked and envied the natural ease with which the red carried herself aloft, gliding lazily on the warm currents of air in the center of her forces. I resigned myself to a graceless landing and ran straight into the tunnel, where I spotted our defenses at the back. I eased my

LARS MACHMÜLLER

bulk through the reduced opening and activated my illusion, letting it look like the tunnel was untouched. "No alliance. Get ready."

At my words, my Crawls and Clenchers sprang into action. They started dragging and pushing huge, pre-prepared blocks of rock toward the opening. Thanks to Creziel's work, they slid easily over the smooth floor until they clicked into place, further reducing the opening to where only the Imps would be able to push through. Once that was done, everybody but myself moved further back down the tunnel, waiting to see what they would do.

I could see the end of the tunnel from my position. First one, then several Imps glanced in to see what was going on. They didn't stay in place for long before retreating, probably to receive orders from their overlord. My mana slowly ticked downward, reaching the halfway mark, and I wondered whether she was going to remain completely in the defensive.

Then, a single Imp started tentatively flying down the corridor. I almost chuckled at the sight. Ruiva wasn't dumb, but still. Being chosen for this kind of scouting duty was just unlucky. I waited until the scout came within my reach and then released a Weakening Fog, enjoying the brief look of horror on the creature's face before it slumped senseless to the ground. Roth sprinted past me, threw the Imp over a shoulder, and ran past me back into the corridor.

I created a new illusion, this time replete with the image of a single Imp moving slowly down the tunnel. This time, the illusion was slightly harder to maintain. The size of the illusion in itself didn't matter much, but keeping the image of how the Imp should naturally move made the process a bit more difficult. As another Imp stuck its ugly head into the tunnel, and I made my Imp wave for it to follow, I was really happy with my Mental Control attribute and with choosing Improved Spell Control as a feat. The control of the illusion felt natural, almost effortless, even with the intricacies of what I was weaving here.

The reward came moments later, as a full quartet of Imps

followed my decoy, and I let them join their brethren in unconsciousness moments later. Unfortunately, that was the last group. Nobody saw fit to join us afterward and after a while, I let the illusion drop and returned to my people.

Creziel was busy manipulating the earth of the tunnel wall, and I just stood and observed him in silence. He had really improved, not only as a person, but very much as a shaman. I shook my head in amazement as the earth flowed almost like water portrayed in slow motion, closing the cave opening and leaving behind a tiny slit at head height. As I watched, Creziel noticed my presence and turned toward me, while the earth kept flowing behind him. Before the walls closed up, I caught a glance of the unconscious Imps inside. Heh. I'd love to be there when they woke up.

I smiled. "You have grown, Creziel."

He nodded, looking at the floor, but then he lifted his gaze to meet my eyes. "Thanks to you, Onyx. They never used to listen to me. Now, when I say move, they actually move. Well, some of them. Roth was always a special case."

I grinned. "No discussion there. Speaking of Roth--how about we go and get the party started?"

We moved past the Crawls who took up guard behind our blockade. Aelis, Tim, and Roth joined us right away. Roth was bouncing on his feet. "Can we do that again? Picture the look on that red's face, when he realizes that a third of his Imps are already out of the battle."

I grinned at the exuberant fighter. "She. But yeah. When she finds out, she's going to blow up. The Imps are tucked away safely for now?"

Creziel nodded. "They should not be able to escape by themselves. Earth is not their element."

Aelis cleared her throat. "May I ask, Milord, what your intentions are with the Imps?"

"Oh, I'm not sure. But I was thinking, if we made it safely through this battle, flying minions with ranged damage wouldn't be a horrible thing to add to our ranks." I didn't even need to be able to sense emotions in order to note the distaste on the faces of the Talpi.

Tim, however, was nodding along eagerly. He *got* me. I indicated the tunnel opening with a claw. "If we can save that for later, we have something a bit more pressing to discuss right now. So, Aelis, you guys were keeping an eye on the Imps from the opening, right? How many are left?"

"Our best estimate is 18, Sire. There may be more. Telling them apart from a distance is frustrating."

"18." I repeated the word, grimacing. "Have you decided how many are going to go out there?"

Roth pointed down the corridor at the Crawls who were keeping guard. "Every single one of those Crawls. I like a good scrap, but they're... obsessed about it. Won't complain, though. They can take a punch." He swung the massive sword around, moving it right through Tim, who jumped with the shock of it. The squat Talpus just showed his teeth in a shit-eating grin. "Our scouts are going too, and Creziel too, obviously, and our fighters."

I did the math. "That's... 14?"

He nodded. "Yes. Plus two more builders who have become decent at handling the *atlatls*. That will leave a few of their Imps unoccupied, but we will have to take the risk."

I grimaced. "I agree. I should have mana enough for that, barely. I prefer we get started now, as opposed to later. Who knows what the red has planned. Now, the Clenchers stay back here with Eamus. There would be no hiding them. They would just charge straight out there at the first sign of opposition. They are here for when I come running. Remember the agreement. Nobody attacks unless I give the signal, all right?" Everything depends on positioning here, and there is no guarantee we will be able to get this right. *If* we get the chance there is just the one shot. One attack and then we run."

Roth shook his head, stamping his foot. "You're not giving us much to work with here, dragon!"

"I know. But the alternative is allowing her to realize what's going on. How do you like the idea of being caught in the open with a furious red dragon who is just looking for targets for her fiery breath?"

He showed his teeth. "Yeah, we'll go with your idea. I just like my ambushes simpler. A lot could go wrong here."

I nodded. "You're not wrong. However, unless we actually mean to lay a siege here, I'm not seeing any other good approaches. The entire island further inland is riddled with Fire towers, and we need to get them all nice and close... and avoid the Bulkbeast at the same time. One shot, then we run. Everybody ready?"

A chorus of assent sounded around me, and I started applying my spells.

CHAPTER ELEVEN

Sometimes we put ourselves in places that only we can get out of! - Howard Ryan, What My Builder Didn't Tell Me.

There is a sensation you get when you've done everything you can and just don't know if it's enough. Returning home after my first job interview. The first couple of times I had a client go over my constructions and assess the quality. It's that weird mix of hope filled with a sensation of impending doom. That was exactly what I was feeling right then. I cast Bestow Camouflage 16 times in a row, fighting my way through a need for a nap as my mana dipped down to hit below a third of my total.

Then, I went first through the tunnel, listening to the cries from the island as they noticed my presence and took to the air. I did not go for the island, but pumped my wings, carrying me gracelessly along the wall of the cavern a few hundred feet. I touched down on a handful of boulders, granting me an overview of the island. The Imps were in clear view, circling and waiting for my approach. The red rested near her hoard, watching me. Even my eyesight couldn't see that far, but I still had no trouble picturing her glaring at me. One Imp started toward me, but was ordered back right away.

Then... nothing. The minutes passed as we watched each other, and they eventually returned to lazy circles, keeping an eye on me. I grinned, staring back at them as time passed by ever so slowly. Every single second they spent staring in my direction was one in which they did not look closer at the walkway. I feared a cry rising up every single minute and now and again felt my pulse race at the sight of a blurred form on the walkway as one of my minions didn't move slowly enough for the camouflage to adjust naturally. The seconds ticked by with glacial slowness, until twelve minutes had passed. I swallowed. My mouth was suddenly dry. If they hadn't been discovered by now, they must have made it to the other side. We were committed now. No turning back.

Beating my wings in a slow rhythm, I slowly rose into the air and threw my mental voice into the wind, shouting for the world to hear. "Ruiva. I would talk." I kept my course low and straight, clearly aiming for the landing right at the end of the pathway to the island. My nerves were shot. Anything could happen right now. If they charged me right away, we might still be able to pull off a partial success. Might. I needed to keep her curious... With all my mental strength, I projected my message. "I was mistaken. I see that now."

Still no response. The Imps were circling closer now, with the gleaming red dragon right behind them. The Bulkbeast was ambling closer, right behind the flying creatures. It was the first time I got a good look at it, and it was positively terrifying. The tall creature was practically a... what did the nerds call those again in the movies? Something like the company. AT&T Walker or thereabout.

The huge difference between that machine and this beast lay in the name. The Bulkbeast was *buff*. The legs were huge, muscled, and clearly heavily armored, and its body was twice my height. The head was small, with tiny, beady eyes and a large, round mouth that seemed more apt for chewing cud than savaging enemies. Regardless, it looked more like a farm animal that had gotten into the magic potions. A single kick from one of those legs would be enough to ruin my day.

I touched down on the ground and waited for everybody to circle around me. Meanwhile, I repeated my request to talk, that I had been in the wrong, that we needed to clear things out between us. I had a moment's flashback to an unfortunate event, where one of the temps had smashed a water main, and I was forced to keep the customer distracted while the entire team worked to clean up the accident and repair it in time for the presentation.

Shaking my head, I swallowed at my situation. The enemy was heavily arrayed against me. On all sides, Imps touched down, spread out to keep me in their sight where they'd be ready to attack at a moment's notice. A few circled around, staying in my blind angle. Straight ahead, the Bulkbeast faced off against me directly. Ruiva touched down gracefully in front of me, head held high as she contemplated my apparent surrender suspiciously. With a sneer, she addressed me. "This was a mistake, *Onyx*. I will not let you just fly away this time. Now, tell me, what was so important that you were willing to play right into my hands?"

I looked her straight in the eye, taking great care to look subservient. Every single second now was one that my minions could use to move into position.

It had been Creziel's idea. My Camouflage was efficient, but we all doubted that it would be able to stand up against the mental attributes of the dragon. The Talpi were used to creating ambushes, and Creziel was convinced that his powers had grown to the point where he would be able to construct a hiding place for everybody in the dirt right next to the wall of one of the constructions overlooking the landing.

Of course, hiding place was a fancy word for moving aside the uppermost layer of earth and hiding everybody underneath a thin layer of dirt, with only a tiny hole to breathe through. Still, right this moment, while everyone, especially the dragon, had their eyes glued on me, my people should be circling around, singling out the Imps and preparing to strike.

I nodded. "I will be honest with you. What I needed to tell you was likely the most important lesson you will learn in life." Blurred shadows moved in the background and then ceased. "It is this: Never trust a Shadow Dragon."

The last part, I mentally shouted and sprang into motion even as the entire landing exploded into chaos. Everywhere within my eyesight, blurred forms came into being as my hidden minions sprang into action, attacking the Imps. I didn't allow myself the luxury to assess the results.

Instead, I cast Shadow Whorl directly at the face of the Bulkbeast and released a Weakening Fog straight at the red dragon. I dug my feet into the ground below me and sprang forward, sprinting right at Ruiva, trying to ignore the size of her bared fangs. I needed to keep her distracted!

Unfortunately, whatever other flaws she had, the red was a fighter. She suffered my Weakening Fog with a shudder, then released her fiery attack straight at me. I was already committed to the attack and could only close my eyes and push my way through the fiery curtain that rose at me.

The pain was horrible, as it burned away a full fifth of my health in a second. One might think that I had already grown accustomed to the pain of a dragon breathing fire from my fight with the other red dragon, but this one was a direct hit, straight on my chest, and it *burned*, expanding to include the entirety of my front legs and upper body. Snarling, I made my way through the inferno, took two bounding steps, and *leaped*. Her muscled form lowered to prepare for my attack, and mid-air, I opened my mouth to release a Deafening Roar.

The wave of my attack spread forward and hit Ruiva right before my outstretched claws did. There was no way it would force her into unconsciousness or even weaken her significantly, but it did unbalance her at a crucial point, and I took full advantage of it. My bulk hit her and forced her to flip over onto her back, and I used my claws to rip and tear into her abdomen, tearing away scales in a bloody mess.

She tried to fend me off, but I had her at a disadvantage. For five seconds, ten, I caused horrible damage to her, until I noticed the trembles preceding her use of her ability. I immediately let go and jumped back, running at large leaps until I was able to get airborne.

A cry behind me was followed by a wash of flame as the red initiated the same ring of fire my former red adversary had used. I dared not look back, beating my wings harder to rise in the air. Then I risked a look. In less than half a minute, everything had changed. Dead and dying Imps lay everywhere, and Ruiva was rising to her feet, hateful eyes following me from within the haze of fire surrounding her on all sides.

A few, the ones at my back, mainly, were still alive, flying about in confusion. The Bulkbeast had been closing on me, but with one target out of the way, the Shadow Whorl seemed to confuse it to the point where it didn't know what to do. Moments later, the beast broke out of its confusion because it started galloping toward the walkway and the blurry forms of my minions who were speeding across the bridge toward the far side and safety.

I dismissed the Bulkbeast from my mind. My task right now was simple: flee back to safety where my Clenchers and ranged attackers would join me to take down my pursuit. That sounded like an easy task, but two long strides had Ruiva leaping into the air flapping her wings to follow. Now, I knew I had to speed it along.

I messed up. I cannot say it any other way. Instead of flying straight back toward the Clenchers, I decided to give my fleeing minions a few extra seconds by taking a longer path back to the tunnel entrance. That's where I miscalculated. I might have landed a few debuffs on the red dragon and was definitely more agile than her, meaning I turned faster. There was just one thing I had not taken into account.

Even with the debuffs from my attacks and her slightly

smaller bulk, Ruiva's Strength had mine beat, meaning her flight speed was faster. Also, with that horrible surrounding fire skill available, she had no need of hitting me, she only had to catch up. The resulting chase was a horrible, heart-stopping rollercoaster of an experience. I was singed more than once, with one of her fiery attacks burning my leg badly.

I didn't stop to look, but from the pain, I doubted I would be able to put weight on that leg, and my health slowly sank to below half. We swooped and dove across the fiery surface of the magma, playing a game of life and death tag. I just needed to make it to the tunnel, but Ruiva knew that as well.

After a panic-inducing minute, I was granted a moment's reprieve as a loud bellow of pain rang through the cavern. I banked into a sharp turn, searching for the red to take advantage. There! The red dragon flew straight, neck turned in the direction of the pathway toward the tunnel exit. I aimed carefully, released a breath attack straight at her profusely bleeding abdomen and veered off even before I could see my attack hit.

I doubted any of the mist would make it through her fiery shield, but it was worth a try. Then, I fled for the tunnel. At this point, my minions were either down or safely back inside the tunnel. Below me, I saw the source of the noise: the Bulkbeast, keening in pain. It had chased my camouflaged minions across the pathway until it reached the part Creziel had weakened and its massive weight forced its legs to burst through the upper crust of earth and deep into the underlying layer of magma.

It pressed on regardless, each pain-filled step causing immense pain as it struggled through the lava. It looked like its tiny mind was unable to comprehend what was happening or go against the order from its master. Through plumes of flame and maddening bellows of pain, it plodded on, even as its meat sloughed off the legs.

I had my own issues to think about. A quick look proved that Ruiva was coming up behind me again. The countdown was over, and I used the opportunity to crane my neck mid-flight and re-cast Shadow Whorl, centering it right at the red dragon's head. My trick almost cost me dearly as a burst of flames heated up the air right above me, but the spell made a world of difference. She might be faster than me, but the whirling shadows and illusions ruined her orientation enough that she took a couple of split seconds to orient herself to follow me.

I eyed an opportunity to punish her disorientation. With my turns already faster than hers, the spell made her every move delayed and confused and suddenly, I was flying circles around her. Seconds ticked by, and suddenly the flames around her flickered and died out. I made her pay immediately.

Once, twice, three times, I hit the beleaguered dragon with my Weakening Fog as we circled, narrowly avoiding the flames of her retaliation. Soon, her wingbeats became more hesitant and beleaguered, and I realized that the extended flight along with her injuries and my breath attacks were taking their toll. Her stamina must have been nearing its limit.

She must have come to the same realization. Without warning, she veered off, making for the nearest spot of land. She had either weakened more than I thought, or she failed to realize exactly where she was, because she did not fly for her domain and safety on the other side, but for the near landing... where my minions were waiting, right inside the tunnel.

The moment she touched down, I hit her with a final breath attack, causing her shoulders to shudder and dip low. I did not want to waste the chance, and shouted my mental message. "Clenchers! Ursam! Attack!"

As I touched down near the tunnel exit, a good distance from the red, I felt an emotion from her for the first time. Stark naked fear. I followed her gaze and watched where the massive bulks of the four unleashed Clenchers came thundering down upon her, roaring with undisguised bloodlust. The sound of the clash was horrible. Ruiva never even got the chance to use her breath attack, before she was falling back, fighting tooth and claw against the hairless bears who tore into her.

I suddenly realized that I had been so engrossed in my own

survival that I had failed to follow the development in the battle. As I took in the massive cavern, I gaped at the development. A stone's throw away from the exit tunnel, a well-known blue form hovered over the remains of the Bulkbeast that was slowly being consumed by the lake.

A few Imps were still alive, but they wisely kept away, flittering nervously about back on the island. That left only us and the red, who was succumbing to the attacks of the Clenchers. I suddenly realized that we were about to miss out on some heavenly rewards. "Everybody, attack the dragon, now. Clenchers, back off. Back off, I said. Move, damnit!"

My Talpi and the Crawls swarmed out from the tunnel, trying to get in on the fight, but the Clenchers simply refused to back away, completely lost to the battle and the bloodlust. A few spears, stones, and other attacks flew through the air to hit the beleaguered dragon, but most did not dare, at the fear of attracting the ire of one of the beasts. I thundered over to force them away, only to see a shudder go through the body of the red as she finally succumbed to her horrible wounds and died.

CHAPTER TWELVE

The rest, as they say, is history. Or cleanup, in this case. I attempted to save some of the Bulkbeast for food, but had to give up. Lifting the heavy body out of the lava required a level of control I simply did not have, which was bloody infuriating, because the scent of the meat sizzling in the lava lake was tantalizing, overpowering the ever-present sulphurous stench.

Then, I took flight, circling the island in an attempt to find a safe place to touch down. Eventually, I decided to spend a while resting and regaining my health, before I dared single out and knock down three Fire Towers one by one to establish a safe foothold, allowing me to beat down the energy shield protecting the hoard and loot it.

Meanwhile, we licked our wounds, enjoying the breather to increase in levels, share our stories. And feast. We shared the meat from the dragon and there was more than enough for everybody, Clenchers included. I also had the chance to have a chat with Timothy.

"That was a pretty risky move, Tim. Standing right out there in the middle of the lake where the dragon and the imps could've attacked you any moment?"

The blue shape flickered. "It was necessary, old man. You should've seen that Bulkbeast. It was just crying out in pain all the time, but it stumbled onward, and I think it would've actually made it to our side. Be real, man. Can you imagine the rocks we've piled up back in the tunnel holding back something as massive as that mountain of meat? Or any of our folks fighting against it?"

He continued talking, not even waiting for my answer. "Anyway, the first attack I laid on it stopped it cold. I doubt it was the damage, but those mental effects must've overwhelmed its tiny mind." He grimaced. "It wasn't nice to look at, though. Damn. Slowly burning up from the legs up is not a destiny I'd wish on anyone but that Necromancer bitch."

I shook my head. "All right. Well done, man. Just... take care of yourself, okay? I'm getting used to having you around." I noticed how I'd turned a bit overly emotional, and forced a grin. "I mean, who else around here is going to understand me and know I'm right when I say that New York pizza isn't real pizza?"

Tim barked a laugh at that. "Now I know why you got stuck in that body. It's because you only used your lizard brain to begin with." He was silent for a moment. "Oh! You're going to love this! So, the Bulkbeast was worth a full 5200 experience, right?"

I nodded appreciatively. "Nice. That's, what? Level 5? 6?"

He grinned. "Oh yeah. Did I mention that I managed to tag the red dragon in the back, too, when the Clenchers went to town?"

I could feel my grin growing to match his. "Niiice. So you got experience from her, too? That's how many levels?"

"All the way to level 7!"

I shook my head. "That's incredible. Tell me what you got, man! Level 5 is one of the good ones, if I remember correctly."

His face froze up as he disappeared into his menus, and then he was back, a manic smile spreading on his face. "Oh, I'm going to need some advice here, man. This is awesome!"

I nodded, waiting attentively until I suddenly remembered. "Oh wow. Level 5 was when I got my choice to evolve into one of the different types of dragons. Don't tell me..."

"Yup. It's the same for me. I'll read 'em aloud. I feel like I'm a bit out of my depth here, and screwing up this choice sounds like a pretty bad idea. Okay, let's see. We have:"

[Ghost:
The most common of evolutions, the ghost differs little from your regular unevolved lost soul. Ghosts remain incorporeal but improve in every single area compared to souls. They are able to pass through wider and taller solid areas, gain a slight resistance to mental and magical attacks and gain the ability to teleport.

Ghosts gain +1 Mental Control and + 1 Mental Power every 2 levels.

Main attack: Improved Mental Attack (Damage focus)

Wraith:
Wraiths are by far the most warlike type of lost souls. These intimidating presences typically look back on violent pasts and are used to conflict and battle. Where the remainder of the evolutions are versatile, Wraiths are typically found in the midst of conflict, trying to deal out as much damage as possible. Wraiths remain incorporeal, but lose their ability to walk through walls. In return, they gain a fear aura, and their main attack improves to the point where the mental effects can influence almost all enemies.

Wraiths gain +2 Mental Power every 2 levels.

Main attack: Improved Mental Attack (Mental focus)

Ectoplasm:

MASTER OF THE MOUNTAIN

Where the other types of souls retain the original form of a body, Ectoplasms gain more control of their substance, giving them the option of how to present themselves. They can condense their essence to the size of a human skull or expand it into a larger area, growing into an intangible mist form. Ectoplasms retain the ability to walk through thin walls and objects as well as their Mental Attack. Their real forte lies in the manipulation of their essence, granting them the chance of imbuing their essence with the strength to either drain or add strength to those touching their form.

Ectoplasms gain + 1 Mental Control and +1 Mental Power every 2 levels.

Main attacks: Mental Attack, Draining touch

Poltergeist:
The common denominator regarding ghosts is their incorporeity. Poltergeists are unique in that they regain the ability to interact with their surroundings, albeit on a limited basis. Poltergeists remain incorporeal, but lose their ability to walk through walls. In return, they gain access to physical touch and, as the only choice, gain access to physical attributes when they manifest on the physical realm.

Poltergeists gain +2 Mental Control every 2 levels.

Main attacks: Mental Attack. Physical manifestation.]

"Wow. That was quite the mouthful. Give me a sec, I'll read it over once again." He returned back into the menus, and I lay down, giving my hurt leg a rest, as he listed all the possibilities. Those were all interesting options, but which would be the best ones? It was hard to tell. Two minutes later, his mental presence was back with me, and he seemed more unsure of himself than he usually was. "Heh. Big choices, eh? Any suggestions?"

I smiled. "Like I could keep my mouth shut... of course, I have suggestions. It's your choice in the end, though. What are your initial thoughts?"

He shrugged. "I don't know. Again, these past days have been like a fever dream. Traveling with strange creatures, struggling for survival. It's like I'm stuck in that old movie, you know the one?"

"Labyrinth?"

"Laby- no. I don't even know that one. I'm not that ancient, man. I was thinking of Lord of the Rings."

I sputtered. "Lord of the Rings? They're not *old!* The hell's wrong with-" I paused, looking at the blue form folded in two, choked up with laughter. "Oh. You're pulling my leg."

He wiped away a translucent tear. "I love saying that to old people. Sorry. I'm just being an ass. In all honesty, this feels a bit like Alice in Wonderland. Like, my life is on the line. There's danger everywhere, but I'm still pretty clueless, and I don't even know *how* to prepare. So I don't know which of these choices make the most sense in this world."

I growled. "Well, apart from you being an insufferable little gremlin, I understand. How about this, though: Are there any of the choices that just don't seem right to you, as in, you would have a hard time getting used to the thought of living like that?"

He answered immediately. "The Wraith. Sure, it sounds powerful and all, but all that about being in the middle of battle all the time? I'm a nerd, not a fighter."

"I can relate. Not with the nerd thing... nerd. Heh. But yeah, while this world is crazy, it's not 24/7 struggling for survival. I can relate to finding a choice that's about more than just fighting."

He smiled. "Yeah, let's scratch that one off the list. Hm. And honestly, let's remove the Ghost as well." He shrugged, the entire body rising an inch or two from the ground. "It's not that it sounds bad per se, it just... pales in comparison to the other two choices."

"I hear ya. So, want my thoughts on the other two?" His

nod was immediate. "Now, as I said, your opinion's the one that matters, but I can see the point of both of these. As for the Poltergeist, that would probably be the most comfortable choice. Regaining the option to touch things now and again--yeah, we'll let that speak for itself. It sounds like the power's limited, though, either in time or power. So, speaking as to its usefulness, that one's probably less impressive. It will, however, allow you to interact with the world on your own. That could be invaluable in its own right."

I frowned. "It doesn't say so in the description, but there's also that other thing that Poltergeists are often able to do in the movies. What's it called? Oh yeah, possession. This is pure speculation, mind you, but so far it seems like our world somehow has some of the elements right of what happens in this world. It's a scary idea, but there might be some sort of bleed-over between our worlds. Anyway, not getting metaphysical here, just saying that some of the abilities from scary movies might be a possibility as you'd gain levels in Poltergeist here."

Timothy snorted. "Yeah. Not sure possession would be my thing. Still, just being able to turn a page in a frigging book by myself without Skeletor at hand--I really miss being corporeal. I was getting used to being able to walk through walls and doors, though. Losing that would be annoying." He laughed, "Damned if you do, damned if you don't, right?"

I grinned at him. "Well you *are* a lost soul, right? Huh. Me too, I guess. Better stop that trail of thought before I lose what I wanted to say. Now, the Ectoplasm would probably take more getting used to. You'd have an entirely new, or at least, more malleable body. The way I see it, that would be the most versatile choice. Being able to drain strength *or* add strength to those you touch? That makes for more choices in combat. You'd be able to join the fight, cause damage, and drain the enemies if they're non-magical, or you could help our forces even if you're staying back with the ranged fighters. You might gain even more possibilities as you grow in levels. Hell, you might even boost our people out of combat."

Tim looked lost in thought for a second. "True. Also, it's not like I classify for the sexiest body alive the way I'm looking right now."

I smirked. "I know I'm supposed to argue right now, but, damn, Tim. Nobody wants a blue blur unless he's named Dr. Manhattan. Or Sonic, I guess. Sorry, man." I held up a claw in front of myself. "Sorry, I'll try to be serious for a moment. In the end, it all boils down to how you want to handle this. My reason for choosing a Shadow Dragon was pretty simple. I wanted to survive, and it sounded like just the thing."

The sides of his mouth quirked up in a tiny smile. "Straight from Maslow's Pyramid of Needs."

"Huh?"

"Nevermind. Please continue."

"Okay... what I mean is, you've got options here. What are you looking for? Do you want to grow stronger, gain levels, and become unassailable? In that case, the Wraith might actually be the right choice. Do you want to spend the time here in as much comfort as possible, maybe hope to gain the power to actually gain a body again, in some way or other? That would be the Poltergeist. If you want the option that would do the most to boost all of us, that would probably be the Ectoplasm. Please don't misunderstand me, Tim. I'm not trying to pressure you into one thing or another, but that's the way I see the options."

After almost a minute of silence, he said, simply, "Okay."

Moments later, his form changed. It undulated and stretched, becoming more translucent and white-grey in color. I took an involuntary step back as the intangible form flowed outward, reaching to fill every side of the corridor. Then, with a sudden snap, it contracted again, until returning to a simple, person-shaped blob without any definition or features at all.

It bopped up and down a few times, before a voice arose from the center. "Holy *crap*, that feels weird." He grew silent, and a pseudopod expanded from the blob to touch the tunnel wall. "Weird, but not unnatural, somehow. I feel *strong*, though.

My Mental Power's already at 29 and my Mental Control at 21. I feel like my mind sort of took a leap in terms of power."

"It was the same for me, when I gained the ability to manipulate shadows inside the domain. It felt like a muscle I'd had all along, I just needed to re-learn how to flex it."

"Exactly." We stood in companionable silence for a few moments, the dragon and the intangible blob. Then Tim spoke again. "It makes you think, doesn't it?"

"No."

"Like, who was responsible for all of--wait, what? Did you say no?"

"Yup. I don't see the point of wondering what could've been. I died and now I'm here. Do I miss my daughter? Of course. Do I miss my ex? That one's tougher. But look at it like this. I was Catholic. Sort of. Now, I was never a crook, but I wasn't exactly an angel either. There was never any real chance of me getting into Heaven without spending a few eons in Purgatory first. So this, finding myself as a Dragon in a world that has weird, fantastic creatures and *magic*? I'll take it. Even if I have to fight for it."

"...You know, this 'not thinking' thing you've got going - you're getting pretty good at it."

"Heh. Stow it, Timmy."

"I'm just saying, maybe it's a good thing that you're outsourcing the braining to those of us who find ourselves deficient in the muscle department... with those large muscles and that small head, there's not bound to be a lot of brainpower left over. You should count yourself lucky you don't drool too much."

I got up and stretched. "Oh, would you look at the time? I had better get going. Large muscles like these need sustenance. I'm thinking a dragon steak. Ultra rare. Should I get you something?"

"Dude. That's low!"

I bared my teeth at him in a savage grin and walked away with a spring in my step.

Our much-needed rest was soon over. Midway through, cries of triumph arose inside the tunnel as the effects from eating the dragon's meat kicked in. I grinned to see the effects.

[Congratulations. You have received a permanent increase to your attributes.

You have consumed the flesh of a being rife with the gifts of Deyra. The mana-rife meat bestows upon you the following:
+1 Toughness
+2 Strength
+1 Agility
+1 Mental Control]

The battle had gained me level 18, and I spent my own attributes immediately. For a second, I wondered if I should dump a handful of points into strength, but decided not to. Hopefully, flying combat would not be a regular occurrence. Three points into Mental Power, two into Toughness, and the automatic two to Mental Control and one to Agility, and I felt *great*. I couldn't wait to see what the system had for me at level 20.

I was starting to see a pattern here regarding the meat. It looked like the attributes we gained depended not only on the quantity of meat we ate, but also on the attributes of the creature, as well as its level. The other red had probably been above my level, and that one gave me seven attribute points total. I shared my theory with Timothy then took to the air.

Fetching the hoard was surprisingly easy, if time-consuming. I tried bringing over a tarp to carry everything, but my claws didn't have the best fine motor skills. In the end, I resorted to simply grasping as much as possible in each claw and taking several trips. I left behind the trash, but every single item with a magic effect, I took with me. On top of that, we gained a full four Mana Crystals. Then I returned to my people, and we rested for a handful of hours before moving on. Sure, the Soul

Carver might be out there, but rushing onward, tired and half-injured, could also end up hurting us in the long run.

I was berating Roth that we didn't need a stretcher for the single Talpi who had gotten herself hurt, she could just ride one of the Clenchers, when Aelis came up to me. Her gaze was empathetic. "Milord. What are you doing?"

Shaking my head in annoyance, I glared at her. "What does it look like? Apparently, I'm the only one who's trying to get this show on the road."

She bowed her head. "Sire, I assure you that I am doing my utmost to move us in a timely manner. Are you not forgetting something, though?"

I frowned at her. "We've loaded down all the meat we can carry and all items from the hoard. I would like to take the time to empty all the stocks from the island, but it's not going to happen. So, no. I don't think I'm forgetting anything."

"Might I remind you about the Imps?"

"Oh." The Imps. The eleven Imps trapped back in the cavern I would need to handle or leave to die. Those Imps. I growled at the inevitable delay and sighed. "Yeah. I forgot. Let's go."

The cave we had trapped them in was way too small for my body, but I didn't envy them the experience. One second, they were chittering away in their own language, fearing for their lives and annoyed with the entrapment, from what I could tell. The next moment, the earth of the wall slid aside like quicksilver, allowing them to look straight at my ugly mug. I did not hesitate to give them a good look at all of my teeth either.

"Greetings. Let's keep this short. Who's your leader?"

They looked at each other, then a cacophony of mental voices assaulted me. "Not me." "You. You're the leader." "No, you."

The loud growl that escaped my mouth contained all my impatience and not a little of the stress from the fight we'd just been through. "All right. I'll make this simple. I do not care to discuss anything. I am not interested in any of your antics. From now on, you are my minions. Does anybody wish to fight this?" The silence was deafening. I nodded. "We are moving off in a moment. If any of you try to escape or act against my wishes, we will kill you all. If you work hard, in time, you can earn your place among us. Now, are there any questions?"

They looked at each other and another conversation arose. This time, however, they were studiously avoiding antagonizing me. In fact, nobody even dared look at me, as they talked among themselves, pushing, gesticulating, and prodding each other. Finally, one Imp was pushed in front of the others. With a nasty look behind him, it addressed me haltingly. "We have a question. Is Ruiva dead?"

I looked the tiny creature straight in the eye. It was even smaller than the Talpi when it stood on the ground. Its body looked tiny and malnourished, spindly legs with bird-like feet carrying the pot-bellied body awkwardly. "Yes. She and the Bulkbeast are dead."

The creature glanced at its comrades and back at me. It was obvious that it didn't know how to compose itself. The nervous burst of joy coming from it underlined the feelings of jubilation and hatred that arose from the group. Finally, the Imp couldn't hold it back any longer and exploded in an ambling deluge of words praising how much she had it coming, how happy they were that we had come, and more. Huh. So, this recruitment drive looked to be easier than expected.

CHAPTER THIRTEEN

Life's a journey. Not a race. - Unknown

Five days. We had already spent five full days taking down a single dragon and her minions. That put us well behind schedule. Annoying. Ah, well. It couldn't be helped. I had no intention of rushing everything if it meant unnecessary risks. Still, a little extra speed on the forced march wouldn't hurt. The next full day, we doubled down on speed, moving as fast as possible along the western edge of the mountain. We encountered no monsters, no signs of anything, and spent little time on any extraneous tasks.

We did take extra care to ensure that the Imps didn't escape, but they slowed us down. A lot. Not only were they by nature extremely noisy, chatting endlessly about every little thing, but Toughness was their dump stat, meaning that we were forced to take breaks every other hour to ensure that they could follow. The good news was that I did not feel any dark intentions coming from them. In fact, if I were to categorize the tiny beings, I'd probably call them... easygoing?

During the long walk, I had one of the Imps join me and

quizzed him... or her, on their race and their lives inside the mountain. Alongside a *long* list of grievances, I did learn a bit about them. Apparently, they were native to the mountain and had been here even before Selys arrived. They were also a collective species that acted and decided among themselves by popular vote, which, as far as I could tell, meant 'whichever side of the argument yells the loudest.' Oh, and they were just as matter-of-fact about their lives as slaves to Ruiva, and now me, as they were about the need to kill to survive.

"No problem. No problem, Onyx. You decide. Of course you do. You won't eat us? That's better than Ruiva. So much better."

"What if you decide that you're fed up with my rule? What will you do?"

The tiny creature stumbled, looking up at me incredulously. "Huh? Nothing. Hope you change? Or that you die? It's the mountain."

He said that last part as if it explained everything - and maybe it did. But then at least that meant that the Imps were likely to accept my rule and whatever changes I'd incorporate later on to make living in the mountain more humane.

At the end of the day, plants started becoming more numerous again, and the heat became less obvious. While everybody was getting ready for the night, Imps falling asleep wherever they dropped, I had a chat with my Talpi and Tim a bit off to the side.

"This does not bode well for our efficiency, Sire." Coming from Aelis, that was about as close to curse words as things came.

Roth did not mince words. "Blasted little critters are lazy, weak, and slow. Let's kill 'em for the experience and get going."

I held up a claw. "Hold up right there, Roth. I get weak and slow--they're definitely not made for protracted marches like this--but lazy, too? That's not what I'm getting from them."

He punched the wall. "Lazy, easily distracted, chatterboxes. Call it what you want. I loathe the Crawls, but they at least know how to shut up and stand in front of me and those who would kill me."

Aelis joined in again. "I agree, Sire. Should we continue as is, we would add at least two extra weeks to the trip."

I grimaced. "That bad?" Then, I forced a smile and looked at the small, furry animals beside me. "All right. I can see that that is an issue. Regardless of my other qualities, though, I'm not a quitter. I don't give up on people, just like that. In the future mountain, there'll be a place for everybody, as long as you can live in peace and obey orders."

The Talpi looked at me like I'd suddenly sprouting tentacles everywhere, and I continued, turning down the platitudes a bit. "Obviously, we need to solve this. But it's not the Imps' fault that they have short, weak legs, and we won't be able to put them through a proper training course until we're back in our domain. So as long as they're working with us, we'll do what we can to find an alternative. Can they ride the Clenchers?"

Aelis grimaced. "They would need to be 3 Imps to a Clencher. The Clenchers would take the load easily, but I did notice Ursam snapping out at one of them when he moved too close." Before I could ask, she continued. "Even if they would accept the task, the Crawls will not be able to carry them for a full day's march, either."

A chuckle from the side made me turn toward the floating blob that was Timothy. Since earlier in the day, he had gained better control of his new body, for lack of a better word, and the bright form had gained rough, but even features, which made him look like a cheap hologram. "Well, the answer's pretty obvious then, is it not?"

"Why have I got a feeling I'm not going to like this?"

The day was off to a sorry start. I'd always been a huge fan of dragons in literature and movies both. I mean, say what you like, whether they're big or small, monstrous or majestic, mean-spirited or noble-hearted, dragons have a certain gravitas to them. They're proud and have a noble bearing. As I plodded along the underground tunnel with 11 chittering Imps reclined on my broad back, that weighed on my mind. Fat lot of good I was doing for the reputation of dragons everywhere. Timothy was having a field day of it, too. The bright form bobbed along merrily next to me, taking in the scenery with way more glee than necessary. "It's so *nice* of you. I mean, not many people would stoop so low as to play taxi for a bunch of noisy critters like those. And a dragon at that? That'll be a story for 'em to tell their grandkids one day."

"All right, you've had your fun, Timmy." With a great deal of restraint, I managed to avoid snapping at him. "Now, please, unless you're trying to give me a second heart attack, this time from sheer annoyance, there is one thing I wanted to ask you"

"Hit me, old-timer."

"I would if I could, Timmy. Heh. Okay, what I would really love for your help with is this: the Crawls are a bloody nuisance!"

He snorted in laughter before he could stop himself. Then he held a glowing hand up in front of his mouth. "I'm not disagreeing here. Although I didn't really hear the question."

"That's the thing. The Imps are annoying because it's part of their nature. I can ignore that, because, well, you can still talk to them. Crawls… Crawls are just dumb. I believe I might not hate them as much if I could just communicate with them. Sign language, writing, clacking rocks together in morse code, I don't *care*. I need to be able to talk to them without wanting to tear their heads off for being bloody slow."

He looked pensive. "All right. Can do. I don't know what I can do, but I promise I'll try. Also, for the record, while this is excellent fun, it's also nice to see. You might not have noticed, but those flying critters thought for sure they were chicken drums the moment you told them they were walking too slow. We'll still have to work on your plans, but whatever you're trying to make of this world, I'm in. Later, oldtimer."

With those words, he floated down the corridor to hunt down Erk. I shook my head in amazement. Where I did have friendly relations with a few of my minions, most still feared me to some extent - and for the rest, I was still the leader. Tim had been with us for less than a week, and people already greeted him wherever he went. Even as a floating ball of fog, he was still a people person.

I wasn't envious of him. I'd agreed to the burden myself, after all, and over the course of my life, I'd found that I enjoyed being the one who called the shots, seeing my plans come to fruition. And a rare few, like Aelis and Roth, treated me like an equal, regardless of size differences. Coming full circle in my thoughts, I considered the tiny weights on my back. It wasn't really a question of whether I *liked* the noisy Imps, and the jury was still out on that one. I wasn't about to throw away a potential tool merely because it was painful for my self-esteem. Sure, when I came back, I'd make sure they got a steady regimen of Agility and Toughness training, but for now, I'd suck it up and act the horsie.

The next two days were moderately uneventful. Tim spent a lot of time floating back and forth, talking with Crawls, Imps, and...everybody. I spent the time learning about our surroundings from Aelis, training with Roth on our infrequent breaks, and improving my illusion skill. It was getting to the point where I could hold a detailed illusion the size of my own body without any strain. If I added movement into the mix, it became harder, but I could hold my own in a sparring match and still maintain the illusion. I found that I was approaching a level of mastery where the real cap lay in my ability to visualize what I needed to project, and I was getting good.

I practiced with my shadows here and there too, and that was simply amazing. With my improved Shadow Control I was able to drown areas in magical shadows at a mere thought. The shadows moved fluently and willingly, and the limits were mostly imposed by the natural shadows at my disposal. With a pitch dark room, there were no shadows. With a completely lit up area such as the lava lake, shadows wouldn't hold up. With a single light from a torch or similar, however, I could split, divide, and endarken my near surroundings just as I liked.

I also enjoyed helping Timothy train his new skills. We quickly found that his ability to imbue his essence with buffs was, in his words, "completely imba," which was, apparently, like OP, only better. Regardless of the slang, I was impressed. He was able to manipulate his shape into a 30 foot circle of fog and it would give a +2 (or -2, if he so chose) to every single attribute of any person within that circle. If instead he concentrated his essence, the effect increased, up to a full +5 to every single attribute if he stayed Tim-sized and just reached out to touch those within his reach. At first, pulling up my personal info, I didn't find the effect that impressive. That is, until Creziel helped me recall that this was a level 5 effect--it could likely grow stronger later on--and that not everybody was a dragon. In fact, a level 1 Talpi only had an average of 5 to all attributes.

When they weren't being obnoxious, the Imps were actually an interesting race. Childlike in their curiosity, attention span, and joy, they were the happiest of races I'd seen to date. They were also almost violent in their insistence to learn and live as much as possible. They were a bunch of scatterbrains, though. Most of them seemed mostly interested in ignoring the past completely and living in the present.

I could hardly blame them, especially since they were punished for showing their natural curiosity back when they lived with the red. What I did glean from their constantly changing, blabbering conversations was that they, as a whole, were a race who lived, bred, and died fast. They were prone to getting into trouble and suffering for it, but they also, sometimes, managed to get away with crazy feats, simply because nobody expected them to try. One of them told me a story about raiding the larder of an entire encampment of Urten and them getting away without a hitch against the much stronger enemies, simply due to the unexpected chaos of their attack.

I was sure he exaggerated, but I could see it. A throng of Imps bearing down upon any enemy, keeping up a constant rain of fire, would be an intimidating sight. Their powers were remarkable, even to the point where it overshadowed the fact that I was playing their personal Uber. Not that the tiny bolts of fire looked like they could do much damage, but the fiery missiles held together way further than what should be physically possible, and they could release the shots *fast*. The idea of a dozen of those shots flying at an enemy at a time from over a far distance was awe-inspiring. They were pretty much the perfect artillery, even if they were frail and slow.

A week after we'd left the domain, Tim came floating up to me, and I could see right away that something had happened. "Hey Tim. You're getting better at controlling your features."

He smiled, holding up a hand in front of his face. "I am? Why, thank you."

"Yeah. Just yesterday, I wouldn't have been able to tell from your face that you're looking smug as hell, but now it's clear as day."

His laughter rang clear across the tunnel. "Oh yeah? Well, I've earned it."

"Well, color me impressed in advance. Did you solve the conundrum of how to move toward our future society?"

His face fell. "Oh. No. I'll get right back to that. Erm. Ignore that, please, and ask me who's solved the riddle of the Crawls. Go on!"

"Really? Okay, this one sounds like it's going to be worth it. Dear Timothy. Who here has solved the riddle of the Crawls and how come they can survive as a species with an IQ the size of a slug?"

"Me! Okay, first off. This is a theory, but I think I've got it right. Unfortunately, there's no easy solution, but things *should* be able to improve in time."

"Any improvement is better than what we have right now. Now tell me, already."

He shook his head, grinning. "Oh no. I get to tell this the right way. Slow and excruciating."

"Like a conversation with a Crawl?"

"...Hah. Exactly. Now, I've talked to every single one of the Crawls at this point. Conversation with them is as painful as you could imagine, but I kept pushing and kept up my attempts to connect, to somehow get through to them. I tried everything, but obviously, I'm not a teacher or anything of the sort. I did learn a lot. Like, their IQ isn't horribly low as such, but their vocabulary, in general, is extremely undeveloped, and if they don't know the words, or the concept you're aiming at, they just won't *get* it. They can't extrapolate from incomplete data, if you know what I mean."

I nodded. "I knew some of those words. The shorter ones." Laughing, I motioned for him to continue. "Heh. Just kidding. So, no intuitive leaps here. What a shock, eh?"

"Exactly. Still, if you keep to extremely simple words and concepts, you can hold an almost normal conversation with most of them. And that's when I made my breakthrough. Or, at least a discovery of sorts. It came about, as I tried talking to one of the younger Crawls, Gert--a teen or the equivalent, who'd apparently reached her majority right before we left.

I was asking her what weapons she liked and she just blanked, completely. No answer. She looked at me, while I repeated myself thrice over. No success. Then, I had the idea to reach out to the nearest Talpi and had them bring their weapons and show them to her. When the fourth Talpus showed her his throwing spear, she nodded, and with great finality, pointed at the spear and said. "Weapon."

I wasn't too sure exactly what in that action triggered it for me, but I had to rethink everything I knew about them. Even Erk, the biggest and, supposedly, strongest, Erk has the vocabulary of a 3 year old. Maybe it wasn't that they were dumb, but simply that they had problems with actually learning words? Like, it was hard for them on a racial basis recognizing words and patterns?

"Now that I had solid proof that they *were* able to take in new words, I figured that, maybe, just maybe, it was a matter of perseverance and stubbornness to ensure that they actually expanded their knowledge and vocabulary. Following that, I took my time talking to everybody to confirm that theory... and eventually proved that I was almost completely wrong."

I had been following his words in excitement but my interest took a hit at that. "Oh."

"Key word is 'almost' here. See, the thing is that I figured out that most of the Crawls are almost completely unable to take in not only new words, but anything. Even constant repetition will just have them staring blankly at you. Buuuuut..." Tim bared his teeth at me in a silent grin.

"Get on with it already, you damn brat!"

"Sorry. I'm just loving this moment. See, it's the age that does it. As is common in almost every intelligent species, age reduces the capacity to take in knowledge, leaving most older people doddering wrecks, unable-"

I grumbled. "All right, you've had your fun. So the older they get, the less they are able to learn?"

He laughed, wiping translucent tears from his eyes. "Exactly. It's like humans, but ten times worse. It would seem that the capacity to learn starts dying when they hit their majority. The younger the Crawl, the more they're able to take in." He shrugged. "I have no clue how this has come to be, evolution-wise. Maybe the body spends all that evolution on their natural defense and instincts or... well, we'll never know.

"Still, they've handled it pretty damn well, specializing in simple skill sets. Say that fella, Erk, is dumb as they come--but he's managed to gain some skills in making decisions and herding the rest. A couple of others have basic crafting skills, some know tracking. They all know how to fight. But I've spent enough time with them to be pretty certain that I'm right. The older the Crawl, the more stunted in their capacity to learn anything. Erk and four of the others here are completely stunted. Two of them are slow, but no more than your regular construction worker."

"Hardi-har."

"Now, Gert, on the other hand, has learned maybe twenty new words today and it feels like she's retaining the knowledge."

"So… insults aside, you're telling me that the kids back in the domain might be able to actually speak normally?"

"I believe so. Maybe. If we get to them fast enough and feed them with enough knowledge that it sticks."

I nodded, impressed. "That is incredible, Tim. To be honest, I wasn't sure that it could be done. That is simply amazing."

"I know." He basked in the praise, but couldn't stop himself from another jab. "That's the gift of youth."

I merely nodded, letting a nasty smile slowly build on my face. "Oh, indeed. And once we're back in the domain, you'll get every chance to use your gift."

He frowned at me. "What?"

"Oh, I mean, we will need a sharp mind to teach the Crawls. So many Crawls, sooo many words and concepts they will need to learn. Obviously, the Talpi have their own language, so they won't be able to help."

His face fell as he realized that he'd painted himself into a corner. "But... but I won't be able to-"

"Oh shush. You'll get it done, Timmy. You're bright and young. "

On the third day after leaving the domain of the red, and the eighth day total, we lost our first minion. We were unaware until our two other scouts came sprinting toward our group, squealing for help. Before I knew it, a group of tall, chitinous monsters ran around the corner, brandishing weapons and charging in without even breaking. Our formation wasn't opti-mal. Following days of uneventful marching, we had started slacking in our security. That's why we were all mixed up, Talpi and Crawls in the front, with me and the Clenchers further back. The tunnel we were traveling was too low for me to fly, and I couldn't see how to reach the front without crushing somebody in the process.

Fortunately, my minions adjusted to the attack straight away. The Imps took off from my back and hovered above me, blasting away at the incoming enemies. Meanwhile, the Talpi moved back. Not much, just enough to ensure that the Crawls took the brunt of the charge and started preparing weapons to join in the struggle. The insect-like adversaries cried out in pain at the fiery assault that met them, but continued their rush, leaving a single Talpus corpse to expire under their tramping feet.

As they smashed into our hastily assembled front, I almost despaired, looking at the numbers arrayed against our exposed frontline fighters. There were at least a full dozen of them, and only four Crawls and a handful of Talpi to take them on. Then, finally, I got my head back in the game. I cast Shadow Whorl right in front of the first attackers and growled in satisfaction to see the immediate result. One of my Crawls took advantage of the insect's sudden blindness to kneecap him and take a step backward, leaving the enemy exposed and blocking access for the enemies behind him.

I started making my way forward, but was overtaken as a bright, floating ball powered straight through my body and sprinted for the front. I had to watch my steps, as some of the Talpus builders were not suited for combat and were rushing back to avoid the frenzied struggle, but I needn't have bothered. The moment Timothy arrived at the center of the struggle, everything changed. He immediately spread out to envelop the entire frontline group of enemies in the translucent fog that comprised his body and started blasting his mental attack at anybody who dared attack our people.

"Imps. Stop attacking." My mental order shouted out through the corridor, as I belatedly realized that some of their fiery attacks were hitting Tim's body, too. Then, with a grunt of annoyance, I pushed another two builders behind me and was finally able to move closer to the frontline. To my surprise, however, there was not much need for my presence now.

While the insects kept advancing, the dual effect of my Shadow Whorl and the barrage of mental attacks that Tim kept up was having a horrible effect on our enemies. The Crawls fought defensively, punishing the insects every time a mental attack or spell effect left them momentarily stunned or disoriented. The Talpi fighters were keeping their distance, sending precise throwing spears with their *atlatls* whenever somebody tried to push past the Crawls. Heh. And Roth was having fun. He was everywhere, his small form managing an impressive range with the two-handed sword as he moved around the corridor, attacking at will, and constantly.

It was my presence that finally broke them. The insects were increasingly pushed on the defensive, Timothy's stunning attacks and draining presence keeping them from launching any form of coherent push. Still they held on. At seeing my long neck tower over the front line, baring my teeth at them in an ear-shattering roar, something broke in them. Within seconds, all enemies were running for their lives, except for the ones caught fighting for their lives at the front. Incidentally, that left a line clear for me to release a Weakening Fog at their retreating backs. After that, it was a matter of minutes for us to finish the still fighting survivors and survey the damage.

It went better than we could have expected, really, especially considering that we had been completely out of formation. We agreed to keep a more fixed formation in the future, with Crawls and Clenchers at the forefront. Fortunately, apart from the single Talpus builder-slash-scout who had been caught by surprise, our people only suffered light wounds. Timothy whined about the Imps tearing him a new one, but when I asked him how bad it was, he had lost less than a third of his mana.

Afterward, as the Talpi were busy dismantling the insect people for food - a grisly sight - Aelis came up to me, wondering aloud. "Sire, this is a rare occasion. I am not sure I understand what happened here."

I squinted at her. The loss of one of our people had left me in a sour mood, but all told I was impressed by the way my people had handled themselves in combat, including the Imps. Nobody else seemed to take the loss to heart. "That makes two of us. Especially when I have no clue what you mean."

"Our assailants. They are Hevrons, Sire. An old race within the mountain, and one which is almost never seen without a master. They *need* somebody to guide them, and I have never heard of them attacking like this, witlessly, without a queen or a master to guide them."

"Oh. This was a witless attack?" I thought at how fast they had appeared and shuddered.

"Very much so. They are known, as a race, for orchestrating large-sized ambushes and for continuing to fight despite over-whelming losses and wounds. These Hevrons did neither."

I growled. That did not bode well. "We will have to be extra vigilant the next time. Maybe we'll figure out what happened.

CHAPTER FOURTEEN

The following day, we figured out what had happened. Aelis guided my way into the intricate tunnel system that spread out ahead, small tunnels ranging off to the sides every ten feet. "Please do enter, Sire. We have explored the tunnels. There is no risk at present."

We walked straight through the main tunnel. It was very obviously not a natural tunnel. Efforts had been made to reinforce the tunnel, and I could see a real doorway far off. The door was hanging off the hinges. As we moved further, I recognized what I was now starting to call a classic underground dragon lair. A large open cave, this one low-ceilinged, with a nice, clean centre in the middle for the dragon to rest and admire his hoard.

Except, the place had been smashed and only bones remained, along with several cored-out Hevron carapaces. The hoard had been picked clean, and soot marks showed where some sort of attack had blackened floors and ceilings. Whatever had happened had been damaging and overwhelming. I frowned at the scenery and turned toward Aelis. "What do you think happened here?"

She looked more calm than she had any right to be in the face of this kind of destruction. Her emotions mirrored the same, resignation and acceptance being foremost. "This would have been the hidden lair of a dragon, I would wager. Did you notice the entrance, Milord? The boulders next to it would have kept the entrance half-hidden, were they dragged in front of the entrance. Obviously, somebody located them regardless and slaughtered them."

She pointed back at the hallway we had passed. "The smaller tunnels would be the homes of the Hevrons. They create these tunnels naturally as they expand. It is in their nature. Now, either they fled through the tunnels as their master, the dragon, was slain, or some of them were outside the lair when they were attacked. That would leave them rudderless and masterless, which is why they were stupid enough to attack us without at least scouting for our entire group first."

"Huh." I looked at the massive amount of destruction, limbs and scuff marks at the center of the cavern. "That sounds logical. So, what about this Hevron Queen you talked about?"

She waved dismissively. "Oh. The Dragon will have killed her before being able to assume mastery over the Hevrons. They can only fathom one master at a time."

I nodded, seeing the development. "So, one of the dragons from my clutch is bound to be relatively close from here?"

"That would be my conclusion as well, Sire."

I smiled. Even in the face of widespread destruction, this was good news. "Great. Let's go hunting."

Our luck persisted. One of the other scouts was able to find marks from where somebody had been dragging heavy items over the ground - presumably the entire contents of a hoard and dragon larder. The tracks persisted going straight northward, and I conferred with Aelis yet again. "How does that route suit us?"

"It could be a lot worse, Sire. There is still a part of the western edge of the mountain that could hold a lair, but we need not all go investigate. It is less populated and as such, a poor hunting ground for a dragon."

"Great. Should we split up into two groups?"

"No need, Milord. Wreil will take on that task for himself and return to us afterward. My presence will be needed to ensure we do not run into any unforeseen surprises near the other dragon's lair."

"If you think it's a good idea, then sure... I mean, will he be all right by himself?"

She nodded. "Most likely, yes. It is half a day for him, but would take a full day for us. Now, given that we are likely about to meet yet another dragon soon, perhaps we should talk about our preparations. I suggest that you cast Camouflage on all scouts, and we will continually circle back when the duration runs out. That way, we are most likely to not be discovered..."

We plotted for a while, and slowly got a rotation going, while Aelis told me all she knew about the part of the mountain we were approaching. The north-western range was one of the most hostile parts for smaller races, and the info she had was second-hand, from a Talpus tribe that had managed surviving inside an elaborate series of tunnels for hiding, not unlike the Hevron tunnels we'd just left behind us.

"The lands here are not optimal for plant life, sure, but not enough to prevent survival. No, the real reason that the place is so dangerous is that the tunnels around here are known for hiding the best veins inside the mountain."

I perked up. "So, metal veins or what?"

"That too. Also stone deposits and crystals that can be imbued with magic. Nobody knows why, but Deyra has seen fit to leave the north-western part brimming with materials."

"So... we'll definitely want to see if we can pinpoint some promising deposits. Oh, and the ones who stay here are the most likely to be able to manipulate the materials?" If I could somehow find and adopt somebody to work iron for me... things would become *much* easier!

"Not necessarily. Some also gather here, simply because the

struggles are harder, and thus the potential for growth is stronger."

"Oh. Of course. That's not exactly a way of thinking that's natural to me."

"Not to us either, Milord."

The rest of the day passed without any further surprises. I kept up a constant rotation of Camouflage on the scouts, ensuring that they'd have the best possible chances of discovering our enemy undetected. Like we learned from the last ambush, surprises could be deadly, and I wanted us to have the best possible chance of survival. Signs of the enemy dragon and other creatures were common, and it became increasingly more obvious that we were getting close.

Following our next period of sleep, we had barely cleared camp when Aelis herself ran back up to us. "We have found them! They are but an hour away. It is a blue dragon."

A blue dragon. I tried thinking back to my initial choice between sub-races and once again cursed the lack of a wiki for the system. "Help me out here, Aelis. Blue dragons? Lightning attack and... good fliers? Does that sound right to you."

"It does, Sire. Very much so. In fact, I can confirm it without a hint of a doubt."

"Oh yeah? Have you seen her flying?"

"No. I have a safe vantage point for us both, Sire. It will explain everything."

The safe vantage point was a tight hole, forming a window into the largest cavern I'd seen in the mountain to date. Several different tunnel exits led from the cavern and it was wide enough that I couldn't even see the far side clearly. The floor of the cave looked completely natural and untouched. No buildings were present, no defenses, none of the regular occurrences in front of a dragon lair. When I took in what adorned the ceiling of the cavern, there was no doubt as to why.

It looked like somebody had taken a stalactite, made it as wide as it was long, then enlarged it by a factor of a hundred. Or the world's largest, fattest ice cream cone. The huge earthen construction pointed down from the ceiling for at least six stories, terminating about 20 feet from the floor. So, maybe the Bulk Beast would be able to reach up there, barely, but most creatures wouldn't. In short, the only way for almost everybody to attack would be by flying. Oh. So that was what blue dragons did best? What a coincidence.

The resident dragon hadn't even been kind enough to allow for some sort of easy access. No, it was all aerial - same for his minions. Right now, I could see a handful of them flying around on the far side of the cave, and a couple were performing lazy circles around the cone. "What are those?" I pointed with a claw.

"Oh, those? Culdren, I believe. Hardy, armored creatures. They are also horribly fast, despite their looks. You will want to look over there also, Sire."

"Are those-"

"Imps? Yes. And there are some other coiled-up horrors inside the construction itself that I cannot easily recognize at this distance. They could be Spinners, but the area around the neck does not look right."

I nodded, contemplating the situation. "So the dragon's been gathering all the flying minions he could possibly find then installed himself where you need to be able to fly to reach. I'm afraid we have an intelligent one on our hands."

Aelis looked forlorn. "Oh, Sire. I am sure we will be able to find a solution. You always wind up--"

I laughed, backing away from the hole to avoid being seen. It wouldn't make a huge difference, but I wanted to make an entrance. "Oh, Aelis. Thank you for trying to comfort me. This one's going to be the easiest yet, though. Messy if the dragon doesn't back down, but easy nonetheless."

She blinked owlishly. "Oh. Well. I had better round up everybody then, had I not?"

I smiled and nodded. This one was going to be fun.

I told Aelis to run ahead and spent a little time considering exactly how we should handle it. We had the right resources, but it was still a question of how to present it to my people, and afterward, how exactly to proceed to ensure that we weren't going to be taken by surprise by the blue because we'd failed to consider some essential detail. Still... I couldn't really see any real issues. Not unless the blue and his minions decided to try and take us straight on right away, and we could prepare for that, too.

When I returned to where our groups had gathered, everybody waited attentively. Aelis had clearly already spread the news of what was going on. Wreil had returned from his scouting trip, too. I addressed him with a nod. "Any nasty surprises on your tour, Wreil?"

He bowed. "No, Onyx. I had to backtrack a bit to avoid some Plague Worms, but there were definitely no dragons around. Actually, I have some information for you afterward. I managed to find a small Talpus tribe and exchange information."

I smiled. "I look forward to it. No urgent information, then?"

"No. Merely a random collection of knowledge we might be able to use. They have fled across this area in search for safer ranges and know a lot about the plants, animals, and materials of the area. From what I gathered, you are the one with urgent news."

I grinned. "You could say that." Turning toward the group, I spent a moment taking in the diversity of the group that was facing me. Tiny Imps chattered, trying to stay attentive, but constantly sidetracked by their own conversations, what somebody else said, or something else from across the room.

In between, a few Crawls were looking at me, unblinking. The rest of them were either sleeping or going about their business. They knew that if something involved them, we would make sure that they were told, or at least, prodded in the right direction. The Talpi, meanwhile, were hanging on my every word. Timothy was hanging about near the ceiling, shining a dull light down on our gathering.

I clapped my paws together, catching everybody's attention. "Good news. We've got an easy one. This time, either the dragon's going to surrender and we'll have our first real ally, or we'll be able to destroy his defenses in safety."

Roth jumped up into the air. "I knew it! Finally, we caught a break. Tell us, lizard. How are we going to take them down? Defensive fight on the ground? Can we ruin their wings somehow? Come on!"

My grin grew, and I could feel the desire to laugh out loud. "No. It's even better. We just need to... dig."

CHAPTER FIFTEEN

All relationships go through hell, real relationships get through it. -
Unknown

The blue dragon was beautiful. Not in the same way as the large red I'd fought, a beauty of fire, danger, and muscles. No, this was an aesthetic beauty, pleasing to the eyes and filled with grace and movement. He was large, too. I mean, there was no way I would be taking him on in a fair fight, but as he glided through the air of the cavern, he made the rest of us look ugly and clumsy in comparison.

I managed to drag the blue out to a peace talk. He could have attacked me, but it would have led to a few nasty surprises for him, not the least, my entire army that lay ready behind the newly erected fortifications right inside the tunnel system. Fortunately, nothing happened. He just took a long, circuitous glide that left him perched from a seat on the lowest layer of the cone with his armies arranged on perches and outcroppings all around him. It was an impressive sight, to be sure.

If it wasn't because I knew I'd be able to make it back to the tunnels before they could swoop down on me, I'd be shitting bricks right now. As it was, I maintained my composure and grinned at the blue as he spread his wide blue-white wings to either side. "Greetings. My name is Onyx, and I have a few things I wish to talk to you about."

I used to read quite a lot. There are some words that get thrown around a lot that you'd never use in real life. Like ichor. Or shenanigans. To date, I'd never really experienced anybody looking at me with scorn. But this blue dragon was definitely being properly scornful. Must be easy, when you're looking down on the world like insects.

With a slight feeling of utter boredom, he addressed me. "I am Creive." The mental pronunciation made it sound more like 'crave.' "I will tell you what I told the other two of our kin to come crawling in supplication: I do not care for these games of yours. Selys will not be my master, and you will not defeat me. So go. Live another day. Or die like the last dragon who insisted on establishing her domain in my reach."

I grinned. I *liked* him. It was a welcome diversion from the other dragons I'd spoken with lately--he was very up front about his wants. "Apologies, Creive. I can't do that. See, the thing is, I'm going to become the master of the mountain myself, and for that to work, you need to either die or, preferably, accept a position as my ally. Oh, and before you act prematurely and attack, there's something you need to know. Unless you become my ally, that impressive construction of yours up there will come crashing down in two days--and there is not a single act you can perform to halt me or my minions in doing it."

I could practically feel his eyes boring into mine. What took me aback was that I could *literally* feel his emotions. With the other dragons I had met, there had been the occasional hint of what they felt, but nothing solid. Here, they were very much present, not crisp and clear like when I was talking to Roth, but muted, in the background, like when I was trying to feel out Arthor's emotions.

Sooo... maybe Mental Power and Control were the lowest stats of the blue? He was affronted, that much was clear, but there was also more than a hint of fear. His mental voice remained as dismissive as anything. "Bravado. How dull. Do scuttle away now and make sure you do not return, or I will be forced to attack. I really cannot be bothered to fight so early in the morning."

I roared my laughter out into the vast cavern. "You think it's that simple? Just tell me to go away, and that's what will happen? I'm afraid I'll have to disappoint you. I will, however, tell you what's going to happen. Do you know Talpi? Weak critters, right? Worth little in or outside of combat. Even if you were to force them to spend every waking hour inside a Training Chamber, I wouldn't want to pit them against any of your impressive specimens."

Creive opened his mouth in a massive yawn. "Is there a point to this long-winded tale of yours?"

"Don't worry. We're getting there. Because even if Talpi are horrible fighters, there is one thing they do better than most other races in the Scoured Mountain - they dig. In fact, they have told me that digging a tunnel beneath the ground of this impressive upside down fortress of yours should be a matter of a day, two at most. Now, unless you happen to have any diggers of your own, I doubt you would be able to halt them."

Surprise and unease. He didn't understand what was going on, but he didn't like it. "Even if that were the truth, why should that worry me?" I caught the faintest brush of unease from him.

"See, that's the other thing that Talpi do well. When they thrive, they breed Shamans. Shamans who have a certain affinity with dirt, earth... and stone. And my Shaman has convinced me that if I install him for his safety in this tunnel below your fortress, he'll be able to bring it down in a day's work or two."

The blue lowered his head, scratching his wings with a tooth. It did nothing to hide the clear burst of fear that escaped from him. "Words. Those are just words. They are exactly what I would expect from a Shadow dragon."

I waited until he looked back up and looked into his eyes

again. Even from a great distance, I could tell that he was rattled. "Are you sure? Are you really asking me to prove myself?"

"I am not falling for some insidious scheme. I told you, I do not care about your power struggles. I merely wish to stay here and thrive. Even if you should be able to bring down my fortress, I'll just travel elsewhere in the Mountain and establish a new hoard." The emotions escaping from him did not back up his self-assured words.

"Yeah, that's normal for blues, right? You're travelers. You move about, see the world, and set down where you feel like. Except, I don't believe you. You're invested here. Not only that, you've decided to put all of your attribute points to your physical attributes. Not a bad plan... as long as you have a safe base. If you have to establish yourself anew, it's something different, isn't it? You'll have to spend *weeks*, just to construct the most basic of defenses. But maybe that's your plan?

"Forget about the fast growth and take it outside the mountain, where the air is clear and the skies are open?" I allowed my laughter to escape into the cavern, as the burst of emotions that rang from him told me exactly how well he liked *that* thought. "If you insist, I will go back to my minions and get started. We can all take our chances and will meet again once the dust has settled. Heh. Get it? Otherwise, you can listen to my very fair offer to *become my ally*, and you can avoid losing everything you've built." I didn't add *you pea-brained lizard*, because I felt like it was implied.

"Ally. It has the same ring as slave. What would that entail?"

"Quite simple. You'll hand over some of your Mana crystals. I'll go through your hoard to see if there are some items I would really like, but I promise to leave you the majority. Then I'll be back once in a while to check in on you. Oh, and you will swear to inform me if you learn anything I should know. In return-"

"What are you not saying? This is merely a ruse. Even Selys would not let me get away so lightly."

"In *return*, I promise to aid you, should you get attacked or otherwise get into trouble that's not your own fault." I looked at Creive, doing my best to appear as earnest as I could. "I know the reputation of my kind. It is not unearned, either. Even so, I do not mean to deceive you--I swear to Deyra. I only want to establish that I'm in charge, give myself a boost, and be able to move on without too much hassle. So, what do you say?"

Of course he turned me down. Of course. It was not the way inside the Mountain. In fact, the massive blue dragon tried to assault me from above, and it took a well-placed Shadow Whorl to disorient him enough for me to rush back to the tunnels and safety. And we got to work--or, at least the diggers did. I had exaggerated somewhat in my stories.

Creziel was not at all confident about his range or his abilities, but I was. Still, the next day and a half was a weird experience, seeing as how, to most of us, it was almost a vacation. Our builders and Creziel were busy with the tunnel. The builders dug, while Creziel hardened the layer of dirt above them, ensuring that the blue wouldn't be able to collapse the tunnel on their heads, or his head, when the time came to demonstrate just what they could do. We had our scouts out in force, one of them constantly keeping an eye on the domain to see if the dragon or his minions left and the rest spreading out to ensure we wouldn't be jumped. But as for the Crawls, Imps, our fighters, and me? We suddenly didn't have anything to do.

We continued with the training. The battle with the Hevrons had taught us that we needed to integrate the Imps into our fighting structure. Most of the Talpi with ranged damage were obviously unavailable, but we could still train with just our Crawls, Imps, and fighters... and me and Timothy, of course.

The Imps were easily distracted, and the red dragon, Ruiva, had clearly not spent much effort teaching them how to fight or work in formation. So, we tried out different formations (and then backtracked quite a bit to ensure that the Imps understood the concept and purpose of the formations in the first place) with different constellations of enemies and did some reworking ourselves to figure out how best to apply the Imps and ensure they could bring their firepower into play without putting the rest of us in danger.

A lot of the work was with the actual planning and figuring out the optimal formations. Like, say, if it was a single, large enemy without magical properties, Tim would take up position near the back of the enemy so he could attack and affect it with impunity. If instead the enemy *was* magical or elemental, like, say, a dragon, Timothy would stay behind the Imps or our ranged fighters, sending out tendrils to buff them and taking potshots at the enemy from a safe distance.

And, if we were attacking a large number of smaller enemies... the different combinations were numerous, and right now we were in the beginning phases, figuring out what worked and then trying it out. Then later, we would have to work on repetition, making sure that our strategies became ingrained in our actions to help ensure that during combat, muscle memory would kick in and become a natural action and reaction.

Timothy continued his efforts to teach Gert how to speak. From the looks of it, there was clear progress too, and he wasn't wasting his time.

We only had to fight once. The blue sent out a group of his Culdren through one of the far exits of the caverns to range around and ambush us. We kept eyes on the cavern at all times, and our defenses held fast. The Culdren were intimidating to be true, tough, fast, and hardy, but against a bunch of Clenchers and Crawls with Timothy and Roth on their side, they were clearly outmatched and soon fled back to the domain with their ugly tails between their legs.

Eventually, a dirt-covered Talpus approached me, dragging his feet with weariness. It took me a moment to see through the layers of grime and realize that this was Creziel. His weary grin gave away his joy, even as he refused to meet my eyes. "You were right, Onyx."

"I love those words. If only I'd heard them once in a while from my ex, maybe we'd still be together."

"Huh?"

"Nevermind. Truth be told, I rarely was. Now, what was I right about this time?"

"My range!" His excitement shone through the tiredness and I could feel the tiny bursts of triumphant joy reaching out from him. "I needed to be a bit to the side so the falling section of the fortress wouldn't collapse my position. A question?"

"Sure?"

"Why not just have me go in from above? I would be able to take everything down from there."

"Oh, that one is simple. Because I really don't want to ruin Creive... just give him a slight nudge to join us. Bringing down his entire fortress and killing most of his minions probably won't have that effect. But showing off by having it crumple bit by bit from below?"

Creziel's eyes widened. "Oooh. I get it. And if he doesn't give in, we can always go in from above." He held up his paw. "Now, Onyx, it is on the outer ranges of my capabilities, and if I take off the necklace, it's completely gone... but I *will* be able to affect the stone of the lowest couple of layers of the dragon's domain."

I shot a wide smile at the tiny, dirty creature. "Oh. Is that the +5 to Mental Power necklace? Arthor lent it to you? That old softie. Thanks for the update. It was just what I wanted to hear. Now, you go and sleep. We will act in the morning."

I could hear the trembling and crashing of rocks, even from where I was staying back in the tunnels, near our defensive fortifications. By our agreement, we all stayed on the defensive, except for Creziel. In case the blue tried something, we'd be ready to range out, but this time, Creziel was the one taking all the risks, even if he'd reinforced the earth above his head and the tunnel was to the side of the intended impact zone.

It was infuriating, really. I hated hanging back and staying inactive, especially when it was clearly time for action. Even so, I had no problem seeing that it was the right way to handle things, I would just have preferred to be part of it. Aelis was standing by right in the tunnel mouth, keeping an eye on everything.

Half a minute passed by after the first rumbling had ceased. A minute. And then Aelis' mental shout reached toward me. "Milord. Come."

It blended with another mental shout - that of the blue. "Onyx, show yourself! I surrender."

I immediately sent a clear message for Creziel to pause his attack. Ambling forward, I waited impatiently while the Clenchers pushed some of the large boulders aside through sheer force to make room for my bulk. When had we become so effective at building fortifications? Aelis met me near the opening and started reporting immediately. "At first, he tried all sorts of attacks. He had the Imps fling fire at the ground, while he blasted the area with Lightning--to no effect. Then he set some minions to digging, until he realized they'd be plastered by the falling rocks. He is out there now, waiting for you."

My stomach rumbled in appreciation. "Please stay attentive and shout if you see any signs of an attack." I composed myself before stepping out into the cave. Dust was settling, covering every surface with a layer of dirt, and I had to fight down a bout of coughing. The blue dragon looked the worse for wear, his bright coloration dulled by a thick layer of grime, and I slowly walked over to him. Above and behind him, the majority of his fortress still hung.

I had to praise Creziel when he made it back out of the tunnel. He had followed his orders to a T. The lowest layer of the upside down fortress was currently lying in shambles upon the floor of the cavern. But even as I stared into the open interior of the lower layers of the remainder of Creive's domain, it looked like the integrity of the structure was still intact.

I got closer to the massive dragon. Seeing him up close, I was happy I'd decided to avoid physical confrontation. He was a goddamn beast. Even though the blue was slenderer than the first, huge red who attacked us, he outdid both of us in length. The play of muscles under his skin was unmistakable, too, and the claws looked like they could carve through my scales without any resistance.

Still, Creive looked like shit. No two ways about it. Even beyond the dirt on him, his shoulders slumped and he had a defeated look on him. I was ready for some sort of final confrontation, but I soon noticed the number one emotion coming from him: resignation. When I made it halfway across the cavern floor, he knelt and pressed his long, sinuous neck to the ground, closing his eyes.

I stopped fifty yards from him. From what I could feel of his emotions, this was real. There was no ambush waiting for me, no monstrous spells or traps about to be unleashed. His flying cohorts weren't about to drop down on me. I was finally about to secure my first ally. Pushing down the burst of triumph that arose from within, I sent a gruff message to the blue. "That's enough of that. Like I said earlier, I want an ally, not a slave."

He slowly raised his neck. "I expected to be punished."

"No. That isn't going to happen, Creive. If you move against me, I *will* strike you down. But as long as you serve my interests and don't work against me, I will not fault you for desiring nothing more than to be left alone. Now, I want your oath, in your own words, that you are not going to attack me or work against me, and that you will warn me if you learn of any large movements in the Mountain."

Gradually, he arose to all fours again. He still wavered and did not meet my eyes, but the occasional pang of hope rang through the feelings of resignation coming from him. When he spoke, his mental message was clear. "I, Creive of the blue, charge Deyra to mark my words as she marks my struggles. I swear fealty to Onyx with all that this entails. I swear that I will place him before me, will not seek his downfall, and will move to inform him of any development within the Scoured Mountain that threatens him and his."

I nodded, looking him straight in the eyes. Personally, I found his speech a bit too grandiose and flowery for my liking, but when in the Scoured Mountain... "In return, I, Onyx of the

Shadows, charge Deyra to mark my words as she marks my struggles. I swear that, in return for his oath of fealty, I will look out for Creive, and will keep him apprised of any development within the Scoured Mountain that threatens him and his. Upon his words, I will fight to protect him as if his domain were mine."

I wouldn't say I expected it. Hoped for it, more like. I will admit that the pop-up that arrived when I finished my vow made my heart beat faster in unadulterated joy.

[**New vassal available**
Another creature who draws from a connection with Deyra has sworn his servitude to you. If you accept the bond, for as long as you both survive and maintain your vows, there will be a bond between you.

Through meshing your connection with your vassal, Creive, you earn a boon from Deyra, but open yourself to additional risks, both associated with your vassal. Any lightning damage you take is increased by 20%.

Accept vassal Yes/No?]

What? The hell was that? Shouldn't my resistance *increase* if I bonded with a blue? Was this the system's - or Deyra's kind of checks and balances? I stared affronted at the notification. Yes.

[Connection with Deyra strengthened. Mana regeneration improved by + 100%

You have accepted a blue dragon as your vassal. Current bond: Newly established. Please select the type of boon you would prefer: Ongoing or one-time.]

Nice detail with the mana regen - that gave me the same as creating two additional Mana Crystals. And the choice was simple enough. I was looking for something long-term here. If I had my way, I'd be teamed up with Creive for longer than I was with my ex. Without the graphic details.

[You have selected an ongoing boon. From now on, you will gain 5 percent of the experience that Creive earns.]

I blinked. Wow. That was worth way more than the debuff I received here. Still, the debuff just meant there were limits to the number of vassals I'd be able to take under me - otherwise I'd end up vulnerable to everything and anything.

Creive looked distant, too, but from the sensations emanating from him, the notifications on his end were looking pretty positive. I nodded at him. "I'm glad you decided to see reason in the end. I would've hated to bring you down when there was no real need. Now, there's no need for me to invade your domain. If you bring the contents of your hoard down here, I'll go through them, and then we will leave you alone. Additionally, I would like to hear all you know about the surrounding areas."

In moments, Creive had his minions drag the contents of his hoard down to us. While the flying minions handled the air convoy, Creive let me in on the surroundings, and I told him the story of how I'd been abducted by the Talpi, sparking the start of our unlikely alliance. Apparently, my Talpi hadn't been way off in their theories about the northwestern part of the mountain. The place was contested, and a lot of different monster groups took the chances and swarmed toward his area, either for the thick concentration of powerful creatures or for the bountiful veins of metals.

"I care not about the mining aspect of it. The creatures roaming the area, however, are a bountiful resource for my growth and for keeping my own creatures equipped. Do you mean to strip my minions of their weaponry, too?" Creive was very nonchalant about the whole thing and I didn't feel any underlying resentment. It was like he'd flipped a switch and already accepted his new situation. Must be the benefit of a clear power structure.

"No. I see no point in leaving you defenseless. You're only good as an ally if you can hold your own. I will take any armor for my stronger fighters. At a later point, I will also send some of my minions to mine some of the better quality stone."

Creive nodded. The burst of surprise was weak, but clearly there. "Thank you."

Eyeing the chance for an easy target, I asked. "Are there any nearby dragons?"

"No. There have been no dragons here in the last two weeks. I am afraid that the rumor of my stance and strength has spread. My hoard shows but a single other domain within range. That one has been present since the first day, and we have failed to locate it. It must be in the higher reaches."

"What were you planning to do when Selys decides upon her successor?"

"Leave the mountain." The answer was immediate. "I know that I am not likely to be able to stay here forever. I may not be able to continue outpacing our brethren, and I do not care to toil under somebody who decides to pit her own children against each other. Still, I would be a fool not to abuse my situation here for as long as possible."

"Good thinking. Now, it looks like your people are bringing the last items, and I'm running out of questions, too. I don't intend to overstay my welcome. I will leave you with something to think about, though." I looked him straight in the eye, trying to impress my earnesty upon him. "I agree. I dislike Selys' approach too--and I would have a mountain where dragons do not need to fight each other simply for the crime of existing."

I was finally settling on some rough ideas for the future. My plans were more extensive than that, but I didn't care to share that at this moment. "This is why I do what I do. And when I am done and find my place as the Master of the Mountain, I would have you remain my ally. I don't ask for an answer right now, but just think about it. There is an alternative to taking your chances outside, where you are unable to connect directly with Deyra's essence."

Creive was silent for a while. Then he spoke, deliberately and slowly. "I will think on your words. For now, take your picks and leave. While we might not end up at each other's throats, I could do without company for a while."

I nodded and went over the loot, paying good attention to Creive's emotions. I wanted to make sure that he was on the up and up and wasn't trying to hide some of the contents, but I felt nothing out of order. He was paying attention, clearly curious as to how much I was going to leave him with. My search for mana crystals was disappointing. He only had four, which left him far below the requirement of seven for a small medium hoard.

I took a single one for myself and then looked at the rest. Intriguing. Where my own hoard was filled with everything I'd been able to get my hands on, with quality levels from pure scrap to the best Arthor could produce, this was top-of-the-line. Here, the pile was nowhere near the size of my hoard, but not a single piece was clearly flawed. And what pieces. There were ornamental bronze daggers that would look right at home on top of a sacrificial altar. Huge iron hammers weighing half of one of my Crawls. Armor pieces that clearly didn't belong on any normal bipedal creatures.

In short, it was heaven for somebody like me, who was limited in possibilities when it came to crafting materials. In the end, I wound up taking enough armor that I could plausibly outfit at least three Crawls with assorted pieces of iron and leather armor. On top of that, I was fairly certain that my people would be able to adapt five other huge chainmail pieces to protect Ursam's neck, head, and legs. As the kicker, I took a single crown. Creive didn't even know where that one came from, but it was going to make for an amazing gift if it gained a few modifiers. In regard to magic skills, the rewards were limited. With his hoard at lower levels, the items did not gain abilities as fast as in my hoard, though one of the armor sets did have a nice +2 to Toughness modifier.

We were about done, and I suddenly came up with a final question. "Okay, one more thing, then we're out of here. How many dragons were in the clutch?"

"Ten in all. Eleven including you. Three reds, two whites, two greens, myself, one shadow and another blue. For myself, after getting escorted to the lower layers, I have only seen two - a white who fled and the shadow dragon I killed. She boasted that she had killed a white herself."

I did the math. I had killed three and gained one ally. That meant, with a white and a shadow dragon dead, and counting myself, we still had four dragons--one red, one white, a green, and a blue--unaccounted for. Those were definite improvements. "All right, Creive. I won't be too positive about this. I know I've coerced you into working with me. But in the end, I hope we learn to work together well. I mean what I said: If you are in trouble, do not hesitate to call for help. I *will* show up, although the time I'll need to get here may prove too much."

He nodded and bowed his head slowly, blue crown of horns surrounding his face glinting in the dark. Then he looked up, serious eyes boring into mine. "I did not expect you to stick to your word. Please be on your way now, but..." his mental words trailed off, like he was considering what to say next.

"We allow most groups and creatures to establish themselves, and then strike when they lower their guards. If you are moving north from here, send your scouts over before you go. I will give them directions. A group of Boost Worms have taken up camp along the way. They are easy experience for one such as you.

CHAPTER SIXTEEN

Creive was right. The twelve Boost Worms were extremely easy experience. They were large, ox-sized worms with acid-covered teeth, who could amp up their own physiology, increase their power, resistance, and muscles for a limited period of time. According to Aelis, an enraged Boost Worm was a match even for a Clencher.

Up against, say, a Shadow dragon, who drained their attributes faster than they could boost them? Yeah. They never stood a chance. We went according to our usual method, ensuring that each of our people got a strike in before we finished them. The experience was bountiful--a full 1500 apiece brought me right into level 19, and I considered my options.

How did I want to evolve now? I had been fighting like a mix between a ranged damage dealer and a scrapper, keeping as far away from the enemy as possible while weakening them, resorting to close combat when that failed. The thing was, I couldn't see my number of minions decreasing as it stood. Talpi, Crawls, and Clenchers multiplied rapidly, and I had no reason to believe that it would be any different for the Imps.

No, whatever I chose, it would have to be in a supporting

role. There was no point in amassing helpers then putting myself on the front line, especially when I had Strength as my dump stat. No, from now on, I would count on the single point to Agility I received each level to ensure that I was fast enough to avoid most enemies, and put all my points into Mental Power, with the occasional point to Agility and Toughness to keep things balanced.

Mental Control--I doubted that I'd need it. My mana regen was already crazy enough that I regenerated my full mana each day. This way, I would be able to back up my fighters with powerful illusions and an effective breath attack, and still ensure that I'd be able to create constructions fast. I wanted to go over this with some of the others to hear their thoughts, but I figured that the premise was solid.

We carved up large portions of the meat. Our stores had been running low, but with this, we would be good for the remainder of our round trip, as long as we didn't take too long. We sent Wreil back to Creive to tell him where the rest of the meat lay and then we took off. The area we were entering was unmapped lands both for the Talpi and myself and we were relying solely on what the other Talpi tribe and Creive had told us. They had been free with their knowledge, though, leaving us with a decent idea of what we were going into.

According to both, there were larger chances of ambushes when we left the outskirts of Creive's domain. He was in complete control of his own area, but further away, larger crea-tures were keen to take advantage of the constant number of creatures traveling through the area to take advantage of the metal deposits near Creive. Hence, the first day we made quick progress, but on the second day, we moved slowly, keeping up a rotation to ensure that we always had a camouflaged scout up front to make sure we wouldn't run into any nasty surprises. It also led to a lot of longer delays, whenever our scouts wanted to be sure that things were as they should be.

We occasionally bumped into smaller creatures and took

them down, where it wouldn't cause too many delays. Following a clash with a small tribe of nimble, but ferocious, four-armed animals, I took great joy in realizing nobody had even gotten hurt. We were growing strong compared to the remainder of creatures in the lower levels. By now, there was little that could stand up to us down here. If it hadn't been for the subtle threat of the Soul Carver, we might have cleared house, taking down some of the larger threats for the experience. As it was, we decided to move forward with a little more confidence than earlier.

The experience was nothing much at level 19. A couple hundred here and there didn't mean much when I needed 20 thousand for the next level. Still, it all added up, and at the lower levels, it was still significant. Timothy kept improving rapidly and hit level 10, choosing an incredible feat that effectively doubled the buffs and debuffs from his touch. At this point, he could already incapacitate smaller or low-leveled creatures with a simple touch, and the combination with my breath attack was simply vicious.

During one of these delays, I was fiddling about with my map, trying to get an idea of the general layout of the area. One thing I had learned from the Talpi by now. You could rarely anticipate anything about the general layout of the mountain. You could have hours and hours of tunnels, constant, boring unchangeable, even similar-sized ones. Then, within the next mile, you could experience underground rivers, lakes, waterfalls, and beautiful mineral deposits that looked like underground forests--hidden, glittering wonders that left you amazed and awed.

Then, there were the ruins. Clearly, large parts of the mountain had been occupied at one point or another, by radically different species. You could spend an hour walking perfectly fashioned tile tunnels, letting you know that civilization had once dominated part of the place, only to have the architecture replaced within minutes by another ruin where dimensions and angles were subtly off and offensive to our senses.

Quite often, we had to take detours to find tunnels that accommodated my size.

Currently, we were having a break inside one of those ancient ruins. A claustrophobic find, with low ceilings and a large number of small, quadratic rooms. We found no information left of their erstwhile inhabitants, but exactly every third room was vibrant, filled with beautiful murals depicting the world above. They promised a huge world filled with all sorts of species and variations of nature and marvels of architecture.

Right at this moment, I wanted nothing more than to spend a few days in the ruins, learning more about other nations and the world outside this underground dungeon, except I knew it was not to be. Not yet, at least. This is why I was completely engrossed in my map, ensuring that I would be able to find my way back here and explore at my leisure, once I had handled the tiny problem of the Soul Carver and Selys. A dragon needs dreams too, right?

My map was a marvel. The visuals were stunning, colors exact, and I could zoom in to almost the exact degree I wanted to, orient it in any way I chose, even switch between layers in the mountain effortlessly, where I had ventured above the lowest layer. Its remaining functionalities needed work. There was no way to add notes or pins to the map, and the moment I left here again, everything would be greyed out.

Hence, I decided to memorize a sequence of locations to help me find it some other time. This time, as I zoomed out, trying to find something memorable to use for later, I was suddenly distracted by something completely surprising. Not the fact that my Talpi back in the domain were slowly digging out another cave next to the Farm--that part I'd been following for a while.

No, it was another area on the map that stayed colored, showing me all its information. Breathless, I zoomed in and laughed out loud in amazement. Bless you, Deyra, whoever and whatever the hell you are! Apart from the increased mana regeneration, with Creive as my new ally, his domain was now available for me to watch. It was amazing!

I forgot all about my surroundings and spent every single available moment going over the blue dragon's domain. Again, I could only shake my head at how lucky Creive had been to find his fortress. It was hard to fathom how it had been constructed in the first place, but from within the map, I was able to stroll along the halls and see that it was very far from a natural construction - in fact, it was criss-crossed with tunnels and stairs, ripe with dust-covered rooms and unused areas.

To be honest, I was surprised by how, even with the threat of Creive relatively close by, the place still remained unoccupied. From the looks of it, there were also a lot of practical aspects to the fortress that remained unused. I saw arrow slits and openings studding the towering construction that would be excellent for defensive measures, all of them unused.

Well, almost all of them. The gaping opening left by Creziel's handiwork was not left completely undefended anymore. While some of the Culdren were working, rather ineffectively I judged, on repairing the lowest floor of the fortress, a platform along the lower edge that had, just a day earlier, been unoccupied, now sported a softly glowing construction--a Lightning tower, if I was to take a wild guess.

All too soon, we had to move on. I promised myself to keep an eye on Creive every once in a while, and we resumed our journey. We were getting close to the northern edge now, pretty much as far as we could come from our own domain and still stay inside the mountain. Our plan was to continue along the eastern edge and then, if we still hadn't found all the dragons, do a shorter circle counter-clockwise around the center of the mountain.

The armor we obtained from Creive was exactly what the doctor ordered. Soon, I had a handful of Crawls decked out in mismatched armor from head to toe and that, along with their natural folds of hardened skin, should make them even tougher than they already were.

When we didn't fight, I didn't see much of Tim. He was constantly on the move, the ball of light bobbing along next to this Crawl or other, completely engrossed in whatever his current project was.

At one point, he did drop back to keep me company. I looked at his form. The vague features on his "body" were really creepy. They were human-like enough that it was easy to tell what they were supposed to be, but they were also see-through and in slight, constant movement, creating some very disturbing effects. Like when I was looking him in the eyes and one entire eye started drifting slowly sideways. He didn't take any heed of his spatial challenges, though, and his mental voice sounded like it always had. "Woooo. My brain is friiiied."

I snorted. "Yeah. I can easily imagine. I've got trouble understanding Southern folks. Learning to communicate with Crawls is so far out of my league, it isn't even funny."

He waved my concern away. "So, I've been doing some thinking-"

"Hence the fried brain. I'm not that slow, Tim."

He rolled his eyes. "About this future society of yours... ours. I've been trying to wrap my head around it, catalogue everything I know about the subject, but I might be approaching it wrong. There are so many different ways of governing and so many approaches that I have trouble narrowing it down to an approachable task. Tell me. Who should be in charge in this perfect future society of yours?"

I bared my teeth. "That is part of my issue. I don't rightly know. Not just myself, that's for sure. I mean, if we were talking about a civilized society, it would be a bit easier. I'd want to work toward our own world, where people have a say in the major decisions of society-..."

He interrupted. "So, a republic or some variant of a democracy?"

"Yeah. That sounds about right. But in here, things are different. We can't just tell Erk that he needs to make decisions for the Crawls and expect for them to be good. Also, if we put somebody like Creive in any form of ruling position, he'd think of his own benefits and nothing else."

"You are right. And just like with history, these things don't just spring up out of nowhere. There might need to be some sort of transitional phase to get people used to the changes." He was silent for half a minute, then asked. "Would you step down yourself, resign your authority? Right now, the buck stops with you."

"Yes. But! Not until I felt reassured that whatever system we erect was ready to take over. I'm not going to let this fall apart."

"Hm. That's fair. Just reminding you, giving up the reins can be hard, you know. At least, 99% of all dictators and other authoritarian leaders seem to have issues with it."

I was about to complain, but caught myself. "Sure. I *am* a dictator right now. I can live with that. And I'll keep that up until we have a working solution in hand and the means to implement it."

Timothy beamed at me. "Thank you."

Weird response. "What?"

"That was just what I needed. Now I know how to approach the task and where to start. The rest is just work. Now I can relax a bit."

Timothy blurred a little, growing wider and more unde-fined. "Oh, that's better. Keeping the body together actually takes a tiny bit of concentration. It's a weird sensation. Honestly, I don't mind the challenge of all the considerations. If only my brain could shut up every once in a while, that'd be nice."

"Heh. Usually, I use beer for that. Making it shut up with alcohol's kinda tough in this situation. I mean, even if we were to invent beer...."

"Right? Who wants to see a dragon drunk off his nuts? My point is... hell if I know if I even have a point. It's just... man, it would help if anybody else here was as into learning as I am. Not just the Crawls, either."

I tipped my head to the side. "Honestly, I think the Talpi

have come a long way already. They're improving by leaps and bounds."

"Come on, man. We've been over this. Learning is everything. There's so much to be learned if we just figure out the system. We can apply logic to this world, sort everything out, and make the system our bitch. And my brain won't give me a goddamn break!"

"Oh. Anything I can do?"

"Kind of you to ask. No. Once I get over the worst hurdle, I'll be able to make my head shut up and actually get to the fun part. You know, abusing the meta."

"...I really don't know."

"No, you wouldn't, would you? We're going to use cheat codes, old timer. The old IDDQD. Up, down, up, down, whatever. Soon, we'll be able to see which actions, prior feats, or attributes are needed in order to get which feats. Then, once we've got that down to an art, our people can pick and choose between the strongest feats out there. Also, every time that you get some new minions, we'll be able to update our base knowledge and learn more."

I laughed. Timothy was a fresh breeze. His optimism was really hard to defeat. "I would love that. Like you said earlier, we'll just have to get some spreadsheets going, then-"

"Oh, I solved that."

I halted in my tracks, gaping at the smart-ass. "You... what?"

"Oh, close your mouth, old man. You'll swallow an Imp. It was a piece of cake, really. I did remember reading about Quipu, ages ago and then-"

I narrowed my eyes. "You're doing this on purpose, aren't you? Trying to make an old man feel dumb."

"...Is it working?" The bright form shivered as he laughed. "All right, so I like feeling clever every once in a while. Sue me. You're going to love this, though. Quipu was a system they used in South America ages ago to keep track of vast sizes of data. And once you've got the basics handled, it's damn simple to use. Even you should be able to understand it."

"Har har. I appreciate that vote of confidence. So, what do we need to invent to be able to use it?"

"String. No. Stop looking at me like that. I mean it. It's leather string and a clever use of knots. I've already got our system pretty well figured out and Eilet is working on-"

"Eilet? Oh, the leatherworker."

"Exactly. He's working on the first handful of them right now. Then, with a Talpus to help me, you know, actually *pick up* the damn things, I'll be able to sort through all our people within a short period of time. We'll have to keep separate notes on paper or bark or whatever to keep the exact details of the feats noted, but that's a bynote. The main thing is this: Once we're back in the domain and I've got, like, a week to sort every-body out, any Talpus can come and ask, '*hey, what options do I have if I want to be a scout?*' and then I can, within a minute or two, show him which combinations are available, which requirements he needs, and how he needs to apply those attributes."

For a moment I just looked at Tim without saying anything. "Are you for real? You just came up with all that from some system you read about ages ago?"

He shrugged. "I do some pretty deep Wiki dives. And some stuff is just interesting enough that it sticks in my brain."

I shook my head in amazement. I didn't know if that was an extraordinary intellect or a mind that worked in twisted ways, and I didn't much care. "Well, if you need anything else, you'll have it. Just ask me. Oh, and while you're busy with Eilet, could you spare some thoughts for this: I still haven't applied my attributes from the last level. I'm planning to stick to Mental Power for the next couple of levels at least. You know, since I'm not planning to fight from the front lines, I figure I should make sure my attacks and skills are as powerful as anything. You're about to be browsing through a lot of attributes and feats, and if you find something that speaks for or against, I don't want to waste my points."

He cackled. "Muahaha. The god of spreadsheets will guide

your path. Er. Sorry. I'll look at it. For now, Eilet and I have what we need, but there's a lot of work waiting for us..."

I smiled and shook my head in amazement. "Great. I can't believe this is what you're going for, though. You'll need many people to work the knots on the leather strips, won't you?"

"Huh? No. One or two helpers should do it. Why would you think that?"

I barely contained my grin. "Oh, nothing. I just wanted to say... *knot* it!"

The white form stared me down for several seconds before reforming into a human form with huge teeth. "There's no doubt you're a father. Horrible dad humor aside, this *is* a big deal! Every adventure requires a first step. Some day, we'll think back to this one and be able to recognize that this was when we started winning."

His words sounded like a quote, but I didn't recognize it. "Sure. Now get to work, ya rat."

"Rat? When I write the history of this place, I'll make sure to make you appear ugly and fat." With that parting shot, he floated off, grinning.

CHAPTER SEVENTEEN

I like the cold weather. It means you get work done. - Noam Chomsky

On the third day after leaving Creive and the tenth day total after leaving our domain, Wreil was the one to give us the news. "We have found him. It's a white."

It took us only seconds to gather everybody. We were already traveling close together and didn't bring the scouts back in. They needed to stay out there to ensure our safety. We were currently moving through a dirt tunnel that was damp with moisture and had heavy roots sticking out from the walls here and there. Most of my minions sat down on some of the roots to avoid the wet ground. I addressed Wreil, "So, a white, you say?"

He nodded. "Without a doubt. It's getting colder. I spotted frost on some walls."

I frowned. "Yes?"

Aelis stepped forward. "What you may not know, Sire, is that the temperature within the mountain is constant. You may have natural occurrences that heat up areas, like the lava areas we have encountered, but naturally occurring phenomenons that cause the surroundings to freeze are rare. According to the stories, only white dragons are able to create frost and snow around them."

"Oh. That is likely to be a construction they can create. Wait, I did read that myself. You're right! Still, that doesn't sound like a good deal for white dragons. Aren't they likely to be discovered right away because of this?"

Roth got the attention of everybody by means of banging a hard claw on his sword. "I've lived that, by means of one of my ancestors. Their presence is easy to spot, but harder to beat. Unless you're made for the cold, the swirling, chaotic white will end you before you even meet the damn lizard. That's what happened to my ancestor, at least."

Tim spoke up. "Still, it sounds a bit like a death sentence, at least in here."

Roth responded with a nod. "You may be right. With all the ambushers around here, getting noticed often means your death. A pack of Clenchers, an Orugal, or another dragon… if you're discovered early on, you're asking to be attacked. Even so, if he's already entrenched, it's going to be hard for us to dig him out."

"Yeah. That would be correct, both literally and figuratively." I waved a paw dismissively at his confusion. "It isn't important, Roth. Now, this makes for a bit of a difficulty, in that we're unable to just send in scouts to see what happens. We're not risking your lives to the cold without reason. Also, in case it comes to a confrontation, we're pretty well set. I reckon the Clenchers and Crawls can handle a great deal of cold, and we also have the advantage of the imps. If we can lure them into a trap, creatures that are accustomed to the cold will not be immune to fire."

Roth wasn't impressed. "Doesn't tell us how we're supposed to talk to him in the first place, does it?"

"Heh. No. Actually, this time, I was just going to go and have a nice chat. No ambushes or traps, nothing. I'm feeling good about this one."

"That's so dumb. It worked with that blue terror back there, sure, but why do you insist on throwing away all the advantages each time?"

"I don't. But we've already got one ally. I believe I'll be able to convince this one that he's outmatched. Oh, and obviously, I'm going to be maintaining an illusion all of the time. If they try to jump me, I simply won't be there!"

"That is... less idiotic. It's still risky, though. Let's at least set it up to make them pay if they say no. We'll be baring our necks like this."

I shook my head. "No. *I* will be baring my neck. Still, let's be clever about this. So, how about we get to planning what fall-backs and protection we can?"

We spent an hour discussing our approach before our scouts started moving on. I was going to be in front, but I wasn't going to be that far ahead. Since our struggles with the red near the lava lake, we had erected defenses every single time we paused to rest for the night, making sure that, even if we were jumped during our rest periods, we would have the terrain on our side and the optimal placement for our scouts. At this point, that meant that, with just five minutes of preparation and the right kind of tunnel, we would be able to create a solid defensive half-wall with raised platforms for our ranged and spear-toting Talpi. Five minutes more would allow us to reinforce the wall and tighten the tunnel ahead of the defenses, creating a funnel to keep any enemies from approaching more than we wanted at a time. We, and by we, I meant Creziel and the builders, usually spent about half an hour on the construction until they were satisfied.

Defenses weren't everything. What we needed more than anything else was knowledge. We needed to know how wide the cold area spread, if there were any patrols or other creatures outside the domain, how many exits and entrances there were to the domain and, if possible, what we would be facing. The scouts were filled in on the development as they returned and sent out again right away with corrected instructions and a fresh casting of Bestow Camouflage to keep them from being discovered.

Over the next handful of hours, the responses started ticking in, most of them favorable. The area where eternal winter reigned was large, maybe a diameter of a mile, and looked to be completely circular. On top of that, the surrounding area half an hour's march in any direction was deserted, lending credence to the idea that the white had been there long enough for all other creatures to learn that this was an unsafe area. They also found tracks. Tons of them. One set belonged to a dragon a bit smaller than me. The others... "Crawls? Are you sure?"

Aelis' emotions mirrored the certainty of her nod. "Very much so. I do not lack for examples of comparison around here, Sire. The final ones, I do not know. They are bipedal and the roughness of their feet indicate claws. I have seen tufts of fur - still, it could be a handful of different species."

"Hmm - so that confirms my theory that the Crawls can handle the cold temperatures pretty well, then. Anything else?"

"Yes. There are at least four different entrances to the cold area - two of those are wide. We will not be able to close it off without them becoming aware. I did find a good spot for us to prepare your entrance."

"Good. We'll keep scouts out to the sides then, in case they try something, but otherwise, I guess... we're ready? Anything more you think we should do, Aelis?"

Aelis walked over to me. Then, slowly and deliberately, she laid a hand on my flank. I could barely feel her touch - even so, her hand felt warm, warmer than her tiny presence should be able to account for. "Please avoid dying, Sire."

I smiled down at the tiny creature. "It wasn't pleasant the first time around. I'll do my best to not repeat the experience."

She nodded and patted my flank. "In that case, Sire, let us go prepare a proper entrance."

The tunnel ahead was dark, filled with specks of white. I stood in the center of the cold tunnel, hard-packed dirt mixed with ice underfoot and tried to penetrate the depths of the billowing snow ahead. Behind me, Creziel and the builders were hard at work, digging into the sides of the tunnel at a frenzied pace in order to loosen the frozen earth. I waited, anxious for them to finish while I tried to spot any movement up ahead.

This would be the worst possible time for an attack. The five minutes turned to ten and fifteen as the Talpi learned that the frozen earth was hard to work with. Talpi pushed the carved-out blocks of frozen earth into position, and I sighed in relief as the ranged Talpi took their places alongside the Imps and Crawls, while Creziel and the builders kept up construction around them. As I moved forward, the world turned white as my sense of orientation disappeared.

For a moment, I wondered at the world and exactly how it could even be possible to create a system that would allow for snow to fall within a goddamn mountain. Then the cold hit me and my thoughts turned to other avenues. Holy crap, it was cold. Within half a minute, the soles of my feet were starting to grow numb. A dragon was a reptile of sorts, right? So, could cold actually kill me?

I shook my head and focused on the mission and maintaining the illusion that placed me and my tracks ten feet to the left of my actual placement. With a glance at the map, I adjusted my aim to walk straight for the center of the cold zone. I pushed away the pin-pricks of cold that threatened to slow down my mind and let my mental voice boom out into the white. At this point, he must have discovered my presence already. "Kindred. My fellow dragon. I would speak with you. I have come alone. Let us talk in peace." The only thing I'd been able to find in common among the dragons so far, had been a penchant for old-fashioned speech, like they figured they were nobles and they damn well better talk like it, too. Well, when in Rome...

It didn't take long for a response to arrive. The mental voice was female, articulate, and surprisingly warm. "A Shadow brother. What an honor. We shall talk. Keep moving straight ahead, and I will meet you."

That was... vaguely ominous. It was the first time I'd been met with kind words, and it was disconcerting. I smelled a trap. Either that, or the owner of the voice was so confident in her superiority inside the freezing cold that she didn't consider me a threat. I shuddered. Fifteen more minutes, and she might be right on that count. This cold was *heavy*.

I plodded forward. The tunnel grew and shrank in turns, with side tunnels appearing from within the disorienting blizzard without any discernible pattern. Even with my map, the place was a veritable maze. The snow lay in drifts now, and entire walls were covered in ice. From time to time, I could feel my footholds slipping even despite my clawed feet.

My instincts were yelling at me to *get out*, and I prepared myself mentally for an ambush. From then on, progress became harder, as I struggled to maintain the illusion even as the cold did its best to freeze my extremities and my mind. At times, I spotted shadows from within the whirling snow, but they always faded away. I was approaching the exact center of the cold area, and suddenly, without warning, the blizzard just... stopped.

The relief was insane as I walked from a thundering snowstorm into a calm winter day, with snow and crunching under my feet. Before me lay a twisted winter wonderland. We were inside a low-ceilinged, large cavern, ringed in on all sides by icicles or frozen stalactites, it was hard to tell which. The calm area was circular and the size of a baseball field, with the storm visibly raging right outside. It felt like I was trapped inside the eye of a hurricane. Right outside, dark shapes moved, half-seen, and before me was the white.

If there ever was a White Queen, this was it. Forget about Narnia. Her skin was a white so bright it was hard to look at directly, and where she moved against the backdrop of the blizzard, it was hard to tell where the snow began and she ended. Her eyes were hard and cold, a brilliant blue blazing at me. The horns surrounding her sleek, deadly face formed a bone-colored, beautiful crown.

She was smaller than me, and Strength and Toughness were certainly dump stats for her, but the pacing of her lithe form betrayed her agility. So her build was approximately the same as mine? Or she was really low-leveled. I couldn't sense her emotions. Not too low-leveled, then. In front of her lay her Hoard. Glittering shapes of her treasures stuck out from beneath a blue protective dome. As she spoke again, the former civility was entirely gone. "So. A shadow brother. Not only that, but an *unknown* shadow brother. Here to trick me and slay me? Of course you are."

I tried to stop the furious words spilling from her and get a word in, but she wasn't having any.

"We all know that shadows are not to be trusted. Good with words, sure, but filled with hate and horrible intentions." Every time I tried to interrupt her, she would just speak louder. In the end, I tried to yell over her angry accusations, but it devolved into a yelling match. Before a full minute passed, she was pacing back and forth before me, tail whipping with frenzied motions into the nearby snow drifts as she spouted her hatred. "You think you get to leave safely? You believe you can tout your lies inside MY domain? Bring troops to MY home? You will rue this day. EVERYBODY! ATTACK!"

I did not wait to hear the final words. As she started with the threats, I turned tail and ran toward the exit. I did not make it more than a handful of steps before the blizzard returned with a vengeance, and the moment she told everybody to attack, the world exploded. Pain erupted in my hind legs as I was struck by something blue, and I almost lost the sensation in my right hind leg.

I fought through the pain and disorientation to maintain my illusion, and that is what saved me. Next to me, weapons exploded from everywhere inside the blizzard to impact right where my illusion was. At least the white was the only one with the attributes to see through my illusions. I did not stay to count my blessings.

With a growl, I lowered my head and ran for my life. Two medium-sized shapes barred my way, but I did not slow down. I cast a Shadow Whorl right in front of them, lowered my neck, and barreled right in between the two on my flight. Something impacted the lower end of my tail, causing me to roar in pain, even as I suffered a nasty slash from one of the large forms. Then I was past, even as my illusion faded into oblivion.

I have never put as much effort into running fast as I did then. Even so, it was a harrowing experience. Everywhere, the blizzard came alive with movement and colors as previously deactivated towers came alive to shoot barrages of ice and pain at me. My health sank in bites and chunks and frost layered itself around my legs and body, causing me to slow and falter, but within a minute, I finally spotted the half walls of my minions ahead and sprinted through the narrow opening with a final dash of speed.

"Attackers!!" I yelled. I risked a look behind me to see forms exploding out from the blizzard, and I met them with a Weakening Fog. Everywhere around me, my people leapt to the defense, Imps and ranged Talpi raining down death on the attackers, while my Crawls and Roth occupied the center of the narrow opening, braced for the clash.

It was a slaughter. The throwing spears took down a blurry form or two, but the fire attacks of the Imps was what really made an impact. A full handful of forms didn't even make it to our defenses, torn down by the constant stream of fiery missiles. I turned to return to the center of the battle to reinforce my fighters, but when I got there, it was already over, and blood colored the snow. I stared off into the whirling snow, fully alert for anything. One harrowing minute went by, and then another, as we stared into the cold, waiting for an additional charge that refused to show up.

Aelis stared at me wide-eyed, looking in fear at the blood that flowed freely from the large wound on my tail. I had lost a full 40 percent of my health, but at least the slowing effects from the frost attacks were fading now. "Sire. Are you alright?"

"Never. Fucking. Better." I sent through clenched teeth. "That goddamn paranoid psycho. She didn't even listen!" I growled a laugh. "Big damn mistake." I roared my frustration out at the world and spotted Roth, hanging back with his two-handed sword unsheathed and a murderous look to him. "Hey, Roth. So you were right. I failed to take into account that apparently dragons have a problem with using their bloody brains. Stupid goddamn critter." I stamped my feet, trying to find some warmth in my body while my temper calmed down a bit. I growled and bared a smile full of teeth at the tiny warrior. "Alright, Roth. What's the single fact everybody knows about Shadow Dragons?"

"They don't listen to reason?" His angry demeanor was obvious, but the admission that it had been a stupid idea seemed to mollify him some.

"Not that. Try this out. We don't do direct confrontations unless we can avoid it." I let that sink in and then continued. "Guess what? We're going in there, right now, to surprise the hell out of that white bitch."

CHAPTER EIGHTEEN

There were objections. Of course there were. Plenty of them. But they got the point quickly. The idea of a Shadow Dragon performing a direct, head-on attack, moments after being put on the run was ludicrous. When I involved them in the details of my hastily flung-together plan, even Roth began to get enthusiastic about it. The white was clearly not going to commit her forces. She was probably intending to wait it out, maybe get me with an ambush when I had lowered my guard some. Or maybe she just thought I'd run off for good with my tail between my legs. Heh. Good luck with that.

Ten minutes later, we faced the blizzard. There were not many of us, but we came prepared and as heavily armed and armored as possible. My Clenchers looked feral. They had been outfitted with iron armor on their legs and necks, leaving only their naturally armored bodies and thick heads uncovered. Erk and two other armored Crawls looked ridiculous, folds of skin alternating with pieces of armor, but I would not want to be the minion to face one of them.

The remaining eight Crawls looked ready, too, bloodlust reflecting in their usually dull eyes. I cast Camouflage on every single one of them, and the shifting, unclear forms immediately became hard to spot in the snow. Timothy trailed after us, ensuring nobody would jump us from behind, and ready to reinforce us if things got heated. Heh. Or not.

We moved out, moving at a glacial pace. Fitting. I held the front and we slowly moved forward, one step at the time. Most importantly, I maintained my illusion. Where my earlier outing had illusionary Onyx wandering proudly and openly right to the side of where I really was, this time, I went for invisibility. To everyone who didn't have the mental power to see through my illusion, there would be only the snowstorm in front of them, when in fact we were a large group of monsters slowly creeping forward with destruction on our minds.

After the first hundred feet, I spotted a trio of large fur-covered bipedal beasts hiding within the snow with large, two-handed spears, and I acted right away. My Weakening Fog shot out, enveloping all of them, and my mental shout had my own Crawls swarming forward to attack. For the enemies, it must have been a harrowing experience, as my minions followed my breath attack, erupting from nowhere to jump the now-weakened beasts. The moment they sprang forward, blue-white spears shot from a tunnel on the right as an Ice tower erupted into motion, and I sent two Clenchers forward to smash it into oblivion. The bulks of my very own monsters soon hid the tower as they battered it to pieces.

Meanwhile, I kept my eyes fixed on the front. My Crawls stuck to the strategy. Two of the enemy beasts died in moments, while the third one managed to slip away inside a side tunnel. My Crawls started to pursue, but I called them back to my side, and we started our forward progress again. My Clenchers came back, one limping from where a blue casing of frost enveloped the armored front leg, and I shifted the other duo of Clenchers forward to handle the next challenge.

We managed to get a full half of the way toward the white's hoard. The enemy fell back before our onslaught or were struck down where they stood. Fear was evident on their features as our people exploded from out of thin air to avenge their treachery. We made it to a place where wide tunnels on either side held an Ice tower each and I had already committed my Clenchers to the attack on both towers.

That is when she struck.

Suddenly, cold spouted from the tunnel in front of us in a steady, unceasing wave, moving from side to side to cover us all in heavy layers of frost and pain. My mental shout rang out, and my Crawls hid behind my bulk, waiting for the assault to dissipate. I gritted my teeth and ignored the pain as best I could, casting a Shadow Whorl straight at the place where the blue-white wave of frost originated from. It did not cease, but the stream became more erratic and missed me most of the time. My illusion finally burst. Faced with the ongoing attack and the pain it created, I was unable to maintain it anymore.

That was apparently the sign the white's minions had been waiting for. From within snowdrifts around the crossing, previously hidden enemies burst forward to charge in our direction. I met them with my own Weakening Fog, but missed half of them as they came from all sides. Ten shapes became fifteen as they kept emerging from their hiding places. This was, obviously, where the cowardly Shadow dragon was supposed to tuck his tail between his legs and flee. Screw that. I had planned for this.

I sprang forward and yelled "Slay them!" with all my force. Then, I barreled right through four enemies and left them sprawling on the ground as I went straight for the white. My speed was limited. The frost encasing my body was starting to weigh me down, and my entire body was starting to hurt from wounds and the mounting toll of ignoring the frost and ice attacks.

In the center of the battlefield, my eyes met those of the white, and her eyes blazed in triumph as she took in the wounds on my body and focused the streaming frost from her mouth entirely on me. It was tapering out, by now, but the pain and debuffs were mounting, and I watched my health tick down, even as I struggled to move onward. Thirty percent. Twenty.

She was only two dragon lengths away now. My left front leg had completely ceased to work. Fifteen. Ten. The stream of ice from her ceased, and she moved forward against me to finish me off... and that's when I activated the Mana Crystal that was affixed to my harness. My wounds itched as they closed, and I locked eyes with the white, shooting her a wicked grin through the whirling illusions of the Shadow Whorl.

The white's visage widened in horror as she realized what I'd done and tried to turn tail. The frost encasing my body still slowed me down, and my attempt to hold her back was reduced to me leaving two long lines of claw marks on her lower back as she fled, Shadow Whorl causing her to slip once in the process. I shot a Weakening Fog at her, hitting her full in the back and enjoying the visible difference in her stride. Toughness was clearly not where she had invested all her points.

I roared, bloodlust keeping me warm even in the midst of the blizzard, and leapt after her. Within seconds, however, I realized that I would never catch up to her. I broke off the pursuit, bounding back toward the ambush. I dreaded seeing dead bodies everywhere, but the situation had turned bad for the white's minions.

My Clenchers were finishing off the Ice towers, while my Crawls were fighting defensively, holding the line against both the enemy Crawls and the fur-covered beasts. To my amazement, they were not only holding their own, but *winning*. The levels they'd gained, along with weeks of heavy training, were finally paying off. Even as I ran, Timothy joined the fray, expanding to envelop all attackers in his debuffs while his mental attacks caused chaos in their midst.

I watched enemies reeling back from the Crawls' heavy strikes, flailing at my minions to no avail and let a Weakening Fog ruin their day even further. The ambush from behind was the final straw, and the furry enemies wailed in panic, trying to flee to all sides. The enemy Crawls, caught up in their battle frenzy, did not flee. Refusing to surrender, even outnumbered and outleveled, they fought on stubbornly, even as they were torn apart. It was a short struggle, and as the Clenchers rejoined us, it took but twenty seconds before the final enemy Crawl dropped to the ground with blood spurting from a savage Clencher bite on his neck.

Silence fell over the battlefield, but there was no time to waste. I ordered one of the Clenchers and three of the unarmored Crawls to go back and have their wounds seen to. Then we moved on. It was a tough, cold, and painful grind for us, with enemies attacking every so often, and a few additional towers spitting ice and frost at us, but she had clearly already spent the majority of her forces. Soon, we were facing down a handful of Crawls in the center of the white's hoard, which had been completely looted. My victorious roar reverberated through the cavern as I realized that she had fled, and the day was ours.

I could have wiped out the Crawls and continued the chase. In fact, it would have been extraordinarily easy. At this point, my Mental Power was high enough that a Weakening Fog had the Crawls severely impaired, heavy attacks reduced to shambling motions, but I didn't *want* to kill them. It would have been a waste. I already had Crawls in my army, and I enjoyed the idea of the enemy's army becoming mine. That's why I ordered my forces back and soon had the Crawls downed and unconscious with my breath attack, while I went on the lookout for whatever caused the damn blizzard to keep raging.

Half an hour later, I had all my people resting outside the white dragon's domain, except for the scouts. I eventually gave up on finding what caused the blizzard and figured that she may have hidden it within a snowbank. The new Crawls were waking up, and my own Crawls surrounded them, slowly letting them in on the new situation. There was little talk and, surprisingly, no struggles.

I wondered if, in the case that I was forced to flee, my minions would be equally pragmatic and quick to surrender to the new overlord. Probably. Hopefully. I wouldn't want them slaughtered simply because they didn't want to let me down. Ten frustrating minutes with one of my new minions brought me up to speed on where the white was fleeing. "That way." New minions, same as the old ones. At least my scouts could tell me that she had only a few of her minions left.

The wounded Clencher had gotten off easy. Once he'd shrugged off the worst of the frost, his leg was only slightly worse for wear. The same for one of the Crawls, who'd had the misfortune of being partially covered by the white's breath attack. The other two Crawls were worse off. Neither suffered from life-threatening damage, but one of them had a shoulder almost crushed by a heavy blow, and the other was going to take weeks recuperating, if he ever was going to regain use of his foot.

I did not feel bad about taking extra time to treat my minions. With my scouts, we were bound to be able to track her down soon, and we still needed to find another three dragons afterward. I needed everybody combat-ready. After the fight we'd had, I didn't fear facing off against the white and what few remaining minions she was left with. My Clenchers and I were going to make short work of them. If nothing else, today had taught me that Mental Power was a life saver, and that skimping on Toughness was a horrible idea.

A couple of hours later, we were off. The Crawls were bandaged as well as possible, one of them arrayed on an impromptu stretcher. The six Crawls from the white marched along nicely, and only their placement squeezed in between two of our Clenchers showed that they were on probation instead of being actual minions.

Aelis got my idea for hunting down the white even before I talked to her about it. "She may be able to outpace us, Sire, but as long as we stick to her trail, we should be able to track her down in time. She is bound to stop running at some point." A smile played on her lips. "Also, Wreil earned a new feat at level 10, after he tracked down the green's lair. It will be hard for anybody to shake him, as long as he is on their trail. He says that he can smell them."

Hence, we were back to the old formation, and Tim had another interesting feat to add to his weird knot database, once he got it going. The scouts kept ranging out and returning to keep their camouflage on. I did not have great hopes for any one of them, should they be spotted by the white, but they insisted that they would keep their distance.

The next two days were not days I would like to repeat. We traveled continuously westward, following in the wake of the white. We almost backtracked the way we had just come from. According to Wreil, there was never any doubt that we were still on the trail, even though she changed her course often, whether in an attempt to shake her pursuit or in search for a place to hide, I didn't know. I started cursing my decision to spend additional time in healing my minions; these delays were costing us even more time now.

The backtracking left us with a lot of uneasy time on our hands, too much so. As the white started veering off northward, we approached unknown lands, and these were rife with stronger monsters, flocking to the edges of Creive's territory in the search for easy pickings.

Trying to take down one monster and getting jumped by a dozen others was not an experience I wanted to have. Hence, we spent a lot of time in waiting positions while our scouts searched for the right way onward. About this time, I was really looking forward to being able to get back home to the domain. A life of constant alert was wearying. I couldn't imagine how it must be for an entire tribe who had known nothing else for their entire lives.

At a certain point, I even started an attempt at using my claws for carving in bone, just to try to find some sort of outlet for my nervous energy. The result was... not pretty. My claws were too rough to create fine detail, and not well-suited for holding any bone in place. In the end, I resorted to spending most of the time fine tuning my spellcasting abilities again. I was becoming quite adept at maintaining an illusion, regardless of what I was doing. I'd gained level 20 during the last battle, and wanted to allocate my points, but reined in my desires. I was going to see what kind of dragon I was up again next. I wouldn't want to choose the wrong kind of skill.

On the third day after forcing the white to flee we finally got the news from Aelis. "We have tracked her down, Sire. At least, we believe so. We have made a circle of the entire area, and unless the white has lucked out on discovering an area with an exit to a higher layer, there is no way out."

"Let's get to it right away, then. Do we have eyes on her?"

"No. We have done as you said. Keep back and do not engage. We are keeping an eye on the exits, but if she does leave, we will hide and let her pass." I gave her a warm smile. I loved how they actually listened and did not take any unnecessary risks.

Ten minutes later, the Clenchers and Crawls strode into the place right behind me, again. The Talpi were hidden right outside, waiting to leap in and join the fight on my command. It was an unremarkable place, more of a tangled dead end of confounding tunnels than an actual cave. I found a decent place and told my people to spread out and prepare. Within seconds, they were in place, weapons ready and eyes on the prize. I raised my mental voice and shouted, "White. Come out!" There was no reaction, and thirty seconds later, I repeated myself. "Last warning. In a minute, we will attack, and there will be no mercy."

Seconds later, her reply came from somewhere inside, defiant and recalcitrant. The tone reminded me of Dina's teenage period. "Why should I? It's not like you mean to spare me anyway."

I couldn't stop my outburst. "You haven't even *tried* to listen. Now, get out here or face the consequences, damnit."

Within moments, I could hear shuffling motions from further within the tunnel, and the white appeared. She kept her head low to the ground, avoiding my gaze, while she shot nervous glances to all sides, waiting for the first attack to land. I growled at her. "What is your name?"

That confused her. "My name? What would you need that for?"

"I need your name because I am not going to kill you unless you actually force me to. Now, my name is Onyx. What is yours?" There we go. I managed not to curse her out and push her into something stupid.

"I am Aelnir. May I ask what your intentions are?"

"There we go. I intend for the two of us to sit down, chat quietly, and find a way for both of us to live in this mountain *in peace*. Which is what would have happened if you hadn't jumped me in the first place."

The talk that followed was long, dull, and contained a lot of repetition on my side, mainly regarding what I didn't intend to do. No, I didn't mean to kill her. Nor enslave her or practice my ghastly shadow magics on her. (Where did *that* come from?) Yes, I did in fact mean for her to be able to continue her life almost undisturbed after I had left, and would only check in once in a while and collect my tribute. At long last, I leaned back and watched as she swore a vow as I instructed her to.

"I, Aelnir of the white, charge Deyra to mark my words as she marks my struggles. I swear fealty to Onyx with all that this entails. I swear that I will place him before me, will not seek his downfall, and will move to inform him of any development within the Scoured Mountain that threatens him and his."

I nodded and looked her in the eyes as I repeated the vow. The update was the same as with Creive.

[New vassal available
Another creature who draws from a connection with Deyra has sworn her servitude to you. If you accept the bond, for as long as you both survive and maintain your vows, there will be a bond between you.

Through meshing your connection with your vassal, Aelnir, you earn a boon from Deyra, but open yourself to additional risks, both associated with your vassal. Any cold damage you take is increased by 20%.

Accept vassal Yes/No?]

Yeah. I knew the risks here. Accept.

[Connection with Deyra strengthened. Mana regeneration improved by +100%

You have accepted a white dragon as your vassal. Current bond: Newly established.

Please select the type of boon you would prefer: Ongoing or one-time.]

This one was a bit different. Even though he was hostile when we first met, I felt like I could trust Creive, more or less. He was selfish, didn't care much about me, but didn't feel like a traitor. Aelnir? That was different. I didn't trust her at all. Any ongoing buff might only last for half an hour, until I left the place and she broke her bond.

[You have selected a one-time boon. You receive a permanent increase of 10% of your newfound vassal's attributes
+2 Strength
+3 Agility
+3 Toughness
+6 Mental Control
+5 Mental Power]

There was only one difference in this and my earlier arrangement with Creive. I took her entire hoard. Each and every piece of jewelry, weaponry, and armor. Her eyes followed mine in avarice and dislike as my Crawls carried the heavy loads past her. "You brought this on yourself, Aelnir. If you had only listened, I would only have charged you with part of your hoard. However, you have not only hurt some of my minions needlessly, you have also wasted my time. Time... is not a luxury I have at the moment. This means that you will have to start from scratch. I am well aware of that."

"But where should I go? My domain is falling apart as we speak. My defenses ruined. My people dead."

In the past, I'd had employees like this before. Not for long, usually. It probably was a defect on my part too, but people who tried to make their problems mine? Not a fan. "Aelnir. Listen to me and listen well. Right this moment, your domain is only falling apart *because you're not there.* Go back, re-establish yourself, find your surviving minions, hurry to increase the size of your hoard again, and take this lesson to heart. If somebody tries to invade your hoard, defend yourself for all you're worth. If they want to talk, be wary, but listen. Not everybody's trying to trick you."

She didn't respond, and when we parted ways shortly thereafter, I felt sure it was a relief to both parties.

CHAPTER NINETEEN

The best laid schemes o' mice an' men gang aft agley. - *Robert Burns*

We spent the following day backtracking toward the east, and I indulged myself in the pleasure of checking out Aelnir's hoard while we walked. It was a good one. Of all the dragons we'd encountered to date, she was the one who most matched me, in attributes if not in attitude. She had obviously spent a lot of attribute points in Mental Control, allowing her to regenerate enough mana to build a lot of structures in her short lifespan.

The result was the large number of Ice Towers, but above all, it was easy to see from the hoard. There were a full nine Mana crystals and the items within the hoard were both numerous and well-developed. I could only count myself lucky that she hadn't found the time to actually equip her minions with all the items, or the result may very well have turned out differently. Creziel asked for the chance to study some of the mana crystals, see if they would be able to build some of their own, and I readily agreed.

I enlisted Timothy's help in figuring out how best to share

the items to our people, and obviously, he devised a new task on the spot to create a list of all our items, replete with effects. More pieces of leather string for his handicrafts project. I was beyond impressed with the quality, however. Every single item had at least one modifier and some had two.

When I distributed the items among my people, they wound up with the equivalent of three or more levels in bonuses on average. Some were even better, like the full set of well-crafted, if rough, leather armor I gave Erk, passing on his old armor to another Crawl. The bonuses on the new armor gave +2 increases to Strength and toughness and a 15% resistance to magical attacks to boot.

My unsightly minion was well on his way to becoming a powerhouse. The experience made me long for my own hoard and for seeing exactly how well items were doing back there. There was no doubt that the time that had passed had worked wonders for their boosts in my absence, and I was seriously curious to see the new gains. Unfortunately, I couldn't use Inspect through the map when I wasn't inside my domain.

Our group was in a great mood. We had two allies now, even if one of them was very unwilling, and we just needed to find three more dragons. Halfway there. It sounded like a huge task, but with everything we'd managed so far, all the increases and levels we'd gained with minimal losses--yeah, we allowed ourselves to pat our own backs. Our breaks were filled with enthusiastic retellings of the battles we'd had and speculation on the future. Some even professed that they were curious to see Fire Peak, Selys' vaunted city. That was impressive to me--Talpi weren't exactly the most curious of species. But they were learning, and as they grew in strength, so did their desires to see the mountain.

We were, on the whole, not slowing down, either. I was impressed by that. All usable weapons and armors we had gotten from the hoards, we immediately shared out between us to equip us as well as possible. Everything else, we loaded onto the Crawls. Mana crystals, jewelry, everything. All other minions would be affected a lot more by the additional burdens, whereas the lumbering pace of my hardy, charisma-deficit fighters didn't change one bit.

We took the same route back. Backtracking meant that we didn't have to spend as much time scouting, and we moved fast. I did remember to check on the map and see the progress both back in the domain and with Creive a couple of times. Creive, it looked like, was doing just fine, and a lot of the time, he was out and about outside the fortress. The one time I spotted him, he was lazing about on top of his fortress, observing a bunch of his minions who were butchering and quartering some huge, thick-skinned monster. Living the easy life.

Back in the domain, things were even better. There were babies everywhere. At least one of the Talpi and one of the Crawls had given birth, and the tiny critters looked too cute and cuddly for their own good, even the Crawls. Meanwhile, Laive was getting comfortable in her new room and still hadn't managed to poison herself, bonus point in her favor.

Two things stood out among the familiar faces. One, they had broken into a new cave, quite a ways farther away from the domain and were hard at work leveling the place to prepare it for farming purposes. Two, part of the new cave was now taken over by a new makeshift enclosure that held a pack of fat, ungainly rodents. When I mentioned them to Creziel, he confirmed my hopes. They'd actually managed to find some meat animals for breeding somewhere--way to go!

I took up the discussion with Tim regarding the future inside the mountain again. I still disagreed with him on some points. For instance, I still saw no point in spending the effort to have a fully fledged system ready, when our situation was as precarious as it was. Still, with the goal getting closer, I admitted that we needed to have some general ideas in place as to what kind of rule we would eventually want to create.

For now, I was keen on the idea of an expanded version of

what I had going with the Talpi--a sort of Council where we would discuss important issues and delegate authority, but with me having the right to veto anything. Tim wanted true democracy, but agreed that it might not be viable right away, especially if we would go adding new species and new complications into the mix. We parked the discussion to think about it before making any final decisions, but I did enjoy the idea of every species being able to bring contributions to the table. Who knew? Maybe even the next generation of Crawls would be able to help, if Timothy was able to educate them.

We were getting close to the white's domain again. She had elected not to walk with us. I didn't complain, and I honestly didn't blame her, either. This tunnel was a weird mix of a cave and a tunnel, rock walls widening and closing in again without rhyme or reason. Some of the tiny offshoots looked like they could open up onto hidden areas, unknown halls and dungeons laying in wait for the adventurous just within reach. I toyed with the idea of opening my map to check whether any openings actually showed up, when I noticed something weird.

A patch of darkness on top of a stack of boulders did not act like it was supposed to. If somebody were to ask me what that meant, I doubt I would have the vocabulary to describe it. Shadows are, for lack of a better word, alive. Even in areas that are supposed to be hidden in pitch darkness, there will be variations that a person with the right kind of eyesight, like, say, a dragon, will be able to pick up on. This patch... did not act accordingly. It looked deeper, more dark, than it had any right to.

Curious, I walked closer and really looked at the area. It was circular, maybe a 10-foot radius and stood stock still. If it had been a monster, I figured it would've jumped me by now. My mind was going nuts with all kinds of theories. A hidden trap. Treasure chests, cleverly concealed behind a fake wall. An opening into a Shadow dragon's domain, hidden by a Gallery of Illusions. I tried to control the shadows, make them act at my behest, but they did not waver. Huh.

At a sudden impulse, I concentrated on my essence and brought up my Mana manipulation skill, forming it into a long pseudopod. I was getting better at it. The tendril I stretched forward was wider and felt more solid. I tentatively touched the outer part of the area. No change. The shadow held nothing out of the ordinary. Disappointed, I let my shadowy pseudopod roam into the center of the area.

Where the tendril roamed, a face looked straight at me. It took me a split second to realize what I was looking at, but when I did, it became obvious, and I sprang back in shock. The pallor of the face was a washed-out white, and it was completely unmoving, statue-like. Everybody had stopped around me and were looking at me like I'd blown a gasket. I ignored them and moved back in.

What in all hells *was* this? I got closer, a few feet from the apparition... and froze. Not of my own volition. Tendrils of insidious, oily power slipped inside my mind, it was the only way I could describe the invasion I was experiencing. I tried to struggle, but the force wasn't having it. Any opposition of mine made the tendrils grab a better hold and solidify, forcing their way into my brain and taking up residence.

Then the face moved.

The lips of the figure twisted upward into a grimace that was somewhere between a carnivorous grin and a smile. A voice spoke inside my mind. Cold, distant but triumphant. "Hello, Puppet. I have been looking for you."

Panic was a mild word for what I was experiencing right then. More like fully-fledged terror. I tried to shake off the control, but found myself unable to act... in any way. Neither mind nor my body reacted to any instructions, and I could only watch in terror as my body turned back to my people, my teeth bared at everybody and the cold mental voice rang out to reach everybody.

"You pathetic worms are mine, now." At first, the reactions were mostly confusion. The shadowy illusion surrounding the pale apparition disappeared, leaving only a tall, dark figure surrounded by a sea of swirling darkness. He wore a long, dark coat, with dozens of bright lights affixed to it. Or, at first, I thought they were lights. Then I realized my error.

They were stones. Rocks and metals of various shapes and sizes, bedecked with glowing runes. As my minions slowly realized what was going on, their confusion turned to panic. Before anybody could act, he raised his hands, displaying a long dagger, carved with glowing runes. Waves of power slammed out from around him, forcing everybody to the ground. Even as I was outside my own control, my body was forced to take a knee.

"I do not give any chances. If you try to flee, you die. I will send my long-lost dragon puppet to tear you limb from limb and reassemble you to my amusement. Then, I will tear apart your souls and have them suffer in the void, outside the touch of Deyra." Somehow, across the tunnel, my eyes linked up with those of Timothy. His glowing form had solidified, and the emotions on his face were clear to read, even frozen as he was. Horror... and recognition.

The Soul Carver had returned.

After the immediate panic was over, the Soul Carver eased off on the magic and had us all marching again. After a while, I recognized exactly where we were going--toward my domain. My people were, understandably, rattled and looked like they were ready to leg it at any chance. Even the Crawls were uncommonly affected, shuffling their feet and shooting scared glances at the tall figure every once in a while. I felt myself forced to take up a place in front of the procession with the Soul Carver bringing up the back. Tim was arranged in the middle, floating along in the center of the silent procession.

While my people were scared silent, I could not claim the same luxury for myself. Even though I wanted nothing more than a chance to gain my bearings, refocus, and somehow think of a way out of this, there was no time and no succour. All the time, while we walked, the Soul Carver was inside my mind, and he was having a grand time.

"Do you have any idea how long it has taken me to find you, Puppet? The link becomes tenuous over the distance, and you just kept moving. I will thank you for bringing along my old toy, however. With the two of you close together, you were easier to find."

At last, I felt something ease up, just the slightest bit, inside my mind. My body was still moving along outside my control, but my mind... "I... uh, I'm sorry you caught me. Who are you again?"

My brain became fire. My entire existence dissolved until I existed in a world of endless pain. Once, when I was young and impatient, I managed to carve a slice of skin off my leg with a planer. This felt like that, only applied to my mind--like somebody, without pause, removed tiny slices of myself.

Below me, I could see my feet slowly walking on, ignorant of the pain I was experiencing. The cold voice spoke up again. "I do not take well to either insolence or ignorance. My old failure, Timothy, will have told you already. I am the Soul Carver, and I have come to reclaim what is mine by right."

I was slowly coming to, after the shock of the pain. "I... yeah. I know who you are. So, what are your plans for me?"

Even from the mental equivalent of several hundred feet away, I could *feel* his smile as he responded. "To use you, Puppet. Use you to fulfil your intended purpose. Soon, you will allow me to gain my rightful place as Master of the Mountain."

I acquiesced. Playing along would be the name of the game until I found a way--any way--to escape from his clutches. "Of course. I'll do as ordered. It's not like I have a choice."

His laughter was terrifying. It was a high-pitched resonance that sounded more like a scream. "I am aware. This is the only way to be in control. However, I will not have it said that I am not magnanimous. Once we have completed our goals, I will release you to your own devices. While I do enjoy controlling you, it is a bother. I do not wish to do so forever, and once I am safely in place, I will let you serve under me."

That, more than anything, scared me. From the writings on

the wall, there was no doubt he was lying. It had said something like his control growing in time, and I'd slowly be reduced to a slave. In short, I needed to find a way to remove myself from his power, and I needed to do it fast. "That's mighty kind of you." He either didn't notice my sarcasm or chose to ignore it. Even so, I had to keep him appeased until I had a plan. "What do you need from me?"

The walk back to my domain was a horrifying experience. I spent the entire time removed from my body, trapped inside my mind, contemplating everything that had gone wrong, the what-ifs and how I could have avoided my current entrapment. My body went through the motions, my head looking down upon the ground and the tips of my claws as my feet slowly ambled forward. Knowing that Timothy was undergoing the same isolation further along in our progression did not help at all.

In fact, it only underscored how badly I had failed.

Maybe I should've gone directly to Selys, told her about her enemy? No, she would have simply killed me. If I was a threat to her, there was no reason to let me live. Then, she could have gone after the Soul Carver at her leisure. And like that, my mind went around in circles, questioning my choices but finding no answers. It was like I had been thrown into this world, only to be steering straight into a course that would lead to my own damnation - and there was not a single thing I could do to avoid it.

In time, I started loathing the sight of my claws again. Those damned reapers, moving back and forth below me, killing machines without any other purpose than ripping and tearing. Not a single beautiful detail to them, unless you gave in to the bloodlust and found grace in the sight of blood and slaughter.

I thought I was past this. I believed I could get used to the fact that I no longer had my hands to keep me occupied, that I would resort to using my head instead. Use my minions and mind to craft lasting beauty in the midst of all the death and destruction of this place, where once I had used my own hands. Except now I had been caught, and I was staring right down at the future I could expect. One of destruction and bestial bloodshed.

When I wasn't lost in self-pity or what-ifs, I was busy feeding the Soul Carver's curiosity. His one order from the start was simple: Tell me about yourself. I did not make it far through my explanation before I learned which things did and did not interest him. My interests? No. The details of my life? My failed marriage and estranged daughter? Very much no.

Whenever I was too long-winded or described something which, to him, held no interest, he would send a wave of pain at me. The degree of pain depended on exactly how bored he was At least, that's what my pain-addled mind reckoned after the sixth nerve-racking, never-ending rush of needles jabbed into my brain. He did care about construction. Not about my own house or the decades I'd spent slowly, lovingly caring for it. Not about the wholesale business of it, either. I started talking about proportions, living space, and material requirements, and didn't get further than two minutes into my explanation when he hit me with another spell. The *specifics* used in construction, however... those were of interest to him.

I spent a surprising amount of time talking about the materials used in construction. Cement, clay, bricks and the construction of bricks, different types of wood, and the ways to treat them to harden them or improve their lifetime. He listened and listened attentively and at that point, it felt like I cracked part of the code.

It might seem obvious, looking back, but at the time, it was a revelation. He was looking for anything that could help him *here*. Any material, construction, or idea which one could theoretically construct in order to give him a leg up and advantage in this world of varying access to knowledge.

With that sudden insight, my rambling monologues went from the personal realm into more theoretical ones. I made sure that I was always very open about my knowledge or lack of knowledge on a topic. I had the feeling that giving him the idea I'd be able to build a trebuchet and then not being able to deliver would be a monumentally bad idea.

Still, with what I'd read and played over the years came to good use, as I told him all I knew about traps and siege weaponry. It was probably a bad idea to lead the mind of a cruel necromancer onto those kinds of ideas, but as soon as I'd exhausted my knowledge on regular construction, my mind was pretty well-set in self-preservation mode.

The Soul Carver spent a lot of time inside my mind, listening and, on very, very rare occasions, asking questions of me. Once in a while, he left me alone, still locked inside my unresponsive body with only myself to keep me company. Right then, I would've chosen better company, if I had the choice.

I lied exactly once. I figured I could lie about my level and have him underestimate me, but he caught on to it immediately. The pain-filled hell that followed was the worst of the torments he subjected me to. When I finally surfaced, he didn't make any mentions of my lies, just repeated the question, and I answered. Honestly.

He returned to me several times over. At a certain point, he apparently got bored with my world, and prodded me to tell about the enemies in the mountain. Later, we moved on to Selys and her machinations, and I had no way of answering those. Finally, he told me to concentrate on my own progress, my skills and levels.

This was my single, tiny victory on the entire march. I figured out that lying by omission worked, and managed to keep the existence of my illusion skill a secret. Once we had completely exhausted my knowledge, he started staying away for longer periods of time, sometimes returning with more specific, detailed questions, often regarding construction or the Mountain itself.

It appeared he had already decided where I would be able to come with useful answers. The long periods of introspection in between did nothing good for me, and I lost myself in daydreaming about better times. Eventually, my musings and daydreaming solidified into one clear thought. I needed to get away. I did not care how, but I had to flee and escape his clutches. How I was going to do that without leaving my minions and Tim at his mercy was still beyond me.

CHAPTER TWENTY

Reclaiming my domain was a nightmare. I had been looking forward to it, waltzing back in, victorious, telling everybody how we had secured the mountain and from now on, things were going to change. That Selys was, obviously, still in charge, but we'd carved out a place for ourself under her. We could work to make the mountain safe, not just for ourselves, but for all intelligent species. It would be possible for those who did not choose to embark on a course of blood and danger to choose so at their own device.

Instead, I walked in front, turned off all defenses, and asked everybody to gather, only to have the Soul Carver stride through all our carefully prepared traps and spells to seat himself on the throne unimpeded.

I will not linger on their reactions. It was heart-rending and completely predictable. They caved and gave in to his every need. How else would they have acted? He was so beyond the powers of my minions and myself, there was no way anybody would be able to stand up to him and live. I was lost in these thoughts of despair and loss, even as my body marched itself to flank the Soul Carver on his right side, with Timothy on the left.

"You will all obey. Anybody who does not will find themselves on the receiving end of my displeasure. In the coming days, I will go over my domain and weigh your futures. If you try to flee, you will die. That is all. Go back to what you were doing."

As everybody went back to their doings, a wave of relief swam through me, as the Soul Carver's tendrils released their hold on me, and I regained use of my limbs for the first time in days. I had to contain myself to not strike out at him with everything I had. Or run for the hills. A sigh from Timothy on the other side of the throne told me that he was experiencing the same.

The voice remained, right there. "This should be fun, my puppet. Show me your hoard."

I blinked. "Erm. It's right there." A sensation like sharpened nails running over my essence ran through me, and I shuddered.

His voice was unchanged as it continued. "You need to open it up to me. Look at it and concentrate on sharing."

I did as he asked. The hoard sprang up with all the knowledge of its contents. When I thought of the word "Share," the Soul Carver must've received it, too, because he didn't torment me further. A moment later, he tossed a black gem in front of me on the ground. "Place this inside the hoard and accept any changes it requires."

I did as he asked. The gem was expertly carved and looked expensive as hell, but otherwise there was nothing special about it - no ominous runes, no waves of spellcraft wafting from it. However, when I placed it right at the center of my hoard, a single pop-up appeared before me.

[Do you wish to grant Selrahc Nead mastery over your hoard? Please note that all construction options will be limited to his approval.

Yes/No?]

With a sinking heart, I selected yes. It felt like a blow to the stomach, and once it was done, I could *feel* the tendrils of mana move from the hoard and lash their way through the pale necromancer.

The Soul Carver, or Selrahc, as I now knew him, did not make any exclamations. In fact, he rarely did. I had to echo Timothy's earlier observations--the guy had been dipping into his own product. He was dead, or at least some weird variation thereof, where his body was partially dead or dying.

I could smell the sickly-sweet smell of the rot without any effort on my part. Now that I could turn my head to observe him, I could also note some things about him that were just plain... wrong. His face was unnaturally still. He did breathe, but it would seem like he did it fewer times than you ought to. There was also an extreme absence of any natural movements. He only moved when it was necessary, never twitching, shuffling, or grimacing like any normal being.

Moments after I pressed yes, he extracted two glittering brick-sized items from pockets within his jacket. They were stones, like the ones held in place all around his jacket. Where the others held a couple of runes, these were layered with tiny runes, end to end, wrapping the dark material with glowing scripture. "Puppet. I want you to take a good look at this. It has cost me a lot of effort to reach this place. But finally, my work has paid off. These are your soulstones. The means by which I hold you and Failure in my grasp." He placed the stones within the hoard, and I watched in dismay as the color of the shield defending the hoard grew opaque. "There is no use trying to reach them, Puppet. They are safe from you."

He stood, and I was left staring at the hoard, mind blank as I realized he was right. There was no way to access the hoard now, and inspecting it just told me that I needed access from the owner.

I spotted a whirling shape growing right next to the throne. It was reminiscent of my own constructions, except the whirling strands of mana here were joined by dark tendrils. Clearly, the

Soul Carver was building something of his own. Without any warning, he stood up and addressed me. "Come. You will show me what you have done with the domain and explain your justifications for each choice." As an afterthought, he added. "Failure. You will move to your prison."

My heart hurt, as I watched Failure--Timothy--glide toward the Soul Circle. As the settings on the circle changed to keep him trapped inside, I wanted to hit something. Poor guy.

The Soul Carver didn't act like it was anything special. He motioned for me to get going, and we started walking through the domain, while I explained my thoughts behind the different constructions. From the constructions supporting our basic needs like the Habitats, larder, and the Farm over the ones allowing us to improve ourselves and our productions--the Training Chambers, Sorcery Chamber, and Laive's room, and finally we got to the defenses. He did not react and rarely spoke. The only times he said anything were to have me explain some things that might not be easy to understand from the explanations on the constructions themselves.

At a guess, I would say he lingered the longest on the defenses. His eyes, at least, were roaming over every inch of them, from the Gallery of Illusions to the fake openings, murder holes, and the pit trap with the retractable floor. I told him everything, leaving out not a single thing--except for one: the Shadow door inside my own room that led to the escape tunnel.

At the moment, it was blessedly closed, entrance blending into the surroundings, and you would have to be able to see through the illusion to spot the door. It was a tiny hope, and not bloody likely, but I held out hope that maybe, I'd be able to escape that way with my minions, if he was distracted.

When we were done with the tour, he sat down on his throne, neck ramrod straight, and nodded, once, mechanical and precise. "I will think about our progress. You will stay with me while I ponder this."

I bowed, keeping my head low and avoiding his eyes. I didn't want to appear as if I had any fight left in me. "Okay. Uh, can I use the time to keep everybody working on their usual business until you have decided? You know, make sure things progress as they should?"

He didn't even appear to have heard me in the first place, but suddenly, his offhanded response came. "Acceptable. Just don't disturb me."

I bowed again and followed to place myself right next to the Soul Carver as he occupied his throne, like a glorified Labrador next to his owner. The image wasn't that wrong, either, except this lab had a bone to pick with his master. Heh. That was horrible. I grinned inside even as I considered my next move. I might be on a leash right now, but at least I had the freedom to speak with my minions and plot. There would definitely be room for plotting.

One other thing I was also able to do was inspect the hoard, as the smelly bastard had his equally putrid minions bring in all the treasures I'd won on my raids. I had to fight to keep from grinding my teeth as they brought in weaponry, jewelry, and armors by the bucketload, only to toss it haphazardly into the hoard, leaving it outside my reach.

The only treasures I was able to keep outside his reach, for now, were the nine Mana crystals I'd pilfered from the white's hoard. Those hadn't been returned to the massive pile of items my Crawls had been carrying, but in Creziel's backpack. It would appear he didn't give them over for the Soul Carver to keep. Clever Talpus.

The accumulated treasures did what I had been waiting for a long time. They propelled the size of my hoard--because it *was* my hoard, damnit--into the next level of quality, with all the improvements that brought with itself.

[You have met the necessary criteria:
- Surpassed level 20
- Contents of the hoard improved
- At least 12 mana crystals owned

[Small Medium Hoard has been upgraded to Medium Hoard.

Your current Hoard size: 22 Mana Crystals (Medium) grants you the following:
- Maximum Population size: 150. Current population: 75
- Domain size: 7000 foot radius.
- Domain detection range: 60 Miles. Domains within range: 5
- Mana regeneration rate is increased by 500% (Total current regeneration rate increase=1400%)
- The possible quality of magic abilities gained from the hoard is increased. Uncommon possibility of multiple magic abilities.

The connection and benefits will remain for as long as your Hoard is active.]

[Criteria to upgrade hoard:
- Reach a minimum of level 25
- Improve contents of the hoard
- Own at least 30 Mana Crystals
- Create one of each constructions]

[Skill has improved: Inspect
- Inside your domain, you are now able to see the weaknesses of enemies.
- You can now use Inspect through your map outside your domain.]

[Skill has improved: Domain Map.
From now on, you may share your domain map with anybody within reach, inside or outside of your domain. You are also able to add and share personal markers and notes on the maps]

[Construction unlocked: Illusion Defense.
This construction comes in the form of an illusion generator covering the entire Domain. It can hide any entrances to your

Domain, envelop your lands in shadow, and severely impact the detection ranges of any hostile domains.

Mana cost: 500

Construction time: 48 hours]

[Construction improved: Growth Boost

This energy field enfolds a malleable area of 60 x 60 feet. Growth of all animals, plants, and vegetables within the area is increased by +100%.
- Efficiency of Growth boost is increased to +125%
- Protective field added. From now on, a Growth Boost will cause a low amount of damage to any intruders within the energy field.
- *Sacrifice ability added. The energy field is now capable of consuming living matter to improve efficiency.*]

[Construction improved: Stone Door

This sturdy stone door can be placed at whichever doorway you want and possibly buy several crucial minutes in a conflict. It is magically keyed to the creator and his minions and can be locked at a touch.
- Sturdiness of your doors is improved. From now on, all stone doors constructed will be twice as hardy.
- *Trap ability added. From now on, you can add mana to your stone doors, adding random trap abilities.*

[Construction improved: Habitat

This construction converts an area of 30x30 feet into living space, optimal for any living creature to move into. Please note: While any race and species may take up the Habitat, not all are able to peacefully co-exist. Increases health recovery for all creatures in the Habitat.

- Your Habitats now add a well rested buff. Any minion sleeping in the Habitat for more than 4 hours will have an 8-hour increase to toughness.

- Your Habitats now improve health and mana recovery.

- *High-level creatures will now have the chance to spawn stronger offspring. The higher the level of the parents, the bigger the chance. Not all creatures have this option.*]

[Construction improved: Training Chamber

This construction transforms 30 x 30 feet of room into a Training Chamber. Inside this area, physical training will allow your peons to improve their physical prowess. If they spend enough time here, they will be able to improve selected attributes. Progress will be relative to the original attributes of the creature and dependent on the efficiency of the training.

- Your minions are now able to improve their attributes even faster. Attribute gain speed increased by +25%.

- *The attribute cap of your minions has been raised. Your minions can now raise their attributes even higher.*]

[Construction improved: Shadow Tower

This construction creates a semi-transparent, small tower infused with shadow essence. The tower acts like an self-aiming defensive ranged fighter, spewing pellets of shadow matter on any offensive fighter within range. The attacks function in the same manner as Weakening Fog, weakening targets to the point where they collapse for lack of strength.

Shadow Towers are not the most durable of constructions, but can often be overlooked in the chaos of battle since they are hard to spot.

- *Improved camouflage added. Shadow Towers and the pellets of shadow essence they shoot are now nearly invisible. It will take a trained eye to spot the towers.*]

Man, that was a handful. I tried to take it all in. So, the domain was now large enough that I'd be able to spot anything entering from a safe distance before they got closer to our constructions. Plenty of room to expand the defenses, should I ever manage to oust my newly found nemesis.

The domain detection part confused me a bit, though. My detection range increased, but the number of domains remained the same? That was until I remembered that the domain of the red I'd killed, Ruiva, must have faded from existence by now. That meant I had Creive, Aelnir, and three others in range. That left one dragon from the clutch missing. Either he was already dead, or the mountain was even larger than I thought.

The map got even better. That one at least, I was still able to use for myself. The Illusion Defense - I wanted it. Right away. If only I called the shots.

As for the rest of the updates, they ranged between insanely promising for the Habitat and really disturbing for the Growth Boost. None of them were bad, though. In combination, they'd prove extremely helpful. I just needed... yeah. That one, tiny detail.

The next day, I lay next to the pale, tall, self-zombified bastard, occasionally sharing short messages with Talpi who passed by. Not many decided to come visit, and I couldn't blame them. Still, now and again, somebody took the risk of infuriating the pale appearance, shooting quick questions about their progress and what to do. They were inane questions, most of them, everyday questions to which they already knew the answers, but I heard the questions underneath. "What are we going to do? Are we going to take action?"

My answer to all of them was the same. "Nothing has changed. We will keep to our usual plans, see what happens, and be ready to act. Tell everybody." I did not need anybody to stir up trouble right this moment. There would be plenty of time for that in the future.

The Soul Carver didn't seem to notice anything as he sat on the throne, unmoving, staring out into nothing. Second-guessing what he was doing was folly. He could be casting a spell, plotting world domination, or just having a nice little nap with his eyes open. I couldn't tell the difference. After half a day's silence, I was contemplating some sort of action against him, when one of the Imps decided to make their entrance. I had been relieved at their absence, so far. Their chatty, noisy personalities seemed like the exact thing to piss off the scary abomination.

The Imp didn't care. Maybe he didn't have the faculties for it, and maybe he just hadn't adjusted to the new world order. He traipsed across the throne room, taking in the area, until his eyes fixed on me. He lit up and lifted into the air, looking like he was going to fly straight across from where the Soul Carver sat. Until now, I had kept my mental voice to a whisper, in order to not disturb the presence next to me. Now, my voice rang through the room: "Leave. Now!"

The Soul Carver acted instantly. Eyes still staring blindly off into the room, he lifted a hand and a translucent wave coursed from him... and slammed into my body, wracking me with pain. Moments later, his head swerved, and he looked down at me. "I told you I did not wish to be disturbed!" After almost a minute of silence, the pain was slowly fading, and I watched an unnerving smile building on his lips.

"I am at an important place in my musings. I will need you to send a group of Crawls--say, ten or so--to the southernmost opening in the mountain. Open your map, and I will show you where. Then, I want to be alone until tomorrow. Do not leave the domain. I will know."

I did not allow him the time to change his mind. Some time away from his oppressive presence was just what the doctor ordered. I quickly left the throne room, ushering the trembling Imp, who was hiding behind one of the pillars, ahead of me.

First, I went to the Crawls' chamber. From the outside, I could already tell what had happened--and for once, looking at my dull minions made me smile. Inside, two newborn Crawls were stumbling around on stubby legs. As they saw me, they both stared, mouth agape, before running straight at me to start climbing my clawed feet. I couldn't help but chortle at their unbridled curiosity. Apparently, they weren't born fearing dragons. If only we managed to get rid of our undead infestation, so we could get to educating these cute critters.

One tedious and unsatisfying discussion with Erk later, I went to find a scout who would be able to take the Crawls along. They were simply unable to understand the directions I gave them, even when I tried to show them on the map. That done, I moved along, deep in thought. What should my next move be? Where to start?

I found the rest of the Imps hidden away next to the Clencher Habitat, chittering and laughing, half-assed going through some training exercises in the Clenchers' Training Chamber, clearly without any idea as to what they were doing. I almost moved on, but then decided that some unbridled positivity was sorely needed.

I caught Eamus as he passed by. The Clencher trainer looked tired. "Eamus. How is everybody?"

"I... don't know. Even the Clenchers are scared of the Soul Carver, though. They recognize him as an enemy, but they're too afraid to move close. What are we supposed to do?"

"Learn from the Clenchers. They may be dumb, but they recognize power. We will plan, and then we will act at the right time. Where's Arthor?"

He answered without hesitation. "In the Sorcery Chamber. He didn't want to be seen."

"Again, wise choice. Could you go get him, Creziel, Aelis, and Roth? After that, I want you to spread the word--to everybody, Crawls included. *Nobody* is to approach the Soul Carver unless Arthor or I say so." It might not work in the long run, but it should avoid any immediate casualties from the trigger-happy mage.

Roth was the last one to arrive. His fur was matted with sweat, leaving no doubt as to what he'd been up to. The usual group was gathered, and we were ready to take on the world. Except, this time, nothing was as it used to be. The mood was somber, and even Roth was subdued.

Arthor, for once, didn't have his stones buzzing about him. He glared at me, and spoke up as the first person. "Lizard, sometimes I curse the day you arrived."

"Me too, Arthor. Me too. I hoped to avoid this." I shook my head. "I don't know how long we have. The Soul Carver could invade my mind any moment. If I growl, that is what's happened, and we will all keep quiet. Now, while we have the chance to talk freely--what do we do about our situation?"

We spent hours, plotting, coming up with and discarding plans and stratagems. We parked our long-term plans, like the construction of a second Farm or the overview of feats and skills, until further notice. Our discussions boiled down to one overwhelming question. With Timothy and myself unable to aid, would we be strong enough to risk an attack?

Roth was in favor. "It's the best we've got. We'll stack the hidden tunnels above the throne room and rain death down upon him. Then the Clenchers can jump him from the sides, Crawls from the other side, and the Imps can fire from the entrance. Who could stand against that?"

Creziel, for once, didn't hold back. "Use your head, Roth. What about the enemy who brought all of us low *with a single spell*. Did you forget that part?"

"No. But if..."

"There will be no premature attacks." Arthor's tone did not invite discussion. "Creziel is right. We are too weak, and I will not throw away our lives like this. We could run away, but I am afraid that the Soul Carver would turn Onyx on us and hunt us down."

"I believe we should chance it." My words were low, but

determined. "Not yet, though. We need him to relax first. Let him believe we have accepted his reign. We will focus even harder on training than before. Forget about building on our defenses, as long as he doesn't command it. What's important right now is that we grow as strong as possible for what we need to do. There will be an opening, and once we spot it, we will act." I sighed. "And if there is no opening, we will attack regardless, but we need to be clever about it.

Roth gave a grudging nod. "Alright. I guess we could increase the training for everybody. It's no secret that our scouts could do with some work, and those lazy Imps, too."

"The Clenchers, too. And you, Arthor and Creziel, will have it harder than anybody else. Not only do I need you to step up your training in the Sorcery Chamber and Training Chamber both, I also need you to prepare everybody else and provide us with weapons and more ammunition."

Creziel frowned. "Ammunition? Spearheads?"

"Exactly. Whatever is going to happen, it is going to be bloody, and I need for us to be ready at all times. That includes having the damn best weapons available that we can prepare. For now, the hoard is closed to us, but we're not going to let that stop us."

"Pfah. That's easier said than done, lizard. If you'd actually done what I asked and brought back some decent materials, things would have looked different. As it stands, we are short on supplies, but we will do our best."

"Good. Talk to Laive, too. She might have finished some poisons that we can use against him. The Soul Carver isn't fully alive, but she might have something that will affect his flesh."

We went back to planning the specifics. I stressed to everybody that Arthor would do the planning and lead all species, since I could very well be immobilized at a moment's notice. I informed the nearby Imps of the same and instructed them to tell the Crawls, too. Then, as the discussion was turning to logistics and specific requirements for food, we were disturbed--by screams.

The horrible, pain-filled screams reverberated from the throne room. I ran from the Clencher Cavern right away, turning the corner of the entrance hallway and almost fell in my haste to make it to the throne room and avert... whatever was going on. I didn't know what I was thinking. As I entered, my body froze right away, as the icy cold tendrils of the Soul Carver took hold and clenched. I was stuck, right there in the opening, forced to watch.

It was Eilet, the outspoken leatherworker who had cussed me out for wasting his precious materials on a collar while I had a perfectly good one resting inside the hoard already. There was no way to know what had led to the incident, but the result was horrifying. The thin creature hung spread-eagled in mid-air in front of the Soul Carver, spinning slowly. The necromancer was on his throne, eyes roaming intently over the Talpus as dark tendrils of power were rending the fur off the poor, defenseless critter.

I wasn't the only one to be drawn to the throne room by the anguished screams, but everybody wisely stayed back. We all watched as Eilet was flayed alive, the fur peeled back like a hunter removing the pelt of a downed animal. Then, the tendrils started experimenting, prodding and picking at the body, while the Talpus spun slowly right in front of the Soul Carver.

Meanwhile, the screams continued unceasing, like an under-lying melody, rising and sinking in force as the Talpus needed to stop for breath. I could feel my mind reeling from the visual assault, trying to escape to a safer place, but it wouldn't let me. I couldn't avert my eyes either, fixed in place as I was. He worked methodically and ceaselessly on the rest of the body, weighing and assessing my minion at every point. At some point, I real-ized that the Talpus had, blessedly, fainted or passed away, and the screaming was merely an echo continuing in my own head.

The investigation became more intrusive, and the tendrils started extracting entire parts now, assessing muscles and organs alike. Finally, the monstrosity on the throne got bored and tossed aside the body. The remains of Eilet hit the floor off to the side, and my treacherous mind couldn't help but notice how the blood slowly started filling in the blood grooves in the floor.

The Soul Carver, meanwhile, lifted his head to look straight at me. This time, his lips were turned down in displeasure. "Too weak." He moved his head from side to side, taking in the creatures standing on all sides, watching him in unspoken horror and disgust. "Disperse."

The word came clearly, and everybody fled. Everybody but me and Timothy, who was locked inside his Soul Circle with his back toward me. I was glad I couldn't see his face right that moment. He'd already gone through this several times, and now he was caught again.

My body suddenly moved, until I was facing the Soul Carver again, then he released control. It took all my self control to not leap at him, consequences be damned.

He spoke like he couldn't see the struggles in my eyes. "Overall, you have done well, my puppet. Your constructions show a good deal of potential. Their shortcomings can be attributed, in part, to your lack of understanding of this world and its inhabitants. We will adjust that now. First off, constructions. There is no need for Habitats. I will reclaim those rooms for my experiments.

"Wasting space and precious mana on the well-being of your underlings--it will not do. The Training Chambers and Sorcery Chambers, we will keep. I will be investigating soon whether my minions can make use of their gifts as well, since they are not constructions available to my class. Maybe it can stave off the physical and mental decay in my minions, but I doubt it."

His eyes roamed over me, as if he were looking for a reaction. I didn't know what to say. It was hard to tell from his tone of voice, but it didn't sound like he cared about my opinion.

"Your defenses are adequate. Outside the mountain, you would have issues with spellcasters. Here, it should be sufficient. I will add a few details myself. I am positively surprised by your research into poison as well. We shall keep that creature, and I will want to converse with it.

"However, there is no doubt as to where you have failed. Your origins have imbued you with a weakness I will soon remedy. Compassion. Failure back there shares the same weakness." A pale hand indicated Timothy inside his Soul Circle, and I looked at the bright form that was currently looking away from both of us. The Soul Carver continued. "We will keep the Clenchers. The Imps also have potential as distractions and elemental damage. The Talpi and Crawls, I will handle. They will be sufficient until we find some stronger bodies."

The casual way he said it almost made me miss the significance of his words. "What do you mean you will handle them?"

The pain shooting through my body disrupted every attempt at measured thought. "I believe I have told you not to interrupt? Ah, well. Telling you will be educational. I have enough low-quality soulstones to convert the Talpi and Crawls into real minions. With a bit of effort, they can be improved. The Talpi will still remain only marginally useful, but at least they will not keel over from every little piece of metal that should pierce their abdomen."

The calm with which he shared his methodical assessment of the situation made me realize something about the Soul Carver. While I had already pictured him as megalomaniacal, cruel, and heartless, I still thought of him as a human being with regular motives.

Nothing could be farther from the truth.

This was a monster in near-human form. And this monster was about to blow out the candle of Talpi and Crawl lives here in the domain, unless I did something. But what the hell could I possibly do? I would have to somehow reach him on his own level. Maybe... "Master?" The word tasted like ashes. "May I say something?"

"Of course." Like he was the soul of courtesy. Damn bastard. "If it is pertinent."

I bowed low and kept my head low. "With all due respect,"

which is not a lot, you rotting piece of offal, "I believe you have misjudged the worth of the Crawls and Talpi."

His eyes fixed on mine. While his face remained impassive, anger burned in those bright blue eyes of his like a bonfire. "Have I now? Are they not weak and slow, then? Do they not only gain a single attribute point each level? Will they be able to hold back an infuriated Tresher?"

"Obviously, you are right, Master." Maybe he could be reached with flattery. I'd try, at least. "However, I believe you are missing some details. The Talpi and Crawls are individually weak, sure. Yet they fight well together and reach a level of efficiency you wouldn't believe just by looking at them, especially with the training they've gone through and the dragon meat they've consumed. When we took down the green dragon, combined teams of Crawls and Talpi held off enemy Urten without any major problems. Also, even if they were completely useless in a fight, I would still keep them--because their real efficiency lies elsewhere."

I had his attention now. His gaze was entirely fixed on me. I used the opportunity and spoke as fast as I could. "First of all, Talpi are excellent scouts. They have to be, to survive for as long as they have with their weakness, like you so astutely noticed, Master. If you want to remain undiscovered, they will be a huge boon."

"Unless I have other ways of scouting that do not rely on weak bodies." He was smiling now. It looked like he was actually having fun, enjoying the game of it.

"There is that, of course. On top of their impressive perception and knowledge of the mountain, they also have an understanding of earth and rocks that is not easily matched. They excel with traps, and half of my defenses have been thought out by the Talpi. If you need a new tunnel created or need one collapsed, they will do a better job than minions twice their size.

"Yet, all that pales in comparison with the final utility of theirs, which lies with their shamans. That is how I managed to capture and train the Clenchers in the first place. They're *one* with earth and rock, making it flow like we would make water move just by moving it with a hand. Even if we ignore the usefulness of that for construction, the possible gains of having their shamans with us in fights far outweigh the issues with their lack of health and strength."

"You make for a compelling case. Now, explain exactly why I shouldn't just convert them? They will retain most of their mental attributes and former knowledge for some time, and the physical gains are unmatched."

Fortunately, the answer to that came straight from Arthor's teachings. "I doubt it would work. Shamans receive their mana and powers from the strength of the tribe. Does the link to Deyra still hold true if they're killed?"

"Converted," he corrected, but didn't even punish me for it. His eyes were staring out into the air, like he was thinking. "No. They would likely lose any shamanic capabilities. Alright. You have convinced me to give them a chance."

"Thank you, master. I assure you, you will not regret it."

"You misunderstand, Puppet. I give nothing away for free. I will give them a chance to *earn* their lives. Ready them. The test is arriving now."

CHAPTER TWENTY-ONE

Choose your battles like you choose your house. In both cases, you're the one most likely to wind up with the bill. - Carl Thurington

It looked like the preparation for some sort of game. Two teams lining up, each sizing up the other team, looking for weaknesses, discussing strategies, and trying to pump each other up. Except the game was deadly and real, and the other team was created of undead monsters. Well. Not all were monsters. Some were just regular undead, bipedal and humanoid, a few even fresh enough that I could still recognize their original race.

Most, however, were just that. Monsters. There were a few skeletal forms, but the vast majority still held onto their original meat. It had taken a while for me to reassure everybody that we were not under attack. I was happy I had--if the undead had decided to retaliate, I did not hold out hope that we would survive. Not against this army. As soon as my people had brought them back to my lair, they ran off to join their own, clearly afraid that they'd be killed or worse.

Because it was an army, not just a small shamble of undead.

There were groups and groups of the walking dead, or flawed souls, to use the lingo of the mountain. A pack of undead wolves waited next to two massive beasts that could originally have been ogres, trolls, or anything with "giant" in front of the name. Massive, reptilian shapes slithered on rotting scales while a large, three-headed monstrosity dragged rotten wings on the ground behind it.

Whatever else I might surmise about the Soul Carver, he was beyond a doubt a subscriber of the good old "bigger is better" club. At least a dozen of his creations had to duck to make it through the huge entrance, and another few, still waiting somewhere inside the Gallery of Illusions, had been forced to give up on entering entirely. Somewhere, the pale bastard had even gotten himself an undead wyvern.

The Soul Carver was in an excellent mood. Or, at least, that's what I surmised. He was as active as he'd ever been since I saw him, moving about between his undead horde, checking them all over. He turned toward me, and regardless of the dead look in his face, his eyes beamed with pleasure. "Excellent. Prolonged absence without reinforcement is always bad for their repair, but they have hardly been touched. It looks like they have made it here without any meaningful struggles. In any case, the Crawls should have scared away anybody inside the mountain so they were not spotted. I doubt anything would have been able to avoid the Roarer's attention."

"The Roarer, Master?" I moved closer, acting interested like a good little minion.

"No matter. What matters now is our challenge. You said that they were able to handle Urten with little challenge, right?"

"Yes. Five Urten, to be specific." Of course, there had been extenuating circumstances. Poison fog, Clenchers, my breath attacks, and a hell of a lot of distractions on either side. I was not certain they'd be able to handle as much entirely by themselves, but... they needed to impress the Soul Carver, or they would be history.

"Five Urten." He repeated it to himself. "That is nowhere near good enough. The defenses surrounding Selys are formidable. We shall need to test a variety of things. Say, speed, strength and... versatility." As he said the words, he motioned for three different creatures to move forward. The first was one of the huge undead snakes that slithered forward, bloated body surrounded with a dark miasma of sorts.

The second was one of the ogre-creatures, and it hefted a huge cleaver with enough nicks and dents that it almost looked like the broken-off wing of a wrecked airplane. The last one was a legless shape hovering in the air, that appeared nothing more than a carved-off torso of a well-armored knight. Each of the arms hefted a normal-sized polearm. The flyer was the smallest, but even without legs, he was half again as large as Erk, the largest of the Crawls. The Ogre was the largest. He had been forced to crawl through the entrance and stood at least twenty feet tall.

I looked from the three monsters to my minions and swallowed. They looked pathetic compared to the huge beasts. Even though they outnumbered the beasts by fifteen to one - more, with the Crawls I'd brought home, I couldn't see how they would be able to even hurt them. I kept it up with my subservient attitude. It looked like the Soul Carver responded best to that. "Master? A question?"

"Yes? You will not plead for mercy. I have made my decision."

"Never, Master." In the end, *you'll* be the one screaming for mercy, you unnatural fuck. "We have one additional fighter who you did not choose to include among the fighters. He has improved a lot. Could we be allowed to use Tim for the fight?"

"Tim?" His eyes moved upward as if he was searching for the connection. "Ah. Failure. Yes. You may. In fact, should he develop properly, I may have to rename him."

In the centre of the throne room, shadows played as the bright light that was Timothy bobbed over to join the Crawls and Talpi. Meanwhile, the Soul Carver sent everybody else away. The two of us ducked into the tunnel toward the Clencher Cavern, where we would have a full view of the entire throne room, where it would soon turn into a battlefield.

The soulless abomination who currently held all our lives in his rotting hand was surprisingly fair about it, even as he prepared his undead monstrosities to slay them all. He gave my people ten minutes to fetch their weapons and armor and talk tactics, but he didn't want me to join them. They were supposed to stand or fall by themselves. On the other side of the throne room, the undead monsters did nothing at all, didn't move a muscle, didn't taunt my people or prepare. Just stood there.

Before I knew of it, the time was up. My people were already divided into groups. Half of my minions were divided into five groups. These were meant for close combat, each with three Crawls in front, one armored and the rest on the flanks, and spear-wielding Talpi in the back. The other half of my people were gathered in a large, chaotic mass in the back.

The Soul Carver let his mental voice rise to where everybody present could hear it. "All right, my pets. Teach my Puppet a lesson!" And the huge undead beings rushed to comply.

A mere glimpse at the three undead monstrosities bearing down upon them was too much for some of my Talpi. Five of them turned tail and immediately raced for the exit, disappearing through the doorway to my room.

The Soul Carver reacted with a tiny chuckle, but said nothing. He was probably looking forward to hunting them down afterward. Except, their flight didn't look that panicked... I quickly focused my thoughts on something else, so the scary necromancer didn't realize that something was going on.

In the center of the room, the giant snake pressed onward, rushing to be the first to get at my people. It was met by three of the five groups of melee fighters and a veritable downpour of throwing spears.

On their left, the other two groups rushed past to engage the giant Ogre, and on their right, a single form moved out to face the floating torso--Roth. I almost screamed at him that this was no time for bravado, but obviously, he already knew. He raised his two-handed sword in a salute and ran forward, straight at the being. Behind him bobbed a glowing form, rushing behind him quickly, looking for all the world like an avenging angel. Bless you, Timothy.

The salute must have been a signal, because at that very point, the ranged damage intensified and spread out. Missiles flew, not only at the giant snake now, but at all enemies.

Their reactions were markedly different. The flying soldier ignored each and every missile, and they just pinged off his heavy iron armor. The Ogre was annoyed with the barrage, but only held up a hand to cover his face from the assault. The snake, with its girth, had no way of ignoring the spears and redoubled its efforts to close with my people.

They clashed in the middle of the throne room. There was no literal clash, however. Erk and two other Crawls crouched behind their long spears, and when the snake descended upon them, they threw themselves back at the last moment, allowing the snake to impale itself on the spears. While they ran back to equip themselves with fresh spears, the two other groups attacked the snake from the sides. While this was going on, the rest of my people closed with the Ogre and the flying torso.

The groups that closed with the Ogre halted the moment they got within melee range and started circling him. The Talpi melee fighters left the Crawls to keep his attention, while they moved around to engage his flanks and back. I had trouble seeing exactly what they *could* do. Even the Crawls didn't reach past the thigh of the huge figure, and the Talpi were even smaller. Roth... had slowed down, and was engaging the flying figure, completely focused as he advanced forward, weapon held up in a defensive position.

The ogre let fly a huge bellow and slammed his massive cleaver at the floor. The Crawl he aimed for jumped for his life and barely avoided the huge weapon. Even so, the force of the impact flung the Crawl to the ground, and while he rolled to get away, the Ogre managed to hit him with a glancing kick, flinging him several feet along the floor. While he was engaged, the other fighters closed in to wreak havoc on his legs, spears and other weapons carving and stabbing into the dark, rotting meat of his lower legs.

The snake did not take heed of the three pinpricks impaling its lower mouth as it tried to slither around to engage the forces on its flank. It could not disregard another issue, as its giant bulk was an issue in the large throne room. When it tried to slither to one side, the Crawls on that side flowed back and hid behind one of the large stone pillars, while the group on the other side took full advantage of the possibilities to try to force their way through the thick scales on its rotting side. They were not causing any verifiable damage, though, and the miasma below the snake sent out feelers toward any of the creatures that came near, sending loving caresses at their skin, to an unknown effect.

Roth had finally closed with the flying monster, and he was being pushed back, hard. Or, at least that's what it looked like. As the monster advanced in a hurricane of steel created by the whirling polearms, it was hard to see any form of combat from the tiny Talpus. Ringing sounds from the conflict clearly proved that he was parrying some of the attacks, even as he ran. The white cloud that was Timothy hung heavy over the flying form, and it was hard to see from a distance where Tim ended and the flying form started. The occasional stutter or hesitation in its onslaught were the only signs that Tim's attacks had any effect at all.

Things were not looking good for my people. It was hard for me to see how they would ever be able to cause damage to the undead creatures. My ranged fighters kept on their unceasing onslaught, to little effect. Whatever else the "conversion" of living creatures to undead caused, it clearly hardened the skin, and the throwing spears had trouble breaking through the skin to cause damage. Then, finally, the Shamans joined the fight. At first, it looked like they merely lugged rocks at the enemies. Rocks or not, they flew true and harder than they had any right to, especially from the spindly Creziel. Within moments, the Ogre and the snake were under a constant assault, as rocks flew straight at their faces, forcing them to keep their head averted from the shamans' projectiles.

Even with that addition, it was hard to see how my people would be able to triumph. Slowly, it was becoming apparent what the miasma below the snake did, as those it touched moved more sluggishly and slower, their strength sapped from them. First one, then three of the Talpi melee fighters were forced to disengage for a break.

Out of the blue, a high-pitched squeal sounded from above, and Roth reacted immediately. He disengaged from his flying attacker, running at full tilt past him toward the entrance of the room. After crossing half of the distance, he braked, skidding on his feet as he slowed, and turned back toward the flying soldier, spreading both arms in a taunting gesture.

Whatever else the flying creature was, it was not immune to being taunted, and it flew to take him down. Where before, the swings of the individual poleaxes blurred together to make them seem constant, unbelievably, the pace quickened and became closer to a 6-feet-tall meat grinder. Roth, to my surprise, did not back down.

He closed his eyes, an inner glow spread around him, and his pace quickened. And quickened. The two-handed sword whirled around him, forming an impenetrable barrier, holding back the heavy polearms. Once, he even managed to pierce the spinning cage of weaponry and land a solid hit on his enemy, but it bounced right off the hard armor.

Then another squeal interrupted the shouts, grunts and cries of battle. Roth did not hesitate, but flung himself back immediately, throwing the sword at his enemy to remove himself as quickly as possible. After deflecting the heavy weapon, the flier moved to follow, but Timothy acted now, laying into the opponent with constant mental attacks... and then it happened.

From above, an expanding mass fell down, splashing straight through Timothy's incorporeal form to hit the flying, armored monster fully, drenching him in a split second. Roth, meanwhile, kept on fleeing, flinging himself back to avoid even the slightest spatter of the liquid as if it were... poison. I had only just entertained the thought as the torso started twitching.

Tiny shaking movements soon turned into full-body convulsions as the liquid made its way between the gaps and holes of the armor to whatever flesh lay beneath. Within seconds, the flying figure flung his weapons away, as full-body shakes threw him to the ground. He lay there, twitching in obvious pain inside the spreading pool of death. Soon the shakes stopped, and he was finally still.

The Soul Carver's gaze focused on the murder hole in the ceiling, where the "fleeing" Talpi had released our container of nasty poisons. He then looked straight at me for several seconds, unspeaking. He gave no indication of his thoughts, but I got the sudden impulse to take a step back. Thankfully, he soon looked back to the throne room, where we could see that the Talpi had moved further along the hidden tunnels above and were using the holes in the ceiling to rain down spears on both the snake and the Ogre. The first enemy was down.

The other fights were not going as well. The Ogre was not a precision fighter. His attacks with the cleaver were large and wide, and he added to them with clumsy kicks and punches. Even I could see that he had terrible form. Still, with his bulk and strength, he did not *need* precision. Even as the flying torso stopped shuddering, he clipped one of the encroaching Talpi, sending him flying against the nearby wall with an audible crack. The tiny form did *not* get back up.

Two other unmoving forms were already dead or unconscious, and one Crawl was trying to wield his spear with one arm clearly broken. The only thing keeping the Ogre from taking out everybody was the constant ranged attacks. Some of the Talpi and Crawls were racing back and forth, picking up discarded throwing spears and rocks and bringing them back to the attackers. Marks on the ogre's legs showed where the attackers had done some damage, but his wide legs were still moving without issues.

The snake was in no hurry. It moved slowly, confident in its bulk and miasma doing enough damage to wear down any attacker. It was right, too. All Talpi had been forced to back off by now, some of them collapsing to be dragged away as their stamina ran out. Only the Crawls remained, advancing on the snake on all flanks, slashing and stabbing and they were clearly having issues, too.

Even as I watched, one Crawl failed to move back fast enough as the snake rolled its massive bulk over, and was trapped beneath the heavy form. The only sign of weakness in the snake was a single throwing spear that had impaled the left eye of the monster in a lucky throw, robbing it of half its vision.

Again, squeaks sounded through the room as Arthor gave his orders. At this point, the attacks of the Crawls were visibly losing some of their strength. It looked like they were starting to succumb to the dark tendrils of the miasma. They were still keeping back the snake, while the ranged attackers and the shamans maintained their constant barrage.

At that point, either the Soul Carver gave an order, or the snake finally got it through its thick skull that the real threats were the shamans and ranged attackers arrayed toward the back of the throne room. The huge animal relentlessly pushed forward, ignoring the tired Crawls that tried to hold it back with inefficient stabs and slashes, then a shudder ran through its body.

Roth had joined the fight with a vengeance, and his heavy slash had torn open a wide gash in the face of the snake, laying open half its face. Acting instinctively, it pulled back, only to be met by another attack, as Erk pushed his heavy spear through an existing wound on the other side, inserting half the spear before twisting and pulling it back out. At the same time, the ranged attackers kept up their assault, tormenting the snake with pinprick attacks to the face, boosted by Timothy's glowing presence.

For five seconds, ten, the snake was reeling, attacked from both sides by Erk and Roth. But then it regained its senses and struggled onward, ignoring two heavy attacks from its opponents to close with the ranged attackers. My Talpi split away, rushing to either side, except for two of them. Arthor and Creziel stood their ground, just feet away from the throne, ignoring its onslaught, sending jagged rocks at its face, while Tim lit them up from behind with his boosts, giving the shamanic duo an almost angelic look.

I almost did something stupid at that moment. Seeing my minions, no, damnit, my friends, staring death in the eyes, while I just stood and stared was almost too much. Next to me, the smile of the Soul Carver warned me off. Any interference, and he was sure to kill them all.

The snake ignored any and all distractions, even Erk and Roth doing a number on its flank while it was distracted. It rose up, towering before Creziel and Arthor, rising up to crush them with its massive bulk. At the very last moment, they acted, springing to either side. Arthor made it fully away, but Creziel didn't, earning a hit on the back to throw him across the floor, like a barbie doll discarded by an offended toddler.

However, the trap had been sprung. When they jumped aside, they revealed what they had been building right behind their backs. Heavy spears were somehow stuck in the floor itself, affixed as if they were part of the construction. Where the heavy form of the snake's front crashed down, the spears tore their way straight through the body, forced through by its own bulk. The snake shuddered and tried to rise again. Tried and failed.

A mere dozen feet away, Arthor stood, concentration clearly written on his face as his focus was entirely on where he had just stood. Creziel was on the far side, pale with pain, but also focusing on the snake... and whatever they were doing, worked.

The large serpent tried to remove itself from the damaging spears, but failed.

It pulled once, then twice, confused with what was going on, and then went completely berserk. It twisted its entire length, trying to force whatever was keeping it down apart, rolling up the body and extending it again at whiplash speed. A loud cracking sound announced that one of the spears had snapped.

The rest of my people weren't just keeping back. They saw the struggle going on, and the entire throne room looked alive, as all Talpi and Crawls except the ones around the Ogre rushed to close with the snake. Within seconds, its second eye closed forever and the huge, undead animal recoiled from the mass of attacks that tore into its entire length. Finally, a high-pitched triumphant yell erupted from Roth, as his heavy strike carved its way *through* a third of its body, and the damn thing finally lay still.

A tired shout had the swarm of tired Talpi and Crawls split again, removing themselves from the fading miasma around the snake. Only Creziel and Arthor remained, too tired to move, along with Roth, who was stumbling around as if drunk, drenched with the rotting insides of the serpent.

Were the undead able to think? I like to think that the Ogre must have felt at least a hint of fear or unease at the sight of the entire remaining force of Crawls and Talpi bearing down upon him. If he did, he hid it well. An ear-splitting bellow escaped him, as he brought his cleaver around in a wide stroke, keeping all enemies at bay. The only thing he got for his troubles was a massive onslaught of throwing spears. One of them tore through his entire cheek, throwing a few teeth to the ground in a spray of rotting meat and black blood.

The huge, heavy-hitting Ogre didn't go down easy. In fact, he managed to hold off everybody for several tortuous minutes. In the end, Erk was the one to make the difference. He kept the Ogre occupied, managing to avoid or deflect the much heavier weapon of the Ogre with his long, heavy spear, allowing the others to attack unpunished.

Eventually, the Ogre did go down, buried in the sea of smaller critters. First, one massive tree trunk of a leg gave out, tendons cut to ribbons. Then, in a mass of attacks, the huge form slowly lost its strength. When, finally, the huge cleaver fell from its hand, my minions arose against the large beast in a massive onslaught. Seconds later, the huge form stopped moving altogether as they methodically dismembered it. The yells of triumph that came from my minions raised my spirits along with theirs, joy letting tears spring to my eyes.

Then the Soul Carver stepped forward.

Silence spread over the room quickly, with a few creatures who were slow to grasp what had just taken place being hushed by their neighbors. All celebration was forgotten and replaced with held breath.

The Soul Carver looked at the room, taking in everything, judging and weighing everybody with his eyes. Eventually, his mental voice rang out. It was as emotionless as ever, but the message was clear. "You will do. I want the Throne Room cleaned by tonight. Now, get to work."

My people kept their heads down and got to work, moving first to help the unconscious and injured brethren. The pale mage had already forgotten all about them as he turned toward me. "Lesser persons would not keep to their promises. You are fortunate that I am not such a person. Your critters will form part of the spearhead that will pierce Selys' defenses. You should be proud."

I should be proud that he'd use my people as the first ones to throw against Selys' forces? Yeah, no. "I am proud, Master. I never doubted their performance, though I did fear that your monsters were too much of a match. Especially that flying one."

His eyes closed halfway for a moment. Was that displeasure? It was hard to read the emotions of somebody who didn't seem to have emotions like the rest of us. "Yes. I wonder how they learned that the Korvan was still truly alive? That poison would not have done any good against somebody already converted.

"Still, it matters not. They handled themselves very well,

making up for their sorry strength with agility, teamwork, and quick thinking. Now. I am going to be left alone for the rest of the day. I have a lot of repair work before me, and will have to see if the Korvan can be converted."

He sounded almost eager.

CHAPTER TWENTY-TWO

The next couple of days were a flurry of activity. We remained unbothered by the Soul Carver, who locked himself inside what used to be the Crawls' Habitat. We moved everybody inside the Clencher Cavern instead. Since the experience with Eilet, we figured that as few chance encounters with the Soul Carver as possible was the way to go. The cleanup went surprisingly fast. Moving the corpses of the undead creatures was the hardest thing, and we were forced to let the Ogre stay where it was. It simply couldn't fit into the side corridor. Fixing the floors and the tilework was up to Arthor and Creziel, and I doubt Creziel disliked the chance to work sitting down. He had dislocated a shoulder and suffered from a sprained leg, along with other minor injuries.

Among the injured, Creziel had gotten off easy. The effect of the dark miasma from the snake wore off after a handful of hours, which left the majority of my melee fighters pretty well off. The groups who had squared off against the Ogre had not gotten off so easy. We had suffered two losses--two Crawls who had taken direct hits from the huge beast. On top of that was a huge number of non-life-threatening injuries that attested to the force, if not the accuracy, of the now permanently dead Ogre. Broken and bruised ribs, arms, and legs were commonplace among those who'd faced the towering beast.

Regardless, we had everybody training. Everybody. Even the ones who were suffering from bad injuries found the energy to sit inside the Training Chambers, performing whichever exercises their injuries allowed them to. The battle we had just survived showed without a doubt that we would all need to grow strong if we wanted to make it.

I still hadn't applied any of my level-ups since hitting level 19. Everything had happened so fast since we reached the white's domain and I had never had that chat with Tim. Now, I had made it to level 20 and even had a new feat waiting, but didn't want to make any final decisions until I was certain about the escape plan. I was going to be clever about this. Still, the impatience was real.

On the day after the battle, I joined Arthor inside the Sorcery Chamber. He was currently sitting in the middle of the room, cross-legged, while four large rocks rested on the floor around him. The emotion washing off of him was of despair. "I made a mistake, lizard."

"What do you mean? Joining forces with me?"

"Pfah. Yes. That too, I suppose. No. In the battle."

Ah. Now I knew what he was hinting at. "We all do, Arthor. You survived. That's all anybody can ask."

Ignoring my comment, he frowned and shook his head. "Pfah. As I require my own to face their failures, so I should accept my own. I should have sent three groups against the brute. I believed it clumsy enough that we should be able to distract it and evade its attacks with ease while we took down the others. Meanwhile, the snake escaped my stone spears. Were it not for Creziel's new feat that lets him manipulate rock with a speed to leave me in the dust, it would have escaped entirely and doomed us all."

I laid down right in front of Arthor and brought my head down to rest on the floor. "Arthor. You and I don't always see eye to eye. By now, you know that I care for you Talpi almost as much as you care for your own. With that in mind, understand that I mean it from the bottom of my heart when I say this: Second-guessing is for suckers. Also, if our roles were reversed, you would be telling me the same. You took a chance, and somehow you managed to come out on top *and* outmaneuvered the Soul Carver himself. That is not a mistake--that is success. Also, if you need to blame somebody for failing, blame me. I gambled everything on returning with Selys at our side, and lost."

He glared at me. "Don't think for a second that I'm not blaming you." A couple of seconds later, he let his head hang. "Pfah. Who am I kidding? You're not to blame for anything else than existing, and that's as much on Deyra as it is on you. We knew the risks when we first learned that the Soul Carver was the one who had been here before, yet decided to make it our home regardless of that information."

He grunted with effort and, one by one, the stones left the ground and wobbled into orbit around him. The tall Talpus sneered and closed his eyes. "Speaking of the Soul Carver, lizard. We need a plan. You saw what he did to Eilet."

"I agree. We need to be ready to act. At the very least, we need a good plan for running, if it comes to it."

"Yes. We believe that we would be able to get away from his creatures if we can just escape the domain. His words are just that--words. Who would care about finding some Talpi?"

"First of all, that's Talpi, Imps, *and* Crawls. You might not like it, but you're together in this now. If you're running, I want you to take them."

The rocks clattered onto the floor, and Arthor stood up, scowling. "The Imps? That's not going to happen. Pfah. Can you even *picture* hiding somewhere with them? We'd be dead within minutes."

I closed my eyes. "Arthor. I was expecting this, but I still want you to reconsider. Think about your answer. Just a month ago, you thought the exact same way about the Crawls. Worse, perhaps. Now, you didn't even complain when I told you to bring them. So consider this: Do you *really* want to let the Imps fend for themselves, when you have the chance to save them and put them in your debt forever? Those flying creatures who have the ability to go anywhere, have no sense of fear when it comes to combat, and who pack a serious punch in ranged combat?"

For a moment, I believed that I'd overdone it, but then he started chuckling. The ever-cranky shaman who was always ready with criticism or a harsh word chortled, shaking his head. "You are so incredibly annoying, dragon."

"I know. And I'm right too, am I not?"

"You are. The potential boons from bringing the annoying loudmouths outweighs the risks, especially if we can come up with a plan for escaping. Has the Soul Carver noticed the emergency exit behind the Shadow Door?"

"I don't think so. He hasn't mentioned anything. Still, I can't be certain. Seeing through illusions is a matter of Mental Control and Mental Power, and his far outweighs mine."

Arthor nodded, lost in thought. "So all we need to do is bring everybody to the exit tunnel at the right time, without alerting the Soul Carver or any of his minions... that might be doable, especially if we establish some sort of distraction. We could arrange a collapse somewhere in the adjacent tunnels, for instance. Maybe bury a few of his minions."

"I like that idea. Work with it a bit, and come back to me with your ideas. We can arrange when to do it. It would need to be soon, I fear. I... can't read him, but I feel that things are going to get worse here soon."

"Agreed." Arthor frowned, then looked up at me. An unfamiliar emotion burst from him. Surely it wasn't... worry? "What about you?"

I showed him all my teeth. "Don't worry about me, Arthor. I can get away whenever I feel like it--well, as long as that freak isn't anywhere near me. I was thinking I would aim straight for Selys, tell her what's going on, and help her finish him off."

Arthor did not look convinced. "Okay. Even if you do manage to run from the Soul Carver and all of his minions-- and he *is* going to come for you, don't doubt that for a second-- what makes you think Selys won't just kill you instead of helping you? You're clearly a danger."

I opened my mouth and then closed it again, expelling a huff of air between my teeth. "Okay, it's not a perfect plan. I mean, you think I like the idea of leaving Timothy behind? Or Ursam and the other Clenchers? I just can't see how to ensure that I get everybody out. It would require for us to get both that pale bastard *and* all his stinking minions out of the domain, and that's just not happening. It's a shitty situation - but it's the best idea I've got right now."

Very slowly, the recalcitrant Talpus reached out and patted my paw. "I understand, Onyx. We will do our best to help. I'll admit that I would be... annoyed to see you go, as well. We have gotten used to your presence by now."

I stared at the shaman. That was the most overt display of emotions I'd seen from him. "The same goes for you, Arthor. I'd hate to not have all these tiny underlings to order around all the time. Even so, if you get the chance to get out, I want you to take it. I will remain safe, at least to begin with. The Soul Carver needs my help for his revenge, whatever he's plotting. It's not like he lets me in on his plans."

"We will, Onyx. We will. If we get the chance, we will tell you."

On my way back from the Sorcery Chamber, I couldn't help but smile. Doing something, even if it was just plotting for an eventuality that would never take place, felt good. I hated this busywork, tiptoeing around the place, hoping that today was not the day where the Soul Carver was going to perform another atrocity. To be fair, though, he hadn't even left the room he'd taken up for his repairs. He seemed to be a bit of a workaholic.

Timothy wasn't doing too good. I found it hard to blame him. After a long period of pain and suffering, he got his first vision of what life could be like if he was allowed his personal freedom. Then, just like that, he was dumped straight back into his old life of servitude and mistreatment. I checked in with him whenever possible, and tried to chat with him about Earth-stuff and anything very much not associated with his present situation as a captive slave.

Today, I had a hard time getting him to play ball, however. "What is the point, Carl?"

"The point is that, if we haven't thought ahead, we'll never be able to introduce a system that works here, and they'll be stuck with an overgrown lizard in charge for eternity. Nobody wants that."

Tim wasn't having it. "Just stop." He flowed to the far side of the Soul Circle, glancing behind me to the far end of the throne room, ensuring, beyond any doubt, that the Soul Carver wasn't in session. "We are so far away from being in a place where we have any actual influence on how the future society of this dump looks, it's not even funny."

"No." I lowered myself to where my head was right before the floating ball of light and looked earnestly into his eyes. "I get what you're saying, Tim. I really do. But I refuse to accept it. Did I ever tell you exactly what my first sensation inside this world was?"

He didn't answer, and I continued relentlessly. "A spear wound. That's how they welcomed me here, trying to poke me full of holes and make me into dinner. I don't know how often I've almost died here--from teeth, weapons, or magic. But every time, I've survived and grown and learned from the goddamn experience. So excuse me if I'm not going to lie down on the job and chant 'woe is me' just because some goddamn freak has my balls in a vise. Now, help me here, man. What's the next step? How do we move on from dictatorship?"

Tim's gaze unfocused and then his eyes screwed up. "Gah. I really didn't need that visual. All right, point taken. We can do this." He closed his eyes and went still for a moment. "Okay. So we picture that the bastard is dead, you've taken over the mountain, and we need to move on. We need..." His mental voice trailed off, then returned, more sure of himself. "We have to create some sort of stepping stone between dictatorship and whichever system we'll be going for in the end. In this way, the different races and tribes can join the power structure, become accustomed to having a say, and you still have the authority to stop them if they get out of line."

"That sounds like a logical next step. Hell, it feels like we've almost been aiming for that anyway."

He looked up. "You mean with the councils and all? Yeah. The only thing we really need to do would be to hand some actual authority over to the others, then formalize the process. Oh, and pinpoint how we select who goes on the council. Then we would in practice have ourselves a working oligarchy of sorts."

"Oh. Yeah, that makes sense. Do you have any suggestions as to how we should choose?"

He shrugged, and his form blurred out into obscurity. "It very much depends on what we want and how far-reaching we want these changes to be. If we want to focus on gaining in strength, we could make a sort of stratocracy, select the highest-leveled among us. If we want to focus on skills and knowledge, we should go for some species of technocracy, select those who are the most adept at their fields."

His softly glowing shape solidified with a delighted grin. "Come to think of it, my recommendation would be to aim for a system where we choose people based on their abilities, contributions, or their honor. Y'know, a meritocracy or... Timocracy."

A snort escaped me. "...Really? That's a horrible joke."

He flung his arms out to the side with an innocent expression. "Hey man, I don't make the rules. I'd ask you to Wiki it, but even back on Earth, you probably wouldn't know how to do that."

I rolled my eyes *hard*. "So, this... meritocracy." I blatantly ignored the other possibility. "I like that idea. That would allow us to select important areas then promote the people who contribute the most and add new areas as things develop."

"Yup." Tim seemed less despondent now as he focused on the task.

We spent a while discussing the possibilities, without settling in on the exact constellation. When I left him, he was deep in thought, and we had boiled the task down to a number of decisions before we were ready to present it to the others.

I swung by my own room. Technically, the Soul Carver's room, but it didn't look like he had moved back in. At a glance, the Shadow Door looked intact and hidden. I sure wasn't going to chance opening it. I continued on, my route taking me further, past where the pasty-faced old necromancer was busy reconstructing his slabs of flesh and ducked under the low doorway to enter Laive's room.

The Soul Carver was an enigma. There was no denying that he was a complete horror, with little resemblance to a human being except for the exterior. However, on certain topics, he was surprisingly progressive. The moment he'd understood that Laive could possibly learn to concoct some combat-efficient poisons, he not only let her survive, he also let her keep the room. Right now, she was hard at work in the leftmost side of the chamber. She was watering a set of troughs that took up about a third of the wallspace. They looked like they contained...

"Looks like you're keeping busy. Is that dirt?"

The no-nonsense Talpus didn't even bother to turn around. "Yes, Onyx. It's just dirt. Just like all the stuff on the other side is *just* poison."

"Great point. Could you show me what you're working on? I would help, but soil is pretty far from being my specialty."

She shrugged and allowed me to move closer. She spent half an hour letting me in on her projects. It was all surprisingly methodical and analytical, more so than what I had expected from the no-nonsense, hard-working Talpus at first. She was currently working on three different projects: one looking into the effects of growing different combinations of crops, one measuring the effects of different moisture levels on different types of crops, and one doing the same with different levels of enrichment by manure. The room smelled ripe. Laive could see my lack of interest in the soil, because she soon moved over to the interesting part.

"I would never have guessed that these tests could be so damn *slow*! It sounds easy, doesn't it? Find poisonous plants and animals, take their poison, and try to combine and strengthen them? Right. So far, it's been a couple of weeks, and I'm still trying to figure out exactly which parts of these twenty plants are poisonous."

I tilted my head. "Why do you need... no, wait, I get it."

She nodded. "A poison created from the full plant is going to be far less potent than the one created only from the poisonous part. Of course, everybody has told me what they know about poison, but we have never had the time to settle in and really learn. That means my tests are going to be... well, practical."

I looked at the new crude stone cages that had been installed at the back of the room. I heard skittering from back there. "I'm guessing that's what those cages are for?"

"Yes. Vourens have some of the hardiest constitutions in the mountain. If poison works on them, it's going to work on everyone."

That sounded familiar from my world. If it could kill a roach, it was bound to work for other insects. Still, I could see some potential issues arising from that approach. "In time, we would do well with a second form of test. For now, this seems like the best we can do. So, have you got anything for me? What was the poison they used for that flying monster?"

"The poison *I* used," she corrected me. "Cherka Root is tasty and filling, but if you boil the tip, it becomes poisonous. I am glad that I got to talk with your glowing companion before he left. I don't know all the plants he referenced from the writings on the wall, but this one is common."

I could feel a grin growing on my face. "Wait a minute. Are you telling me that you used the Soul Carver's own recipe to kill his minion?"

She shrugged. "Yes. It's not perfect, and needs large doses to work, but as you could see, it does kill. I needed to use all the Cherka Root we had, and still had to dilute it in order to have a decent quantity. It was a huge risk, but we must have managed to get some inside its orifices."

I shook my head, impressed. "How did you know it would work?"

"Ask Wreil, if you care to know about the flying creature. It's his memory to share. Now, this is one of the two only effective poisons we have to date. But, unfortunately, it doesn't hold up to being out in the open. You cannot apply it to your weapons unless you use it right away. I hope to find a way to make it useful on spears... perhaps a paste of some sort, sealing the effect until it pierces a body." She shrugged and pointed at two other containers. "I am going to work on these two in the near future. Marretseeds paralyze instead of killing, and the stalk of the Tealcore causes horrible, instantaneous indigestion. That last one, I can tell you about from experience, if you would like."

I looked at Laive from out of the corner of my eye. I felt nothing but businesslike earnesty from her. Really? "No thank you. I would love to hear about any major updates and breakthroughs, though. You said you knew one other poison already?"

"Yes. Calben root. The leaves of the plant are edible and tasty. The root, meanwhile, kills if you eat it. It is not dangerous to the touch." She shrugged. "I will work to see if I can refine it further. For now, I have given a handful of large examples to our scouts. They may be able to kill enemies by planting the root inside some meat... or however they tend to handle their traps. Aelis sounded like she had some ideas."

I nodded. "Well done, Laive. I am impressed by your work."

I stuck my head outside the door, glancing down the hall before continuing, "Has the Soul Carver been bothering you?"

She shook her head. "Quite the opposite. He showed a lot of interest in my work. Rather logical, that. His unliving minions are not affected by most poisons. You could apply a contact poison to an undead Talpus, for instance, and our speed, small size, and agility would be enough that we would be able to apply the poison and kill far larger enemies."

I tried to hide my disgust at her words. Was she getting friendly with him? Her next words dispelled that fear.

"He smells wrong, though. Unnatural. I don't want him near us, if you could do something about it. Can you?"

I let out a sigh of relief. No need to start watching over my own people. "I'm trying my best, but I doubt it. There's one thing you can do to help. If you have any new discoveries, don't tell him unless he specifically asks. If he does, tell him everything."

She nodded, matter of fact. "I will."

I was soon back in the Clencher Cavern. The noise level was impressive. There was plenty to hate about the current situation, but I could find one good thing about it: Everybody was so fed up with the current situation that they took their training seriously. Even the Imps were hard at work, performing mock fights against a handful of Crawls inside the Training Chamber.

CHAPTER TWENTY-THREE

In any war, the first casualty is common sense, and the second is free and open discussion. - James Reston

The next day we spent exploring the bond between the Soulstone and myself. Except, that description is inaccurate. No, the right thing to say would be that the Soul Carver had a hoot testing out the limits and capabilities of the Soulstone on me. I was there for the fun and games, but the experience was very much not fun for me.

"The experience," the Soul Carver intoned, as he had me running around the throne room, "is like trying on a new glove. You know how a glove works. You may know the materials and even the method of construction used to create the glove. Still, before you try out the glove for yourself, it is an unknown. Is the fit comfortable? Will it need to be widened? Is the grip acceptable? Does it adjust itself well to hard use? Only a few hours of tests will be able to answer these questions."

I was stuck inside my mind, fuming. I was going to wear *him* like a fucking glove. Wait. No, scratch that analogy. Even as I rebelled in my mind against the force of his mind taking over and leaving me trapped as an observer, I started doing something I should've started the first time he caught me. I observed and learned.

First off, I worked to find the edges of his control. Exactly to which degree was he able to contain me? Were there any limits and how would I be able to challenge them? Were there any subconscious routines I could take over to impede him at the right time? The answer here was, unfortunately, no. I spent a while lamenting my decision to not choose the feat that improved my mental defenses.

Still, it might not have made a difference, as the results of my experiments were irrefutable. His control over my body was immediate and absolute. As long as I was within his reach, he was able to control me, seemingly without any effort on his part. Certain parts were beyond him, like using my wings properly. That, or he just didn't care to use the time necessary to learn it at the moment.

One single thing I did take with me was that he didn't need to touch the Soulstones to play around. Having them safely back in the hoard was enough for him. That seemed like a useful thing to learn. Knowing how to use it to my advantage was another thing.

He mastered the use of my breath weapon within minutes. Not only that, he quickly learned to adjust and efficiently distribute the tiny droplets of my attack. Even furious as I was, I was impressed by the intellect that lay behind the absolute raving lunatic. I knew I didn't take to it that naturally. However, there was one part that evaded him.

"Tell me about your other abilities, in detail this time."

Damn. I'd better be careful. Couldn't give the game away. "Well, they are somewhat limited and not as direct as other dragons. I am able to manipulate shadows within the domain, for instance, and create a layer of illusion to camouflage my minions anywhere." He relaxed his control, and I showed him what I meant, enveloping a passing Crawl in illusionary shadows.

"On top of that, I am able to create a Shadow Whorl, impeding the vision and confusing the senses of any attackers." Again, I showed him, creating a whirling ball of furious, moving shadows further down the corridor. "I will be honest with you. My survival to date is not due to the power of my abilities. Sure, they have helped. Still, my success is mostly due to my focus on constructions and good use of my minions. If I hadn't had this domain to start from or creatures that complimented my own weaknesses? Things would have looked much worse for me."

The Soul Carver looked at me for a long time. His eyes betrayed nothing and his emotions were, as always, walled away. "There is no sense of deception from you. I would have expected that by now. I may have to change my initial plan." He was silent for a while. "You are a means to an end. Understand that. I did not single you out or select you. I do not *care* about you. I care about efficiency.

"This is why I wanted to become the master of the mountain in the first place. I need good materials in order to experiment and improve my Soulstones, and the mountain has those in spades. Also, it would make a good staging point for creating a proper kingdom. When Selys brought up her silly requirements for becoming her follower, I realized I would not be able to follow through with my plans as her vassal. I would need to replace her instead.

"I might have been able to defeat her back then, had it not been for the fire. I was and remain stronger than her, but her fire attacks and those of her minions are supremely damaging to my minions, and she never risked a battle where I would be able to pin her down and overwhelm her with numbers. It was far easier for her to just torch my forces and wait.

"While it is easy for me to obtain bodies inside the mountain, the conversion takes time, and she was faster. In short, I need to get close to her in order to end her and take over the mountain." His lips contorted upward in what could, with a great deal of largesse, be interpreted as a kind of smile.

"At first, I believed you would be like the other dragons, treacherous and short-sighted. However, it would appear that your old world has allowed you to remain a creature that is ruled by logic instead of emotions. Hence, I will change my approach. My original plan was to sacrifice you in order to gain the optimal advantage against Selys. Now, as long as you cooperate fully, I will let you live as my second in command."

He would let me live? How extraordinarily kind of him. I tried to quell the fury inside of me and speak only the truth. At this point I felt confident that whatever his Mental Power was, as long as I didn't outright lie, he was unable to see through nuances. "I will do my utmost to survive, Master. I do believe that you are very capable of letting yourself be ruled only by logic." Twisted, nutjob logic but still....

He nodded. "You will still have to face Selys and survive. That is a difficult task. Still, I will let you have free rein in the battle to distract and avoid her attacks as you wish. Then, if you succeed, you will be able to reign the mountain below me."

"That is very generous of you. I had not expected that, to be honest." It was true. I hadn't. In fact, I still didn't. I counted on the pale bastard to change his mind on a whim and do exactly what suited him at any moment, and if I disagreed or slighted him in the least, to turn me into an undead dragon.

He nodded. "I would not offer that to just anybody. Yet, I believe we will be able to usher in a new era of efficiency to this world. There is so much waste and inefficiency here, areas ruled by petty warlords and people without even the most basic mental capabilities."

Of course, this did not mean that we were done with him dominating me. No, we spent another half day before he was satisfied with his control over my body and capabilities. He also reached a decent control over the Shadow Whorl, but he did not figure out that I hadn't told him about my Illusion skill. His control over those abilities, however, was less thorough, and it felt like I might be able to tear control from him in a stressed situation. Still, my main focus during those hours lay in the Soulstone.

As the Soul Carver toyed around with his control, struggling to gain access to my spell-like abilities, he took it out for me to see for the first time. With my body fully subsumed by the damn necromancer, I was unable to focus on it as much as I liked, but at least, I was able to catch some glimpses of it every now and again.

The word "stone" was misleading, I soon learned. In fact, it looked more like a bar of brownish metal. On all sides, the metal was adorned by dark runes, seemingly burned into the metal. It was hard for me to control the hatred inside myself. If only I was able to destroy that damn thing, we could run off, and the Soul Carver would have no way of catching up with us. He didn't let the metal bar out of his sight for a moment, though.

Understandable, when it was the lynchpin to his plans here in the mountains. Still... watching yet another tantalizing glint of the damn thing from inside his coat sparked a plan into being. No, at this time, it was just a hint of a plan. Maybe there was an alternative to running for the hills and hoping for the best. I just had to make sure that I remembered exactly what the damn thing looked like.

When the Soul Carver let me go that day, it was with another unnatural smile on his face. If I didn't know better, I would think that he was trying to be companionable. Well, I was going to milk that for all it was worth. And, in the meantime, I would plan his downfall. Any ideas of just swiping the soulstone were crushed, as he placed it carefully back inside the hoard, when we were done. Still, I knew more now and had an inkling of a plan. A brief discussion with Arthor had him agreeing with the concept, and soon, a custom order would see the light of day.

Later that day, I chanced upon the Ogre again. He was standing inside the throne room, placid and with an empty look on his face--business as usual for the undead minions when they weren't working. He was ugly. Heh. Even uglier than he was before. His legs especially had been savaged in the fight. It looked like somebody had taken the flesh on his legs and forced it to flow, until it covered the damaged places. The same went for all the other stab and slash marks - they had been filled with the same gel-like material, like somebody decided to repair a stab victim with silly putty. It worked, though. There'd be no denying that. And while the strength and durability of the Ogre might be impaired, I still had no intentions of going up against him.

Now that the Soul Carver was done with his reparations, he spent more time around the domain again. His first glowing construction inside the throne room finished, and was soon joined by a second one, inside my old room. I selected Inspect, and was rewarded with the nasty realization that those blood grooves weren't for fun. In fact, the first construction was a center of dark energy, constructed exactly where the grooves joined in front of the throne.

[**Essence Siphon**.
This Siphon works to transform the spilled lifeblood of any being into temporary power for the creator. As the domain improves, so will the boons and duration of the increases.
- *Duration of temporary increase is doubled.*
- *On top of the increases, lifeblood will also replenish the life and mana of the creator. If he is already fully healed, the health and mana will be added as temporary points on top of his current points.*]

Yeah, I wouldn't be attacking him straight-on any time soon.

I was discussing the progress with Aelis in the evening. The Talpi were currently keeping up their scouting around the domain, but were not allowed to range further. She wanted me to argue with the Soul Carver to expand their routes, to ensure that we wouldn't be attacked by roving forces. I, on the other hand, just didn't see the point. If, by some miracle, any attackers managed to get all the way through our defenses, they'd still be obliterated by the Soul Carver. The quiet voice that slithered into my mind interrupted that discussion quite nicely. "Puppet. Join me."

There was no gainsaying that. I got up and rapidly moved toward the throne room. He was conspicuously absent. A cold sensation moved up my spine. The door to my old room was wide open, and a pale white sheen came from inside. As I entered the room, the first thing that became apparent was Timothy. He was unnaturally quiet, translucent body collected and looking straight toward me. The look on his face was uncommonly easy to read: starknaked fear.

As I walked on, the reason for his distress became apparent. The Soul Carver was busy working on his walls again, expanding on one of the sections that he had left unfinished. It looked like he was back to his old research. That paled next to what stood right next to him. A dark entrance beckoned, from where the Shadow Door stood open, illusion dispelled. Fuck. He found the escape tunnel.

"Ah, Puppet. Would you care to explain this?"

With a sinking heart, I did my best to act as if I didn't know what he was talking about. "The Shadow Door? It was my idea. I thought that an emergency exit would be a good idea, in case we were to be attacked by a superior enemy. It leads to a remote area slightly above ours."

"Solid reasoning. Now, explain why you did not tell me about it in the first place."

"I forgot." "I didn't think you would care." "I wasn't going to use it anyway." All these lies sprang to mind and got rejected in a split second. He would see through me instantly. I decided to try something else and faced him, putting on my most earnest face. "Backup. Basically, I had no way of knowing whether life under you would be unbearable. Not mentioning the Shadow Door meant that I would have a viable escape route in case I decided it became too much."

He mulled it over for a moment. When he talked again, his

voice was contemplative and cool, but it did hold a side note I found hard to place. Admiration? No. Maybe? "This is the trouble with intelligent assistance. Intelligence and loyalty do not go well together."

I didn't say anything. What could I say? "I wasn't going to use it?" Yeah, right.

"I will have the exit demolished by tonight, and my guard will be doubled. There will be no escape for you." His lips jolted up in that not-quite-smile of his. "I will grant you this for your honesty. When we defeat Selys, you will still be allowed to survive."

I bowed, as low as my body allowed. Damn. It was bad enough I wasn't getting away, but this ruined everything for my people. "Thank you, Master."

"Good. As for now, you knew what your risk would entail, did you not?"

"I did. I decided taking the chance would be worth it."

It was not worth it. Not in a million years.

The following torment was worse than when I tore off three of my nails on my left hand. Worse than when an errant piece of machinery laid my leg open to the bone. Through decades of working with tools and in situations where accidents do happen, I've established quite a pain threshold. It was not up to the task.

My body was frozen, but I could feel the waves of pain tearing through me, pulling away strips of my sanity in the process. It did not end. Wave after wave hit me, each one cresting higher, leaving me itching, hoping, *begging* for unconsciousness to take me. When, at long last, the pain subsided and I was allowed control of my own body, I curled up into a small ball and just lay there, shuddering.

The Soul Carver's mental voice was devoid of intonation. "In a month or three, you and I will take a handful of your tiny minions as bait and go out to defeat the rest of the dragons, including those you call allies. We do not need allies for my plan to succeed. We need you to be strong. Now, I will need you until we reach Selys. However, if you try anything like this again, I will take my chances without you, carve out your soul, and have you join the rank of my flawed minions."

I found it hard to come up with any good answers to that. A while later, I was allowed to leave.

CHAPTER TWENTY-FOUR

The domain was destroyed. Bodies of dead minions lay everywhere, constructions torn apart, and every pile turned over in the search for anything useful. I was in a state of shock. I had made it a habit to check in with my allies each morning and evening, check out what was going on.

Creive was doing well, rebuilding and improving his upside-down fortress slowly, while maintaining his stranglehold on the area. Aelnir was also restoring her domain, slowly and sullenly, clearing up the debris from our battle, but spending most of the days inside her old, half-destroyed lair. Only, when I checked in this morning, there was nothing half-assed about the destruction bestowed upon her domain. I watched, engrossed in the gore and ruin of the scene as Aelnir fled from unseen assailants, bleeding from several long cuts on her flank and with caustic goo sizzling on her hind flank.

Her pursuit came into sight soon. It was an entire horde of minions large and small, towering Urten lumbering along next to smaller minions crackling electricity from their clawed hands. Others were hidden in shadows or crawled along on the ceiling, evading my vision. Finally, following the wave of smaller minions, the real threat came. A small, sinuous green, walking with his head respectfully lowered beside a large, powerful blue.

Arthor tried to catch my attention, but I shushed him. This was important. What happened next was inevitable and gruesome both. I held no hope that they would spare my unwilling ally, but I did not expect them to spend as long as they did tormenting her. Not just with pain. No, they were clearly interrogating her.

Aelnir surrendered the moment the two dragons caught her, but they spent minutes playing with her, while an unheard conversation took place between their minds. Damnit, why couldn't I talk telepathically with my allies? The duo battered the frightened white back and forth, sheer panic obvious on her face while she tried to curl into a ball and act subservient.

Whatever their argument was, at some point, the blue tired of it. A blinding bolt of lightning spat from within his maw, enveloping Aelnir in a full-body web of electricity and stunning her. Then, in a fluid, graceful movement, he sprang forward and sealed his teeth on her neck and clamped down. The blood ran in rivulets from between his teeth as he sawed back and forth, but it still felt like a long wait until life finally left Aelnir's mistreated body. The notification left no doubt as to the finality of the moment.

[**Vassal defeated**
Your sworn vassal has been defeated and your bond with Deyra weakened.

Connection with Deyra weakened. Mana regeneration reduced by -100%]

[**Vassal bond destroyed**
You suffer backlash from the destruction of your bond with your vassal, Aelnir. Your attributes are reduced by 5%.

Time remaining: 5 days]

I blinked, looking down at Arthor's annoyed frown. "I think we're in trouble."

Minutes later, I had the usual suspects gathered inside the Clencher Cavern. Erk represented the Crawls, and the Imps had finally decided upon a representative, bickering and discussing for ages until the loudest, most insistent specimen made himself heard. His name was Grex.

I looked at each of them in turn. "All Talpi here know how close we came to destruction when the big red dragon attacked us. That was some time ago, with our defenses more simple and without all our allies. Except, this time, two dragons have allied, and combined their minions, from the looks of it. That is not all. They just killed Aelnir, my white vassal, and I would be very surprised if she didn't give away our position in an attempt to have them spare her life." My mind was in turmoil. As if we weren't in enough trouble already.

Creziel looked shaken. "That is horrible."

Arthor, on the other hand, looked contemplative. "Could be. It could also be exactly what we need."

Grex was in constant movement. The tiny Imp fluttered around our group, hanging on our every word, "What does that mean? What does that mean, though? Exactly what we need? Do Talpi need attacks from large dragons? Are they suicidal? That must be it."

I ignored the tiny Imp and looked Arthor in the eyes. "You would use the attack as a diversion?"

"Yes. Pfah. I don't like it any more than you do, Lizard. However, the alternative is even uglier. Remain a slave for months until we get used for bait? After the Soul Carver collapsed the exit and started guarding the front entrance. We have made no headway at a decent plan for us to simply slink away. We could start digging a new tunnel, but... I fear he would discover us. So, let us plan and aim to use their likely attack in a way that benefits us. What do we need?"

I shook my head, trying to clear the negative thoughts from my mind. "The very best thing would be if we could get the dragons and the Soul Carver to kill each other. I somehow doubt that the Soul Carver will do us the favor of taking on the attack by himself. That leaves us either with the chance to escape during the battle or try to obtain an advantage for us during the chaos."

Grex was loving it. "Great plan. What does that mean, though? Do we still stay here? I don't think the pale one is going to be happy if we run. We can't run well. Can we sit on your back again? That was fun!"

Roth was the first to shake his head. "Trying to escape during a battle? Insanity. Now that he's collapsed the escape tunnel, we'd have to fight our way through both the Soul Carver *and* the forces of the attackers. No. Tell us about that advantage."

I took a deep breath. "It would be a huge risk, but if we can get access to the Soulstones, I will be able to replace them with illusions and free myself and Timothy from the Soul Carver's influence at will. We may not be able to make use of it right away, but it will give us a surprise."

Arthor was not convinced. "That's still a flimsy chance. Even if we are able to secure them, why wouldn't he simply see through the illusion? He spotted your tunnel."

"I don't know *anything* for sure." I snapped at him. "We're trapped here; all our options are looking like shit to me right now. Run? Only part of us are going to get away, if we're lucky. Fight his minions? Fight *him?* He can freeze Timothy and me with a thought and use us to tear you apart and dominate the rest of you with a single spell. This is the only way I can see of securing an advantage for ourselves. There are no easy solutions here. Still, if we actually manage this, we will be able to break his hold over us. At the very least, it'll allow us all to make a break for it. Plus, once we leave the domain to face Selys, we should all be together. We might catch a break there."

Arthor frowned but didn't comment. Roth was bouncing about on the balls of his feet, shadow boxing. "At last, a chance to do something. I'm in. How do we break that damn blue shield?"

I smiled. "That part, I've got an idea for. Listen. This is what we do..."

Then it was just a matter of waiting. Under the circumstances, that was easier said than done. The days passed by slower than the bureaucratic phase on a public construction project. My people threw themselves into training again. The Crawls mostly eschewed Agility and worked only on Toughness and Strength. Meanwhile, every single Talpus spent most of the day exploring the paths they had chosen, Builders and Fighters working on their Strength or Toughness, Scouts on Agility and Toughness and Shamans on... everything but Strength, really. Neither Creziel nor Arthor were looking good these days with all the work they had on their plates.

The Soul Carver did not pass the time relaxing either, but if he noticed the frenzied pace at which my minions were driving themselves, he didn't comment. He finished a creation within the room where he worked on his minions.

[**Mana focus**
This construction allows you to enter your mana and apply it, concentrated, in the forms of runes on the face of weapons or other appliances. The runes will allow you to add magical effects onto dead material]

I was intrigued. This could be a potential game-changer, ensuring everybody had magical equipment. Along with a Training Chamber, plenty of levels, and lots of dragon meat, it would allow anybody to gain a lot of strength. It did not seem that the Soul Carver saw the same possibilities. He proceeded to use the construction to create soul stone after soul stone. Not like mine or Timothy's. Those had been embedded with runes on all sides, glowing with ample magic. These were simpler things, with one or two runes each, possibly for reviving simple creatures.

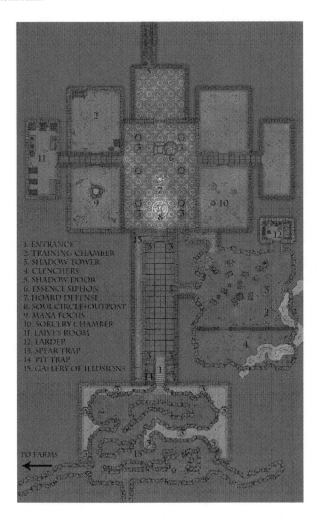

1. ENTRANCE
2. TRAINING CHAMBER
3. SHADOW TOWER
4. CLENCHERS
5. SHADOW DOOR
6. ESSENCE SIPHON
7. HOARD DEFENSE
8. SOUL CIRCLE+OUTPOST
9. MANA FOCUS
10. SORCERY CHAMBER
11. LAIVES ROOM
12. LARDER
13. SPEAR TRAP
14. PIT TRAP
15. GALLERY OF ILLUSIONS

TO FARMS

A handful of days later, it happened. I had started wondering if I'd been worrying for nothing. Out of the blue, an out of breath Talpus scout ran into the entrance hall, screaming as he came. "Attack! An attack!"

I managed to intercept him and debrief him first, and moments later, I found myself before the Soul Carver. "We are under attack, Master. They have not reached us yet, but they will within an hour. There's tons of minions, Urten, tiny electrical ones, and even some shadow jumpers nobody here has heard of before. And two dragons. A smaller green and a large blue."

The silence stretched until it became almost unbearable. His eyes bored into mine, as if searching for verification of what I had just said. Then his smile grew, stretching the skin on his face taut until he resembled a murderous clown more than anything else. "How wonderful."

Okay? That was *not* what I had expected to hear. The terrifying creature in front of me ignored me, talking like it was obvious.

"That will save us a lot of time in the long run. So, by your count, there will just be a single one left when we are done, as well as the blue in his fortress? Excellent. Now, this time, I will allow you to control your own forces. That way, they will not be alerted to my presence. Draw them in, hurt them in the process, and do make sure to lose a minion or ten in the process. Having their approach look too hard might make them back up. We do not want that."

Yeah right. Fat chance of me doing that. "But... what happens when they do pass the Gallery of Illusions? They will come right here. They have more minions than we do, if only slightly, and there are *two* dragons."

He nodded, slowly and gravely, with the smile still in place. "I will handle that. The most important part is that we ensure that they all make it in here. If anybody should escape, they could ruin my plans. You do not want to test my displeasure if that happens, Puppet."

"Yeah. Yeah, I reckon you're right about that."

After a brief battle council, everybody got into place, and I found my own spot right outside the exit from the Gallery of Illusions. Inside the Gallery was the pale glow of Timothy, who was getting ready for his first real test, along with a number of torches that had been lit for the occasion. Everybody else had been retracted into the domain and assigned their own places. The few undead who were too large to fit had been sent... elsewhere. The Soul Carver hadn't said, and I didn't ask. We were tensed up, ready for anything.

I caught them on the mini map before I heard them. The domain had grown to the size where the first tunnels were far enough away that no sound arrived. But I could see them arriving, like waves licking the sea shore. The first ones to arrive were scouts, moving slowly and cautiously, testing the waters. Then they started finding signs of our presence--the abandoned tunnel opening to where the new Farm was going to be, plenty of obvious footprints in the dirt of the tunnels, signs of recent construction. The wave pulled back, rejoining with the main group before expanding again. This time, they came in force and with speed, spreading out to overwhelm and investigate the entire area.

The first screams must have arrived at the same time, when they started encountering some of our old traps. The results were pitiful--a few injured, and one of the small electrical creatures dead from an unlucky dive into an old pit trap. The rest rejoined the main force and spread out again as they found the right way into our domain.

Now, the noise was growing, and I could hear them from the Gallery. Shouted commands, roars of anger and, behind it all, a single, overwhelming roar of challenge. I checked the map again and yes. There they were. Behind all the minions, the two dragons came, pushing their expendable fighters before them.

I finally got a good look at one of the shadowy figures. To me, it looked like they held a permanent, upgraded full-body Camouflage effect, fading in and out of focus constantly. Their physical bodies were frail, but held long, razor-sharp claws the length of their hand.

[**Stick Kin**.
Health: 75
Weakness: Fire]

"Everybody. The shadow creatures are weak to fire attacks.

Let the Imps handle them, if possible. They look dangerous up close." My mental shout rang out to those hidden everywhere around me and I steeled myself for the first wave to arrive--and arrive they did.

The Stick Kin came first, almost unnoticeable, spindly creatures sneaking along the walls. They made it less than ten feet inside the Gallery before the illusions started taking hold. I immediately thought back to the single Orugal that we had tested the illusions on earlier. He had been completely enthralled, panicked, and pretty much gone insane by the end. This was different. The Stick Kin were affected, obviously, but they didn't completely lose control or lose their sense of direction.

"Time to amp it up a bit!" I thought and started working on my innate shadow control. Throughout the Gallery, patches of unnaturally deep illusionary darkness sank down over the intruders--and *then* they started to lose it.

Still, they probably would have gotten over it. I spotted one Stick Kin continuing onward, hands held out ahead of itself in an attempt to stave off any contact with a wall or something, and another was blinking, like his Mental Power or natural resistance to shadows was slowly fighting down my influence, except, that's when my minions opened the paneled windows, and the fight started in earnest.

All the way along the edges of the Gallery, Shadow Towers spewed their weakening essences at the intruders and right alongside them Imps fluttered, raining fire down on our enemies, while my ranged Talpi flung throwing spears at the intruders. And Timothy... oh, Timothy! He dove straight into the center of the incoming groups, spreading his essence to affect as many as possible, while pouring his mental attacks indiscriminately onto anybody nearby. Wherever he moved, Stick Kin halted and almost faltered, easy targets for our damage dealers.

Had the Stick Kin been alone, I reckoned that they would have been fleeing or eliminated within the first minute. Minute and a half, tops. Alas, they were not alone. Far from it. The small, electricity-wielding creatures joined the fray, while Stick Kin and the occasional Urten kept coming in ones and twos, striding forward with no sense of tactics, but plenty of rage. Soon, the place smelled like thunder as the small, wiry, bipedal critters flung electrical discharges everywhere, hitting their own more often than not.

Large Urten joined the battle as well, roaring with battlelust as their blades burned bright with the fury of their innate fire gifts. I continued overwhelming them with unnatural shadows, robbing them of their sight, while the Gallery of Illusions betrayed their other senses and my people and Shadow Towers kept up their attacks.

Still, their enemy had the advantage of numbers. Timothy was forced back, slowly and surely, out of fear that the elemental attacks would take a toll on him. Also, despite their confusion, the enemies were simply too numerous. We did not dish out enough damage to stop them. Within the next couple of minutes, they were slowly finding their way across the crowded Gallery. The occasional enemy was downed by our defenders, but overall, they ambled forward, weakened and confused, but numerous. Timothy joined me near the entrance, concentrating and buffing my attributes with a touch.

His unclear features did not portray his emotions, but his mental voice rang with excitement. "Hoooo, yeah! This is goddamn *awesome!* Old man, you have no idea how much I needed this." The first of the enemies--a wildly flailing Urten-- stumbled blindly around the corner, and Tim met him with a Mental attack, straight to the face. The Urten screamed and froze, dropping the flaming mace from his grip.

I followed Tim's attack with a Weakening Fog, grinning in surprise as the brute tumbled bonelessly to the ground. Heh. It must've been hit by a Shadow Tower or two on the way. "Really? You needed to get into a huge battle, risk your life, and kill some people?"

He cursed, as his next shot went wide and missed a Stick

Kin. The thing halted and gazed around, trying to find the origin of the shot... and found my next Weakening Fog instead. "Exactly, yes. Guess whose face I'm picturing on each and every one of 'em?"

"Heh. Not the toughest challenge ever. Sounds like fun! I'll join you for a game of shoot the freak." It felt like a game, too. More and more enemies were moving in our direction, and it was getting harder and harder to keep up with the pressure. Still, it felt like an old-time shooting game, with our enemies mostly oblivious about our existence. The few remaining Stick Kin were wising up to us, and it looked like they were preparing for a serious push, yelling orders back to the other assailants. "We're moving back now, Tim." I said, and followed my own advice, moving down the decline and into the entrance corridor leading to the throne room.

We took some shots on the way, as the attackers slowly figured out the right way to move. Those electrical attacks were no joke. Every time I was hit, it was like the body part short-circuited, and it was a second or two before I was able to move again. Even so, the attackers moving into the corridor also meant one thing: They were bundled into a tight place, perfect for my breath attack. My first Weakening Fog took out six attackers, allowing us a breather to move a bit further back. At the other end, two Urten peered into the corridor, blinking in surprise at the open, shadowless corridor before them after the avalanche of shadows and illusions they'd had to fight through. Behind them, more followed.

While we retreated, Tim did not pause for a moment. Every few seconds, he fired off another Mental Attack, spewing obscenities at our opponents. As the number of attackers slowly grew, he started shooting glances at me. "Uh. Old man? Right about... now, maybe?"

I fought to keep a wicked grin from my face and failed, utterly. "You youngsters need to learn a little about patience. " It looked like we were about to be overwhelmed. Attackers rushed down the decline into the tunnel, charging at us with abandon.

The translucent Shadow Towers inside the corridor took potshots at all enemies but were nowhere near enough to do any real damage.

I took two careful steps back, cleared the side tunnel from the Clencher Cavern, and roared. The din of my roar spread outward, as I gave a mental yell, "Now. Now! Slide it open! Cavalry, charge!" The savage joy at those words made me laugh, a bloodthirsty, coughing rumble erupting from my mouth. Then I underlined my message with a Weakening Fog at my assailants.

Three things happened in quick succession. First, a full fourth of the enemies dropped from my breath attack, like a featherweight boxer sucker punched by Mike Tyson. Then, the pressure from the enemies faded to nothing, as the floor dropped the hindmost enemies straight into the pit trap below. I spared a brief thought of compassion for the poor bastards. Inside the trap, the few minions who managed to survive the drop and the waiting spears below would be easy prey for my waiting Talpi and their spears, as they attacked them from their hidden places beyond the wall of the pit. For a moment, the air was torn with pain-filled cries. Then, the sounds were drowned out by the third development, as the Shadow Door slammed up and the first ever squad of Clencher Cavalry rounded the corner from the Clencher Cavern, thundering down at the remaining intruders.

I had problems believing that we had actually found volunteers for the job. However, it was surprisingly easy. Having been at the receiving end of scorn and violence from the entire power structure inside the mountain for generations, the Talpi were apparently ready to accept any risk to be those in power for a change. And the sensations coming from them, as the new Clencher riders thundered past me down the corridor, long spears lowered, were ones of sheer, savage glee.

Some enemies tried to flee. I couldn't fault them. If I was looking down at the lowered spears of four maniacs riding Clenchers side by side toward me, I would have done the same.

To their horrified realization, there was nowhere to escape *to*. A few unfortunate attackers tumbled down the pit trap to join their friends below before they understood their predicament. Meanwhile, their wavering front line was inching backward. Timothy and I followed behind the charging Clenchers.

The clash as the Clenchers hit the enemy line was deafening. The line was buckling already, but at that point it broke completely. The towering Urten did not surrender. However, we had instructed the riders to aim for the large beasts first, and the impacts killed three Urten outright. The remaining attackers simply could not stand up against the bulk of the huge ursines trampling into them. For a moment, it was all chaos. While the Clenchers tore into enemies left and right, their riders lay into anybody nearby with their short spears, long spears discarded immediately after impact.

Then, their momentum slowly disappeared as the hindmost third of the hostile survivors started pushing back and the electrical bastards overcame their shock and started firing. The stopping power of their attacks was impressive. Even through their thick skin, my Clenchers took the attacks hard and stopped, struggling to get their stunned bodies moving. One careened into a wall, and the rider cried out in pain, as his leg was stuck between the Clencher and the wall.

I acted immediately. I threw up a wide swath of shadows separating the attackers and my Clenchers, as thick as I could possibly make it. "Back! Move back!" I commanded, even as I strode forward. I stretched my neck and delivered a Weakening Fog over the heads of the cavalry. The fine droplets acted immediately, taking the fight out of a handful of the weaker enemies.

Upstairs, behind the pit trap, I could see their numbers increasing again, and more than one was eyeing the pit trap, as if wondering whether to jump over it or chance jumping into the trap itself. "Close the trap." I shouted, even as my Clenchers started pulling back one by one.

It was not a clean retreat. Whatever training we'd managed to bestow upon them, Clenchers were wild animals, and their savagery was hard to quench. With the combined efforts of their riders and my calls, we were able to finally withdraw them all. The last one had the rider physically beating down upon it to have it stop savaging a downed Urten.

Then I roared straight into the faces of the remaining handful of enemies inside the corridor - and retreated myself. Timothy was right there beside me, throwing Mental Attacks at everybody. The few enemies inside the tunnel dared not move against us. They hid behind downed comrades, shooting nervous glances between us and the forces arriving above. With a grinding sound, the pit trap finally slid closed again, and the second wave tentatively, trying to avoid stepping on the slab of the trap itself, launched themselves forward and down at us.

As we ran past the Clencher Cavern, I closed the Shadow Door, reactivating the illusion. I did not want the enemies to go the wrong way. Looking over my shoulder, I realized I may have hesitated too long, as the foremost Urten were right on my heels. Kicking up speed, I sprinted down the corridor, entered the throne room, and tried out my new trick. Behind me, I heard roars and crashing noises, as the intruders finally pinpointed the Shadow Towers inside the entrance hallway and smashed them to bits in quick succession.

So, my Illusion skill required that no enemies were watching straight at the illusion in order for me to activate it in the first place? Annoying, right? Except now, I had the power to create shadows at will. Once inside the throne room, I jumped to the side, hit the entrance with the heaviest blanket of shadows I was able to summon, instantly put my new illusion into place, then removed the shadows again. Mere seconds later, the first two Urten came roaring into the throne room and then just... stopped. They glanced around, beastly faces blinking confused when they spotted a completely empty throne room, devoid of... anything.

I had deactivated the Shadow Towers inside the throne room, saving them for the ambush. The Urten debated their approach, then proved that they did have a couple of brain cells between them, as they decided to move back outside the room to wait for their comrades.

The trap was set. Everything was in place, and the Clenchers were raving for a second round. Everybody was here. Tim was hiding inside one of the tunnels near the ceiling along with a bunch of Talpi. I chanced a look at the map overview. Good. A full third of our enemies had dropped inside the corridor or down the pit trap. On top of that, additional bodies lay strewn like chaff everywhere inside the Gallery itself. At least half their numbers were gone, and we had almost no losses so far.

A deep, heavy roar sounded from up ahead, and I flinched. A bit early to count this as a victory. Now, the major players entered the scene. Flanked by a handful of well-armored Urten, the green and the blue finally strode into the Gallery of Illusions. My minions dropped everything and hightailed out of there, back toward us, while the Gallery of Illusions was turned into a shooting gallery.

This time, it was one-sided in the enemies' favor, though. The green didn't seem to be affected by the illusions at all, and the blue looked more distracted and annoyed than confused. My Shadow Towers kept up their attacks, but they were torn down and reduced to ruins within moments. We had debated having our defenders close the panels before they fled, but I didn't mind the task of rebuilding if it meant that the attacking dragons were slightly weakened--and none of the attackers were small enough to enter the crawlspaces to attack us that way.

For now, the attacking dragons' minions were huddling at the far end of the corridor, refusing to budge. However, as the dragons got closer, they saw them keeping back--and were not satisfied with their minions' lack of progress. Within seconds, huge roars chased them onward into the throne room, where they slowed down and spread out, scouting nervously in all directions after signs of traps or defenders.

I waited for as long as I could, until the minions were well spread out throughout the throne room. The effort to maintain the illusion was becoming harder and harder. Not only was it one of the largest illusions I'd handled, I also had to maintain it in a semi-circle around the place. It was worth it, though. When I finally sent "*Now,*" activated the Shadow Towers, and released control of the illusion, the shock was absolute. What they had seen as an empty throne room instantly converted into a room lined with my minions on all sides. Crawls stepped forward in front of the ranged Talpi and Imps, presenting spears, Clenchers and their riders built up speed for a renewed charge from the back of the room near the throne and I... I sprang straight forward toward them and released a Weakening Fog along with a Shadow Whorl placed at the center of their group.

The wave slammed through them like a storm hitting a field of wheat. A third of them either dropped entirely, strings cut, or were forced to their knees, fighting against the debilitating effect of my breath attack. A half dozen extra started moving erratically, their sight and senses ruined by the Shadow Whorl. The rest still stood, bogged down, but holding, right until everybody else joined in the ambush.

Throughout the room, the attackers were reeling, under siege on all sides by towers and minions alike. We allowed them no reprieve. Death and destruction rained down upon them from my ranged attackers, even as the Crawls got in close, pressing in with nasty jabs from their spears, melee Talpi lurking at their backs to abuse any openings. A few Imps were placed too far to the back of the Throne room, and their attacks hit the blue sheen of the Hoard Defense, as if by accident as they were shooting at the enemies. From a distance, it would be hard to tell that I had placed them there by design to weaken the shield.

Even hard-pressed, our enemies didn't take it lying down. Those who remained standing pushed outward, fighting for their lives, striking down indiscriminately at anybody, and with the tightly packed forces of my people, they could hardly avoid hitting somebody. Electrical discharges flew wild, flames from the Urtens' weapons obscured the vision, and the few remaining Stick Kin slashed furiously with the long claws.

Still, the pressure on their troops was immense. My forces pushed hard from either side, and the exact moment their momentum seemed to stall, was when my Clenchers hit them with their charge. This time, they caved entirely. I could feel the victory right within our grasp... but that's when the dragons arrived.

They came with a roar of thunder, and a massive lightning bolt impacted in the middle of my forces. The effect was instant, stunning some and sending others tumbling across the floor. Meanwhile, the enemies' minions scrabbled to regroup and gain some semblance of formation. I yelled at everyone. "Back. Move back! Toward the back of the room."

This time, there was no discussion. Nobody seemed to want to stay as the last defenders up against two towering forces of nature. I couldn't blame them. The huge Urten filed into the room in orderly fashion, sweeping past their own to form a defensive measure in front of their masters. They made for an impressive honor guard. Not only were these armored in what looked like crude cast iron breastplates, they held large, unwieldy shields and moved like they had fought together before. The dragons strode in like they owned the place, the majestic blue ducking under the gate to be able to enter.

CHAPTER TWENTY-FIVE

In the midst of chaos, there is also opportunity. - Sun Tzu

"There he is, Heivax. The one who has been causing us so much trouble." The mental voice sounded obsequious and hostile, and I immediately placed it as the green.

"I have eyes. I do not need you to point out the obvious." The blue, on the other hand, sounded just like he looked. Majestic, powerful, and in charge. "My shadow brother. An impressive defense. I would speak with you."

I glanced at the map. The last minions of the dragons were rushing in now. The trap was ready. No harm in sharing a few words. "Sure. I mean, it would be easier to just come yourself instead of trying to wreck the place."

The blue, Heivax, smiled. It was a proud smile, not the least apologetic. "Oh, I know. Yet, I have found that setting the right tone immediately is important. Isn't that right, Voidun?" The green bowed his head down deep. Oh, there was *history* there.

Interesting. So they weren't just trying to kill me? I smirked at the blue. "Tone for what? Right now, it looks like you were just setting the tone for a resounding defeat."

MASTER OF THE MOUNTAIN

The blue looked down at the numerous corpses surrounding him. "Oh, I disagree. I must congratulate you on your defenses. You have done an impressive job at defending yourself from a superior foe, with paltry minions on your side." He shook his head at the look of the Talpi, Imps, and Crawls surrounding his forces. "Still, here we are, and you have nowhere further to flee. So, allow me to line up the possibilities. You either accept your defeat and join me as my pawn, or die and strengthen me in death. These are the options. Now, choose." As he spoke, he moved slowly forward, towering above me.

I had to swallow at the sight of his white-blue majesty, scales glinting impressively in the light from the torches. "I have a counter-proposal. Heivax, was it?"

"No counter-proposals, I am afraid. The last red we encountered also tried to bargain for his life. I killed him slowly. We will have no ruses."

"Oh, so you don't even want to know who you're really up against?" The undead forces had been moving about on the map for a while now, encroaching from their hiding places in the surrounding caverns. Even as I spoke, they spilled out, undead monstrosities emerging from the side corridors, from my room, the Clencher Cavern, and more from outside the domain itself. For the first time ever, I had an honest smile on my face as I said the words, "The Soul Carver."

I have never seen a dragon panic before. It's not a pretty sight. Especially on somebody as impressive-looking as the blue. His face fell, leaving a naked look of horror on his face for a split second, as the undead monstrosities appeared from all sides. To his credit, he gathered himself quickly and, with a guttural growl, lunged against me. "Traitor!" He flung the word at me.

I saw it coming. The lightning built up inside his mouth, and he telegraphed his intentions very clearly. There were a few options available to me. I could have shrouded the entire hall in shadows, flung up illusions, or cast Shadow Whorl straight at him in an attempt to distract him. But the Hoard Defense was still up, and I needed to do something. My choice probably wasn't the wisest, but it was what I could come up with in the heat of the moment. I started backing away, as if uncertain exactly how to handle this.

The moment his lightning struck me, I was flung back with impressive force. A full twenty percent of my health evaporated instantly. Even Heivax looked shocked when I was propelled back across the throne room, slamming with furious power into the shining shield surrounding the hoard. I hit the shield hard and bounced off, growling at the damaging spark that sprang out at me from the blinking blue shield. In my effort to get back up, my legs flailed furiously for traction, and I hit the shield again, once, twice. Each time resulted in another damaging spark, but the last time, the blue shield actually burst and died.

"The Soul Carver is going to be furious that you ruined his Hoard Defense," I sent at the blue, glancing at the rest of the room. My minions were pulling back now, ranged attackers still firing away, but the rest of them wisely decided to let the undead take the punches for them.

The green took a glance at the huge monstrosities ambling toward him and turned tail, running for the exit. He reached the edge of the throne room when two of my strongest builders hidden inside the walls finally got the chance to unleash my largest weapon: the huge, magical stone spear lovingly crafted by Arthor and Jazinth in combination. One second he was running for his life. The next, he was keening, trapped in the doorway on the barbed ends of the spear, flailing in panic at his unseen foe. With an impressive effort, my minions managed to tug back the spear, and the green limped back down the corridor, bleeding profusely. I did not envy him the experience of meeting the Soul Carver's most powerful minions who were too large to even fit inside the domain. I could see undead monstrosities on the map, right outside the domain, just waiting.

The blue growled and watched as two of my Imps, understandably, stopped attacking him and hid behind a pillar instead. Around us was a circle of peace, the only calm place in the throne room. "Coward!" he spat at the retreating back of the green. "So the Soul Carver will be angry? Let him come and show me himself how angry he is. Unless... is this a trick? Shadowkin, are you doing this? If I slay you, will this... fade?" With a roar, he sent another Lightning attack at me.

This time, I didn't just take it head on. I dove away in a graceless evasive maneuver while placing a Shadow Whorl straight at the blue's nose. Then, I covered the space between us in the deepest shadows I could muster. My flank was still hit, stunning my leg, but the damage wasn't too bad. My health still hovered above half. Still, I let the dodge take me straight at the hoard again, except this time, there was nothing to stop my forward momentum.

Weapons, jewelry, and Mana Crystals were flung to the side, as I barreled through the pile of precious items. Safely on the other side, my eyes rummaged around. There. That one. And that one. I kicked the glittering soulstones to the side of the room. Now I just needed to-

Even blinded and with his senses half messed-up by the Shadow Whorl, the blue kept up stalking me. I sent a Weakening Fog straight at him and leapt out of the way. I needed to get some distance between him and me. Two large jumps had me almost barreling into a Talpus and approaching my old room behind the throne. Where *was* the bastard?

I had just had the thought when I felt it. That sensation of somebody pushing down upon my entire body, forcing me to kneel. Crawls and Urten, Stick Kin and Clenchers, survivors were forced to the ground across the entire throne room. The only ones to continue unaffected were the undead creations. A dark lance shot out from my old room, impaling the blue straight in the chest, and the Soul Carver strode out. I thought for sure that was it, but Heivax proved his strength.

As scales flaked off his chest, he rose to his hind legs, roaring defiance at the world. When he lowered himself to all fours again, a sheen of living electricity enveloped him, covering his entire body, making him look like the center of an electrical storm. It must have revitalized him as well, or else he must have had high enough attributes to ignore the Soul Carver's spell, because he leapt straight at the stitched-up pale sorcerer, claws first.

Heivax went for the throat, and for the shortest moment, I thought the blue was about to end all my trouble for me right there. However, instead of landing the attack, his wild slash bounced off an invisible protective facade. As he fell to the ground, twisting like a cat to land on his feet, the Soul Carver hit him in the flanks with another dark lance. I decided to use their face-off as the chance to get some distance between me and the two fighters. Fortunately, as their duel intensified, the pressure from the Soul Carver's spell lessened, so it must be something that required at least some attention to function optimally. I managed to drag myself to the far end of the throne room, downed minions lined against either wall. Then I felt safe enough to turn around and watch the duel.

I had figured that the Soul Carver was a certain winner, what with him being impervious to damage. At first glance, that was what it looked like, too. The huge, blue dragon leapt straight past the spell-caster, letting his front claws screech off the surface of the invisible shield. As he passed by, his tail followed, slamming into the barrier and rebounding inaudibly. None of the impacts left a scratch, and the Soul Carver's face was impassive as always. Yet, where his natural weapons failed, the electrical storm surrounding Heivax *did* penetrate the shield-
-and where it landed, it did horrible damage to the stitched-up humanoid. Tiny blood veins burst near the surface of his skin, and drops of blood were spilling as tiny ruptures emerged on his face.

That's when I finally got to see the efficiency of the Soul Carver's Essence Siphon in practice. His undead creations had been busy, tearing into the remaining minions of the blue and the green. Even as I watched, the last, giant armored Urten stabbed furiously into a large undead centipede, ripping and tearing as his own lifeblood was being spilled from the three other monsters that were piled onto him.

The blood spilled and pooled until it hit one of the blood grooves and joined with the lifeblood of all the other minions, slowly moving toward the throne and the Essence Siphon. Where before, the construction was just a large, slowly swirling vortex, now it changed to a tornado of dark energy. Slowly, the top of the tornado thinned out and started tipping in the direction of the Soul Carver.

As soon as the magical construction tipped to the side, the change sped up. The tornado elongated, stretching into a long funnel that went straight from the Siphon to the Soul Carver. The results were instant. Right away, the tissue on the spellcaster's face started regenerating. His spell started weighing heavier on my back as well. Then, slowly, that unnatural grin appeared on his face again. "You really thought you could challenge me? Me?"

He stepped toward the blue and slowly brought his hands together in grasping motions and pulled down, furiously. Heivax did not notice any change and sent a lightning attack straight at his enemy. Then he gathered his feet under him to spring to the attack again. The heavy lightning hit with a clap and a reek of ozone, but the Soul Carver hardly even noticed the impact on his chest. And when the huge dragon tried to spring to the attack again, he fell. The look on his face was almost comical as he stared in horror at the single leg that was not moving at all.

The Soul Carver released yet another dark lance that bored straight into the chest of the blue. "Not many people realize this, but bodies have a mind of their own. It is simple, admitted, but a body part knows what it's supposed to do. Have you ever had your mind awake in the middle of a dream? Even though your mind knows that you are awake, your body is aware that it should still be sleeping, hence it refuses to act.

"What is even more interesting is that you can actually learn how to instruct other bodies how to act with the right use of magic. Prod a nerve, and it contracts. Inform a leg that it is asleep, and it refuses to act." The Soul Carver looked horrible. Even with the healing, veins had burst all over his body, leaving his hands and face an unnatural, bruise-colored, blood-covered mess. If the damage had any real effect on him, you could not tell from his face, as he walked forward, unperturbed. His hands made short, clenching, jabbing motions as he walked. "If you know what you are doing, you can even tell a body that it has a *cramp*."

The last word impacted the proud dragon. One moment he stood there, and seconds later, he sank to the ground in anguish as both his hind legs started contracting with short, sharp cramps. He tried to power through it, but another dark spear emerged from the Soul Carver's hand. This one, he simply held in his hand as he walked forward and then, with great satisfaction, he pushed his hand forward, plunging the spear deep into the chest of the downed blue.

Heivax did not go down easy. His single working front leg clawed at the Soul Carver, but was repelled by the shield. Lightning sprung from him toward the necromancer again, but the raging storm subsided from its initial torment, diminishing until it only remained in place around their two forms, like it was caressing two lovers.

Slowly, even that light dimmed and along with that, the life of the great blue. The majestic form of the huge blue dragon was soon carving uselessly into the air, unseeing, as his remaining life pulsed along the spear and into the Soul Carver. Seconds later, he died, and the body slumped down onto the floor.

The silence that followed was only broken by the cries from some of the injured. Moments later, the burden on our backs lightened, and we were able to breathe again. From across the room, I met Arthor's questing eyes, and I gave him a single, sharp nod. Then I turned toward the Soul Carver. "Did the green escape?"

The rictus of his grin was still there, frozen in place, as he turned his judging gaze on me. "No. His broken body lies outside the lair. He was weak. Not like this one. The blue has earned the right to fight at the forefront of my armies."

I nodded. "It would seem fitting." It would also ruin my plan of escaping during our travels. Acting as if I suddenly had a thought come to me, I asked. "Maybe I could come up with an alternative, and better approach, though?"

"Are you questioning me?"

"Well, yeah. I mean, it depends on your plans, but if it takes you a long while to raise the dragon, maybe we would be better off marching straight for Selys, while you have the effects from that Siphon activated? Also, I doubt that the benefit from the dragons being converted outweighs the risks of being discovered by Selys. You have plenty of large minions already."

His eyes bored into mine, narrowing. "Not many who have handled the same level of punishment you have would still be able to challenge me." Then, he turned to look at the downed dragons. "You may be right. Though the blue would be a powerful addition to my forces, I am not sure that I have a high enough quality Soulstone for his body at present." He let his eyes roam over his minions. "Hardly any damages for me to repair, either." After a long pause, he continued. "Very well. It has been decided. Tomorrow, we leave."

CHAPTER TWENTY-SIX

Of course, it wasn't as simple as that. Even though he had made the decision, and the rest of us just had to obey, there was still so much to be done. The very first thing I did was confirm that we'd done it. After I smashed the Hoard Defense and kicked the soulstones off to the side, Aelis had rushed in to pocket them. They were safely hidden in Arthor's packs right now. We'd agreed on our initial plan. If the Soul Carver found out that the soulstones were gone, Arthor was to destroy them, and we'd all bolt right away, disperse, and make our separate ways to Creive's domain as best we could. If we got lucky and he *didn't* discover the deception, we would wait until we found a good opportunity to destroy them and flee as a cohesive force.

Following the battle, we took a look at the losses. We had done a lot better than I had expected. A few sported broken limbs, and one Crawl lost an eye while gaining a handful of impressive scars from what had to have been a Stick Kin. Miraculously, after all that carnage, nobody died.

Next was the question of preparing for the journey and ensuring that everybody was ready, including the injured and pregnant ones and pups. While the Necromancer allowed the

Talpi and Crawls to live, I doubted his largesse would expand to granting extra care to anybody who was too ill or weak to travel.

The Soul Carver came by to confirm my suspicions. "We are taking everybody and everything, Puppet. It has been a good domain, but we are not likely to be back. Make sure that you carve enough flesh from our attackers that your requirements for food is covered. Are there any who cannot travel? I should be able to convert them in time."

I shook my head vehemently. "No. We are ready. A question?" Seeing as he didn't complain, I continued. "We'll want to divvy everything inside the hoard out, don't we? I mean, there should be some pretty good increases on the items by now, and they won't be of any use there in the hoard."

"We will. However, it will not happen until we start the battle. While the majority of the items will go to my minions, there should be some for yours as well. I have learned the hard way, that you should limit the offensive capabilities of unruly minions. It is an unnecessary risk. My minions will pack up and handle the hoard."

"No problem. If you don't mind me asking... That sounded like there was a story behind it."

"There was." He remained silent for a while, then clearly made a decision. "There may be a lesson worth telling the story." His facial expressions remained as impassive as ever, but his eyes were clenched shut, the pain in them evident. "You know a little about leading people. You have had responsibility over workers in your world and have learned, here and now, what leading a group of minions directly means.

"Still, that is a far cry from being a ruler. I was a ruler. Admittedly, I was not a good one. I was a wastrel, bending my ear to anybody with a convincing sob story. My rulings and laws showed the same. I ruled from the heart, not with my brain. As a consequence, the land suffered, and my people did as well, even though I did it all for them." He paused. Right at that moment, even with everything he had done, I was not looking at the monster.

He was hurting, bottled up with all the regrets of his former life. "How did they reward me? I will tell you. They burned me, cut me, and dragged me out to die. *Down with the tyrant.* Those were their words." He shook his head. "I regret what I did to them, but I will not regret the path I have chosen. Trusting in those below you to know what is best for themselves is folly, and I am no longer a fool. Neither, I believe, are you."

How could I respond to that? Like I was going to follow his example? He would know it, if I lied. "I have trained and led many people. I'm well aware that a lot of people seem unable to make smart choices in their own lives. Sometimes, it even seems like they try to ruin it for themselves. So, what exactly is it you are searching for here in the first place? I doubt that you are just looking for materials or revenge. You don't seem like the type to hang on insults from years back."

He looked at me, unblinking for long seconds. Then, a slight smile appeared. "You *are* insightful. A delightful surprise. And willing to chance my displeasure in order to learn." Then, as if trying out my name for the first time, he said, slowly, "Carl. If you continue like this and start trusting me, we could end up like real partners. I have to warn you. I will need you to stop trying to work against me and preparing alternative plans. Join me, completely, and we will rule this place properly."

I simply nodded. "Is that your real plan? To rule this place?"

"It is. This is the perfect place to start a proper stronghold. Outside the mountain, in civilized society, nothing much ever changes. The grand powers remain unflinching, unblinking, and in charge. But that will change. The power structures are in place here for me to take over, and when I do, I can use it as a stepping stone to grow and take over all the stagnant forces of the outside."

"So, if you intend to take over, you don't mean for everybody here to be... converted?"

He shook his head. "It would be a waste. Now, do not misunderstand me. Anybody resisting will become a part of my forces. Also, the people, regardless of race, inside the mountain, are so used to the current power structures, that they will need heavy controls in place. That is what my flawed souls, my unliving minions, will be for. They will ensure that the people know their place while I make the hard decisions. So, I need to know--are you with me or not?"

Fuck. Not good. I couldn't just deflect that. "I'll have to be honest with you here, Selrahc." He nodded and I continued. "I dislike your methods. We have plenty of examples from my world where horrible, torturous regimes are born from the best of intentions." I shook my head. "Even so, I realize that this world is different. And I'm learning something else--that if you want to change the world you're in, you need to make sacrifices. I will join you."

The smile that lit on his face was, for once, reflected in his eyes. That did not make the grimace look any less monstrous.

I kept my own face studiously blank. If he learned that the last part about having to make sacrifices was meant as a comment on my own situation, I didn't care to experience the reaction.

The Soul Carver,turned his attention inward, and so did I. I wasn't going to call him Selrahc in my own mind. Even knowing what he'd gone through, I did not want to humanize him any more than I needed to.

"I have a gift for you, Carl. It feels like the thing to do, in order to celebrate our future. It also adds to the chance that we will both have a future, when we face off against Selys." It was not the first time I'd experienced him laughing, but it was still no less disturbing. The sound reminded me of an untuned violin. You could hear what it was supposed to sound like, but it was still wrong.

The gift was a meal. Well, a lot of meals, actually. The Ogre and another, huge, bipedal undead monster dragged in the corpse of the green and left it right next to Heivax's earthly remains.

"For me?"

"Yes. Also, I know what this means. I have my minions share

all their relevant knowledge before the mental decay becomes too much. It is a common secret within the mountain that the meat of dragons gifts some of the attributes they held in life. Yet, it is no use to my body. It can no longer take in sustenance the same way."

"Well... I won't say no. This can make a huge difference."

"Good. Your joining me would be useless, if you do not survive the matchup against Selys. This should help you."

I almost felt bad. Almost. He was like the kid who'd never had any friends, and now he was trying to bribe me to get me to like him. Except, my mind kept going back to the memory of him picking apart Eitel, methodically picking and prodding at different parts of the body as if he were investigating an insect. That was not somebody I would be able to talk sense into. No. Our original idea was still good. He needed to go. We just had to find the right time and place.

Soon, my belly was filled to the brim. I had consumed what I could from the two dragons then had seconds. I felt like, if I moved, I was going to explode. Not only that, but I was fully rigged. For the first time ever, I actually felt properly outfitted. I still wanted some actual dragon armor at some point. Hell, I understood why regular dragons didn't put on armor--flying with a lot of weight would be death.

Still, inside the mountain? I could sport full plate armor and still move around at a decent pace. I'd like to see a bloody monster bite through that! Unfortunately, my leather workers weren't up to armor creation. They had done a decent job, though, especially considering the schedule. The Talpi had provided for me, finishing exactly what I had asked for some days earlier in record time. With their help, I was soon bedecked in a criss-crossing leather outfit that started with a leather neckband and combined a large number of stitched-together animal skins with leather hand and footholds. From what I could tell, it looked rather martial. There were few defensive boons to take from the creation, but I chose not to care about that. It wasn't important. The functionality of it was what I was after, and like this, anybody unable to walk or needing to rest would be able to ride on my back. All told, it would ensure we didn't have to leave anybody behind.

Aelis observed me while she tore into a slab of dragon meat. After a while, she asked. "Onyx, are you not going to be punished for sharing? It was a gift for you."

I shrugged. "What he doesn't know won't hurt him. Besides, it's not like he told me not to. Heh. And it's kind of a tradition by now, you know? Even if some of the joy is gone this time around."

"The joy's gone? What do you mean? Huh? My brain is celebrating. My mouth feels like it's leveling up every other second. This is the best meal I've ever had! How could it be better than this?" Grex hovered above us, eyes closed in bliss as he munched his portion.

Roth gave a rough laugh and punched the tiny Imp in the leg, watching him lose his balance and almost faceplant. "You just wait a couple of hours from now, and it'll be better yet. Still, Onyx is right. It's one thing with stolen joys like this one--eating of the body of an enemy you yourself helped beat is another thing entirely."

Arthor had been staring at me for a while. "Why share, though?" I could feel the earnesty burning off of him. This was not a casual question.

I looked around. Most of the usual suspects were present. Weighing my words, I didn't face the serious Talpus at first. My gaze rested on Aelis. She, my very first enemy inside the mountain, now friend and staunchest ally. I smiled at her. "We have come a long way since that first day inside that tiny tunnel south of here."

She nodded, smiling with her entire body.

Arthor didn't smile. "Pfah. I am aware, Lizard. Do you have a point?"

I grinned. "Not always. This time, I do. A lot has changed since that first fateful day. I have grown. You have grown. Our relationships have evolved from that very first agreement, but we have not discussed it."

"What's there to talk about? Situations change. People die." Roth shrugged, starting in on a new stretching routine.

"No. This is important. I can't remember my first words to you, when I first asked you for an alliance."

Creziel stepped in. "I require your obedience. Any internal decisions in your tribe are for you to decide. But I'll be your leader, and if I require you to do something, you do it."

"Hah. Thank you, Creziel. That is my point exactly. It made sense at the time. But that is not what needs to be discussed. See, I've had Tim hard at work to help me. For a while now, I've had you by my side, assisting with ideas and suggestions. Any success we've had is because I've been able to rely on you. But it will not do in the long run. If I am going to improve the way this place is run, I cannot continue to always make all the decisions singlehandedly. Rather, I want it to be at your side, making the decisions with you."

Arthor frowned, standing up. "Now? You want to discuss how we should run the mountain now? We will be led into battle soon, led to the slaughter like we always knew would happen. What is the point, Onyx? For Deyra's sake, what is the point?"

"First of all, we are not going to die. We are going to make it through these struggles, cheat that cursed freak, and end up on top. Second, when we make it, and I become the ruler of this goddamn death trap of a mountain, I'm not going to want to lord it over everybody. We have already been working toward this, but right here, right now, I don't want to leave it unsaid.

"We are going to create a society where we make the decisions together and share the responsibilities. I'm still hazy on the fine print, but you will be part of the creation. The important part is this: We are in this together, and I want the Talpi on my side, not as my peons. And the Imps. And the Crawls. This is why I share. If we survive, I don't want a kingdom of subservient weaklings under me. I want equals, strong equals to back me up. And I want you to know that this is what I'm offering." I looked Arthor straight in the eyes. "So. What do you think?"

He didn't lower his eyes, searching for something in my gaze. "I think I've said this before, Lizard... you're broken. Having the weaker races of the mountain help make decisions alongside a dragon? It's unheard of." The tiniest hint of a smile played around his mouth. "But I don't hate it. And we've been doing it on a small scale for a while now. At the very least, it will give us something to talk about while we march to our doom."

A few short hours later, the effects from the dragon meat kicked in, confirming my theories.

[Congratulations. You have received a permanent increase to your attributes.

You have consumed the flesh of a being rife with the gifts of Deyra. The mana-rife meat bestows upon you the following:
+1 Strength
+3 Agility
+1 Mental Control
+2 Mental Power]

That had to be from the green. Pure agility, no toughness, and a mix of the rest.

[Congratulations. You have received a permanent increase to your attributes.

You have consumed the flesh of a being rife with the gifts of Deyra. The mana-rife meat bestows upon you the following:
+3 Toughness
+3 Strength
+2 Agility
+1 Mental Power]

Woo. Now, I wanted to know what level Heivax had been and what his stats were. Nine points? What a powerhouse. I realized it was time. I needed to make *the* most important decision. I had hit level 21 after the recent battle. Now, I knew what had to happen. I had one main task. I needed to stretch my mana in a way that would allow me to maintain my soulstone illusion until we managed to flee from the Soul Carver, perhaps even until we reached the upper reaches of the mountain and Selys herself. And I needed to fix it now; my mana was already ticking downward.

I checked over my attributes.

[Personal Info:
Name: Onyx
Race: Young Shadow Dragon. Level 21 – experience toward next level: 2700/21000
Size: Very large

Stats and Attributes:
Health: 365/570
Mana: 512/610
Strength: 32
Toughness: 57
Agility: 71
Mental Power: 61
Mental Control: 79
Mana regeneration rate: 1248/day
Health regeneration rate: 57/hour]

I liked the growth, but that wasn't what was important to me. The mana regen was. As it stood, keeping the illusion active at all times, which I was, right now, cost me... 2880 mana a day. Damn. I clicked level up, watching my Mental Control automatically rise by 6, and dumped the full 15 points from my last three levels into Mental Control, ending up at... 1600 mana/day. With my nine mana crystals, that would give me four and a half days to come up with a solution. Now, more than ever, I needed the perfect feat. Come on, Deyra. Don't let me down.

With trepidation, I brought up the waiting notification.

[Feat available. You can select one feat from among the following:]

[Improved Breath Weapon. Your Weakening Fog improves. From now on, the attack has the chance to add a temporary stun effect upon any enemies.]

[Improved Hardiness. You grow faster through your struggles. Your Toughness receives a one-time boost of +10.]

[Improved Power. Your mental capabilities improve with use. Your Mental Power receives a one-time boost of +10.]

Ordinarily, this might be a tough choice, but right now it was a no-brainer. I selected Improved Power immediately - that would net me maybe a day more, due to the increased mana.

To my surprise, a final notification was waiting for me.

[Congratulations. You have evolved.

A dragon grows both through years, experience and violence. You are starting to become settled and are growing in power and wisdom. From now on, you are a Young Shadow Dragon.

Innate ability gained: Shadow meld. When you are hidden in shadows, physical damage will be halved.]

Initially, I was unable to see or feel any differences. However, letting the tip of a claw slide over my scales, I noticed it. A slipping of sorts, like an almost unnoticeable gust of wind playing over my entire body. I realized that my scales had taken on a different hue as well, darkening to shape themselves to the shadows surrounding me. Then, I realized just how overpowered this ability was. Outside the mountain, it would only be effective at night, and only then outside the reach of cities and light. In here, we were almost perpetually wrapped in shadows. No wonder most dragons disliked Shadow Dragons. There was no fighting fair with us. Now, I just had to survive.

CHAPTER TWENTY-SEVEN

After climbing a great hill, one only finds that there are many more hills to climb. - Nelson Mandela

"So. How are we going to handle this?"

"It is simple. We need to make it to the top of the Mountain. I know the route and some of the challenges that we will meet along the way. Then we enter, with me hidden and you and your tiny minions playing the act of Selys' loyal subjects. Then we take her down and establish my rule, with the aid of *my* minions."

Oh yes. His minions. That cavalcade of shambling, undead monstrosities that were right now walking in the middle of our procession. It wasn't like they needed protection, but we had come to the agreement that they shouldn't be spotted before we were there. Rumors of undead traveling the mountain would be a good way to get the assembled wrath of Selys' reign brought down upon us.

It didn't improve our prospects for an escape, though. "All right. That seems pretty straightforward. What are we going to encounter on the way? I know that you said that our scouts are to stay close, but if they know what we are supposed to look for, it will make their efforts easier."

He nodded. "I will make a list. The first day should be easy. We travel to the center of the mountain, and then we move up."

I walked next to the Soul Carver. We were well past our usual haunts on the first day of our mission, and he had been directing our travels for the entire day. For me, much of the time had been spent managing our efforts, ensuring we had a safe way of progressing and ensuring that the Soul Carver was occupied. Oh, and keeping my concentration. Right now, the illusionary soulstones were resting back inside the Soul Carver's jacket. I doubted that my illusions would be able to keep up with his Mental Power if he decided to scrutinize them in detail, but until now, that hadn't happened, and I intended to keep him distracted as well as I could.

Still, having to keep up the illusions at all times was draining, and not just for my mana. The knowledge that he may at any time see through my stratagem and punish me was... distracting, to say the least. Oh, and I needed us to hurry without it appearing like I was rushing.

On the good side, our last talk had done a world of good. He might still choose to slay any of our minions at a moment's notice. Still, as long as the rest of them kept their distance, and I was the one to walk alongside him, he seemed less... homicidal now.

"...You have done well in keeping us from being discovered so far. I have not had to intervene yet."

"Thank you. We are going to need some help soon. My Talpi know a lot about the lower layers and share info with other Talpi whenever they get the chance, but they rarely move further up into the mountain."

He walked on in silence for a while. "My studies on creatures from within the mountain has been valuable in learning about the interior. As in the world outside, the stronger creatures are drawn to power. Hence, the higher we travel, the more dangerous monsters and settlements we will find. Paradoxically, we will also see fewer outright predators the higher we travel."

"Huh. That seems weird. Why is that?"

"Consider this. The higher we travel, the closer we are to Selys' reign. She, as the strongest, or at least, most constant, force within the Mountain, has no interest in being beset by roving monsters every time she leaves her throne. Hence, all the larger settlements near her are only made with her approval. That does not only create peace near her surroundings, but further down the layers as well. It took me a long time to understand."

"Oh. I get it."

"You do? Then explain."

"It's the Law of Chad." Fucking Chad. Why did he always have to be right about these things? "I'll have to see if I can recall his exact words. 'You have the exact power that people think you have.'" He had followed that sentence with "If a broad thinks you're the boss, you *are* the boss, if you catch my drift." I was pretty sure most of his lessons hadn't been approved by management. I shook my head, erasing the image of Chad from my mind's eye. "Basically, if the nearby settlements have been approved by Selys, it's not a far cry for them to make it appear like they are untouchable themselves, and that an attack on them would be an attack on Selys." However much I disliked Chad, he had been right about too much, and I could see it in my own employees back on Earth. Outside, and often even inside, a clear and fixed hierarchy, informal positions of power would appear, and clever people would take advantage of it to better their own positions.

"I should like to meet this Chad. That is the exact point. The closer we come to Fire Peak, the less likely we are to have roaming monsters, and the power struggles are less out in the open. Only the most powerful, desperate, or elusive monsters roam these areas."

I nodded. "That makes a lot of sense. I will inform the

scouts, and they will know what to look for, and make sure that we become more vigilant as we move upward."

He gave a slight, approving nod. He spent the next ten minutes reciting the forces he had seen back when he made the journey toward Fire Peak and Selys.

I was taken aback by the sheer number of battling species living inside the mountain. The place was, without doubt, larger than Mount Everest. Hell, it had to be larger than that big-ass mountain on Mars. I had to hand it to the Soul Carver, though. His memory was excellent. That, or he had spent a lot of time obsessing over his plans. On second thought, I knew which it was. As his explanation finally stopped, I inclined my neck. "Thank you. If you don't mind, I'll inform everybody."

I moved along, talking to Imps as I passed, and a few of them flew up to sit on my back. They had improved already. With the dragon meat and the training, most of them had already gained enough Toughness and Agility to keep a decent speed for at least an hour at a time without help. As for the rest... I gave a nod to Timothy as I passed him. He was a vague mist encompassing the group of Imps, boosting their stats and ensuring that they kept up. They still needed the occasional break, but we were definitely getting there.

I passed by the Clenchers, smiling at the sight. Each of them had a stretcher attached, carrying our wounded, and on top of Ursam, a brave Talpus pup had braved the temper of the animal, riding him like the world's largest pony. Tim also used them as rechargeable batteries, draining mana from them to keep going. Best pets ever.

I sent a wave of approval at the big beast, even as Aelis made her way through the rows of undead toward me. "Sire. Good thing you are here. The scouts just reported back. We have found a pack of Higher Water Banes. Their home is straight in our path. We might have to backtrack for an hour in order to move around them undisturbed, but it should be no hassle."

I nodded, spent a while telling her about the Soul Carver's

observations, then dropped the Imps off and retraced my steps back to him to let him know about the detour.

His reaction wasn't what I had expected, though. "Wonderful. We are going to attack them."

I stared at the Soul Carver, who looked back at me with his usual emotionless expression. Even his eyes showed no reaction. "But... I thought the point of our progress was to ensure that we didn't get spotted?"

"Yes. We do not want me and my forces to be spotted. However, that is just half the point. The closer we get to Selys' city, the more numerous and powerful our opponents become, and the more complacent. The other half of the point is that we *want* the mountain to be in turmoil. You creating havoc while you proceed is a good thing, and it will prove your power in the eyes of Selys. Finally, in order to succeed, you and your minions could do with additional levels, and I would not mind additional material. As long as we are doing the ambushing, we will take all the chances we get to improve without large risks."

I shut my mouth and considered the task. Obviously, there would be no debating it with him. But if we were to do it, we might as well be clever about it. And I needed to hurry the hell up. Even if I managed to keep the illusion alive, my mana kept counting down every other minute. I had already had to use two Mana Crystals to stay afloat. "All right. Can you assist with the attacks? And how long do you have until that boost from your Essence Siphon runs out?"

He smiled. "Wise of you to factor that into your considerations. I still have four and a half days until it runs out. The boost is not irrelevant, and we should try to make it within that time. Of course, I will be joining you in the attacks. I will remain unseen to avoid any risk of being recognized. From what I know about these Water Banes, it should be a simple thing to send in your minions to distract them while you and I damage them."

Damnit. That was exactly what I feared. I did *not* want the bastard to use my people as cannon fodder. How to phrase this?

"Of course, Master. Would you mind if I spend a short while discussing the possibilities with the Talpi? They tend to know a lot about the creatures in the mountain and how to take them down with little wasted resources."

He waved me off, and I quickly gathered the others. Minutes later, I was back with an alternative approach. "We were fortunate, Master. I believe that I know exactly how to progress. We should be able to clear this place within half an hour and move on."

"Half an hour? For the attack, maybe. Converting any of them will take at least an hour apiece afterward."

I grinned at him, affecting camaraderie. "Oh, we can do so much better. This is what we do..."

I forced my way into the enemy lair, each step feeling like I was wading through molasses. The air itself pressed down upon me, trying to force me to the knee. However, if I was affected, the Banes had it worse. The tough, rubbery bodies of the creatures lay prone everywhere around the basic village, pushed to the ground, panting in effort like breathing in itself was a challenge. Despite the struggle, I grinned. This was not a fight. This was clean-up duty. The tour of the place was five minutes of back-breaking work, where I gathered every enemy inside the village, while the Soul Carver stood still, observing me.

"I am running out of mana. You have three minutes more." The words were delivered flat, not as an apology, merely a statement of fact.

I grunted, pulling one more of the unwieldy beasts after me. I was glad I did not have to fight them. Their rubbery, thick skin resisted almost all attempts at piercing them and their bulk was large enough that they should be able to overwhelm even my Crawls simply with their weight. Flipping it next to the fifteen other beasts, I sighed and moved into position. Then I breathed. One Weakening Fog after the other, as soon as the countdown was over, and two minutes later, I asked the Soul Carver to drop his spell.

There was no movement. Not a single twitch from the downed beasts.

The pale spellcaster observed us without comment as my people filed in. The process went without hitches, each of them quickly and efficiently performing a single attack on each downed beast. The Imps saw it as one large game, buzzing around and chittering in joy while they repeated the efforts of the others, until I moved in and admonished them to stay still and behave. Then came the time for the execution.

I did it myself, using my bulk to force my sharp claws through the thick skin of their necks. Within moments, the lair rang with exclamations as we all received a staggering amount of experience. 22,300 experience points, to be exact. Enough for everybody here, including myself, to level at least once. I dumped everything into Mental Control right away, earning myself another half day of respite.

When we left the cavern, twenty minutes later, I looked like a particularly gory pack mule. Every bit of space on my back was taken by the Banes, except for the centre, where the Soul Carver sat, in the middle of a spellcasting process of some sort. An hour later, I heard his mental voice from behind. It was teeming with curiosity. "You are an interesting sort. No other dragon would allow such an attack on their dignity, yet you actively encourage it. Why?"

I started shrugging, then changed my mind. Didn't want to push him off. "As long as my own people are involved, I don't care about looks, only efficiency. If this gets us to our target faster, with less risk and less chance of deaths, why would I oppose that? Sure, I wouldn't want to appear weak in front of enemies, though."

"We are alike in that. I also care more about expedience than looks. You are setting yourself up for disappointment in the long run, however. Sharing that much experience with your underlings can only lead to mutiny and suffering." He paused, then continued, in a creepily cheery tone of voice. "But there is

no need to worry. I will help you look out for any hints of insur-
rection."

I simply nodded. It was hard for me not to shudder at the
thought. Good thing we had already agreed that everybody
should stay unobtrusive and not do anything that looked the
least bit suspicious. "So. Would you tell me about the kingdom
you mean to create? I'm not a history nerd, but I still know a bit
about different types of governments and their successes.
Maybe there is something to be learned."

We continued on our way. Holding a conversation with the
Soul Carver was a draining experience, especially given that I
couldn't tell him what I thought about the horrors of his dream
regime and had to look out for the way I phrased things inside
my mind. At the same time, I had to maintain the illusion. And
it was a horror in the making, to be sure. He was basically going
to create a police state, keep everybody in check by means of his
undead minions, and ensure that nobody leveled too much--all
in the name of protecting them, obviously. It might work too, at
least to begin with. The differences between low-level and high-
level creatures here were huge. Where, in the real world, it took
weapons and a crazy level of control to keep the common man
under control, here, he could theoretically manage simply by
keeping everybody from leveling.

Obviously, there would be pressing questions that could be
weak points to his plan--limits in distance, how well he was able
to gather information from his minions and how well they held
up over time, just to name a few. However, when I asked him
about details, he clammed up and started acting suspicious. It
appeared that there were limits to the camaraderie between
us yet.

The Soul Carver finished the conversion of his new minions
quickly. Within half a day, the final form slid off my back and
ambled unsteadily back to the remainder of his army. By then,
it seemed that he had also had enough of my company and
joined his minions, only moving back up when he had a
command or a course correction to share with us.

We were all looking for an opportunity to arrange our flight, but it refused to show up. The Talpi were allowed to range ahead and behind us, with most of the Crawls set up as a second set of defenders in case anybody were to attack us from either side. The rest of us, including the young ones and their mothers, were too close to the Soul Carver and his undead to allow for a quick getaway, and we were being driven hard. On the rare occasion that we were allowed to sleep or take a break, we rested right where we were.

Over the next two days, we traveled at a decent pace, for me, at least. For my people, it was a lot more taxing and grueling, especially those who hadn't invested heavily in Toughness. By day three, the Imps spent almost all of the time on my back, and even some of the Talpi started needing rests. Turns out that, without proper pauses, you get a debuff to your Toughness. Huh. We took down two additional groups on the way. One was a huge gathering of Dweelers. I shuddered to think what would have happened, had they surprised us, instead of the other way around. With the debuff from the Soul Carver, we barely paused to slay them before continuing on our way.

The second group was an unknown race. Even the Talpi didn't know them. We proceeded as earlier: the Soul Carver went in first and pacified the ugly creatures, who looked like a mix between the abominable snowman and wookies, and then I followed to round them up and weaken them to the point of fatigue. I hadn't even made it into the cave, however, when they surprised us with an ugly ability.

After a few seconds of lying on the ground, their bodies started shining. At first, it was just an almost unnoticeable sheen from each of the downed creatures, but it turned into a blinding glow, like a full-body LED headlight, then they started getting up and flinging themselves at the Soul Carver with abandon. Of course, he didn't seem to care. He just stood there with his shield activated and took the attacks, while I hesitated in the opening.

I stood there indecisive for a minute. For one, it didn't look like they were doing him any damage. With God as my witness, I wouldn't mind them striking him down and eating his remains. However, I did not want to incur his wrath--and not coming to help him might be the exact thing needed to do just that. Even so, if the frenzied monsters were strong enough to ignore his spell, would I even be able to make a difference? The beasts were going absolutely batshit crazy. The light came from cracks in their skin, or their fur, making them look like kaleido-scopic strobe lights and, if anything, the lack of reaction from the Soul Carver aggravated them even further.

Before I came to a final decision, I noticed the light dimming slightly. Not only that, their attacks also slowed some-what. Then I realized. This was just temporary. A momentary buff or physical reaction that allowed them to boost their abili-ties manyfold or ignore spells, whichever. However, it would not last, and it was just a matter of waiting. Right enough, two minutes later, the light disappeared from the last of the beasts, who dropped boneless to the ground before the Soul Carver and I marched in to weaken the beasts and reap the rewards.

Later I stood, reveling in the experience that ticked in. The 14,300 experience was almost enough to hit the next level. The Soul Carver approached me, and I had to ask. "Weren't you afraid? I mean, with the light and all, their attacks might have been elemental attacks and be able to force their way through your shield. You could not have known beforehand."

He intoned. "I have plenty of tools at my disposal. Besides, fear is a matter of the body. I control my body. Not the other way around."

CHAPTER TWENTY-EIGHT

Our course would look erratic to somebody who hadn't been here before. One thing was for certain, however. We kept moving upward and the local traffic became less and less. I cursed every minute of wasted time, as I watched my mana slowly dripping downward. Even with my impressive regenerative abilities, I was unable to keep up with the mana demands needed for maintaining the illusion. Two and a half days passed as we climbed the mountain, and I burned through my reserves of Mana Crystals. Just two more to go.

Still, maintaining the deceit was essential. I despaired at the thought of what would happen if I lost my control of the illusion for just a moment, and the sensation of the soulstones pressing against the Soul Carver's body from within his jacket went *poof*. Every time I talked to him, I searched his face for a hint that he was just toying with me and had long since discovered that the soulstones were safely in the hands of Arthor. My mood wasn't improving, either. Whatever else you could say about the need for sleep of dragons, going for days without sleep was taking its toll.

That's how I almost let the Soul Carver string Wreil up. I

mean, I did notice, as if it were far off, the fact that he hurried back toward us and was explaining something to the Soul Carver, but it took me at least five seconds to wake up from my trance and realize that he stood over the tiny talpi, releasing dark energies into his prone form.

"What the hell? What's going on?" I rushed forward, and the Soul Carver released the energies. A tiny whimper coming from Wreil told me that whatever the Soul Carver had been doing wasn't permanent. Still, I edged forward, forcing the necromancer to face me instead of my downed minion.

"Your slave doubted me. I was just explaining to him that this will not do."

What? "Wreil? What is this about?"

He was slowly picking himself up from the ground. "The Soul Carver says that the tunnel is supposed to go straight or left here. As you can see, it only goes left. The other scouts are out to--"

"He said I must have remembered wrong. I would not misremember something like this."

From the hatred wafting from the mistreated scout, he did not see it the same way, and it looked like he was not going to just let it go.

Fortunately, Arthor spoke up before Wreil said something stupid. "The Soul Carver is right."

Everybody turned to see the tall shaman stride through the grouping, ignoring everybody to tap at a section of the tunnel where it curved off to the right and downward. "The earth has been displaced here. It was well done, but I can sense the tunnel continue on the other side, maybe 30 feet away. Sometimes, these things happen naturally - this did not. It was manual labor."

"Manual labor?" I could feel a frown building. "Why would anybody close off a tunnel in the middle of nothing? There's not supposed to be anything here. Not unless-" The sound of cries arose in the distance. "Damnit. It's an ambush!"

I turned around to start issuing orders, but the Soul Carver

MASTER OF THE MOUNTAIN

acted first. "Send the Crawls and the Talpi to fend them off. The rest stay here, while your shamans and builders reopen the tunnel. Oh, and keep the scouts here, too."

There was so much wrong with that. "Yes master. Could we perhaps send-"

"Was my order unclear, Puppet? Do you doubt what I meant? I am not wasting any of our good slaves on a distraction. Now move!"

I didn't need to be able to read their emotions to tell what they wanted to ask. Their glances said it all. "Do something!" I gritted my teeth and obeyed. "You heard what he said. Crawls in front, ranged Talpi behind. Roth, you keep charge of everybody. Make sure to come back safely. Wreil, you follow. Send for us if things go bad."

They ran off, the Talpi looking as recitent as the Crawls looked eager. Meanwhile, Creziel and Arthor started in on reopening the tunnel. Within seconds, we could see the earth start running like a mudslide, straight down to where our builders were rushing in with tarps, buckets, and other containers to carry the dirt away and open up the passage.

"Master, should Timothy and I not join the fray? It would be a waste to let our minions die if the ambushers are creatures that Timothy or I could easily defeat."

He thought about it for a moment. "No. You keep confusing the realities of this world with your own world. This will be a useful lesson for you. Yes, you could act like you prefer to, taking a personal interest and taking unnecessary risks. Here, however, these risks get you killed. This is exactly what your minions are for. Taking your risks for you. Where we are going, we will need the Imps and Clenchers. There will be plenty of heavy fighting and open areas where the Imps will be useful. The others are dispensable."

I wanted to argue, but didn't want him to teach me any further "valuable lessons." Instead, I stood, undecided, glancing between the growing tunnel opening and the other tunnel, where screams and sounds of battle started to ring.

At this point, it became clear to me just how much my shamans had grown. The earth flowed constantly, and there was barely a delay as heavy rocks dropped down to the earth. Creziel and Arthor stood shoulder to shoulder, speaking little as they toiled. Around them, builders flowed effortlessly, carrying heavy loads further down the tunnel at a near sprint.

Two tense minutes passed, and Wreil came jogging back. He looked nervously from the Soul Carver to me and back. "They're pushing us back. It's Ethium. A huge pack of them. Their spears and bows are hard to handle for the Crawls."

The Soul Carver smiled. "Ah, good. I made the right decision. They are tool users, clever, lithe and fast--and they would likely love nothing more than running to Selys with news that I am back."

"But they are not a threat for me? Then I can go back them up, make sure we do not lose any fighters unnecessarily."

He shrugged. "A lucky arrow would always be a threat, Onyx. No, there is no need. We are already halfway through the tunnel. They will hold for a few minutes more. This is what they are for."

I watched Wreil as his shoulders dropped and he slunk back to tell the fighters to hold.

The sounds of the battle increased in intensity. Our people were clearly pushed further and further back, and a few injured Talpi stumbled back around the bend toward us. Our shamans increased their pace, the intensity oozing off of them, even as they pushed harder against the mountain itself. The builders sprang at Arthor's yelled commands, almost sprinting with their heavy loads to clear the area. It was going to be a tight fit for me.

I hated this. Waiting without anything to do. I wanted to rage against the Soul Carver or just run off and defy him. It was just so goddamn unnecessary. He was probably also putting me in my place so there was no doubt who was in charge. The animal part in me agreed, fury boiling inside to be let out, and I had to clamp down hard, while the noises of battle intensified.

Finally, Arthor's mental shout rang clear through all the noises. "We're through!"

Immediately, I sent out a mental shout at top volume. "We're ready. Get through right away."

The Soul Carver nodded and motioned for me to follow. I walked right behind him, anxious to get moving. Meanwhile, he walked like he had all the time in the world. I had to duck my neck and push my bulk through the tunnel opening on the far side, but I made it, dirt spilling on all sides. Once we were on the other side, he addressed me. "Get your scouts out to ensure that we're not running into any surprises. Then Clenchers and Imps. My minions will follow behind them, and you can stay here to ensure that the tunnel is closed properly. Do not enter the fray."

Finally, some action. My commands rang out, and within seconds, the scouts were sprinting ahead of us, with the Clenchers and Imps following right behind. Way too slowly for my liking, the Soul Carver's minions followed through the tunnel. It might have only taken a couple of minutes, but felt like forever, because the shamans had to widen the opening even further to allow the largest of the Soul Carver's abominations to push their bulk through. At long last, I was able to send the command for my poor Talpi and Crawls to retreat toward us.

Again, we had to play the waiting game as the battle lines slowly flowed back toward us. Cries and clashes grew in intensity as the Talpi started returning in ones and twos. Some of them were injured, but all-told they looked better than I had dared to hope. Roth arrived as the last one, jogging backward through the tunnel to keep his eyes on the far end, where the conflict was yet to arrive.

"Where are the Crawls, Roth?"

He spat on the ground. "Back there. I told them to make sure that we got away clear. They did well, poor bastards."

"WHAT?" My mental shout shot immediately. "Erk! Flee right now. Everybody, come back here."

Five seconds passed, ten... then the first Crawl tumbled into the tunnel, bleeding from multiple places, almost stumbling as an arrow hit the wall right next to him. Then they arrived, all at once. My Crawls were fighting defensively, taking damage with each step back. Even as I watched, a Crawl was pushed off balance by a spear impacting the folds on his neck and fell, as an arrow struck him right in the head. Erk was in the center of it all, moving slowly, but holding them back with each methodical, precise strike of his heavy spear.

I finally saw the enemy. They looked like elves, if elves were dark-skinned with multi-jointed limbs. They were heavyset, but agile, and the way they moved seemed flowing and unnatural, never standing still. The pressure against my Crawls was constant. Behind the spear-wielding ones, archers appeared. I acted immediately, flinging an illusion into being behind my Crawls like the tunnel was covered in complete darkness. The spearwielders were so closely intertwined with my Crawls that I couldn't do anything, so I stepped back from the tunnel opening and sent the ranged Talpi forward to intervene.

Within seconds, throwing spears flew from *atlatls*. Few struck home, but they did make the Ethium pause and back off to reassess their situation. The Crawls used the opportunity to strike out furiously and, at my repeated insistence, finally disentangle themselves from the close combat and move toward safety. Erk moved last, staying in the thick of things, bleeding from a dozen places, but taking one sure step after another in the right direction. He was just fifty feet away from the other end of the tunnel. I deposited a Shadow Whorl in the center of the attackers, disturbing their choreography. Meanwhile, the first of the Crawls stumbled to safety beside us now.

"Get ready." I told Arthor and Creziel.

Arthor sneered at me, as he sent a rock flying to strike an attacker in the torso. "We aren't blind, Lizard."

With a loud shout, Erk moved his heavy spear through a figure eight, pushing his attackers away and allowing him to take a few steps back unopposed and stumble into a heavy jog.

"Move it, Erk. You're almost there." The second to last Crawl stumbled past us, panting, covered in blood.

My words were accomplished by a rumbling, as Arthor and Creziel started pulling down the ceiling.

Erk kept up his slow, patient jog as he moved backward, spear punishing all attackers. He was just thirty feet away and the attackers were staying back now, sending glances between him and the rest of us who were waiting. Clearly, they were having second thoughts about their chances.

I don't know what happened. Perhaps a single Ethium managed to break the illusion. Perhaps it was just a lucky shot. Regardless, a single arrow came flying through the air to impale Erk's right hand with a meaty thunk. For a second, the only noise in the tunnel was the clattering sound of his spear as it hit the ground. Then they went on the offensive. Within a second, spears flickered out to punish the, now unarmed, Crawl. Even like this, he refused to flee, taking stoic steps backward toward the tunnel opening and safety.

I yelled something, I'm not even sure what. First, a spear-head tore through his calf, dropping him to a knee. Then, weapons shot out in quick succession, carving into his other hand, elbow, and neck. Finally, with great finality, his heavy body slumped defeated to the floor, blood spreading around him.

The rumbling went unnoticed at first, but as the first rocks started tumbling from the ceiling along with cascades of earth, the Ethium started panicking. Too late, though. I bared my teeth at them, as my shamans buried both Erk and his attackers in a tomb of dirt.

I stalked away, looking for my target in between all the bloody, dirt-covered Talpi. There. "What the fuck? You left the Crawls to die? Why?"

Roth was bandaging up a long, shallow cut on his arm. He looked up at me and growled. "What do you mean, why? That's what the Crawls are for! You have said so yourself, haven't you?

You'd rather have all meat shields die than Timothy, right? They served well."

I stumbled back, mind in disarray. He was right. The little bastard was right! I'd lingered in developing the society, so they took my careless words at face value and left the Crawls to die for nothing. It was my fault.

As we slowly got reorganized and moved back into marching positions, I followed along. My body was there, but my mind was elsewhere, going in dark, self-recriminating circles.

CHAPTER TWENTY-NINE

When the Soul Carver exclaimed that we had made it to the top of the mountain, I could scarcely believe it. We'd made it! I was at a third of my mana with a single Mana Crystal to spare. Our scouts had worked their butts off for the past half day, leading us along winding tunnels in secrecy to avoid the monsters living here.

Three mighty settlements took up the space on the level right below Selys' home, but the Soul Carver had deemed that the monsters residing there were too powerful for us to spend our time attacking. The possible gains this near to our goal were not worth it. Right now, Arthor and Creziel were busy carving into a side wall, assisted by our builders, where an unopened chamber beyond should be able to hide us for a while. The Soul Carver waited for me ahead.

He did not react as I moved up next to him, merely stared straight ahead. I joined him and took in the vista ahead of me, where the climbing tunnel opened up into something new. I gasped as I took in the magnitude of what lay ahead. My two encounters with red dragons had prepared me for opulence, a love of glittering things and scenes replete with lava like they were set in the lower layers of hell. I was not prepared for civilization. But that was what met me. Sure, the Talpi had told me that Fire Peak was a large city, but I had still been thinking in terms of a large hoard inside the mountain, surrounded by buildings and the like. The scene before me was not that.

It was a city. No, scratch that. It was a metropolis, placed out in the open for everybody to admire. Dead center on a gigantic rise, it showed off a gigantic fortress in the center of the city, dark crenellations sporting huge bonfires at even intervals, with large buildings ranging out toward a large wall surrounding the city. Around the fortress, needle-thin towers rose at intervals around the city, though none dared rise as high as the crude, towering fortress itself.

The numerous fires around the city covered the view in a vibrant sheen, and I couldn't help but feel a certain foreboding. We were going to attack *that*? The look of the ominous city had made me tune out the surroundings. But when I looked around, my jaw dropped. "She has cored out the entire peak of the mountain?" The walls of the mountain were visible on all sides now, set miles apart, underlining exactly how large the scene was and allowing anybody on the walls or inside the fortress above to spot attacks from miles away. Finally, high, high above us, I was met with something I hadn't seen for months. Daylight, blessed daylight poured in from where the cap of the mountain was missing.

The Soul Carver spoke, slowly and ponderously. "She did not create the city or the surroundings. That one lingers from earlier generations. I believe humans once ruled this place, or dwarves. However, it serves as a powerful reminder that the power that gathers here, at the peak of the Scoured Mountain, is not to be underestimated. When last I was here, Selys' numbers were less. The towers are also new, and I do not know what they do. Now, we have a lot of work ahead of us."

I could see what he meant. Even at this distance, I could see that the walls surrounding Fire Peak teemed with armed creatures and the skies above the city held numerous flying defenders too, zipping to and fro. Inside the city, there was movement everywhere, and the multitude of buildings promised a huge number of inhabitants. Even with a conservative guess, the inhabitants of the city would have to outnumber us ten times over.

And those towers... I had no way of knowing, but with the regularity of their placement throughout the city, they had to have some function. "I can see that. So, my minions and yours hide out here and the two of us go in? Then, when Selys is dead, we can send in the troops?" Heh. more like I would be able to use the chance to betray him and laugh as Selys set him on fire.

"That was my initial plan. Now, looking at their defenses, we will have to adapt the plan. This is going to take a while."

Such simple words. Yet, I fought to keep my concentration as they kicked over the plans I'd been haphazardly building since the Soul Carver took over. "What do you mean?" I tried to keep from revealing exactly how unsettled I'd been.

"There are too many of them. Even with their leader replaced and the element of surprise on our side, we will struggle to establish dominion over them all. We will have to establish the hoard here and arrange an alternative attack plan."

He started sounding out his tentative plan. It seemed sound. He would establish a grinder here, in the layer just below the entrance leading to Fire Peak. Here, my minions could lure the enemies near, combining his and my structures, weakening and defeating the enemies while falling back all the time. With the majority of Fire Peak's forces occupied chasing my people, he would use his own abominations to breach the city.

With the powerful enemies weakened and outside the city, he believed that it would be an easy task to conquer for us to invade the city and slay Selys. Then, we would hold the city against any attackers while the Soul Carver converted Selys and the other fallen enemies into undead to join his cohorts.

I had trouble concentrating on keeping up the facade while

we spoke. I needed him to go in with me now! Everything would fall apart otherwise. "Aren't you afraid of being spotted here? You said it yourself. Whispers that undead are roaming the place could ruin everything."

He waved a hand dismissively. "My minions need no comfort. They can stay inside the hiding place we are building. Your gifts and the earth powers of the shamans should help hide the place. Any of your minions who are spotted can be sacrificed easily. Now, let us take a look at where we will be hiding. I am sure that your construction skills will be useful in altering the place to fit our needs."

I followed in his footsteps, coming up with ideas on the spot and adding on to his initial ideas. Hidden within the walls, we would work feverishly to turn the entrance tunnel into a series of deadly traps. Once we were done with the mundane preparations, we would establish the hoard and start on every construction we would be able to construct before they discovered our presence. Obviously, once we established the hoard, it would be a matter of time.

If Selys' domain ranged more than about three miles to the edge of the upper layer, where we were established, we'd be discovered straight away, and she could send her minions right at us. If, however, we were outside the domain itself, it would all depend on how often she checked her domain. Hell, we might go days without her discovering that a new domain had been established right outside her city.

No matter what else happened, these considerations were beside the point. There was no way I'd be able to handle the mana regeneration necessary in the handful of days or more it would take to prepare the area for an optimal defense. In two hours from now, I would have to use my final mana crystal, and about fourteen hours later, our chances would implode along with my illusion. I had no intention of finding out how the Soul Carver would react.

So. What to do? Try to swap the real soulstones back? Destroy the stones and run for it? Neither of these choices were good. Even if I managed to swap them back and he didn't notice, and that was a major *if*, it would lead me straight back to the path I wanted to avoid in the first place. Even if he actually held up his side of the bargain, the position as second in command to the Soul Carver was not one I wanted to pursue.

Running for it might work, if I broke the Soulstones. But we were straight back to the earlier considerations. Even if they were staying out of sight, the Soul Carver's minions were every-where. Even now, a hulking behemoth rested right next to me, unmoving yet threatening. The odds of everybody making it outside the necromancer's reach before he figured out what was going on were abysmal and a fight was out of the question. Heh. And Selys wasn't just going to let us all in. No, I needed something... some kind of diversion.

Right then, I was not good company. Once the Soul Carver was done planning, he let me go to let my people in on the plans and get them started on the undertakings. I avoided people milling about in the caves and polite inquiries alike, just staying in the background, taking in my people. Things were progressing fast. The cave they had unearthed was huge. Even with the size of the Soul Carver's minions, we had no problem fitting everybody inside. Right now, the young Talpi and Crawls alike were running about under the oversight of their parents while everybody else was making use of the chance to rest and have something to eat.

From the explanation of the scouts, we should be safely hidden away from the sight of any wandering minions. In the distance, our scouts were out in number, keeping an eye on any movement going our way, while our builders were preparing the surroundings. My mind was in turmoil. Do or don't? Risk it all? Start living on the run, like the Talpi had done their entire lives?

I was far away when Aelis patted my leg and brought me back to the present. "Sire? We brought you something to eat. You have not been eating today. Deyra will guard your soul, but you need to take care of your body yourself."

A tiny smile made its way to my lips. Aelis was becoming a

mother hen - and the thought of this tiny fur ball looking out for me who was twenty times her bulk made me chuckle. Damnit. Her simple presence helped me. I knew what I had to do. "Aelis. We'll need to gather everybody. We have some important decisions to make."

Fifteen minutes later, we were gathered in the far end of the cave. Around us, my favorite people were gathered. They looked subdued and lost as they looked to me for an explanation. Two builders were digging into the far wall next to us, providing us with a cover story in case the Soul Carver wandered over to see what we were doing. I took a deep breath and said, "You are fleeing tonight."

Arthor did not beat around the bush. "You? What about yourself? And what happened to the plan?"

"It was a long shot to begin with, and it was all dependent on our making it here in time and attacking before I ran out of mana. Now, that's not happening, and we'll have to act before tomorrow. I don't know what will happen when my illusion runs out, but I don't think it's something we want to experiment with. As for myself, I will attempt to flee, too, but I'm not going with you. I'll try to lead him away from you." Their horrified exclamations interrupted me, and I had to shush them down.

"Keep it down. We do *not* want him to notice what's going on. Now, I've made my decision. I'll try to get away and improve your chances to flee. I'd love for you to come up with a better solution, but I'm just not seeing it. The thing is, if we all run for it, together, we'll have all the minions as well as the Soul Carver right behind us. If we run in separate directions, he'll definitely go after me. This should give you the chance to get as far away as possible. Heh. And I have my illusions. That rotten bastard might be able to see through them, but I doubt all his minions can."

The feelings coming from Aelis were of both shock and heartbreak. "But Sire. How can we make it without you? You have changed so much for our tribe in so little time."

I looked at her fondly. "Thank you for those words. It can't all be attributed to me, though. You have seized the opportunities, worked hard and risked much to make it this far. This is why I know you're well set to continue. You have the setup to make it far, as it is. You already know how to handle the Clenchers and with the Crawls at your side, you have all the defensive powers you need to hold back any enemies while you bring traps, magic, and ranged weapons into play. Besides, if all goes well, I'll be back to you before you know it. If not, you'll still have Tim."

Timothy's form blurred and distorted. "Wait one goddamn minute. I'm staying with you!"

"Like hell you are. The Soul Carver doesn't need you for his plans, and you won't be able to help me if you stay. But our people do need you. With you on board, they'll have excellent protection against mundane attacks, and they will need you *for* the future. If I'm not around, who's going to help ensure that everybody gets along?"

The bright form distorted even further. "But I'm not a leader."

I nodded. "That might be true." I didn't add the words *for now*. Tim sported an impressive amount of growth, and he might get there... eventually. "Arthor will handle that part of it. But you are clever and hold a lot of knowledge in that convoluted mind of yours. Knowledge that our people will need in order to stay together and improve for the future. Besides, if you're not around, who's going to finish that string project of yours?"

He didn't answer. Arthor was quick to enter the discussion, however. "I will handle all leader responsibilities, will I? That's awfully easy to say for you, dragon. Pfah. Well, we are not going along with this. Not unless you tell us why." Underneath his accusing words ran an undercurrent of worry and fear.

"It's simple. I've thought over every version of this, and the only way I'm getting away from the bastard is if I'm letting some of you guys take the fall. Even with my illusions, there's no way we can all escape free of harm. A month or two ago, I would've taken the chance, but not anymore. Despite what I sometimes tell you, I've grown fond of you."

Sensations of empathy pulsed back toward me from the Talpi present. "I've called myself a leader since the start, but I haven't really been one, have I? Being a leader can seem easy. You just shove people around and tell 'em what to do, then you reap the rewards for yourself. Well, sometimes, being a leader also means that you need to take responsibility and face the music on behalf of those you intend to lead." I looked at each of them in turn, then I showed them my most ferocious grin. "Besides, if you think I mean for that stinking old corpse to actually catch me, I've got news for you. I don't know how, but I'll stick it to him good."

The assembled group fell silent. Aelis was the first to speak. Her mental message was accompanied by strong feelings of fondness and loss. "Please make sure that you do that, Onyx. And you need to make it back to us afterward. Whatever you say, we do need you. Life without you will be less."

The emotions from the group were variations of the same. Sadness, first and foremost. Well, except for Roth who, as usual, didn't hold back. "That's the way to do it, Onyx. And if he does catch you, kick him in the teeth on your way down."

CHAPTER THIRTY

*I feel like getting married, or committing suicide, or subscribing to
L'Illustration. Something desperate, you know. - Albert Camus, A Happy
Death*

We left shortly after this. While I knew what I had to do, there
was still no assurance that I was going to get away with it. Also,
the clock was ticking. Mere hours before I'd have to let the illusion drop.

The Soul Carver was busy. One of the Water Banes had not
been converted properly, and he was working on it. This boiled
down to him standing stock still with a low-quality soulstone
floating in front of him, while his fingers followed intricate
patterns in the air ahead. Ever so slowly, a rune formed on the
stone, burning bright with power. "Yes, Carl. What do you
need?" His mental voice relayed nothing about his attention to
the work in front of him.

"I would ask a favor."

"Yes? That is intriguing. Why would you believe that I am
interested in granting such?"

"Honestly? Because you are better than I initially thought." I didn't need to lie about this part. He *was* a better person than I'd figured at first, if only because I figured him for nothing but a murderous psychopath. He was that, but with human-like tendencies. "You have proved that you can handle not being right about your approaches and change from it by letting my minions live, even if you didn't see their usefulness at first. Now, I would show you that living creatures have advantages to undead at times, but that it takes some additional compromise."

He let the soulstone hover down to the floor. "Aha. Asking for a favor by telling me that I am wrong. That is a novel approach. How do you propose to teach me my errors?"

"Well, I believe that you've been removed from the lives and desires of living creatures for a while." I turned around, motioning at a group of nearby Talpi, toiling away without pause. "My minions have worked without pause since you joined us. They have been in several battles, have almost been killed--by your own creations, none the less--and know that they're soon about to risk their lives again."

"True. As was to be expected. If they were not worthy minions, there would have been no reason to let them live. A life under my rule will include constant struggle and conflicts. I do believe they have had plenty of time to recuperate."

I nodded. "Agreed. However, they will need more than physical rest. They also need the chance to improve their spirits. Just a short while ago, your minions fought to crush them, and now they are forced to travel alongside them constantly, creatures that, until recently, only existed for them in legends. So this is my proposal: Give my minions an evening of rest, away from your minions. This will allow me the chance to tell them that everything is going to be all right, that we are working for a better future, and that their assistance is essential."

The pale creature's facial features were still as usual, but his mental voice betrayed a hint of curiosity. "So you would lie to them in order to improve their efficiency. I must admit that I doubt the usefulness."

"Well, I will vouch for the approach. Well-rested minions who fight for what they believe in will be a lot more efficient than ones who struggle only for their own survival. In fact, let us make a wager. If you admit that they prove more efficient after this chance to rest their spirits, you will grant me back control over my hoard once we've taken down Selys." Not like that was ever going to happen, but let the bastard think I was in this for the long haul...

His disturbing laughter screeched at my ears. "I appreciate your humor, Carl. Of course, that is not going to be possible. Still, I might be convinced to let you join in on the construction decisions... if you win. What is in it for me if you lose?"

I considered his words. It wasn't like I had a whole lot of bargaining chips. "Me acknowledging that your wisdom super-sedes mine will not be enough? Fine. How about this? If you win, I will let you decide my path. My attributes from the next three levels and next feat will be yours to select."

"Acceptable." He pondered the situation. "We have enough food for at least a week. Let us dispense with the work on the corridor, close off the entrance so no one finds us by chance, and create an enclosure for your minions."

My spirits soared as I hurried back to my people. This was excellent. Maybe there was hope for our escape. In record time, we had the builders and Crawls moving dirt from the side walls to the center of the cave. There, Arthor and Creziel shaped a wall, creating a large room separate from the rest of the cave. The wall was thin, but sure to hold. Meanwhile, they started planning the next moves, searching for the right place to create an emergency exit that would allow all of us to flee. We would be operating under heavy time constraints, but if anybody could do it, it would be the combined labor of the builders, shamans, and Crawls.

To keep up appearances, I had everyone start working to prepare a feast. Soon, a huge fire soared, warming up the room and spreading the appetizing smell of roasted meat. I smiled to see some of the younger Talpi start playing with one of the younger Crawls. Good to see that they could shed their worries for a while. If only it was that easy for the rest of us, as well.

A short while after the last piece of wall was erected, Arthor reported to me. They had found a route that would allow them to create a tunnel within only a few hours. We would need to start digging soon. But before they got started, I needed to ensure that the Soul Carver wouldn't come crashing in at any time. I could just envision him spotting the tunnel right when we were nearing completion.

Approaching the Soul Carver was always an intimidating experience, this time made worse by the fact that we might finally have a real chance at freedom. The cave felt oppressive to me now, where escape was in sight and having the Necromancer's minions lurking motionless on all sides didn't help. A few shuffling undead worms were busy reinforcing something near the wall while the Soul Carver himself was back to converting some of the yeti beasts we'd slain.

"Carl. Good. I was about to send for you. We will be talking about Selys tonight. My past struggles with her taught me some things about her. You should learn how best to handle your attacks if you want to survive the battle."

What? "Uh, Selrahc. I was just about to thank you for the chance, then go to improve the spirits of my minions?"

"Oh. I see how you could be confused. Our agreement concerned your minions, not you. You will get the chance to tell them your pretty lies about their futures, but then you will come straight back here and help me with the preparations. After all, I would not want you to abuse my good humor, right?" His eyes glinted with dark humor.

Had he seen through my deception? He obviously didn't trust me fully. There was no time. "I must admit, I had been looking forward to improving my own spirits a bit, too, but if you insist. I'll be back soon."

"Make sure that you do."

My clawed feet had never felt heavier, as I dragged my bulk

toward our part of the cave. Aelis and Wreil parted the huge pelts that covered the entrance and welcomed me with cautious smiles. The smiles died immediately as they saw the look on my face. I told them the bad news straight away. "Change of plans. I'm staying."

They didn't take the news well. Within moments, the cave was filled with desperate plans of immediate attack, other, even more desperate plans of holding back the undead forces while they dug the tunnel in haste. I had to carve through the mental suggestions flying through the air. "Enough! We don't have time for this. If I don't return to the Soul Carver soon, he'll wonder what's taking me so long, and the opportunity will be lost for all of us."

Aelis couldn't stop herself. "But Sire. We--"

"No buts. I am staying behind. The Soul Carver insists. It's for the best, really. This way, I'll be able to do what I can to distract the bastard while you run for it."

Arthor cut off the rest with a sharp gesture. Beside him, the circling rocks slowed down and crumbled apart as the tall Talpi frowned at everybody. "He is right. There is no time. Onyx. I haven't said this, but we will forever be thankful for the time we've spent with you. We are different now, from when you first met us. Our sight is aimed higher. I hope that... no. Deyra be with you and guard you. That is all."

"This world wasn't exactly what I had expected of an after-life, but you were a huge positive surprise. Please stay safe and continue improving the way you have. Also, please, do not continue the way I have. Do not push each other down. Instead, work together and create a world where you lift each other up, make the most of all of your talents. You can do it, I have no doubt. You, all of you, may be small, but your spirits are strong."

Of course, I didn't leave right away. A lot of my people wanted to say goodbye in person, and we needed to spend some time to ensure that we had the plans ready for their escape.

Finally, however, I had to bid them goodbye and walk the heavy walk back toward the Soul Carver and my doom.

The fount of all my problems didn't notice my mood. He greeted me with a nod. "Ah. Carl. Your minions will be able to improve their spirits by themselves now?"

"They should." Inside my mind, I added, "*Getting away from you should do the trick.*"

"Good. Now, we have a lot to prepare for. You had some protection against elemental damage, did you not?"

The minutes went by glacially slow as I tried to focus. The Soul Carver elaborated on not only Selys herself, but also her two human sorcerer pets. All fire based and adept at ranged attacks, their forces were incredibly predisposed to dealing with the Soul Carver and his creations.

"Still, my time outside the mountain has not been entirely in vain. While growth is harder and targets are far between, there is also a larger variety in species and, if you know where to look, a lot of intriguing characteristics to add to my tools." Even with all I knew about him, hearing him talk about killing something and raising it again as something akin to handling a tool gave me the chills.

"You may have seen the unassuming worms back there? They have some interesting features--the ability to slither along ceilings, poisonous teeth, and an impressive resistance to fire. When Selys sends out her underlings, they will find some nasty surprises waiting for them."

We went on to discuss the logistics of the plan itself. I had to admire that it made the huge task of taking over the rule of the mountain seem more realistic. We would lure out their armies, grind them down and weaken them, but refrain from getting bogged down in any close engagements. When my minions had pulled their armies far enough away from Fire Peak, they would try to pull a disappearing act and circle around.

Meanwhile, the Soul Carver would waltz in unseen alongside me, as I returned, apparently triumphant in my given quest to subdue the other dragonlings in the mountain. We would take down Selys, let in our armies when they'd circled around to avoid the pursuit, then hold the city against any comers, while using all the corpses to strengthen his armies. His memory was impressive, too. He sketched an elaborate map of the city from scratch, complete with plans for where to place the different forces.

I knew I should keep my trap shut. Selrahc had shown that he was damaged beyond repair. Still, I couldn't help myself. There were enough glimpses of humanity left in him, that I had to ask: "Have you considered a different approach?"

"I am open to suggestions. I do believe that your minions will be best used on or near the battlements, however. The Talpi, together with the Imps, should be decent ranged defenders, while your builders together with the Shamans and Crawls can shore up and fix any breaches. My minions will defend the gate from any large attacks."

"That's not what I meant. What I mean is... how about trying it my way? Trust our people and lift them up at our side. Keep your minions for defense only and rule the world alongside them?"

Even with his face blank, the creases around his eyes showed how hilarious he found the idea. "As equals? The Soul Carver and his dragon, ruling alongside a Talpi? Come now. Don't be ridiculous. It's all well and good while you're fighting together. However, the moment that your interests start diverging, their daggers will find your back. No, mine is the only way. You should be happy that we are keeping your minions, even if we are bound to lose a good number in the coming battles. Still, Talpi are like Vouren. A few months of peace will have their numbers up again."

He went back to plotting as if I had never spoken. I swallowed my regrets. I had known that it was implausible to get him to change his mind. I wanted it to happen, but still... he had struggled to get his vengeance for so long that it was illogical to think it could change.

I could tell the exact moment my people started fleeing the

cave. In the middle of a sentence, the Soul Carver stopped and started staring in the direction of the other end of the cave where, right this moment, my people were pouring out the escape tunnel, soulstones in hand. I hardened myself against his obvious confusion and opened my mouth wide, putting my entire being into the Deafening Roar that erupted from me.

I followed up with a Weakening Fog, then jumped straight at the Soul Carver. My claws tore at his throat and found... nothing. I growled in frustration as my attacks bounced off an invisible barrier. Damnit. Too slow! Behind me, undead abominations turned toward me, reacting to unheard commands from their master.

He was clearly not unaffected by my ability. Staggering, he slowly stood up to his full height and his presence slammed into my being. Predictably, pain rode along on the wave and his words reverberated inside my head. "What have you done? How did they get your soulstones? Why did you attack me?"

I fought against the pain. "We just wanted to get away. That's all." The pain subsided, and I continued talking, both to keep him occupied and to keep him from hurting me. "It was all we ever wanted. You could have listened, Selrahc. Hell, if you'd come with a plan for building a decent world, I might have even joined you. As it is, I needed--"

"STOP talking." Another wave of pain flooded me, followed by even more, agony building in higher and higher waves. His voice shouted inside my mind, drowning out everything in an overwhelming wave of fury. "I trusted you! I was going to give you a place at my side! But you stabbed me in the back, just like the others. Just like *him*!" His words continued, as did the pain... but then, suddenly, the pain subsided along with his presence.

I shook my head to clear the vestiges of the agony and looked around. The Soul Carver's minions towered at my back, ready to jump me. In front of me, the necromancer stood stock still, not a muscle moving on him.

I took a great deal of pleasure in gloating at him. "Did the connections disappear? Yeah, I told them to break the soul-stones as soon as they left the caves. It's the best thing about the Talpi, really. They know exactly how to handle rocks. So they're gone now. Deal with it. Sure, you can hurt me all you want, but it will be in the old-fashioned way. My soul's my own now!"

CHAPTER THIRTY-ONE

To my surprise, I was actually left alone for a while. Well, to a certain degree of "alone." A handful of the Soul Carver's abominations were left to physically restrain me and make sure I didn't flee. An Ogre and a many-legged monstrosity literally sat on top of me and held down my neck. Fat chance of me using my breath weapon now to escape.

I should be feeling something, but in truth, I didn't mind. I didn't allow myself to think too hard. My future wasn't looking too good, but I had chosen this route for myself, and I was going to stick to it. At least, this way, I got to ruin the rotten bastard's day *and* ensure that Tim and the others lived to make something of themselves.

An hour went by. Two. With every ticking minute, my mood improved. The Soul Carver could only risk so much time outside in the tunnels before his forces were spotted and Selys would unleash her forces and fury upon him. Finally, shuffling noises from the tunnel announced their return, and the monsters started filing back into the cave.

The Soul Carver came last, but I barely noticed him. My attention was fixed on the hulking, feathered abomination in front of him. The monster in itself was nothing special, a bipedal creature that was all claws, rotten plumage, and foul smells. I was completely unable to avert my eyes from what it was carrying in its massive forearms.

There, like a perverted image of a babe resting with its mother, lay a form I would recognize anywhere. The tiny creature, dressed, as always, in soft dark leathers, could have been any of my Talpi, but the dangling arm with the missing appendage gave it away, even from a distance.

Aelis.

The Soul Carver's voice sounded like a purr inside my head. "Let us talk."

We had underestimated the Soul Carver. Several times, he had mentioned that he had his own ways of scouting. He had refused to elaborate on it, and with the skills of the Talpi, he had never been forced to disclose them. Now, the trio of disgusting body bags on the wall and ceiling gave away his secret. Their natural camouflage abilities made them fade into the background whenever you looked away.

When I did manage to catch a glimpse of them, the hideousness of the amorphous blobs riddled with long hairs, suction cups, and eyes made me wish I hadn't. According to the gloating of the Soul Carver, they were horribly inefficient at actual combat and mostly took down sleeping prey, but they had enough poison to immobilize, say, a small one-handed Talpus who was acting as rear scout.

"This is quite simple. Simple enough that even a traitor like yourself should be able to understand it." Venom oozed from the Soul Carver's words. Oh yeah. He wasn't taking my people's escape well. Because, even if he had caught Aelis, the rest of them had evaded his grasp. "You value these weak critters above a world where people are safe? Well, I will put that to a test. You get to choose. You can either help me defeat Selys and put me on the throne, or you will get to see me flay this sorry waste of flesh alive and convert it into my ranks."

I knew what had to happen. Obviously. The health of one

damaged Talpus was nothing compared to the horrors that would ensue if the Soul Carver managed to win the throne. I had to give her up. Still... as I watched her form, sleeping off the effects of the soporific poison in the arms of the horrid beast, I knew that I couldn't. Aelis was the one who'd been with me from the start, supported me all the way and cared for me. I looked into the eyes of the pale monster in front of me and could feel the hate burning inside.

"All right. You win."

We did not waste any time. The moment a crestfallen Aelis awoke from her slumber, we were placed before the towering form of our adversary again. His smile looked as disturbing as ever. "Welcome to the ranks of the living, young critter. Now, I am going to use you to prove a point to our reptilian *friend* here." He spat the word. "Attachments will only cause you pain in the long run. I realize that I have been reticent in showing off my powers. You may believe that my magic is only defensive and that I need to craft soulstones in order to control my minions."

His smile grew even wider, stretching the pale skin around his lips as light formed around him. Floating motes rotated around him, solidifying into lengthy ropes of dark chains. They grew and stretched in length, elongating soundlessly. The tremble in the rictus smile of the Soul Carver betrayed his concentration as the chains moved outward, settling in long cords around my bulk and that of Aelis.

Round and round, the chains circled my body, until finally pulling taught on all sides and slowly fading away from view. At first, the sensation was just weird - the sensations of the links against my scales were not metallic and cold, but warm and living. However, the moment they disappeared, pinpricks of pain grew from all sides of my body and, beside me, a cry of pain arose from Aelis.

The high-pitched sounds of the Soul Carver's laugh accompanied her cry. "I do not use this spell often. It is so much easier to just convert minions. And yet, there is a certain enjoyment to be found in it. Make no mistake. The chains are still there. They will be invisible to the view of others, but they are mine to command with but a thought.

"Against a tough dragon like you, Carl, the effects are limited. Yes, I can have you weeping with pain, but they are likely insufficient for killing you by themselves. For our furry friend, the prospects are different... I can carve you into pieces with but a thought. Keep this in mind, my treacherous follower." He looked us over before nodding. "That should be it. Now, with your betrayal, all our preparations are useless."

It must have been a strange sight. The mighty dragon and the tiny furred wolf-mole hybrid walking out in front, with the pale humanoid form following behind like a particularly nasty chaperone. I was lost in dark musings and Aelis was brooding as well, eyes sunken in her head, staring at the huge city towering in front of us like she was walking to her own execution. It probably wasn't too far off from the truth. The Soul Carver, however, sounded disturbingly upbeat. "I will disappear from view now. Don't you worry. I will still be right here to help keep you focused." A tiny laughter erupted from him. "I should thank you, Carl. I had been losing sight of my vision lately. Keeping my focus will be easier from here on out."

We walked in silence for a while. Before us, cries arose from the towers next to the huge gate leading into the city. Looks like we'd been spotted. The Soul Carver's mental voice returned. "I admit that I am annoyed that our plan will not work now. It would have been a lot less work for us to take over the city right away, while they were off hunting our distractions. Our combined forces would have been able to take out their diminished armies. Alone, this is impossible. Still, as long as Selys falls, my victory is certain, if delayed. We will let them fight for succession while we bide our time. Then, once they have whittled down their forces, we will attack."

I let my mind wander while he talked. The conflict seemed far off and intangible. So much had changed in the last couple of days that I had trouble adjusting. Was I doing the right thing? Actually, scratch that. I knew I wasn't doing the right thing. I just couldn't bear the thought of losing Aelis. I would have to figure something out. Do something. If only I knew what.

"Ah. There they are. The welcoming committee. It looks like a visiting dragon earns you the attention of one of Selys' own sorcerers. I will fade back a bit, but never worry. I am right here with you. Just keep to the first part of our original plan, and all will go well."

Go well for him, maybe. Still, we had gone over this part so many times that, at the very least, I knew what to do. Convince the enemies that I was a friend and that I was coming in peace. It was that or watch Aelis die a gruesome death. As we got closer to the gate, I noticed the shapes in the gate as well. At first, I almost overlooked the single humanoid form in the center of the group. He was smaller than the others and unarmored.

However, the closer I got, the easier it became to see that he was the leader of the group. The monsters surrounding him were impressive--huge, well-equipped monsters of several races, all bedecked in red uniforms and gold-embossed armor--but they held back and formed a semi-circle around the male. The glances they shot at him, showed that their respect was laced with a good dose of fear.

The robed figure was unarmored. The full-length crimson robe covered him from head to toe, and the only ornament was a golden dragon mask, hiding his features. He held up a hand, and I froze in my tracks. The mental voice was imperious and demanding. "An unknown dragon, approaching the gates of Fire Peak? Explain yourself or face the might of Selys."

I bowed low and saw Aelis throwing herself to the ground next to me. This would be tricky. I would have to assume that, like the Soul Carver himself, the sorcerer before me had a high enough Mental Power that he would be able to see through any outright lies on my part. "I have not been introduced, but I am not unknown. A single egg was stolen from Selys' clutch, with me on the inside. My name is Onyx. I have returned victorious now, to announce that I am ready to accept the mantle as her successor."

He stared at me through the slits of the mask. A pregnant silence ensued. "That is quite the claim. Still, Selys was waiting for something of the kind, ever since the hoards were culled to just two remaining. You will explain your statement as we walk. Bring that pathetic Talpus of yours, too."

We walked slowly through the city, while the sorcerer quizzed me on everything regarding my life and struggle inside the mountain. Aelis, meanwhile, kept her eyes fixed on the ground. Fear and self-loathing rang from her. Answering his questions about the first part of the struggle was simple enough and gave me time to take in the city.

I wasn't sure what I'd been expecting, but the city was a visual overload. Following the towering, well-constructed gate, the buildings started shooting up on all sides. Three stories or more, they were all made of burned bricks and of solid construction, leaving me impressed by the level of their knowledge on construction. They were unpainted, leaving the color of the buildings drab, but decorative murals and clay statues in niches carved into the buildings themselves helped set the buildings apart from each other.

Not only were the quality of the buildings beyond what I had expected, the number of different species in the first courtyard after the gate also surprised me. On our brief walk, I spotted dozens of different species walking, toiling, and lurking alongside each other. Every so often, we'd pass by large bonfires, smokeless flames burning white hot from out of large pits in the ground, with no apparent fuel to feed them.

I was about to revise my preconceptions about Selys as a heavy-handed dictator, right up until I started noticing the little things. A handful of cages stood off to the side, packed with bipedal creatures of a race I didn't know. Their faces were beaten and empty, and the chains on their hands and feet left little doubt that their future looked bleak. As we walked, we passed a scene to the side of the paved road, where an Urten was beating a downed creature. I couldn't see which species it had been, but it was bloody enough to tell that life had left it a while ago.

I returned my full attention to the sorcerer who was repeating something. "Apologies. What was that again?"

Clearly annoyed by my lack of attention, he repeated. "There was one anomaly. Two hoards faded out at the same time. Did you have anything to do with it?"

"I did. Apparently, two dragons noticed that I was taking out the competition and decided to band together and take me down. They underestimated me and my allies and traps, however."

The small human almost tripped. "Allies. Are you telling me that puny... thing at your side is your ally?"

The words exploded from me. "That *thing* is the reason I'm still here today. I doubt your hooded ass would have been able to protect and aid me half as well as she and her people have."

He paused in the middle of the street. Monsters and people of several species made sure to go a huge way around his robed form, while he looked at me incredulously. Damn. Did I just manage to ruin everything? Then he spat at my feet. "Do not test my patience. Selys wants somebody to look over the mountain, but she will not take insolence from a hatchling."

I bowed my head and didn't respond. Fortunately he took that as subservience, because we went back to walking. Apparently, he was done asking questions, and I took the chance to really take in the way the city was arrayed. My first thought was that the city planner ought to be fired, if he had ever existed. Buildings were erected with no consideration to the general layout of the city or the aesthetics. While the buildings were well-constructed, their placement and internal layout was haphazard at best. The only things that seemed to be planned out were the major roads, which moved ramrod straight toward the fortress, and the thin, tall towers. Smaller roads and alleys wound every which way. As we passed another open courtyard, this one apparently dedicated to the wholesale slaughter and butchering of animals, I could see one of the towers on the far end, and the next one over behind that one. It seemed that they went all the way around the city.

We moved on. The climb became steeper and the sorcerer's breath became laboured. I was approaching some ugly conclusions about the city but had trouble keeping my mind focused on the topic. I was still no closer to a solution that might save Aelis. At this point, even if she did get away from the Soul Carver and his chains, she'd be stuck inside a hostile city where she'd be carved up for food within minutes. No, I needed to keep her close and... and what? I asked the sorcerer. "What is your name?"

"You will not need that. I am Selys' tool."

"Alright, *Tool.* Then tell me this: Where are we going? Am I going to see Selys today?" Whatever else happened, I wanted this to end. The period under the Soul Carver had been one excruciating challenge of change and uncertainty. I had been optimistic, clueless, and sure I was doomed several times over. At this point, I just wanted to get it over with.

He huffed. "I am going to deposit you under guard in the Palace. Then, I am going to see if Selys can find the time for me and inform her about your arrival. I am not going to make any guesses as to what she is going to do about you." He stopped and faced me. "I *will* recommend that you learn to rein in your temper and demands. I am but a slave. I can deal with your complete lack of subservience. Selys is harder to predict."

CHAPTER THIRTY-TWO

Eventually everything connects - people, ideas, objects. The quality of the connections is the key to quality per se. - Charles Eames

My robed caretaker was true to his word. We took the rest of the walk in silence and soon entered the bottom layer of the large fortress. As the huge gates slammed open, we entered a world of opulence that left even somebody of my size feeling insignificant. Statues and riches adorned every hallway and the ceiling was tall enough that it almost felt like being out in the open.

After a confusing walk through winding hallways, always moving up, Aelis and I were left on our own inside an unassuming chamber bereft of furniture and other trappings. Layers of dust attested to the chamber not being used often. The doors slammed shut behind us and were immediately locked. Seconds later, heavy footsteps and clanking announced the arrival of whoever was supposed to guard us.

Aelis turned straight toward me, asking urgently. "What are we going to do, Sire? Can we escape? Fly away?"

I shook my head. "I doubt it. Even if we could make it out

of the fortress, I'm pretty sure Selys would see us running as a declaration of war. Besides, the Soul Carver would stop us."

The voice sounding inside my head made me grit my teeth. "You are not as stupid as you look, Puppet. You would have made for an excellent helper, had you not chosen to throw it all away." I tried to find a response that was not an insult, but he talked on. "Regardless, I can feel the minds of those outside. Simpletons, one and all. There is no risk that we are overheard in here.

"Now, I will make this as simple as possible: We are almost there. Once you are summoned before Selys, I will follow. Make sure you take the amputee with you. Then, I need you to keep her occupied. I don't care how. Brag about your accomplishments. Tell her about where you're from, for all I care. I need a solid couple of minutes, however. Then, once I give the signal, you will attack her with everything in your power. This, and only this way, will I spare your tiny helper and her tribe."

I looked to where I believed the voice came from. "What guarantees do I have?"

The answer was prompt. "None. But I do not care about your insignificant Talpi. Never did. As long as they stay out of my way, I have no reason to go after them."

His answer rang hollow to me, and I decided to call him out on it. At this point, what did I have to lose? "I will need your word on that."

"You will... what?" The disembodied voice sounded equal parts amused and affronted. "Oh, Carl. There is such a thing as leverage. You do not have it."

"I disagree. If I am to help you become the new master of the mountain, I will want my allies and Aelis to be safe from you." I watched my friend. She sat on the floor, hiding her face in her single paw. So very unlike her. Even from the start, she had faced what happened stoically, but right now, she emanated loss and hopelessness so hard the sensation almost overwhelmed me.

For a full minute, there was silence. Then, Selrahc's bored

voice rang inside my head. "Forget it. You will acquiesce, or you will watch as my chains tear your companion apart, little by little."

Bastard! Did that mean he was lying? Was all of this for nothing?

Minutes turned into hours as we rested inside the dusty chamber. At first, my mind relished the chance to escape from having to deal with the situation, but soon restlessness took over. I started pacing around the place, taking in the architecture. It was all pretty well created, if boring. However, I could tell that the builder needed to work on his construction technique. He clearly hadn't soaked the bricks before laying them, and the mortar was crumbling in places. Before long, I ran out of details I could use to distract the mind and started trying to get a sense for the others in the room. Aelis was an open book. The former fear coming from her was slowly turning into something else. Resolve? I hoped she wasn't planning on doing something stupid.

The Soul Carver remained invisible and silent. What was there to talk about anyway? We had all made our decisions, and we were way past second thoughts. I tried to fight down the feeling that I was making a horrible decision and focused on planning my timing against Selys for when everything inevitably went south. Maybe a Shadow Whorl, followed by a Weakening Fog. Sure, the Soul Carver said I was supposed to fly straight at Selys, but with a big red, that would be suicide. Perhaps just a feint, then...

Eventually, they came for us. The sorcerer threw the door open and waved for me to follow without preamble. "Selys will see you now."

I started walking, Aelis right next to me. To my surprise, the sorcerer didn't comment on her following. And we moved on and up. At this point, the corridors we followed were wide, spacious and, now and again, interrupted by huge stairways. I said nothing, but knew that, somewhere behind me, the Soul Carver followed, ready for violence.

Aelis was the one to break the silence first. Half-jogging to keep up with the pace set by the sorcerer, her mental voice sounded tiny as she spoke up. "I never thanked you, Sire."

I looked down at her. Her face was downcast, but I spotted tears in her eyes. Her mood was somber. I answered softly, "What for, Aelis?"

"Remember that time, when I finally woke up after I lost my hand? You sat with me, told me about where you come from. You made me feel safe and happy. That means a lot to me."

My smile was probably more of a grimace. "You know I would do a lot to see you safe."

She nodded. "I know. Too much." She shook her head. "I just wanted to say that I appreciated the gesture." Her uninjured paw slid inside her leather vest, withdrew again.

We did not speak until the sorcerer pulled up before a pair of huge, closed iron gates adorned with gold filigree. There, he turned back toward us and stared at me for a moment. "You would do best to pay attention in there. If you are to follow in her footsteps, you have much to learn."

"Wait. So, Selys has no titles? How should I act with her?"

He shook his head. "What need does she have of titles? Act as you want. She does have a temper, however." With that said, he slowly pushed open the gates and stood off to the side, allowing us entrance.

I believed I was prepared to see Selys. I had heard so much about her. Her might and splendour. Her unrivalled strength. In a way, I was. My experiences with red dragons had given me something to compare with and an idea of how much larger, more powerful, dragons looked. I was not prepared for the sight of a red dragon in her prime. She was huge. Perhaps three times my size. With my recent growth and speedy leveling, it had been a while since I felt small, but she made me feel tiny. Insignificant.

The red gold of her scales sparkled in the light of the myriad of candles surrounding us in her room. Even at rest, her coiled muscles looked powerful, like she was ready to pounce at any moment. Admiring her body, I marveled at the form-fitted armor that adorned the length of her shape. Her face was arrogant, lined by a backward-reaching crown of horns half my height. Her eyes bored down upon me from above like they were weighing a prospective meal, but there was a shrewd intelligence in there.

The Sorcerer motioned for me to enter and moved to stand next to the dais. Positioned around the room, hulking, armored beasts of various shapes and sizes guarded Selys. I knew I had to get moving, but hesitated. This was a turning point. If I did this, there would be no turning back. Even if it worked, I might be able to save the Talpi, but would resign myself to a life of servitude. I took a deep breath, bowed, and crossed the threshold, walking closer to introduce myself to the reigning dragon queen.

To my surprise, her voice was warm and melodious. It blanketed me in nice sensations, sparkling with good humor. "A tiny shadow hatchling, claiming to have defeated all others, and in such little time, too. I almost believed my pet was making fun of me. But he was not joking, was he? There is a strength to you. Come in, and talk." Welcoming as she was, the pressure in her words were evident. Even though I could tell there was no sorcery used, her voice carried weight and the idea of refusing her was non-existent.

I made my way toward her, swallowing as her form slowly grew larger above me. If this was what my people usually experienced when they talked to me, I couldn't fathom why they weren't more nervous. Looking up at the huge mouth filled with razor-sharp teeth that smiled down at me was intimidating as hell. I was supposed to attack *that?*

As I walked, I slowly began to take in the details of the rest of the room. It was a huge, semi-circular chamber. At the back, a raised dais held Selys in all her splendour, surrounded by her hoard. If Selys by herself was intimidating, her hoard was visually overwhelming. My eyes slid over the assembled wealth of the mountain, from brilliant gemstones over glittering weapons to full pieces of armor, all arrayed to portray them favorably, and all against the backdrop of a sea of jewelry and coins of silver, gold and rarer metals.

I took in over the ceiling of the room. It depicted a series of murals, showing, in detail, the construction of the fortress and defeat of all other contenders for the throne. I shied away. It was simply mental overload. Too many visuals to take in at once. I lowered myself to my haunches and bowed my head, centering my eyes on Selys again. "I'm sorry for gawking like this. I'm not used to this kind of splendor. Thank you for the chance to stand before the mightiest power in the mountain."

Her chuckle rang through the room. "Oh stop. If I want flattery, I will summon one of my pet humans. I am curious. Your kind usually stay back and only engage if you are forced to. Tell me how it came to be that a Shadow Dragon came to outpace everybody else."

"All right. The very first part of my story was a lucky coincidence. See, the very reason that I didn't start my life hatched with the rest of my brethren was also what gave me a step ahead. My very first experience of life inside the mountain was a spear piercing my egg, seeking my life blood..." I started my story, but this time I tried to make it as detailed as possible in order to give the Soul Carver the time he needed.

To my surprise, Selys was a good listener. She paid attention to the details and did not interrupt, chuckling at the way I managed to find my feet and defeat the Soul Carver's remnants. All the time while I spoke, I believed I could feel power building up behind me, from where the Soul Carver was preparing his attack. When I got to the place where I offered my Talpi an alliance, she interrupted for the first time.

"With Talpi? Why would you do that? They are weak and at most they are good for food and digging. Is that why that scrawny thing is hiding behind you?"

I smiled fondly down at Aelis. "Do you recall what I said when we first met? I recall my sentiment, but not the words."

My smile died, as I felt the emotions pouring from her. Sadness, decisiveness and fondness.

She looked down. "You called us weak, Sire. Then you told us that you needed our skills for hiding, digging, and building and offered your protection in return." Aelis looked straight up at me and smiled, a brilliant, tearful smile even as she took her hand inside her leather shirt and produced something. I did not recognize it at first. It was a tiny item and it almost disappeared inside her paw. "I disagree on our weakness, however. In fact, I believe sometimes we have reserves of strength to do what you are unable to." It was the poison! The poisonous plant Laive had given to the scouts!

Selys sat up straight, showing off her incisors. "What is this ridiculous critter-"

Looking me straight in the eye, Aelis smiled and reverently placed the piece inside her mouth, chewing carefully before swallowing.

I almost lashed out in an effort to stop her. It was too late, though. I could feel the pain starting to blossom from within her. She smiled at me through the pain. "Make it worth it."

I roared in distress. Selys had pulled back and her former smile was replaced by a growl as fire danced in her eyes. My sight bounced back and forth between her and Aelis as I hesitated. I could save this. I could claim that Aelis had gone insane. That she was acting out of fear and lost her mind at last. I could... My mental shout rocked the mountains as I screamed out my fury. "The Soul Carver! He is here! The Soul Carver! The Soul-" The chains surrounding me pulled taut and my world exploded into one of pain and fire.

CHAPTER THIRTY-THREE

I don't know how much time passed by with me lost in the depths of pain. When I came to, the scenery was radically changed. I was sprawled out on the floor, hog-tied by dark, pulsing chains that carved threads of shadow and suffering across my entire body. My limbs felt weak, and my mouth was dry. As my eyes roamed the room, I could see why. Selys' guards were downed everywhere inside the chamber. The human sorcerer was still conscious, breathing hard inside a dark bubble I wagered was a protective shield. Seemed like the Soul Carver had cast that massive debuff of his to weaken everybody. Had I warned them in time? With an effort, I lifted my head and saw Selys.

She stalked around the room, seemingly unaffected by the debuff spell. The golden armor moved with her, amplifying the flames that erupted from her mouth and illuminating the room even as she raged. "Show yourself, Selrahc. You dare attack me? This time, I will not let you get away." As she raged, small fires erupted from thin air around the room, seemingly from nothing. Just like I had the ability to manipulate shadows, it would seem Selys could craft fire from nothing. The Burning End indeed.

A high-pitched laughter filled the room, coming from all sides. "Oh, I dare. I dare much. Even if my Puppet here gave the game away, it almost gave me the time I needed to prepare. May I say that you are looking just splendid, Selys. It would be a shame if somebody were to, oh, *flay you alive*."

With that outburst, two swirling centers of flowing quicksilver came alive and moved down each side of the chamber toward Selys. The floating masses solidified and turned into blurred, whirling blades, twirling at high speeds around the liquid center, like high-speed blenders. Where they touched upon any of the downed guards, the result wasn't pretty. The blades cut deep into any exposed flesh, ripped and tore at their armor and dragged them across the floor. The swirling centers increased in speed as they crossed the room and *slammed* into the body of Selys. Scales were ripped open and blood spattered the floor where the blades carved into her abdomen.

"Tricks and manipulation. You think to harm me with *this*?" In truth, none of the attacks looked like they carved deep into her flesh, and I could see her body already knitting itself together. Selys was not without her own tricks. Her guards, however, fared worse. Only a few looked like they were still alive and the human sorcerer was down on his knees and looked like he had trouble maintaining the shield under the combined pressure of the debuff and the attacks.

The disembodied voice let loose with another shrieking laughter. "You think this is an attack? It was merely a prelude. *This* is an attack." The pale spellcaster dismissed his invisibility, facing down his gigantic adversary from across the room, dagger held above his head in a two-handed grip. Selys acted immediately, breathing a swath of fire at him, so hot it was almost white.

The Soul Carver, at the same time, cast a wide, pulsating beam that sliced into being from his dagger with an angry hiss, covering the distance between himself and Selys in an instant. I had to close my eyes to avoid being blinded by the bright light, but grinned at the after-image of the pale spellcaster wreathed in fire.

I opened my eyes only seconds later, to find the Soul Carver shrieking and Selys charging straight at him, beam still affixed and moving between the two, like a perverted image of an umbilical cord. Before she reached the fire-wrapped form, his shrieks turned to hysterical laughter, as a dark pulse traveled at top speed across the beam from Selys to the Soul Carver. When it hit him, his smouldering form started healing as if the flames had never even existed.

Selys ignored the sight, or didn't have time to take it in. She was airborne and glided through the air to strike down upon her target with the full impact of her massive weight. Right before she hit, I had a notion of what would happen and cried out, "Don't!"

I never had the chance to say anything else. The moment of the impact looked like a dump truck smashing into a bridge. Her hind body overtook her front and she was flung to the ground several feet away. Meanwhile, he did not move an inch. Damnit. So, he was immune to her physical attacks right now, and it looked like those beams of his were siphoning strength off Selys and healing him?

"Selys the Mighty? Ridiculous. I have agonized over this moment. Would you really fall for my trap? Allow me the time I needed to affix my Life Drain onto you? Would you not just leave and return with armies upon armies? Instead, you charge like the moronic animal you are." The Soul Carver moved his hands, and a set of dark orbs traveled straight for Selys, slamming into her bulk.

I lay panting, almost incapable of movement. Aelis' corpse lay in front of me, taunting me with its stillness. I had to do something, or her sacrifice would amount to nothing. But what *could* I do? I couldn't even get up.

Another swath of flame traversed over the Soul Carver and almost hit me in passing. Again, another bead traveled down the beam and he was fully healed seconds later. He mocked her.

"Nice try. Your powers are useless against me, Selys. Why not just lie down while I finish your minions?" Another set of spheres came into being and started their tearing, carving route down along the walls to finish the few surviving guards along with Selys' sorcerer.

Selys didn't just take it. Her mental shout hurt my already aching head. "Ignore *me?* Prepare to see the real power of the mountain!" She stopped mid-stride and slammed her front paws down on the ground, lowering her head. Everywhere around the room, the fires died down and were swallowed, leaving my eyes struggling to get reaccustomed to the sudden darkness. There was one exception to the sudden darkness in the room however--Selys.

All of a sudden, she seemed to glow from within and grow even taller, stronger. Her defiant roar reverberated through the chamber, and her eyes burned as she turned them on the defiant necromancer again. "Now, see if you can take on the Mountain." The blast of fire that emanated from her lasted twice as long as the last time, and I could *see* the flesh sloughing off the Soul Carver. To no avail. Even mid-attack, a bead traveled through the inferno, healing him and, again, four or five seconds later, another bead regenerated the last of the horrible damage.

I got an idea. A desperate, crazy idea, but still. If I wanted to avenge Aelis, I had to do something. "Selrahc!" I shouted. "Aren't you forgetting something?" He turned his head, and I launched my illusion, watching it spring into being. Now, I just had to maintain it, even though the entirety of my body wanted to go to sleep.

He looked away from me again to fling a dark orb at Selys. "Forgetting something? I doubt it. I have not forgotten about your treachery, either. I will make sure to punish you along with your pathetic minions. You will be allowed to watch." An intricate movement with one hand made the chains around me convulse, and pain exploded everywhere.

I fought to stay conscious and keep the hold on my illusion

as my vision blurred from tears. When the wave of pain had passed, the Soul Carver had turned back to Selys. At least, he needed to focus his attention on me when he manipulated the chains. Selys looked undaunted still, even as a dark lance from the Soul Carver tore into her flank. She leapt around the room, switching between attacking his shield and sending fiery waves at him, but her feet were dragging slightly, and her speed was not as impressive as it had been initially.

It was no good. I couldn't just lie here. The effects of the debuff were as harsh as they always had been, but I found that the chains, constricting and painful as they were, were just that. Pain. I struggled to my feet and focused on the blurry form of the Soul Carver and let fly with a Shadow Whorl, even as I forced myself to move.

He reacted to my affront immediately, letting fly a dark bolt that hit me in the side of my chest, stripping me of a third of my health. "Stay out of this. You are not in a league to play with us. And I *will* end you."

I growled, watching as his form disappeared in another wave of flames from Selys. The moment he reappeared, I sent a Weakening Fog his way. That one seemed to make it through the shield. "Well, go ahead then. If it's that or a lifetime under your horrible leadership, I'll go with death. Maybe Deyra will let me be reborn somewhere far from you."

The chains tightened once again, and the pain made me grow dizzy. I dug down deep, however and the next time he sent a dark bolt my way, I managed to roll out of the way, barely. "You'll have to do better than that, you filthy piece of shit!" I started running along the edges of the room, dodging and weaving to present as small a target as possible.

The Soul Carver laughed mockingly. Selys slammed into him again, and he turned back toward her and spawned a new set of spheres, sending them rolling toward her. "Die already, you lowly worm." He pointed straight at my illusion. "Look toward your trusted human pet and despair. You will end up broken like him!" he growled, and turned back toward me.

"And you, Carl. You are making me change my mind. I wanted to keep you alive so you could watch your minions get slaughtered. But now, I think I will just slaughter you and spoil your chances for rebirth." An expansive gesture tightened the chains around me, causing me to stumble, and he sent another, bigger, bolt straight at me. A desperate leap made it hit my shoulder instead of my body, but it still brought me below half health, leaving me limping on that leg.

"Do your worst then, freak!" I spat, continuing my run. I yelled at Selys. "Keep attacking him, Selys. We will wear him down!" As I passed by the throne, I sent a mental message into the illusion. "Wait here. Don't move yet." Then I stopped and reversed course, trying my best to evade the Soul Carver's shots. Behind me, the doors to the throne room slammed open, and a group of guards rushed in, only to be met by a set of spheres that struck them down within seconds.

While he was distracted, I sent another Weakening Fog at him. I still couldn't see any effect, but it was only a matter of time before they started taking their toll. Unless the beam healed him of the debuff as well. Nasty thought. If that was the case, I was probably screwed.

He ignored me, sending a verbal barrage against Selys. "Oh, you wonder why your guards aren't coming? They are busy defending themselves from my minions. I was going to hide my presence, but Carl here ruined that. So if you are hoping for assistance, forget about it. Come here and finish it already!"

The Soul Carver's constant attacks against Selys were starting to have an effect. She looked the worse for wear, panting and dragging her hind leg, as she kept up the constant movement against his dark bolts. She hesitated and took another bolt to the flank, growling in pain. Then she turned and affixed her eyes on him. "Finish it? Very well. But I have said this before. The only end you will find here... is the Burning End."

Then, a fire shield erupted from her, surrounding her in

flames as she leapt forward toward the Soul Carver. It wasn't too early, either. She was at forty percent health, and it was dropping for every moment the beam stayed affixed to her. The fire shield did nothing to remove the beams, but did obscure her entirely, making it harder to target her.

It also cast the room in a bright glow, throwing shadows every which way, shadows I needed. For the next few adrenaline-surging moments, I used every ounce of concentration to wrap myself in shadows while I evaded the Soul Carver's attacks and stayed as far away from Selys as possible to avoid becoming toast. The huge room suddenly didn't seem that large.

The Soul Carver, meanwhile, turned defensive. However much confidence he had in his regeneration forces, it wasn't enough to risk a constant ring of fire, combined with a breath attack to the face. A handful of intricate hand movements had him floating into the air and soon, he flew around the place, keeping as much distance between him and Selys as possible until the fire shield died down.

If he had displayed any finesse at controlling his flight, we would have been completely out of luck, but it was more like him being turned into a particularly ugly puppet, and the puppet master threw him around the chamber by his strings. Speedy, but no control. It made his attacks less constant, but also made him a lot easier to target when he paused to unleash his own attacks.

At this moment, the battle inside the chamber would have been completely confusing to watch for any onlookers. Selys dominated the space, wreathed in fire, while the Soul Carver zipped around the place, throwing dark bolts at either of us. Meanwhile, I wrapped myself in shadows, doing my utmost to avoid both. I did pretty well, avoiding all dark bolts while I did manage to tag him twice with a Weakening Fog. I told myself I was starting to see some drag in his shoulders, but it might have been wishful thinking. Selys, in turn, seemed unable to catch him with his unpredictable speed.

At long last, Selys stopped her hunt, coming to a panting halt back near her hoard. To my dismay, her fires were dying down, and she was looking almost done in, while the Soul Carver remained completely unharmed. Things were not looking our way.

Clearly, the Soul Carver had the same idea. He released his spell, lowering himself to the ground, and started walking toward her. "You see? It was inevitable. Do you regret not giving me the mountain now, Selys?"

Selys backed up, rummaging around her hoard. "Not for a second. My only regret is not crushing you when I had the chance. That, we will remedy now. Attack, Onyx." Then, she grasped an item on the floor, and a split second later, I marvelled to see her wounds close up. I used Inspect and grinned at her health, which was once again at max. A mana crystal. Clever.

Acting out her order right away, I sent a Weakening Fog at the back of the Soul Carver, and got to moving. Circling the chamber, my panicked jump evaded another dark orb, as the Soul Carver tightened the chains around me again. Despite the fog of the pain, my mind was in overdrive. The timing would have to be *just* right. The Soul Carver's regeneration was crazy enough that we couldn't produce enough damage to take him out right away.

Also, clearly the Soul Carver's shield would last for as long as he had mana. Back in the fight with the Water Banes, the shield only lasted a handful of minutes, and that had passed already. The only conclusion I could come up with was that his beam would only fizzle out, if his concentration was broken, or if Selys died. The first didn't seem likely and the latter... impractical. If only his attributes were lower, I would be able to weaken him into unconsciousness, but seeing how a single hit of his bolts could carve a third off my health, that was a horrible bet. No, we needed to combine our powers.

"Selys. Set him aflame every chance you get." My shout was not really needed. She had already taken to keeping her distance from the Soul Carver, burning him every time she could use her fire breath. It didn't have any lasting effects, but it did give us a blessed second each time, where he was out of commission as he regenerated the damage. As long as I got the timing right, that meant I could land my Weakening Fog without resistance. This time, I was certain I could see a difference. The Soul Carver appeared wearier than he had since the start of the battle. A little slower.

Unfortunately, he came to the same conclusion as well and stopped giving Selys his attention. "Oh no, my traitorous helper. This will not do. You will not wear me down. Lesser creatures might fall for that, but not I. It is past time I finished you off." The moment his hands started moving, I scrambled to get away, pulling shadows toward me to hide while I placed a new Shadow Whorl straight at his ugly forehead.

Little did it help. When he inevitably tightened the chains again, my foreleg started cramping from the pain, and I crashed to the ground. A split second later, two shining spheres tore through the darkness, aiming to disembowel me. My shadows were the only thing that saved my scaly hide, since I was hiding on the edge of the darkness instead of in the center. Even so, a few hits from the blades on one sphere tore into my scales, carving 20 percent off my health, leaving me at less than a third. I fought my way up again, getting back at the Soul Carver with a Weakening Fog. This time, he visibly hunched over, though he straightened back up immediately.

"Enough!" he roared at the room. "I did not want to use this, but I am not failing now!" With a flourish, he tore off his dark coat. A few soulstones tumbled out from under the heavy coat as it flew through the air and it landed on the floor with a clattering sound. I widened the distance from him, creating a large area of shadows where I could roam undisturbed.

Good thing I did it, too. Within seconds, his coat inflated as the rattling sounds increased in strength, revealing a whirling mess of bones, flying together to form a stick-thin skeleton that stood up and started moving toward my dark hideout, even as the few remaining bones liberated themselves from under the coat to attach themselves to the fragile form.

Selys acted right away, blasting a breath of fire at the newly-formed skeleton. The wide swath of flames enveloped the clunky form completely, leaving it hidden for a moment. Then it reappeared, completely untouched, and started throwing its own dark bolts in my direction.

Great. A fire-immune skeleton mage. Just what we needed. I sent a Weakening Fog at the Soul Carver and leapt at the newly formed skeleton, building up a sprint in order to destroy the flimsy form in one blow. Of course, that's when the damn Necromancer decided to pull my strings.

Mid-stride, the pain kicked in and my legs locked up. The good news was that I'd gained enough momentum that, even falling, I was able to keep sliding straight toward the skeleton mage. The bad news was that it left me wide open for his bolts to slam into my bulk, one after the other. The two projectiles struck me straight on, and then my bulk hit the skeleton, tossing bones in every direction like a particularly powerful strike in a bowling alley.

Only a graceless dodge sideways at the end of my fall allowed me to avoid the Soul Carver's own dark bolt, and I limped away as fast as I could, while I gathered the shadows around me again. Unfortunately, my retreat was accompanied by the scraping, rattling sound of bones as they pulled them-selves across the floor, jumping and leaping across the floor to slowly reassemble the mage's form again.

The Soul Carver's laughter sprang into being again. He was definitely moving slower now, bent over like an old man. "Do you like it? I made it especially for you, Selys, if you turned out more difficult than expected. Who would have expected that I would have to use it on my own follower?"

Fuck. The skeleton's attack had me down to less than ten percent health, and Selys' health was ticking below the halfway mark, too. There was no way we'd be able to avoid both their attacks while I debuffed him properly. It was time to roll the dice. "We need to attack him at the same time! You too! On my mark." I gathered the shadows, not around me, this time, but at the back of the room.

Slowly, laboriously, the Soul Carver straightened. The haughty sensations in his response were clear as day. "You idiot insects. Do you not get it? You can't harm me. Do your worst!" He spread his arms, and the silver sheen of a pair of spheres reflected in the pale, broken skin of his face. This was it. My final attempt. I sprinted toward him and shot off a Weakening Fog, shouting. "Now! Hit him now!" Then I flung myself sideways, leaping for my life.

Selys acted immediately. Her fire impacted immediately after my Weakening Fog. This time, the damage was gruesome. I could see the bleached bones of his skull, contorted in horrible agony. The beam, still attached to Selys, pulsed, once, twice, then a bead started forming and moving across the beam toward him.

The sorcerer was faster than the bead. My illusion burst apart, as he sprinted on faltering legs toward the Soul Carver, fire spilling from him as he ran. Where Selys unleashed her fire like an ocean, waves of uncontrollable power spilling from her to overwhelm everybody, he wielded it like a whip.

With pinpoint accuracy, the tight fire whip lashed out and wrapped itself around the neck of Selrahc and stayed stuck. For an infinitely long moment of torture, the Soul Carver endured it, fire burning away to seemingly no effect. Then, just as the bead of healing power was about to return to him, his fire-blasted visage gave a curt nod to the world at large... and his head tumbled to the ground, no longer attached to his body.

The beam unraveled, bursting into intangible strands of power, like dark fireworks bursting into the night sky, and the Soul Carver's pale body hit the ground, dead.

CHAPTER THIRTY-FOUR

Freedom is a state of mind. - Walter Mosley

I was in prison. Or rather, in containment, chained in place at the very top of the fortress, carefully watched on all sides by guards with weapons close at hand. The guards were clearly nervous. Whether they were unsure what was going on, rattled by the attack or simply unused to prisoners, I couldn't tell.

I also didn't care much. Below me, I could see a city that was recuperating from an unexpected attack. Clearly, the Soul Carver's minions had ranged far into the city. Dead and dying people lay in the streets, and fires were common. I could not spot a single standing undead minion, however. They must have died along with their master. Hopefully, their souls could gain some peace now.

Peace. I watched the sun sending its first rays of light into the mountain above me. I hoped that Aelis was in peace, wherever she was now. Maybe, Deyra would see her reborn. If it were up to me, she'd have the form of a dragon. She had the courage for it, that was for sure. I did not know what was going to happen now, but I was sure about one thing.

If I survived, I was going to heed her words. I was going to make her sacrifice worth it. I was going to ensure that this place would see changes and that my minions would be at the front of a new and better world, where might was not the only answer. I would sit down with Timothy and carve out a system that would lead to peace and equality. Heh. I just had to survive the attention of Selys first.

In the aftermath of the battle, things turned chaotic, and I'd been led here by a great many guards who (rather sheepishly) came storming into Selys' chambers once it became apparent that the battle was over. I couldn't find it in me to care, however. My mind kept going back to the look in Aelis' eyes as she popped the poisonous plant into her mouth. So much sadness and kindness in that look.

Suddenly, Selys strode up from below. Apart from the exhausted look in her eyes, she almost looked like the battle had never taken place. Her armor was scuffed in a few spots, and if you looked carefully, her movement hinted at wounds beneath that had not yet healed. Still, there were no obvious signs that, a few hours ago, she had almost been killed. The massive red wasted no time, towering over me. "So, you joined my worst enemy in ambushing me?"

I nodded. There was no use denying it. "He was forcing me to, but yes."

"And you were about to go through with it, but didn't...why?" Her mental voice had something lurking beneath the anger. Curiosity?

I didn't think. At this point, my head wasn't up for it. I just gave her my honest reply. "He threatened that he would kill Aelis, unless I complied. Then she killed herself to free me."

A tight frown appeared on her face. "There is more to that story. A lot more. Still. You betrayed me. What do you expect from me now?"

That was exactly what my mind had been worrying about. I was still no closer to an answer. I went for broke. "Either you kill me or appoint me your successor? I fail to see any other endings."

A brief look flashed over her face. Was that bemusement? "So, those are the only possibilities? How would you know? Your amassed knowledge of the world? Your centuries of life?" She huffed a brief laughter.

I smiled a smile bereft of humor. I knew I shouldn't be so nonchalant on this topic, but my impression was that she took better to straight talk. "I believe so, Selys. I would say that I proved my capabilities pretty well back there. And I did defeat or co-opt all other dragons in the clutch. The only real question is exactly how much I managed to anger you. Believe me when I say that I never wanted to attack you in the first place."

The way she shook her head told me her response even before her message landed. "What happened to you? Shadow dragons are never this direct. It matters not. You will answer my questions, and as long as I believe that you will not turn against me, you will live." She paused for a moment, as if considering, then continued. "Your minions are a point in your favor. They ambushed Selrahc's flawed souls as they charged the city, reducing the damage by a lot. If I find you worthy, you will learn that I care little about methods. Results are what matter. And I need a competent replacement, and do not care to wait long."

I lowered my head. Inside, my mind raced. Why would they do that? I had told them to get away, flee for their lives. They had defied that order and turned on the Soul Carver. That was almost akin to suicide.

Focusing on Selys again, I asked meekly. "I will answer any question and pay for any damage I've caused you. Do we need to hurry? It sounds like we are under time constraints."

She tilted her head. "You are quite the insightful one. No, there is no real rush. But I have spent the past many years in preparation. I am anxious to get moving. I will let you in on a little secret. Many races within the Mountain believe that it is the best place in the world, close to Deyra, easy growth once you find your niche. They are fools. So very limited in their vision."

She indicated the clear skies outlined above us. "Out there is an entire world, just waiting for our kind. Prove yourself as Master of the Mountain, and you will see it, too." She bared her teeth in a ferocious grin. "While you handle the Scoured Mountain, I will tame the skies and lesser species and carve a place for our kind to re-enter the world."

Wow. So, Timothy *had* said something about her expanding elsewhere, but this... was pretty damn ambitious. "Of course. I'll make sure I handle everything according to your demands." Out of sheer curiosity, I had to ask. "So... what is out there? New realms? Warring nations? Old kingdoms?"

Her grin was all teeth as she stared at me. "All of that and more. A multitude of species, entrenched in their tiny power struggles, unchanging since my birth. Elves. Ca'ernin. Humans. They all look to make the world theirs and rule. Little do they know that they are but prey."

Oh. Oh fuck. My stomach sank. I took in the sight of the behemoth before me. She darkened the skies above me, her shadow spreading over the fortress top as she raised her head to the heavens at the thought of world domination.

Really? Now, I was supposed to enslave all humans? I needed a goddamn *break*.

ABOUT LARS MACHMÜLLER

Lars Machmüller lives in Denmark with his wife and three kids. Family comes first, and as such, he spends a lot of time perfecting the art of packed lunches, cleaning food off the floor and delivering kids to and from school, kindergarten, playdates and whatnot.

Whenever somebody is *not* crawling on his shoulders, he dedicates every waking moment attempting to exorcise all those LitRPG plot bunnies that keep finding a place to live within his skull.

Whatever little time remains, he distributes evenly between his towering to-be-read pile, his trusty PC, and music.

Connect with Lars:
LarsM-Writes.com
Instagram.com/LarsMachmuller
Facebook.com/groups/357145749698735
Patreon.com/Moulder666
Mailchi.mp/94863280f513/Cranky-Chronicler

ABOUT MOUNTAINDALE PRESS

Dakota and Danielle Krout, a husband and wife team, strive to create as well as publish excellent fantasy and science fiction novels. Self-publishing *The Divine Dungeon: Dungeon Born* in 2016 transformed their careers from Dakota's military and programming background and Danielle's Ph.D. in pharmacology to President and CEO, respectively, of a small press. Their goal is to share their success with other authors and provide captivating fiction to readers with the purpose of solidifying Mountaindale Press as the place 'Where Fantasy Transforms Reality.'

Connect with Mountaindale Press:
MountaindalePress.com
Facebook.com/MountaindalePress
Twitter.com/_Mountaindale
Instagram.com/MountaindalePress

MOUNTAINDALE PRESS TITLES

GameLit and LitRPG

The Completionist Chronicles,
The Divine Dungeon,
Full Murderhobo, and
Year of the Sword by Dakota Krout

Arcana Unlocked by Gregory Blackburn

A Touch of Power by Jay Boyce

Red Mage and
Farming Livia by Xander Boyce

Space Seasons by Dawn Chapman

Ether Collapse and
Ether Flows by Ryan DeBruyn

Dr. Druid by Maxwell Farmer

Bloodgames by Christian J. Gilliland

Unbound by Nicoli Gonnella

Threads of Fate by Michael Head

Lion's Lineage by Rohan Hublikar and Dakota Krout

Wolfman Warlock by James Hunter and Dakota Krout

Axe Druid,
Mephisto's Magic Online, and
High Table Hijinks by Christopher Johns

Skeleton in Space by Andries Louws

Dragon Core Chronicles by Lars Machmüller

Chronicles of Ethan by John L. Monk

Pixel Dust and
Necrotic Apocalypse by David Petrie

Viceroy's Pride by Cale Plamann

Henchman by Carl Stubblefield

Artorian's Archives by Dennis Vanderkerken and Dakota Krout

Made in United States
Troutdale, OR
08/30/2023

12506492R00217